Dear Target Guest,

At a time when it feels like we're all way, way too busy—with work (and work-related email!) that never stops, family obligations, making time for friends, grocery shopping, laundry, some kind of exercise (I guess?), attempting to follow (let alone process) the news—it can be next to impossible to find an hour in your day to feel simple, relaxing, uncomplicated joy. And even if you could find the time, what could possibly make you so happy?

For me, the answer is reality TV.

People tend to be surprised when they learn this about me. After all, I've spent most of my career doing Serious Stuff as a writer and digital strategist working to advance women's rights, advocate for LGBTQ equality, and help to dismantle systemic racism (among other things!). So I can see where it might not make sense that my favorite way to unwind is pour a big glass of rosé and spend an evening with the fabulous, over-the-top personalities who populate the frothy world of guilty-pleasure television.

But you know what? I don't feel guilty about loving reality TV! I think it's *good* to spend time doing/reading/watching things that make you happy, to escape your life for a little while and imagine yourself in the world of your favorite shows. And the show that makes me happiest of all is *The Bachelorette*.

A lot of people watch *The Bachelorette* for the drama, but as a total romantic, my favorite thing about it is that, every so often, you really and truly get to see people take a leap and fall in love. The show is an addictive little optimism machine, where two people can be perfect strangers on night one, but if they just try hard enough, and get vulnerable enough, and ignore all of the cameras (and all of us watching at home), within a few short weeks, they can find their happily ever after. It gets me every time.

So when I started writing *One to Watch*, I wanted to bring the beliefs that drive my life's work into the romantic fantasy world I've adored for almost twenty years. Because on *The Bachelorette* and shows like it, love only looks one way, only happens one way—and we all know that's anything but realistic. Most important, I wanted to re-create the rush of joy I feel every time I flip on some reality TV (and unless you're an exceptionally quick reader, it'll hopefully last longer than an hour!).

I'm thrilled and humbled that *One to Watch* has been selected as a Target Club Pick, and I'm even more excited that you've chosen to pick it up. Especially when we're all way, way too busy, it means so much that you would choose to spend some of your precious free time in the world of this novel with me.

I hope you have a wonderful, relaxing, joyous read, and in the meantime, I'm sending all the love and sequins in the universe. You deserve them.

xx, Kate

Praise for **ONE TO WATCH**

"*One to Watch* drew me in from the first chapter; this book was relatable, incredibly smart, and thoughtful about body image and the way the media treats women, and just plain entertaining. I adored this extraordinary debut and had so much fun reading it!"
—JASMINE GUILLORY, *New York Times* bestselling author of *The Wedding Date* and *The Proposal*

"Bea Schumacher is an irresistible heroine, and *One to Watch* will win you over just as quickly. Its clever skewering of reality TV tropes is balanced by a sweet sincerity and real belief in true romance. *The Bachelor* should be so lucky as to land a Bea of its own."
—HEATHER COCKS and JESSICA MORGAN, bestselling authors of *The Royal We* and *The Heir Affair*

"A delicious and whip-smart page-turner about the complication of being a complicated woman in the world today."
—JO PIAZZA, bestselling author of *Charlotte Walsh Likes to Win*

"*One to Watch* is a powerful story about the love we have for ourselves and others. It's a vibrant, tender, stylish, sexy, and outrageously joyful book, and I couldn't bear to put it down for one second."
—HANNAH ORENSTEIN, author of *Love at First Like*

"A fast, furious read, one that is brimming with wit but also packs a serious punch. The compelling narrator—Bea Schumacher—won my heart immediately, and Stayman-London's storytelling sizzles."
—FIONA DAVIS, national bestselling author of *The Chelsea Girls*

"Stayman-London's charming debut is chatty and fun, brilliantly capturing the highs, lows, and drama of reality TV. . . . This smart, delightful page-turner is a great way for dating-show fans to pass the time while waiting for the next season."
—*Publishers Weekly*

ONE TO WATCH

A NOVEL

Kate Stayman-London

THE DIAL PRESS

NEW YORK

2020 Target Edition

Published in the United States by The Dial Press,
an imprint of Random House, a division
of Penguin Random House LLC, New York.

THE DIAL PRESS is a registered trademark and the colophon
is a trademark of Penguin Random House LLC.

Random House Book Club and colophon are trademarks of
Penguin Random House LLC.

Library of Congress Cataloging-in-Publication Data
Names: Stayman-London, Kate, author.
Title: One to watch: a novel / Kate Stayman-London.
Description: New York: The Dial Press, [2020]
Identifiers: LCCN 2019045514 (print) | LCCN 2019045515 (ebook) |
ISBN 9780593230350 (trade paperback;
acid-free paper) | ISBN 9780525510437 (ebook)
Subjects: GSAFD: Love stories.
Classification: LCC PS3619.T39 O54 2020 (print) |
LCC PS3619.T39 (ebook) DDC 813/.6—dc23
LC record available at https://lccn.loc.gov/2019045514
LC ebook record available at https://lccn.loc.gov/2019045515

Printed in the United States of America on acid-free paper

randomhousebooks.com
randomhouseebookclub.com

2 4 6 8 9 7 5 3 1

Book design by Jen Valero

For Dede, who thinks it wouldn't kill the women on
The Bachelor to wear pants to a cocktail party once in a while.

Thanks for choosing Dad and me to be your family.

But love is blind, and lovers cannot see
The pretty follies that themselves commit.

-WILLIAM SHAKESPEARE

We've all been dumped. We've all fallen for the wrong guy or girl.
We've all made mistakes. But we all want that thing at the end.

-CHRIS HARRISON

ONE TO WATCH

PROLOGUE

Paris, France

Ten years ago

The flea market at Clignancourt was at the far northern edge of the city, a few blocks past the final stop on the number 4 Métro, where the Parisian architecture grew more simple, more mundane—a reminder that not all of the city was steeped in centuries of history and romance. Some of it was just where people went to work and took their kids to school and bought their bread in plain old supermarkets instead of quaint boulangeries.

Bea had come to the flea market in search of gifts for her family—maybe some lace for her mother or vintage records for her brother Duncan—but she also hoped she might find some etchings for herself, or, even better, some children's books with hand-tipped illustrations to read with her stepfather to her new baby nephew. Her friends in her study-abroad program had raved about their flea-market finds, so Bea thought it was worth a trip, even if there was no chance of buying chic vintage clothes like the ones they had modeled for her. It was hard enough for Bea to shop in America, let alone here in Paris, where it was almost unthinkable to see a woman on the street who couldn't be described as "bird-boned."

After years of practice, Bea thought she'd mastered the art of being large and invisible at the same time—the dark, baggy clothes, the quiet manner, the downward gaze. When she arrived as a freshman at UCLA and found herself surrounded by lithe, toned Californians, she was afraid she'd stand out like a bulbous blemish on a glassy complexion, but the L.A. culture of self-obsession made it easier than she expected to slip by unseen.

In Paris, though, she felt eyes everywhere she went. The city was so beautiful, Bea's favorite place she'd ever been—yet she couldn't shake the feeling that the entire population was noticing her, judging her, preferring, silently, that she would leave. Waiters and booksellers in cramped cafés and shops, narrow aisles stuffed with tables and wares, Bea stepping carefully sideways to avoid toppling someone else's plate of pain au chocolat, salivating at the sound of those crunchy, buttery pastries that waiflike Parisians relished each morning without a second thought. Whenever Bea stepped into a patisserie to order something for herself, there were ripples of sideward glances, even occasional bald stares, the accusation always implied: *It's your own fault you look like this.*

It was easier when she got farther out from the center of the city, into the diverse neighborhoods by the canal where the streets were wider and the pace was slower, where groups of students laughed and drank wine from paper cups on big concrete blocks by the water. It was similar at Clignancourt, Bea thought as she made her way down the few blocks from the Métro to the flea market while people hurried by, too focused on their own lives to pause to sneer at her.

Bea couldn't tell what the flea market was like from the outside—for a solid block she could see only the back walls of the stalls, dark slabs of plywood and plasterboard, and she started to feel skeptical that this market could possibly be as extraordinary as her friends had insisted. But once she found the entrance, she understood: It was like stepping through Alice's looking glass into an entirely other place where everything was wonderful and strange.

The market was a maze, with pathways that cut at haphazard diagonals—whichever way Bea turned, she never seemed to pass the same stalls twice, each new alley bringing untold bins of brass knobs and walls of antique oil paintings and spools of silken ribbon. The stalls themselves didn't feel makeshift—some were covered in ivy or string lights, others had stucco walls and wooden shelves piled high with leather-bound books so dusty Bea imagined they'd been there for decades. Wandering the market's aisles, Bea felt a sense of belonging she'd never experienced anywhere else in Paris. Or maybe, she considered, it was just that everything there was so lovely and bizarre that nothing and no one could be out of place.

Before Bea realized how much time had passed, the sun was starting to set, so she made her way toward the edge of the market as proprietors packed up their stalls. Bea hadn't stopped by a single clothing purveyor, but near the market's exit, one stall caught her eye: It was filled exclusively with capes—racks and racks of heavy brocades and soft furs and embroidered silks.

Bea cast the stall a longing glance, but it wasn't any use. She was sure that no cape in the place was big enough to cover her body, that instead of cocooning her in luxury, the capes would simply hang off her back like a child playing dress-up with a beach towel fastened at the neck. But the shopkeeper, a reedy, androgynous Frenchwoman in her sixties in oversized black glasses, saw Bea looking and took a step toward her.

"*Vous désirez?*" she asked with a quick flick of her eyebrow; her voice was deep and throaty.

"*Non,*" Bea apologized in her muddy accent. "*Merci.*"

"Ah, American." She switched to English immediately— Parisians always did. "What is your name?"

"Beatrice"—Bea pronounced it the French way, *Bay-ah-treez*—"but everyone calls me Bea."

"*Enchantée,* Bea. I am Jeanne." Jeanne took her hand and clasped it firmly, and Bea immediately warmed to her; she smelled like spiced wine. "Tell me, Bea, who is the woman whose style you most admire?"

Bea's mind went immediately to the black-and-white movies she'd spent hours watching as a kid on basic cable in her family's rec room. She'd taken a couple of film classes at UCLA, and she was thrilled to discover that Paris had dozens of single-screen cinemas with little paper tickets and red velvet seats that showed classic American movies (with French subtitles, of course) every night of the week. Bea frequented these theaters whenever she had a free evening, delighting in the escape of elegant starlets and breakneck banter. As she considered Jeanne's question, she thought of the different actresses she revered: She could never be twee like Audrey Hepburn, nor statuesque like Katharine. In her wildest fantasies, she imagined herself more like a femme fatale of film noir—a mixture of soft and hard, of danger and intense vulnerability. In Bea's opinion, there was one actress whose style embodied that ideal more than any other, who effortlessly combined sensual laces and silks with angular sunglasses and sharp-shouldered blazers.

"Maybe this is silly"—Bea ducked her head—"but I think I would choose Barbara Stanwyck?"

Jeanne smiled knowingly, her whole face creasing in fond crinkles. "*D'accord—un moment.*"

She disappeared among the racks, a few moments of rustling and the jangle of sliding hangers before she emerged with a floor-length cape fashioned in plush velvet, a dark forest green. It was hooded, lined with silk, and clasped at the neck with a silver brooch fashioned to look like lilies of the valley, with clusters of tiny freshwater pearls where the flowers would be.

"Oh," Bea breathed as Jeanne draped the cape over her shoulders, the fabric gently cascading.

Jeanne led her to a floor-length mirror, smoky with age, and Bea felt a sharp twist in her chest—it was like looking at a glamorous stranger. Bea never had a sweet-sixteen dress, never went to prom, convinced her parents to let her wear jeans to graduation (since, she argued, she'd be covered up by her cap and gown anyway, tentlike and maroon), and reluctantly shoved herself into a series of appalling bridesmaids' dresses for her brothers' weddings. In her entire life, no garment Bea had put on her body had ever made her feel like this.

"How much is it?" she heard herself asking, her voice choked and small.

"It is two hundred," Jeanne offered, but she paused when she saw the look of panic cross Bea's face.

"How much do you have?" she asked kindly.

Bea opened her wallet—she had forty euros and change, which was also her money to eat for the next week. She'd already spent too much at the flea market, and the credit card from her parents was only for emergencies. Two hundred euros was an unthinkable sum.

"I'm so sorry," Bea whispered, and reached to take off the cape, but Jeanne put a hand on her shoulder.

"Perhaps," she said, "there can be an arrangement."

Bea didn't understand what she meant. "Arrangement?"

"I will make you a gift of this cape, and in return, you will wear it all over Paris, and you will tell everyone you meet about my shop, yes?"

"What? No, I couldn't possibly accept—"

"*Bien sûr*, of course you can." Jeanne deftly snatched the cape from Bea's shoulders and removed its handwritten tag. "You would like a bag, or you will wear it now?"

Bea's face flushed, and she looked down.

"I don't understand why you're doing this," she mumbled.

Jeanne tenderly placed the cape around Bea's shoulders.

"The way you dress, the way you hang your head? I think perhaps you are hiding," she said quietly. "But in this cape?"

Bea looked up to meet her eye. "In this cape, what?"

Jeanne's lips curled at the corners, the barest hint of a grin.

"You will be someone who everyone must see."

❧

AGREEMENT

Los Angeles, California

ONE TO WATCH: FASHION BLOGGER BEA SCHUMACHER
by Toni Santo, TheCut.com

The Internet was ablaze this week when pop star Trish Kelly took to Twitter to complain that multiple designers refused to dress her for the Grammys—because she's a size 8! Bea Schumacher is all too familiar with this conundrum: With more than half a million Instagram followers and a blog (OMBea.com, a play on OMG) that logs millions of visitors each month, Bea is one of today's most popular fashion bloggers—but because she's plus-size, almost no high-end designers make clothes that fit her.

For this week's edition of "One to Watch," we caught up with Schumacher to chat about her thriving career, enviable travel schedule, and hottest tips for rocking a red carpet, no matter your size:

TS: How did you get started as a fashion blogger? Have you always loved fashion?

Bea: *(laughs)* God, no. When I was in high school, I wore exclusively baggy black pants and T-shirts and sweaters. I didn't want to stand out; I didn't even want anyone to look at me.

TS: When did that change?

Bea: Junior year in college, I spent a semester abroad in Paris—that's where my fashion addiction began. I was totally broke at the time, I spent the semester digging through vintage shops looking for treasures. I found so many great things that my friends encouraged me to blog about them, a little fashion travel diary. My best friend in my program was a photography major, and she took pictures of me in flowing dresses and floppy hats drinking wine by the Seine. I didn't know the first thing about launching a website, so I just made a preformatted blog on Tumblr—that was the first iteration of OMBea. At first, I just posted pictures, but then I started writing more about my life and the challenges of searching for great clothes as a plus-size woman; it became a really important outlet for me, particularly after I moved back to Los Angeles with its totally monolithic beauty standards.

TS: Was the blog an overnight sensation?

Bea: Hardly! In the early days, it was really only for people I knew. After college, I went to work at a Hollywood agency; I thought maybe I would be a stylist for movies and TV shows one day, and it seemed like a good way to learn the ropes of the industry. I was an assistant there, and one of my boss's clients was a really famous actress who always loved my outfits. We got to talking about my blog, and she tweeted about it—that's when things really blew up. I got tons of new followers, and I started being included in magazine roundups of who to follow, things like that. Once my reader numbers started getting big, I was able to pound the pavement to find sponsors and advertisers.

TS: All while you were working a full-time job?

Bea: Yeah, it was pretty nuts. But after a year of hard work, it really paid off: I was able to quit my assistant job and become a full-time blogger, and I've never looked back. It's been more fun than I could have dreamed.

TS: Tell us more! What's a typical day like in the life of Bea Schumacher?

Bea: It's always different—that's one of the things I love about my job. I might be meeting with a plus-size brand about a potential collaboration, or heading off to a fashion party in London or New York, or doing a photo shoot in my own backyard to show readers how I'm planning to style new looks for summer.

TS: But you don't just write about clothes—you also write about the experience of being a plus-size person who loves fashion.

Bea: I think it would be dishonest not to. It's only very recently that a lot of companies have begun to make clothes that fit me—and especially when it comes to high-end designers, many brands that do claim to offer "plus-size" clothes only go up to a size 16! Which I find ridiculous, because size 16 is essentially *average* for women in America. Within the plus-size community, I identify as "medium fat," so I still have a lot of privilege when it comes to finding clothing options. It's much harder for women just a few sizes larger than I am, which is infuriating, not to mention senseless from a business perspective. I want to shake designers and say, *Hey, do you guys hate fat women so much that you're willing to cut out two-thirds of your potential customers? Do you really see our bodies as so unworthy of wearing your clothes?* But the hard truth is that a lot of people in the fashion world would really prefer that I weren't in it.

And I think a lot of plus-size women feel that way in our day-to-day lives. For us, something as simple as posting an outfit-of-the-day selfie is a political action, and we have to live with all the people who feel entitled to comment on our bodies, to tell us we're ugly, or unhealthy, or grotesque.

TS: People actually say that to you?

Bea: On my blog, and on my Insta and Twitter comments? All the time! So many people have this vitriolic hatred of women in the public eye—especially women who have the audacity not to conform to conventional beauty standards—and on social media, they can deliver their hostility directly to our mentions. I wish I could say it never gets to me, but sometimes it does. It hurts to have strangers echoing the worst things I've ever believed about myself. But I love fashion so much because it has the power to make me feel strong and beautiful. Ditto for my closest friends and my amazing community of readers.

TS: What about romance? Anyone special who makes you feel particularly beautiful?

Bea: Not right now! My schedule is pretty hectic, and I haven't had time or energy to put into finding a great relationship. But who knows, maybe I'll figure that out soon.

TEXT MESSAGE TRANSCRIPT, JUNE 9:
BEA SCHUMACHER & RAY MORETTI

Ray [9:48am]: Guess . . . what . . . I have

Bea [9:53am]: A spaceship. Ten rubies. Oh my god, is it a pony????

Ray [9:54am]: Nope, better than all those things

Ray [9:55am]: I have, in my possession . . . a plane ticket to Los Angeles.

Bea [9:56am]:

Bea [9:56am]: Is this really happening? I haven't seen you in so long I forget what you look like

Ray [9:57am]: Ouch. (You're right, I deserve that)

Ray [9:57am]: But yes! I get in the afternoon of July fourth, and then I'll spend the night at your place (if that's okay?) before I head to San Diego the next morning for Sarah's folks' anniversary party. Does that work?

Bea [9:58am]: Definitely! Want me to poll the old crowd from the agency to see who's around?

Ray [9:59am]: Up to you, but I'd rather just catch up with you than split time with a whole group

Ray [10:00am]: I know I had to move to Atlanta to "be supportive of my fiancée's career" or whatever, but I hate being so far from you, Bea.

Ray [10:00am]: I really miss you.

Bea [10:04am]: I miss you too.

Bea insisted she wasn't nervous to see Ray, but the deep breaths she kept taking (air hissing in through her teeth, then pushed back out past lips pursed in a Lamaze-shaped "ooh") as she sat in traffic on the 10 told another story. She reassured herself that she was a different person now than the girl who spent all those years obsessed with him, the shy Hollywood agency assistant in love with the most handsome guy in her mailroom class.

How unbearably cliché, Bea thought of her younger self as she pulled off the highway and into the winding, moneyed streets of Westwood, where quaint Tudor houses that looked airlifted from a Grimm story lined every block. She'd rather have stayed in her hodgepodge neighborhood on the east side of Los Angeles, but her favorite wine shop was here, nearly an hour away in traffic. For her one night with Ray (pretend though she might that it was no big deal), she knew she had to make the trek.

Les Caves was easy to miss with its unobtrusive sign and rough-hewn wooden door, and still easier to ignore when one peered inside briefly to see scattered tables laden with disorganized clusters of bottles. But Bea loved it here—loved speaking her broken French with the shopkeepers, loved delighting in the quirky wines they put aside for her, mouth-searingly dry Meuniers and sharply honeyed Savennières.

"Bea, *bon matin!*" Paul, who owned the shop with his wife, was pudgy and ebullient. Bea often joked that Paul had turned her into an insufferable wine snob, but he always laughed heartily and corrected her that she should be proud to be a connoisseur.

"*Bonjour, Paul,*" Bea said with a grin.

"*Et qu'est-ce que tu désires aujourd'hui?*" he asked. "Perhaps something very light, dry fruit and mineral? It is so hot!"

"*C'est vrai,*" Bea agreed—L.A. was experiencing its annual July heat wave, the few days a year when even the desert nights barely dipped below 90, rendering the entire city unlivable. It had been like this, too, the night Ray kissed her. That one perfect, terrible night five years ago, when he was stumbling drunk on the sidewalk in front of Chateau Marmont, his breath stale with cigarettes and whiskey, tears streaming down his face as he told Bea his mom was sick again, maybe terminally this time. He put his arms around Bea's neck and whispered, "I can't do

this without you." She replied, "You don't have to," not understanding whether he meant as friends or something more.

After all the countless nights of drinking together, sharing
hushed secrets and whispered observations, feeling so starved
to be physically close to him, clamping down nausea as she
watched him flirt and kiss and leave whatever bar they were
in with yet another gorgeous aspiring actress/model/singer, finally, *finally,* he was looking right at Bea.

It was too hot, and everything was damp, and she knew it
was wrong when he leaned in to kiss her—he was too upset,
too drunk, too distracted. But she didn't care, because she had
wanted this so much for so long, and she felt like she had
somehow managed to wrench her life onto the right track by
sheer force of will.

After the kiss, she expected him to say something
profound—or something earnest, at the very least—but he
just mumbled that he needed to call a car, he had an early
flight.

"Oh," Bea had stammered. "Sure. Of course."

He flew home to Minnesota the next morning. He was
only supposed to be gone for a few days, or maybe a few
weeks, but he never came back, except to pack up his things
and drive east. He spent the next few months at home with his
family, watching his mother die; then he moved to Virginia
for law school; after that, it was off to a fancy firm job in New
York, where he met his girlfriend, Sarah; he followed her to
Atlanta when she won a coveted promotion; that was where
they got engaged.

And somehow, Bea still couldn't believe any of it, as if the
last eight years of her life had existed in some kind of stasis.
Three years of knowing Ray, dreaming of Ray, yearning for

Ray, believing with all her heart that he must feel the same. One night of blissful, agonizing confirmation. Five years of wondering whether any of it had been real.

She'd dated other men in the intervening time, of course, but she never found that same spark—no one so movie-star handsome, so quietly funny, so utterly captivating. Of all the app dates and setups, no one else had that thick, dark hair and those smoldering Brando eyes; no one else could run a finger along her arm and make her entire body feel weak.

And anyway, Bea's primary focus was on other aspects of her life—career, friends, travel, family—she didn't mind waiting to find another love as passionate and exciting as what she'd felt for Ray. She was sure one would come eventually. And in the meantime . . . well, in the meantime . . . was it really so bad to live in her memories? Her fantasies?

But today wasn't a memory or a fantasy: Ray was on a plane right now, probably somewhere over the Midwest, hurtling toward Los Angeles, where he was spending one night in Bea's guest room before catching a train to San Diego the next morning for some kind of anniversary weekend for his fiancée's parents. Bea and Ray hadn't seen each other for more than a year, not since a stilted meet-up in a crowded bar (with Sarah in tow, no less) during one of Bea's whirlwind trips for New York Fashion Week. It had been loud, Bea had been exhausted, Ray had been sour. But tonight could be different—just the two of them, no noise. A chance to rekindle the connection Bea so desperately missed.

"No." Bea shook her head when Paul produced one of her typical bottles, a crisp twelve-dollar white. "For tonight, I need something special."

Three hours later, Bea paced the wide, uneven floorboards of her bungalow in Elysian Heights, a rickety little rental perched precariously on a hillside overlooking Elysian Park. The place was filled with creaks and cracks where faucets were rusty and doors weren't cut quite long enough, but Bea loved it all the more for that; she vastly preferred a homey, colorful aesthetic to anything too modern or tidy—which, to her eye, lacked character.

Now, though, with Ray in a cab just minutes away, she began to see her home through his eyes: not artful but ragged, not welcoming but pitiful. She smoothed down the full skirt of her black corseted sundress (affectionately nicknamed her "slutty goth milkmaid ensemble" because of the off-the-shoulder neckline that showed off her cleavage in Oktoberfest proportion) and wondered if he'd see her the same way.

"This is idiotic," Bea muttered, stopping in front of her hall mirror to tousle her meticulously mussed waves one more time, her hair nearly as dark as the perfectly smudged kohl eyeliner that rendered her bright blue eyes electric. She sucked in a breath: He was just her friend, just Ray, just visiting. Him coming here didn't mean anything—just as their kiss, their whole history, all of it, probably never had. It was all in her head, as usual.

Except the second she opened the door and he threw his arms around her, she knew that she was wrong.

"Bea." He exhaled, dropping his bag on the floor with a thwack so he could fully encircle her with both arms, hugging her tightly against him.

"Hiya, stranger." Bea beamed up at him, and God he looked the same, straight nose and soft lips and those eyes that drank in every inch of her, his hungry gaze that always made her face flush with heat.

"I missed you." He gave her a little squeeze, leaning down to kiss her temple gently.

"I've been here this whole time," she retorted, surprising herself with the edge in her voice.

"You're right." He took her hand. "I'm an asshole. I should visit more."

"Well, you're here now," Bea said quietly.

"And you're . . . happy about that?" He met her eye, not letting her duck the subtext.

"Come on, Ray," she demurred. "You know I am."

"So?" He moved his body against hers, giving her a little nudge. "What does a guy have to do to get the ten-cent tour around here?"

"Oh my God, you've never been here before. How strange is that?"

"Unbelievably strange." He grinned. "Stranger than long-form improv in the basement of that chicken place on Sunset."

"They should have called it longest-night-of-our-lives-form improv," Bea joked, and Ray laughed appreciatively. "Anyway, this is the living room. Do you like it?"

Ray wandered through the cozy room, perusing the treasures from all Bea's travels that crowded every available surface—a carved wooden elephant from Siem Reap, a hand-glazed vase from New Orleans, her laminated LACMA membership card. Ray picked up a glass figurine she'd found in Paris, turning it over in his hands.

"You bought this in college, right—at that flea market you loved? You used to keep it on your desk at the agency."

"Good memory," Bea said, her voice suddenly mottled with emotion.

"This place is great." Ray shook his head. "You should see our nightmare condo in Atlanta—everything shiny and new like a perfect little HGTV prison. Kind of a great metaphor when you think about it."

Bea wasn't sure what to say to that—or if she was meant to say anything.

"Um, do you want something to drink?" she ventured. "I have some rosé chilling."

"Sounds amazing." Ray let his fingers brush against hers, and Bea realized that *this* was the idiocy—the idea that she had ever been remotely over him.

Their plan was to head to a rooftop party at her friends' loft downtown, but Ray wanted to shower first. So after their glass of wine, Bea waited on the couch, listening to the water run and dragging her mind forcibly away from visions of Ray's naked body wrapped in one of the fluffy white towels she'd laid out for him. A shiver went up her spine—or maybe it was just the air conditioning kicking into overdrive.

"I feel like a whole new human," he remarked as he breezed into the living room.

It was unfair—unholy, even—how good he looked in an easy pair of khaki shorts and a soft white linen button-down. Black hair, damp skin, like James fucking Bond climbing down from a yacht and wading ashore.

"Plane grime," Bea forced out, her voice an octave higher than normal. "The worst!"

"You sure you want to go to this party?" He plopped down on the couch beside her, his arm casually leaning against hers—they were a little too still, like they'd both noticed the contact but had no idea what to do about it.

"Oh, um," Bea stumbled, "did you not want to go out?"

Ray shrugged. "I dunno. We could just hang here. If you wanted."

Was he suggesting—what? Nothing? Anything? *Something?* She had to get out of this house. Being here with him was making her paranoid, so desperate for his attention that she was reading imagined prurience into every harmless sentence.

"My friends are expecting us." She hopped off the couch and grabbed her phone to call a car. "It'll be fun, I promise."

"If you can brave the heat, I guess I can too," Ray groused good-naturedly.

Bea nearly exhaled audibly. He just wanted to avoid the heat! He didn't want—

Me. She made herself finish the thought. *He didn't want me.*

Well, good. He was engaged to another woman. Nothing could happen, even if he did want her. Which he didn't, so. That was that.

Bea hit the button to confirm her cab. Their driver would arrive in seven minutes.

The party was just a touch on the wrong side of fun—everyone a little too drunk, a little too hot, quippy comments that otherwise would have made for light banter landing somewhere closer to ornery, tempers running thick and foul, the heat hanging darkly even after the sun went down.

"Who's *this* tall drink of water?" Bea's friend Mark asked with a leer.

"He's Ray, and he's straight," Bea snapped.

"But not narrow." Ray winked, flirting—as he always did, with everyone, making every person he ever talked to feel special, when the truth was that no one ever was.

"Excuse me, I need another drink." Bea rolled her eyes and flounced off to refill her glass of punch. Why had she wanted to come to this party? Why had she wanted to see Ray in the first place? After so many years of missing him so much, she thought seeing him would feel good, but it was awful. Just an acutely painful reminder of how much she still wanted him, and how completely he would never, ever be hers.

"Hey, are you okay?" Ray came up behind her, a hand at her waist. She jumped away, the contact too close, too intimate.

"Don't do that," she chided.

But he reached for her again. "Tell me what's bothering you."

Above them, the first firework exploded—flashes of green and gold, and appreciative gasps all around them as everyone looked skyward. But not Ray. His eyes were trained on Bea.

"Nothing's wrong," she insisted. "I'm fine."

"Don't lie to me," he said firmly, but there was a note of desperation there. "I know you're not fine. Bea, I'm not either."

Cracks and booms echoed around them, red and blue and silver, as he circled her wrists with his fingers.

"Bea . . ."

She shook her head. "Ray, what are you doing?"

He pulled her closer. "You know what I'm doing."

His fingers were grazing up her forearms, her biceps, her shoulders, his hands were in her hair. She heard him ask "Is this okay?" and it wasn't, it fucking wasn't, he knew it wasn't, but she felt her head nodding as if a puppeteer were bobbing it with unseen string, and then he was kissing her. It was so intense, his body pressed against hers, his hands pulling her face closer and closer, his teeth nipping at her lips, and she couldn't breathe, and she didn't care, and when he said, "Can we go home now?" she nodded again. This time, with agency. With intent.

The car ride was unbearable, his hands on her thighs, standstill traffic on the 101. When they finally got to her house, she thought they wouldn't even make it to the bed; he threw her against the wall so hard and ripped the damn dress off her. No one had ever wanted her that much. She was so confused, even as it was happening—had he always wanted this? Why hadn't it happened sooner, when they lived in the same place, when he was single, all those years that she was so in love?

It doesn't matter, she told herself. *He's here now. After all this time, he's here.*

He was on top of her, kissing her gently, and a smile lit up her whole face.

"What is it?" he asked, smiling too.

"Nothing." Her heart swelled, the joy of the moment so expansive it was almost painful. "I'm just really, really happy."

"Me too." He kissed her again, and she breathed in his reassurance. "Bea, you're all I've wanted."

TEXT MESSAGE TRANSCRIPT, JULY 5:
BEA SCHUMACHER & RAY MORETTI

Ray [7:23am]: Hey

Ray [7:23am]: Are you up?

Ray [7:24am]: Sorry I didn't wake you before I left

Ray [7:26am]: On my train now, should be in San Diego around 10, and then it's a lot of brunches and things with Sarah's folks

Ray [7:27am]: But I'll call you later?

Bea [1:31pm]: Ok

JULY 8

Bea [9:25am]: Hi

Ray [9:28am]: Hey

Bea [9:29am]: You never called the other night

Bea [9:29am]: I really think we should talk

Ray [9:31am]: Oh yeah

Ray [9:31am]: Things got really busy

Ray [9:32am]: This week is crazy, let me get back to you

TEXT MESSAGE TRANSCRIPT, JULY 8:
BEA SCHUMACHER & MARIN MENDOZA

Marin [9:33am]: "Let me get back to you"?!?!?!?!?!

Marin [9:33am]: No

Marin [9:34am]: No

Marin [9:34am]: I'm sorry

Marin [9:34am]: No

Marin [9:34am]: He did not say that to you!!!!

Bea [9:36am]: He . . . did

Marin [9:36am]: What did you say?

Bea [9:37am]: Nothing. I didn't say anything

Bea [9:37am]: I don't know what to say to him

Marin [9:38am]: What do you want to say?

Bea [9:41am]: I don't know, hi Ray, I think we've loved each other for almost a decade, even though it was always some new excuse for why you had to live in some new city, be with some new girl, and now you're engaged, but when we slept together it felt like my whole life suddenly clicked into place, like maybe my story was finally ending, or starting, or something, and then you just left like you always do, because you're a coward, but I love you anyway. And I wish I didn't. And I wish you'd just come back.

Marin [9:42am]: I don't think you should say that.

Bea [9:43am]: I hate my life

Marin [9:43am]: Stay right there. I'm coming over.

FOOD2YOU DELIVERY RECEIPT:
ACCOUNT HOLDER–BEATRICE SCHUMACHER

DELIVER TO:

Beatrice Schumacher
1841 Avalon Way
Los Angeles, CA 90026

Stouffer's frozen meals: Macaroni and cheese (25 units)
LaCroix Sparkling Water (Pamplemousse flavor) (6 cases)
Doritos Corn Chips (Cooler Ranch flavor) (10 bags)
Doritos Corn Chips (Nacho Cheesier flavor) (10 bags)
Skinny Cow Ice Cream Sandwiches (original flavor)
    (6 boxes)
JIF Extra Creamy Peanut Butter (5 jars)
Original Saltine Crackers (5 boxes)
Diet Coke (12 cases)
Z-quil Sleep Aid Medication (2 boxes)
Cottonelle Rippled Toilet Paper (18-roll pack)

NOTE:

Do not ring bell. Client waives signature requirement. Leave
    groceries at front door.

TEXT MESSAGE TRANSCRIPT, AUGUST 25:
BEA SCHUMACHER & MARIN MENDOZA

Marin [2:28pm]: Hey, have you left yet? Sharon made this white peach sangria and it's VERY GOOD you should def get a car instead of driving

Bea [2:30pm]: I think I might just stay home? I'm so behind on work stuff

Marin [2:31pm]: Bea, NO! You didn't come to Sneha's thing yesterday either, she was pissed!! Did you go on your date last night?

Bea [2:35pm]: I couldn't

Marin [2:36pm]: Okay

Marin [2:37pm]: But babe, you're not going to get over him if you never meet anyone new

Bea [2:38pm]: I know. I'm just not ready.

Marin [2:38pm]: I wish you'd come to Sharon's. We'd all really love to see you.

TEXT MESSAGE TRANSCRIPT, AUGUST 25:
BEA SCHUMACHER & RAY MORETTI

Bea [7:48pm]: So are you really never going to respond to any of my emails? Not one of them?

Bea [7:48pm]: I'm not trying to ruin your life. I just want to talk.

Bea [7:49pm]: I hate this, Ray. I miss you.

SELECTED MESSAGES FROM THE TINDER MESSAGE FOLDER
OF BEA SCHUMACHER

Jim: Yo!!!!!!!!!!!!

Bea: Hey there:)

Jim: GIVE. ME. THOSE. CURVES.

Bea: I . . . what?

Jim: GIMME EM BEA GIMME THOSE CURVES

user unmatched and blocked

Todd: sup b

Bea: nm, T. how are you?

Todd: can I come over

Todd: address?

Bea: do you think we maybe skipped a couple of steps there?

Todd: wut

Bea: Hey, Alex! Love that Paris pic. My fav city. :)

Alex: Sorry, I don't think this is going to work.

Bea: Excuse me?

Alex: You need to show your body in your top photo. A headshot is dishonest.

Kip: Hello, Bea. How's your week going?

Bea: Hi, Kip! It's pretty average, a little work, a nice hike now that it's actually starting to feel like fall.

Bea: (Oh god, am I the boring girl who talks about the weather? Sigh.)

Bea: How's your week?

Kip: Ha! As residents of Los Angeles, I think we're legally obligated to mark the seasonal transition from high of 84 to high of 78.

Kip: My week's alright. Would you like to meet for a drink?

Bea: Sure, I could do that. Thursday?

BLOG POST FROM OMBEA.COM
7,849 Reblogs ↻ · 22,378 Likes ♥

Hey OMBeauties! Okay, I need to level with you: I'm smiling in this photo, but I'm not feeling great right now. I went on a Tinder date tonight—my first date in a while, in fact. As you can see, I wore my patented First Date Uniform: faded black skinny jeans and a form-fitting V-neck top from Universal Standard that miraculously flatter curves on *every* body, Stuart Weitzman ankle boots fabricated in the Technicolor floral tapestry of my fantasies, and bright-green statement earrings I found at a street market in Barcelona last summer. I wear nearly this exact outfit on every first date (future suitors, be forewarned!), because I find that when you're stressed and anxious about meeting someone new, having a go-to look that makes you feel comfortable yet confident, laid-back yet sexy, can alleviate some of the nerves.

And beauties, I *did* feel great tonight—until I walked into the bar my date had chosen.

Usually, when I go out with dates or friends, I'm the plan-maker. I pick the restaurant or bar so I can make sure it has comfortable seating (seriously, can we ban bolted-down booths forever?); I order the car and pay the surcharge for a sedan or SUV so I won't feel cramped and claustrophobic in the back seat of an itsy-bitsy hatchback.

But tonight, my date was pumped to try a chic new cocktail bar in our neighborhood: a crowded haunt with cozy little high-top tables for two sprinkled throughout the narrow space. The entire time I was there, I felt like a pariah mumbling, "Sorry, excuse me," to every person I inevitably bumped into, praying I wouldn't accidentally cause even a drop of drink spillage, feeling like no matter where I stood, I was always in someone's way.

Going on a first date can be scary for anyone, but I find that for me, natural insecurities can spiral into an echo chamber of all the horrible things society has ever implied (or outright declared!) about my fatness. Even though my date tonight didn't say or do anything to make me feel unattractive, being in that bar surrounded by thin people (ah, Los Angeles), it was perilously easy to backslide into this ubiquitous idea that I'd be so much happier if only I looked like them. As though if I could make my body fit on one of those tiny barstools, I'd be in a perfect, fulfilling relationship instead of forcing myself to get through this date, wishing I could just disappear.

Of course, I know that none of that is true. That I can't change my body type (and don't even want to!), that thin women are no more happy than I am, that these insecurities are seeded and tended in my brain by the weight-loss industry, which profits from our collective self-loathing to the tune of $70 billion every year—despite the fact that 97 percent of diets fail. (Side note: What if we put all that money toward solving actual health problems instead? Could we cure ovarian cancer, like, tomorrow?) I *know* all of these things. But sometimes, like tonight, I just can't feel them.

Okay, beauties, enough rambling from me—I'm off to bed. Thanks for keeping me company; you guys brighten up even the dreariest night. More soon.

xoxo, Bea

Comment from Sierra819: Sorry your date was a bummer Bea!!! But you look amazing!!!!

Comment from djgy23987359: youre lucky anyone would date you go see a doctor before the diabetes kills you

TEXT MESSAGE TRANSCRIPT, OCTOBER 3:
BEA SCHUMACHER & MARIN MENDOZA

Marin [10:53pm]: Just saw your post—you ok?? How was Kip??

Bea [10:56pm]: Hey, I'm fine. He was fine. It was all fine.

Marin [10:57pm]: That's the most terrifying the word "fine" has ever sounded.

Marin [10:57pm]: Do you think you'll see him again?

Bea [10:59pm]: No, it was awkward. We didn't really have anything to talk about.

Marin [11:00pm]: Give me a break, you could banter with a cardboard box if you had to.

Bea [11:02pm]: I don't know. I just felt like there was lead in my chest, I couldn't get out of there fast enough. Maybe it was too soon.

Marin [11:03pm]: Ugh, I'm sorry babe. Do you want me to come over?

Bea [11:04pm]: You're an angel, but I'm okay. I'm gonna kill the rosé in my fridge, watch some old eps of Brooklyn Nine-Nine and go to sleep.

Marin [11:04pm]: Yessssssss I love this plan!! Watch as much Rosa Diaz as possible and become a queer woman so you never have to date men again!!

Bea [11:06pm]: Is that how queerness works?

Marin [11:06pm]: Listen, was I born gay, or did Julia Stiles in 10 Things I Hate About You *make* me gay? It's literally impossible to know.

Marin [11:06pm]: Get some sleep, and don't stay up until all hours drafting emails you'll never send to you-know-who, okay?

Bea [11:08pm]: I won't. I promise.

UNSENT EMAIL FROM THE DRAFT FOLDER OF BEA@OMBEA.COM

FROM: Bea Schumacher <bea@ombea.com>
TO: [no recipient specified]
SUBJECT: [no subject]

Dear Ray,

I don't know what to say to you, but I feel like I have to say something.

I still miss you. So much, not every day anymore, not every minute, not like it was, but when I remember for half a second how good it was, God, I'm just gone. Isn't that ridiculous? That after all these months and years of you jerking me around, disappearing from my life and dropping back in when it suits you, of doing anything and everything I could think of to put you out of my mind, you still infest my flesh, my blood, like you're some vital chain binding me together. And I fucking hate you for it, and I fucking hate myself for being party to this absurdity. Because, what, what, am I an idiot? Am I this pathetic that the second a smart, handsome man shows me attention, no matter how bad he is for me, no matter how deeply I know it, I fall for him anyway?

I feel like you're a pit I can't climb out of. The clawing and craning skyward to try and find some shred of light is so exhausting, and it's so much easier to let the ghost of your arms pull me down and down and down. If I let myself remember how you taste, my breath gets hard, my body heaves. If I let myself consider you inside me, I can't function.

I don't know how I handed you this power, it makes me so insane that you have it. And I fucking know, I know it's probably just me and my own shit, that you don't have a damn thing to do with it. You're just some vessel holding all my sadness, glowing with the nuclear energy of my loneliness. If I try to imagine you letting me go, I don't feel free. I feel untethered, unbound. Like I'm nothing and nowhere.

But if I imagine you holding me, I crumple. Ray, I'm running out of ways to exist.

This sounds so crazy, I know I sound crazy. I'm not sending you this. I would never send you this. But God, Ray. Don't you miss me? Not this mess I am now, but the me who was, until recently, your best friend?

I don't know where I am, Ray. I don't know where we are.

TEXT MESSAGE TRANSCRIPT, OCTOBER 14:
BEA SCHUMACHER & MARIN MENDOZA

Marin [4:15pm]: So tonight, 7:30? I'll bring wine, you order takeout?

Marin [4:16pm]: I'm kind of feeling that good bougie Thai

place, the one with the crazy pad kee mao? But idk
I could be talked into burgers. OOOH OR DONER

Bea [4:22pm]: ?????

Marin [4:23pm]: IT'S MAIN SQUEEZE PREMIERE
NIGHT BEA OR HAD YOU FORGOTTEN

Bea [4:26pm]: I . . . had forgotten

Marin [4:26pm]: Well great news we're watching at your house
so there's no appropriate way for you to cancel.

Bea [4:27pm]: I'm gonna order vegan

Marin [4:28pm]: Ugh don't be spiteful. See you soon!!

TWITTER THREAD FROM USER @OMBEA

@OMBea Hey there, OMBeauties! Totally forgot tonight was
@MainSqueezeABS premiere night, but now my bestie and I
are on my couch with tacos & tequila and we're ready to live-
tweet every plot twist! Join us?

@OMBea Is it just me, or do the people on this show keep getting more boring? Jayden is the whitest white man in history
and every one of these girls is basically performance art of
straight femininity.

@OMBea Like what would happen if one of these women wore
PANTS? Or had SHORT HAIR? Would the world end?

@OMBea And obviously they could NEVER be above a size 4,
Jayden's poor sad penis would break beneath the crushing
weight of an average-sized woman.

@OMBea My friend @MaybeMarin wants to know if we should
drink every time one of the girls says she needs a man to com-

plete her life. I say no bc we might get real real wasted, but what say you???

@OMBea WHO IS THIS GIRL TAYLOR AND WHY IS SHE SAYING ALL THESE FACTS ABOUT PERSONAL FINANCE MARRY HER JAYDEN

@OMBea (we're doing the drinking game)

@OMBea Ok here's another thing though. These women are supposed to be "real" but these bodies are not realistic AT ALL. Who actually LOOKS LIKE THIS?

@OMBea Before you come for me about that one plus-size girl who was on the show one time a) she was A LITERAL MODEL and b) she got eliminated the first night so don't even

@OMBea And obviously I know, it's just TV, it's all staged and fake, but they bill it as reality! Here are real people, finding real love! Except you, all 95% of humans who look nothing like this.

   @CisforCatie PREACH, BEA!!

   @dcfan822828 you actually won't find love tho so like . . .

   @EmmaCsYou love this!!!!!!!! more please!!!!!! can you do a post about this????

TEXT MESSAGE TRANSCRIPT, OCTOBER 15:
BEA SCHUMACHER & MARIN MENDOZA

Marin [7:29am]: Uhhhhhhhhhhhhhhhhhh

Marin [7:29am]: Are you awake

Marin [7:30am]: Probably not, right, okay

Marin [7:31am]: When you wake up . . . maybe look at Twitter

Bea [9:41am]: Oh god why, who's canceled now

Marin [9:42am]: Bea.

Marin [9:42am]: After I left last night . . . you wrote a blog post?

Bea [9:43]: Well my laptop is currently upside down on top of a pile of lipsticks (?) on my kitchen counter (??), so . . . it's possible?

Bea [9:43am]: Oh wait, yes, I definitely did

Bea [9:43am]: Wow I was really feeling my rage, huh????

Marin [9:44am]: Please just check your Twitter.

VIRAL ROUNDUP OF THE WEEK: 10/18
by Patrick Matz, mashable.com

We thought for sure the most shared content of the week would be an already-infamous video of a tabby cat being catapulted off a seesaw by an overexuberant toddler (if you haven't seen it yet, do yourself a favor and *click here*), but a late-breaking surge of support has brought us a new champion: Plus-size blogger Bea Schumacher's scorching critique of reality romance juggernaut *Main Squeeze* has now been shared more than a million times across Facebook, Twitter, Tumblr, and Instagram. We estimate the viral post has reached more than 15 million people, a staggering 3 million of whom have clicked "Like." Read on for the rest of the week's viral content, including a can't-miss tweetstorm detailing the conspiracy theory you never knew you always needed about Hillary Clinton's dogs.

"PACK YOUR THINGS AND GO":
PLUS-SIZE BLOGGER ANNIHILATES *MAIN SQUEEZE*
by Danielle Kander, bubblegiggle.com

Plus-size blogger Bea Schumacher loves *Main Squeeze*—and she's not alone! Who among us can resist watching one man or woman choose from 25 potential suitors, narrowing the field week by week until we're left with one lucky winner for a fairy-tale proposal, a whirlwind engagement, and a low-key breakup six to eight weeks later?

But I don't love the show's total lack of diversity—and neither does Schumacher. Monday night, she went on her blog OMBea (if you're not following her, you're doing the internet wrong) to post an epic takedown. She addressed the show's "appalling" lack of racial diversity, its "perplexing" erasure of queerness, and most of all, its "abject refusal to include any woman who wears above a size 4, despite the fact that two-thirds of American women are size 14 and above."

"*Main Squeeze* is the most successful romance reality show in history," Schumacher wrote. "It defines what it means for 'real' people to find love—except according to its own standards, fat people aren't real. We aren't worthy. We don't even exist."

So far, Schumacher's scathing post has been shared more than a million times on social media, resulting in a flood of new traffic to her blog and Instagram, where she now has more than 600,000 followers. For our part, we're THRILLED that more people will see Bea's body-positive message, and we can only hope her post will lead to some actual change on *Main Squeeze*—and on television.

SELECTED DIGITAL HEADLINES
RUN DURING *MAIN SQUEEZE* SEASON 13

MEET THE WOMAN TAKING DOWN ROMANCE "REALITY"
Bea Schumacher is plus-size and proud!

ONLINE PETITION PUSHES ADVERTISERS
TO BOYCOTT *MAIN SQUEEZE*
The petition, launched on the website change.biz,
has more than 40,000 signatures.

"I LOVE MY THICK BLOGGER"—WOULD YOU BANG A BIG GIRL?
According to our new survey, 60 percent of men
say they'd sleep with Bea Schumacher.

ANGRY INCELS SEND CASES OF SLIMFAST TO PLUS-SIZE BLOGGER
Twitter war explodes after Men's Rights Activists
publish Bea Schumacher's home address.

PLUS-SIZE BLOGGER DONATES HUNDREDS OF CASES
OF SLIMFAST TO L.A. FOOD BANK
"They're the exact same thing as Soylent,
you misogynist turds," says Bea Schumacher.

SCANDAL: FORMER *MAIN SQUEEZE* CONTESTANT
REVEALS DIETING PRESSURE ON-SET
Gina DiLuca claims women on-set encouraged diet pills
and laxative abuse: "It was a literal shit show."

IN TEPID FINALE, *MAIN SQUEEZE* RATINGS HIT 5-YEAR LOW
Notorious producer Micah Faust is reportedly in hot water at ABS.

CAN *MAIN SQUEEZE* SURVIVE WITHOUT WOMEN VIEWERS?
Amidst controversy and dangerously low ratings, rumors fly that ABS may cancel the reality juggernaut.

LAUREN MATHERS NEW EP
IN MAJOR *MAIN SQUEEZE* SHAKE-UP
by Tia Sussman, deadline.com

Following waves of negative publicity and a five-year low in ratings, *Deadline* can confirm exclusively that executive producer and showrunner Micah Faust is OUT at *Main Squeeze*. Producer Lauren Mathers—long seen as Faust's right hand and effectively running the day-to-day on-set—has been promoted to the top spot and will take over immediately, according to *Deadline*'s ears at ABS.

"The brass at ABS have been looking for an excuse to ditch Faust for a long time," said our ABS source, speaking under condition of anonymity. "Alyssa [Messersmith, senior VP of unscripted at ABS] hated Faust's shit—the drugs, the women, the risky behavior on-set, the production shutdowns."

Faust's bad-boy antics have been infamous for decades, but few believed he would ever actually be ousted from his own signature franchise. As for his successor, Mathers has kept relatively under the radar in the industry, working her way up the ladder at *Main Squeeze* for the last five years. I hear she's respected on-set and well liked by the crew. At just 28 years old, she's now one of the youngest showrunners in town—but my source says not to underestimate her.

"Lauren is strategic," the source explained. "She knew this

was the moment to make a play for Faust's job, and that she had the ally she needed in Alyssa." But Mathers shouldn't get too comfortable in Faust's chair. The source went on: "If Lauren can't bring the ratings up for the spring season of *Main Squeeze,* there's no doubt in my mind that Alyssa will fire her ass too. There are plenty of people in town who would love to run a show as big as *Main Squeeze.*"

INSTAGRAM DIRECT MESSAGE EXCHANGE, JANUARY 6: @OMBEA AND @LMATHERS1116

LMathers1116 Hey Bea, this is Lauren Mathers, the new executive producer at Main Squeeze. I'd love to meet and talk more about your piece. Can we have coffee? Where in town are you?

OMBea Hi, Lauren. Well, this is unexpected! I'm in Echo Park.

LMathers1116 Of COURSE you are! I'm in Venice.

OMBea Ha, a world away. Would a phone call be easier?

LMathers1116 No, I'd really love to see you in person. Let's meet in the middle—drinks by the pool at the Standard in WeHo? How's tomorrow at 3?

OMBea Sure, that works. See you then.

Ever since the Fourth of July, Bea felt like opening her eyes each morning was some kind of emotional slot machine: 5 A.M., awake. Flip. A pressing, horrific dread: Ray's arms, his smell, already present. No. Can't start the day like this—pull the lever again. Another twenty minutes of sleep, maybe forty. Flip. Okay, this is better, just another day, just Tuesday. I can live with this. Let's go.

She went through this exercise every morning for months, the wish and foreboding of it mingling each night before bed. Maybe tomorrow will be better. Maybe it will be the same.

What drove Bea truly insane was her total lack of control in the whole scenario. No matter how good a day she had, how productive she was or how many friends she saw or how much she cried in therapy, there was no apparent correlation to how she would feel when she woke up the next morning. Or twenty minutes after that.

There were a few weeks during the height of her *Main Squeeze* post going viral when she was so inundated with texts and DMs and emails and press requests that her frazzled, cluttered existence almost didn't leave room for him. During those weeks, she wouldn't wake up thinking about him; instead, he'd snake into her consciousness later, always buzzing at the periphery, waiting for a few minutes between calls or an unmoving lane of traffic to strike.

Bea knew that pining after him was fruitless. One drunken, sloppy kiss five years ago; one perfect, awful night six months ago. He wasn't the love of her life—he wasn't even returning her texts. So why the hell couldn't she move on?

Bea dragged herself out of bed and ran through her calendar for the day—more or less empty since L.A. was slow to get back to the grind after the holidays. Nothing until her meeting at the Standard at three.

Lauren Mathers. How totally strange.

When her post blew up, Bea vaguely expected—okay,

fantasized—that someone from *Main Squeeze* would reach out to her, maybe invite her to consult on the show, participate in some way? But the show's producers had refused to acknowledge Bea's post at all, not even with a bland press statement. Their strategy had been to ride out the criticism in silence—and it had worked, more or less. Bea's post was only a story for a couple of weeks; there'd been a subsequent bout of thinkpieces debating the impact of the lack of body diversity in pop culture, but then those died out too.

So it was incomprehensible to Bea why the new executive producer of *Main Squeeze* would be reaching out now that her post was all but forgotten. Bea had emailed her agent, Olivia, immediately after Lauren DMed her, but Olivia couldn't dig up any dirt from her sources at ABS, so Bea was going into this meeting essentially blind.

It's probably just a get-to-know-you, Olivia had emailed, *to make you less inclined to drag them through the mud again when the new season starts in March. Which reminds me—we should DEF get you booked on some morning shows around the premiere. Maybe some late shows too. You're funny, right?*

Figuring out what to wear to drinks at the Standard was a futile endeavor. That particular part of town was the epicenter of L.A.'s looks-obsessed culture, where everyone was either an aspiring movie star or aspiring to sleep with one—people who couldn't possibly fathom that Bea could be proud of her body. But Bea was determined to go to the meeting in a bold, dare-you-to-look-away style, so after an hour of weighing options, she settled on one of her favorite looks: lavender coveralls with a playful snake pattern from Nooworks, cinched with a top-stitched taupe corset belt to suggest a more defined waist, decadent cognac booties with a stacked wooden heel, all topped off with her favorite Tom Ford aviators and oversized rose-gold hoop earrings studded with rhinestones.

She arrived ten minutes early, but Lauren was already waiting—she rose from their table and rushed to greet Bea as soon as she walked out onto the pool deck.

"Bea! So great to meet you." Lauren's voice matched her appearance: rich, sharp, and deliberate. Rail thin in skinny jeans, a silk tank, a hunter-green blazer, and sky-high mules, Lauren looked every inch the moneyed Yale grad Bea had Insta-stalked earlier that day. Her glossy auburn hair was thick and straight, her skin creamy and freckled, her hazel eyes vividly alert—it was instantly apparent to Bea that this was a woman who missed nothing.

"Lauren, hey." Bea smiled, instinctively patting down her own wild waves (made more ungovernable by her universal insistence on driving with the top down on her clunky vintage Saab convertible, which was avocado green and affectionately nicknamed Kermit the Car).

"So you're early to everything too?" Lauren asked as they got seated at a table overlooking the pool and the sprawling Hollywood hills beyond. "Not the way people roll in this city."

"Not usually," Bea admitted, "but traffic was nonexistent. I love L.A. from Christmas to Sundance."

"Oh God, same!" Lauren laughed. "The only thing better is Coachella—it's like every asshole in the city gets raptured and you can park wherever you want. Hey!" She turned to the waitress Bea hadn't seen approach. "Can we get some chips and guac, and maybe some of those good off-menu summer rolls? And I put in an order for two French 75s with the bartender—are those coming?"

"Yep! Let me grab them for you."

"Great."

Lauren handed their unopened menus to the waitress, who bounced off without bothering to engage with Bea at all. Bea turned to Lauren, her suspicion rising.

"So you know my favorite drink?" Bea asked.

"Bea, I think you're going to find I know an unnerving amount about you."

"And why is that?" Bea asked, unable to quash her curiosity. A delicious smile spread across Lauren's face.

"What would you say," she said slowly, turning the words over in her mouth, "if I told you that you're my pick to be the next Main Squeeze?"

"Excuse me?"

"French 75s!" The waitress was back, depositing their drinks. Lauren lifted hers to clink glasses with Bea, but Bea couldn't think, let alone move.

"Okay," Lauren said gently, "I'm seeing now that maybe I should have worked up to that a little better. But fuck, Bea, isn't this exciting? You're going to change the face of reality television."

"So . . ." Bea's throat felt dry. "You're saying . . ."

Lauren put down her drink and leaned in. "I'm saying, I want you to be the next star of *Main Squeeze*. I want to hand-pick twenty-five men to compete for your attention, and I want you to get engaged to one of them on television. I want to transform the way America sees plus-size women. I want to explode your career and change your life."

At this, Bea burst out laughing. "I'm sorry, I'm really sorry, but just—*why?*"

A busboy dropped off their appetizers, and Lauren helped

herself to some guac, as if this were a totally normal drinks meeting and not the most absurd conversation Bea had ever had.

"Bea, your piece was absolutely spot-on. Everything you said about the way the show totally ignores women who don't subscribe to one specific hyperfeminine beauty standard, about how we systematically erase every kind of diversity. The guys who used to run the show, the guys I worked for? They *hated* you. And you know what? I fucking hated them. I hated how smug and callous they were about women, how they think we're such idiots that we'll swallow their garbage version of Cinderella year after year, that we can't possibly want more for ourselves—or expect more of the men we fall in love with. Beauty queen, wife, mother. As if that's the totality of everything we could ever want to be."

"So it's true you staged a coup?" Bea asked. Lauren leaned back in her chair, a satisfied smirk twitching on her lips.

"I wouldn't say 'coup.'"

"What would you say?"

"I'd say that I've been overseeing the day-to-day operations of *Main Squeeze* for the past four seasons. That I've made myself indispensable—and that the cast, the crew, and the network all work with me a lot more than they work with certain men whose primary roles at the show have devolved into acting like pigs and cashing huge checks."

"And you convinced the network that it was worth losing the pigs to save themselves the checks."

Lauren tapped her nose—bingo.

"So why rock the boat?" Bea asked. "If you're finally running the show, why not just go with the old blueprint and keep your job secure?"

"First of all, the old blueprint isn't working—last season

was our lowest-rated finale in five years. Second, what's the point of putting me in charge if I'm just going to execute someone else's regressive vision? I told the network that I'm going to shake things up and deliver higher ratings, and I'm working on a lot of exciting ways to do that."

"Such as?" Bea prompted.

"Eradicating spoilers, for one."

"What? How can you humanly contain them?" Bea was extremely skeptical—ever since the advent of cell-phone cameras, the twists and turns of every season of *Main Squeeze* were captured by rabid fans and spread across the Internet well before they ever made it to television.

"By changing up our shooting schedule. Instead of filming the whole season in advance and then airing it afterward, we're going to kick things off with a live premiere, and then film our episodes on a nearly real-time schedule: The dates we shoot each week will air the following Monday."

"Holy shit." Bea was genuinely impressed. "Is that even possible?"

"Sure! There are British reality shows that air new episodes every *day*—it won't be easy, but I know our editing unit can turn around an episode per week no problem. Getting rid of spoilers is one half of my strategy—casting you is the other. America has never seen anyone like you lead a show like this. We're going to be right in the middle of the zeitgeist and send our ratings through the roof."

"Even if that's a sound strategy, why would you choose me? I'm sure the fact that I have a built-in fan base is a plus, but why not cast someone who hasn't, you know, openly vilified the show? Don't you think people will see me as some kind of fame-seeking hypocrite if I do this?"

"The fact that you have a lot of followers is huge for us,"

Lauren admitted. "But Bea, your piece is the *reason* I want to cast you. You wrote about why you watch the show in the first place—how much you connect with all these silly people risking looking like idiots on national television because they really do want to find love. You felt let down by the fact that the show was saying that not a single one of those silly idiots could look remotely like you. If you come on the show, it's a chance to prove that you—and, by extension, millions of women who look like you—*can* find love. And that you deserve the spotlight as much as any other woman."

Bea picked up her French 75 and took a deep drink, letting the fizzy, astringent liquid prickle down her throat.

"Can I ask you a question?" Lauren gazed at Bea with her piercing eyes. "Bea, why *wouldn't* you do this?"

"Being a fat woman in the public eye isn't exactly a cakewalk," Bea replied. "I got a taste of massive trolling when my piece went viral."

"I read about the SlimFast shakes." Lauren scowled. "Fucking disgusting."

The shakes had been terrible. What started as a daily laugh with Dante the UPS guy morphed into full-blown mortification as hundreds and eventually thousands of shakes arrived at her doorstep. But they weren't the worst of it—not by a long shot.

"I couldn't post anything on Twitter without getting rape threats and death threats. They posted my home address all over the Internet, sent revolting text messages from anonymous phone numbers, dick pics at all hours of the day and night, strange men telling me they'd force me down and make me squeal like the pig I am. And that was just from one blog post! If I do this, with all the exposure . . . I don't know. I just don't know if it would be worth it."

"People think fame makes your life easier," Lauren reflected, "but everyone who's been in the limelight knows how hard it can be. People project their insecurities onto you—especially men, the fragile little shits."

"Not exactly reassuring," Bea said pointedly.

"But think of it this way: You went through all that garbage as a relatively anonymous person, with no one to protect you. If you do our show, you'll have our whole team at your disposal—not to mention millions of fans, all the celebrities who watch the show, the feminist journalists who'll write thinkpieces in your honor, bless their hearts." Lauren peered at Bea. "Besides, you wouldn't actually let pathetic Internet misogynists keep you from doing something you wanted to do, right? That doesn't seem like you."

"It definitely isn't—but I'm not actually sure I want to do this."

"Why, Bea? Why would you turn down a chance that could be so huge for your career?"

"How about because I don't trust you?" Bea responded. "I've watched this show from the beginning, and I've seen you make fools of people who didn't deserve it. You have your own agenda, and you have the ability to manipulate anything I say or do in the way you edit me. Why would I hand you the power to destroy my reputation?"

Lauren couldn't help chuckling at this—though Bea didn't understand what was funny.

"Sorry," Lauren apologized, "I'm just so used to people begging me to put them on camera, grabbing at fame for fame's sake. It's kind of a pleasure that you're actually thinking about the step that comes after that. But listen, Bea, our interests are aligned here. I need to breathe life into a flagging franchise, and if I make you the new face of *Main Squeeze,* it does me no good whatsoever to do anything that would harm your image. If you agree to do this, it will be my job to make sure everyone in America loves you—that means magazine covers, endorsement deals, millions of followers, an entire lifetime of career security in exchange for just two months of filming."

"That doesn't sound . . . terrible," Bea conceded, her anxiety rising as she realized she was running out of plausible reasons to say no.

"So why are you still hesitant?" Lauren put down her drink. "Why don't you tell me what's actually bothering you?"

Bea looked at this beautiful stranger—how was she supposed to confess to Lauren the things she could barely admit to herself? Her creeping notion—often dormant, never gone—that the reason she'd never had a proper boyfriend was that there was something fundamentally wrong with her, and that Ray's disappearance was, finally, the proof that this notion was true?

"I don't have the easiest time with dating," she said carefully.

Lauren nodded, unfazed. "You've been single for a while now."

"Well, I'm always busy with work—and fashion, you know. Not a ton of straight guys in that world. Unless they're trying to sleep with models."

"You're on the apps, though."

Bea narrowed her eyes—exactly how extensive (or legal) had Lauren's background check been?

Lauren laughed, as if reading Bea's thoughts. "You blogged about your Tinder date last fall."

"Oh." Bea flushed, feeling silly. "I thought maybe you'd hacked my phone."

"No, definitely don't put that past me. So it hasn't gone well?"

"Are you on them?"

Lauren tossed her shiny hair. "Yeah, but you know, more for a laugh than anything else. I work so much, it's nice to have someone around if I get bored."

"You don't have a boyfriend?"

"And spend my fifteen seconds of free time every week handling some man's emotions because he's not capable of dealing with them himself? Um, no."

"I know. It would be one thing if I ever met anyone who made me *want* to settle down, but . . ." Bea trailed off, hoping this would put the conversation to rest.

"Do you want to get married at all?" Lauren asked.

"Am I allowed to say no?"

Lauren let out a bark of laughter. "Of course! I don't need you to actually want to get married to be on this show—I just need you to be willing to *say* that's what you want."

"I mean, it's not that I don't want that eventually— marriage, kids, a family—I want all those things. It's just that dating has been so bad lately, I've kind of sworn off it altogether. Doesn't really seem like the best time for me to star on a dating show, does it?"

"You know what?" Lauren pondered, working something through, "I actually think this could work really well."

"How?" Bea blurted despite herself.

"The most annoying part of my job is dealing with the mess of people's actual emotions. All these desperate husband hunters—you watch the show, you know how high-strung and impossible they are. But if you're not really looking for a relationship right now, we can keep this simple. You'll meet your men, you'll have fun with them, go on all the fabulous dates, but you'll take things slow. We'll monitor audience reaction and keep the most popular guys around, and toward the end, you can pick your favorites for the overnight trips, saying 'I love you,' and the engagement, obviously."

"And, what? It'll all be fake?" Bea tried not to sound scandalized.

"Why not?" Lauren asked calmly.

"Because there's an audience of millions!" Bea was incredulous. "Won't people know if I'm not—you know, not to be trite—if I'm not doing this for the right reasons?"

Lauren laughed, delighting in Bea's naïveté. "You tell me. Do you think it's a coincidence that half of our couples break up six weeks after we finish airing? How many of the relationships from the last five seasons do you think were actually real?"

The more Bea thought about it, the more she realized she had absolutely no idea.

"Bea," Lauren intoned, "I'm great at my job. It's good for both of us if the public buys your story. And if you actually find someone? Hey, so much the better—those wedding specials are ratings monsters. But if you'd rather play it cool and not take the romance side of things too seriously, then we can be straightforward with each other: We'll make a great TV show. We'll show America that plus-size women deserve to be the leads in their own stories. And you'll be a fucking star. I'm not seeing a downside to this—are you?"

For the first time in the conversation, Bea had to admit she really wasn't.

On her drive home, Bea decided to take a detour through Griffith Park. She put the top down on Kermit the Car and made her way through crooked residential streets into the parkland hills, where tall trees and long grasses rustled in the dry desert wind. She turned up the radio and thought about life before Ray. Was it better? Was it good? Or had this unhappiness been there all along, just waiting to be drawn into the light?

Not doing the show seemed like the safe option, but it wasn't, really—it was just knowable. More weeks and months of missing Ray, making dates and canceling the morning of, feeling like her love life had been cursed with external misery, of hustling constantly and scrounging for advertisers to keep her business afloat, never able to rest easy.

Bea couldn't know what would happen if she did the show—whether she would meet someone wonderful or be thrown headlong into a pit full of snakes, whether she'd be a hero or a laughingstock. All she could know for certain was that if she said yes, her life would change. In the end, that was enough.

A CONTRACT

WHEREAS <u>Beatrice Schumacher</u> (hereafter referred to as the MAIN SQUEEZE) has agreed to appear on the television program <u>Main Squeeze</u> (hereafter referred to as the SHOW),

WHEREAS the MAIN SQUEEZE agrees to participate in principal filming to commence on <u>March 2nd</u> and remain available for at least <u>ten weeks</u>, with a tentative filming completion date of <u>April 20th</u>, as well as a reunion special tentatively scheduled for <u>May 18th</u>,

WHEREAS during filming, the MAIN SQUEEZE will meet, "date," and ultimately choose one of twenty-five SUITORS for a long-lasting and romantically satisfying relationship, and where "long-lasting" is defined as no shorter period than such a time until six weeks after all episodes of the SHOW are broadcast,

WHEREAS filming will begin with a LIVE PREMIERE SPECIAL, continue with episodes broadcast each Monday night that detail the events of the previous week, and end with a SEASON FINALE where the MAIN SQUEEZE will choose a "winner" for an engagement or similar,

WHEREAS the MAIN SQUEEZE will not disclose details of filming to any person or persons not appearing on or employed by the SHOW or the <u>American Broadcasting System</u> (hereafter known as the NETWORK), particularly not members of the press or digital media, including entertainment magazines, gossip magazines, or "bloggers," any unsanctioned interaction with whom will result in legal action for breach of contract and immediate termination of said contract, until such time as all episodes have aired,

WHEREAS the MAIN SQUEEZE agrees, to the best of her ability, to explore deep, soul-searching love in complete honesty and without any "emotional walls" (though if she is experiencing the aforementioned "walls" she is encouraged to discuss them and their potential origins in detail with production crew), through intense interpersonal communication and, as often as needed, physical connection, including physical intimacy if determined appropriate by the MAIN SQUEEZE and her Producers,

WHEREAS the MAIN SQUEEZE agrees to defer to the Producers in all matters that may affect the overall quality or outcome of the SHOW,

WHEREAS the MAIN SQUEEZE agrees to incur any financial burdens borne by the SHOW or the NETWORK if they are in direct consequence of her actions or breach of contract,

WHEREAS the NETWORK retains exclusive first rights to published photographs and other materials relating to any future Weddings, Honeymoons, and possible Dependents resulting from relationships formed on the SHOW,

WHEREAS the MAIN SQUEEZE will, if possible, find True Love, potentially resulting in an Engagement, Marriage, and Everything She's Ever Dreamed Of,

Beatrice Schumacher will hereby fill the role of MAIN SQUEEZE on the 14th season of the SHOW, Main Squeeze.

Signed and dated,

Alyssa Messersmith,

Senior Vice President of Unscripted Programming, American Broadcasting System.

Beatrice Schumacher,

Beauty & Style Blogger, owner of OMBea™ and OMBea.com.

PRE-PRODUCTION

Los Angeles, California

FROM: Lauren Mathers <lmathers@kissoff.com>
TO: Bea Schumacher <bea@ombea.com>
SUBJECT: RE: Contract and next steps

Bea! So thrilled contract and legal jargon is all squared (blech), attaching a few more things for you to look over—tentative production schedule, calendar of pre-prod meetings with camera, sound, makeup, wardrobe, PR, marketing, and I want to get you in a room with some of the other producers to give them a sense of what you're like, what kind of men they should be scouting (can you tell us more about your type??), etc. Plus we've got a standard NDA for you to sign—please please PLEASE note that we are not announcing you as the next Main Squeeze until five days before air, so I just cannot impress upon you how careful we need to be to make sure the news doesn't leak before then. This rollout is going to be spectacular, and I'll frankly kill a man if that self-important motherfucker Reality Stefan scoops our mutual coming-out party. So please, take the NDA seriously!! (Sorry to be a shit about it, but you know. It's for the good of the show!)

——**Forwarded Message**——

FROM: Bea Schumacher <<u>bea@ombea.com</u>>
TO: Lauren Mathers <<u>lmathers@kissoff.com</u>>
SUBJECT: RE: Contract and next steps

Hey Lauren! This all looks good (I mean, overwhelming, but good!). Re: my type of men, smart and funny and kind are the most important things, everything else is optional. And diversity is obviously a big deal to me!! Body-type, race, background—I want these men to bring a new look to the show the same way I am.

NDA signed and attached—full disclosure, I already told my best friend Marin about the show, and assuming it's okay to share with my family? Truly not worth the headaches if my mother hears about this from anyone but me. Thanks again, talk soon!

——**Forwarded Message**——

FROM: Lauren Mathers <<u>lmathers@kissoff.com</u>>
TO: Bea Schumacher <<u>bea@ombea.com</u>>
SUBJECT: RE: Contract and next steps

You haven't told your mom yet?? BEA! Call her right now—and btw will you send me her contact info? We're def gonna need to shoot some b-roll with your parents and figure out which week works for you to bring the guys home to meet them.

⁂

"Real TV? Like actual TV? The kind we get?"

Bea's entire family was gathered in front of her stepdad's desktop computer in the second-floor office—her mom, stepdad, three brothers, their wives, and assorted nieces and nephews all jostling for position in front of the globular webcam affixed to the top of the monitor.

All three of Bea's brothers got married in their mid-twenties, and with the arrival of Duncan and Julia's new baby just a month ago, now all of them had children. Bea's parents—Bob and Sue—were both elementary school teachers who absolutely adored kids, and Sue in particular wasn't shy about letting Bea know that she was eager for her to follow in her brothers' footsteps as quickly as possible. Sue strongly believed that Bea was standing in the way of her own future marital bliss; she'd once read a book on self-sabotage by an author named Abyssinia Stapleton that she now quoted at Bea with the same regularity that other people's parents quoted scripture.

"Abyssinia says that when you sabotage yourself in love, you dig two graves."

"Mom, that's Confucius, and he wasn't talking about love, he was talking about revenge."

"No, Beatrice, it's different! Abyssinia means the graves as a metaphor."

"Confucius meant it as a metaphor, too, Mom."

"One grave for you, and one for the spouse you'll never find."

"If I never find a spouse, why does he need a grave? Isn't that just wasteful?"

"Beatrice, that's why it's a *metaphor.*"

Bea wasn't worried that her family would disapprove of her going on *Main Squeeze*—if anything, she was nervous they'd get *too* excited. But she'd put off telling them for two weeks, and it was time to let the cat out of the bag. So that Sunday night, she saddled up to break the news via Skype at their family's weekly Sunday dinner. Since her brothers and their families all lived in Ohio, they all showed up in person every Sunday, and Bea was always expected to join them for ten minutes of video chat—which could be a real headache if she was traveling in Europe or Asia. Even when she got annoyed, though, it meant a great deal to her that her family always wanted her to be included.

"So what's the show?" Bea's oldest brother, Jon, asked expectantly.

"It's, uh . . . it's *Main Squeeze.* You know. *Main Squeeze?*" Alone with her laptop and a glass of wine, Bea felt a pang of wishing she were with them. It was freezing in Ohio, so her stepdad, Bob, had probably made a big pot of chili, and the brothers would all watch football while the wives gossiped and crushed a few bottles of Cabernet.

"What, like *Main Squeeze,* the real one? The main one? Are you going to be a commentator or something?" Bea's middle brother, Tim, loudly snapped his gum.

"No," she corrected him. "I'm going to be the Main Squeeze. The person who dates twenty-five people and chooses a winner."

The family was dumbstruck, looking back and forth at one another and Bea's face on the monitor, letting out errant gasps of disbelieving laughter.

"Holy moly, Bea, that's a big deal!" Tim's wife, Tina, was a petite brunette with streaky highlights and a singsong Minnesota accent. "Do ya think you'll get *married?*"

"Oh my God, *married?*" Bea's mother lit up, her initial skepticism now tinged with euphoria.

"They get married on the show? Do you have to?"

"No, not *on* the show, but she's supposed to get engaged! That's the whole point!"

"Is that true, Bea? You're getting engaged?"

"Do you know who the men are yet? Have you met 'em?"

"Do you really date *all* of them, or do you just pick one at the beginning?"

"You're not going to have S-E-X on TV, are you?"

"Mom, not in front of the kids, please!"

"Hi, Aunt Bea!!"

"Hi, JJ!" Bea waved to her oldest nephew, Jon Junior, who was now eleven and already a Pop Warner star, just like his dad had been all those years before him.

"So Bea," Jon chimed in, "does this mean you're going to be, you know?"

"What?"

Jon made a weird sort of wiggling gesture with his fingers. "*Famous.*"

Jon's wife, Carol, hit him on the arm. "Bea's already famous! She has six hundred thousand followers on Instagram."

"Yeah, but that's Instagram famous," Tina countered. "This is *real* famous."

"Now, hold on just one minute," Sue interrupted. "Are *we* going to be on television?"

Bea sighed. "If you want to be, yes, I think you are."

At this, the entire family started hooting and cheering until one of the nieces jumped up and down and hit her head sharply on the computer desk, which caused a general commotion and premature ending of the call without a formal goodbye. All in all, Bea thought the whole thing had gone much better than expected.

But a few hours later, Bea's phone rang—it was her step-dad, Bob, who'd stayed mostly silent on the group call.

"Hiya, Bean."

"Hi, Bop." Bea loved that she and Bob still used their nicknames from her childhood. "Everyone go home?"

"Ah, yep, it was a little too much excitement around these parts, the kids burnt themselves out pretty quick."

"You mean you didn't all have a calm, quiet dinner after I hung up the phone?"

"Bean, when has this crowd ever had a calm, quiet dinner?"

"Ha, you make a point. But . . ."

"What is it?"

"Really, though, what did everyone say after we talked? Do they think this is crazy?"

"Well, sure, it is a little crazy, isn't it? Not every day someone in the family is going to be a big TV star. To be honest, I think Tina's a little miffed you beat her to the punch."

"What about you, Bop?" Bea asked softly. "Do you think I'm nuts to do this?"

"Bean, you've been charting your own course the whole time I've known you, and that's since you're four years old. Your mother about had a panic attack when you announced you were going to college in Los Angeles, and then a semester in France. You wanted a big life for yourself, and you're making one. That's not an easy thing to do either."

"So you don't think America is going to hate me?"

Bob laughed. "America makes all kinds of bad decisions—there's no accounting for taste. But no, I think they'll love you just as much as we do."

"All the way up the beanstalk?"

"And all the way home, my magic Bean. You're gonna knock 'em dead."

As filming drew nearer, the demands on Bea's time grew increasingly intense: prep work with a PR specialist to craft talking points for her impending media blitz, practice sessions with a media consultant to perfect the delivery of said talking points, endless test shots with wardrobe and makeup and lighting and camera, and network photo shoots that should have been fun but were mostly just exhausting.

"Can you smile a little bigger?" Lauren urged. "You know, like you're about to find love?"

Bea did her best to look overjoyed, but from Lauren's mutterings about "making her look happy in post," Bea guessed she hadn't quite hit the mark.

There was one part Bea loved, though—the time she spent in wardrobe with her favorite person on the *Main Squeeze* crew: a no-nonsense tyrant named Alison who looked like a mild-mannered English major who sold hand-knit scarves on Etsy but who ran her department with the efficiency of an elite counterterrorism unit.

Bea had been nervous that her stylist for the show would be some typical Hollywood waif without the first clue how to dress a body like Bea's, but Alison was a surprise in the best possible way: She was absolutely stunning, with sea-green eyes and honeyed hair, her style was gorgeous and muted with soft textures and earthy tones. And she was a good few sizes larger than Bea. The two women burst out laughing and shared a tight hug the very first time they met.

"Bea!" Alison laughed with delight. "I'm so happy to meet you!"

"Oh my God." Bea nearly cried with relief. "I'm so happy to meet *you*."

"Not as happy as you're going to be when you see the clothes I pulled." Alison grinned. "I've read your blog for years; do you know how excited I am to dress someone who actually understands fashion? Who might be willing to wear, you know, pants?! I have such great stuff for you!"

It turned out Alison had already reached out to nearly every high-fashion house that made plus-size clothes to send everything they had in Bea's size—Derek Lam dresses and Prabal Gurung slacks and Veronica Beard blazers that retailed for more than Bea's rent.

"Holy shit," Bea said, trailing her fingers along the racks of spectacular garments, unable to fathom that they could really all be for her.

"I know you love a bold print, but we can't do too much pattern on camera, I hope you understand," Alison explained as Bea picked up a Yigal Azrouël blouse detailed with pleated hammered satin.

"Of course," Bea murmured, noting that the blouse perfectly matched a blush pencil skirt in laminated lace. Was this heaven? Was she dead?

"We tend to do a lot of sparkle for cocktail parties," Alison went on, "but I refuse to make you look like a disco ball, so I'm embellishing a lot of things myself." She showed Bea a Dima Ayad maxi she'd hand-embroidered along the bust with lace appliqués.

"This is so beautiful," Bea gushed. "I'm getting '90s Thierry Mugler vibes."

"That's exactly what I was going for! I want to do so much boudoir for you, too, really hit the nail on the head that you see yourself as sexy, and you want America to see you that way too."

"And when the show is over . . ." Bea could barely bring herself to ask the question.

Alison grinned. "You get to keep everything."

Spending so much time with Alison, trying on so many wonderful things and feeling more beautiful than she ever had, Bea could almost believe her press rollout—now just one week away—would be as smooth as the buttery Lafayette 148 white leather moto jacket Bea wanted to wear every day forever.

Usually, the star of *Main Squeeze* was announced well in advance of filming, and the suitors auditioning for a chance to be her husband knew full well who they were competing for. But this year, everything was different: Not only did Bea's suitors not know who she was, Lauren was sequestering them and putting them on total media blackout for the final five days before filming began—the five days when Bea's role as the next Main Squeeze would finally be made public. Meaning that the very first time Bea and her men would lay eyes on one another would be on the live season premiere of the show.

"Don't you think that's a little risky?" Bea asked Lauren, anxiety crackling at the edges of her already frayed nerves.

"We want them to go in with a clean slate—with open minds," Lauren explained. They were doing a walk-through of Bea's soon-to-be bedroom at the Main Squeeze Mansion, a garish affair overlooking the Malibu coastline. Bea detested the plasticized knockoff Pier 1 furniture, but she couldn't deny that the view of the Pacific was stunning. She tried to imagine how it would feel to stand with a man and gaze out at the horizon, to kiss him as the waves rolled in, feel his hands at the small of her back. Try as she might, she couldn't picture anyone but Ray.

"The thing is"—Lauren's voice sliced through the daydream—"we're anticipating some mixed press, and we don't want that to poison the well with your suitors. Of course, we think the balance will be overwhelmingly positive, but there's bound to be some, you know. *Controversy.*"

"Which is part of why you cast me. Controversy breeds publicity."

"Our ratings are going to be enormous." Lauren gave Bea a sly smile. "But I don't want you to get too in your head about what people are going to say about you—let them talk. You can laugh all the way to the bank."

"Totally," Bea agreed with more conviction than she actually felt. "Besides, it's not like they'll be saying anything I haven't heard a thousand times before."

Lauren gave Bea a sympathetic nod. "Listen, I'm going to do everything in my power to ensure this rollout goes as well for you as it possibly can. We're going to give *People* the exclusive—you'll be on the cover—so that will be a great outlet for you, they'll post the story online first thing Wednesday. You'll go straight to *Good Morning, USA!* for your first live interview, and then we'll have you booked back-to-back for three days solid before we go to ground to prep for the premiere. It's going to be grueling, but then, so will our two months of filming. You can handle it, right?"

"Of course." Bea met Lauren's eye. "That's what you're paying me for."

The shoot for *People* went off without a hitch. They photographed Bea in a gorgeous Marina Rinaldi gown, black with a deep sweetheart neckline and long sleeves made of sheer mesh embroidered with oversized black polka dots. With Bea's hair in a sky-high beehive (and fake lashes almost as long), the whole look was very Jackie O meets Andy Warhol. After the photo shoot came the interview, and the reporter they'd chosen, an energetic twentysomething named Sheena, lapped up Bea's commitment to body positivity for herself and her legions of fans.

"I just think you are *so* freaking brave."

"Thank you, Sheena, I appreciate that. But I don't think we should overstate what I'm doing here—I'm going on a reality dating show, not going off to war."

"Ugh, and humble too?? I swear, Bea, you're just *perfect*. Real talk, though"—she leaned in conspiratorially—"are you nervous? I would be *so* nervous if I were you—dating twenty-five men at once is so much pressure!"

"Honestly? Yeah, of course I'm nervous—who wouldn't be?"

"Can you tell me more specifically about what makes you most anxious?"

That every man would remind her of Ray? That none of them would? That everyone would see through her feigned flirtations and call her a liar and a self-serving hypocrite? That whatever had kept her from having a serious relationship for her thirty years on Earth would be laid bare for all of America to see?

"I guess it's two sides of the same coin, really," Bea said carefully. "A show like this presents such an amazing opportunity to make a connection, but you also have to face the possibility that you won't meet that special person. I think everyone at *Main Squeeze* is going into this with the best intentions, but at the end of the day, it's just twenty-five men in a whole world of people, you know? I want to keep my mind and heart open to the possibility I could end up marrying one of them, and I am. But I also want to be realistic—we're all just people, and people are messy and complex. Life isn't often a fairy tale, even on a show that aims to create one."

"Was there a particular fairy tale you loved growing up? Any princess you identify with?"

"Is there a fat princess I don't know about?" Bea laughed. "No, even as a kid, all that princess stuff felt like it really wasn't for me. My stepdad and I always used to read 'Jack and the Beanstalk'; that was my favorite."

"So you prefer adventure to romance."

"I developed my romantic side when I got a little older—I read *Gone with the Wind* so many times the pages started falling out."

"And now you're looking for your real-life Rhett!"

"Hopefully he won't be a war profiteer, but I did always love how Scarlett and Rhett were each other's equals. Their fire, their tenacity, their intellect—I hope to find all that in a partner."

"Well, Bea"—Sheena lifted her glass of sparkling water in a toast—"here's hoping you meet your Rhett on *Main Squeeze*—and that you realize you love him instead of spending all your time mooning over some guy who's with another woman!"

Bea choked on her iced tea. "Excuse me?"

"You know, how Scarlett was obsessed with Ashley Wilkes even though he was married?" Sheena affected an atrocious Southern accent. "Oh, Ashley! Ashley!"

Bea did her best to laugh naturally, but she didn't come anywhere close to pulling it off.

Three days later, before dawn on the morning of the big announcement, Bea was in a posh hotel room in midtown Manhattan, pacing back and forth and repeating her talking points for what felt like the millionth time.

"I'm just so grateful for this opportunity. I've always put my career first and it's thrilling to have a chance to focus on love. It's thrilling, thrilling, I'm so thrilled, just thrilled." She took a deep breath to make herself slow down, but these nerves were like nothing she'd ever experienced.

She'd gotten the photo of her cover of *People* the night before—she thought she looked great, and the headline was bold and punchy: " 'Is there a fat princess I don't know about?' The next Main Squeeze redefines real-life fairy tales!" She was meant to post the photo along with a link to her interview as soon as it went live on all of her social channels while *People* and ABS cross-promoted on theirs. All of this had been preapproved and coordinated by all the corporate players involved, including the social-media team at ABS who were, Bea was horrified to admit, now in possession of all her passwords.

They'd spent hours going over a calendar of preapproved content for the team to put out at regular intervals while Bea was filming the show and on complete Internet blackout. But this first post, the announcement post, sure to be the most widely seen post of Bea's life, she insisted on sending with her own two thumbs. It felt like something she needed to do—to have some kind of agency over this tectonic shift in her existence, in some small way, to break the news herself.

So at exactly 5 A.M. Eastern on Wednesday, February 26, once the *People* interview was up, Bea sat at her laptop—which would so soon be contraband—closed her eyes, and clicked.

@OMBea Overjoyed to share I'll be starring in the next season of @MainSqueezeABS! Read all about it in this week's @People. Can't wait to start this incredible journey.

> **@CounselorKaruna** ahhhhhhh THIS IS AMAZING CONGRATS BEA!!!!

> **@DearJohn01209** I don't understand. Is literally every other woman married?

> **@Bucky909** does this mean I'm actually going to have to watch #MainSqueeze this year?? So many conflicting emotions!

> **@weaver77** if I were single and looked like that I would save us all some time and just kill myself

>> **@HetToToe** @weaver77 she doesn't need to kill herself shes gonna have a heart attack soon as she has sex

>> **@weaver77** @HetToToe in that case I think she's actually safe

@LondonReb Bea, you are such an amazing role model! Good for you!

@Delaney333 Wow Bea way to sell out everything you stand for and join the people who make women feel incomplete without a man!! Hope it's fun!!!

@SSSSSScooter is this bitch stupid or just blind, no one's falling in love with her

> **@halpmeout772** @SSSSSScooter idk id tie her down and rape her then at least you wouldn't have to hear her talk

> **@SSSSSScooter** @halpmeout772 you don't even need to rape her bc she'd never say no

> **@halpmeout772** @SSSSSScooter that's the best part about fat bitches, always grateful

MAIN SQUEEZE CAST ITS FIRST PLUS-SIZE LEAD, AND WE ARE HERE FOR IT!

by Sonia Sarsour, teenvogue.com

The next leading lady of *Main Squeeze* is plus-size blogger Bea Schumacher, and the Internet is losing its mind. After more than a decade of trotting out size-zero girls who seem like they lose another eight pounds to be on the show (Are they shaving down their cartilage? Where is the weight even COMING from?!), we're finally getting a woman who looks like someone people outside Hollywood can actually relate to—and some of the biggest stars in Hollywood are all about it:

@TheEllenShow Love is love—any gender, any size. Rooting for you, @ombea!

@JameelaJamil Oh for fuck's sake, they've NEVER had a plus lead before??? ABOUT TIME, @MAINSQUEEZEABS! Cheers to @ombea for breaking a boundary that never should have existed!

@ChrisEvans81 wait that Bea girl is single? DON'T GO ON THE SHOW CALL ME BEA

The hashtag #CallChris trended nationally, so if things don't work out for Bea on *Main Squeeze,* she might just have a backup plan! That said, we wish Bea nothing but the best on her journey—her season premieres with a live special on Monday night, and we think it's *definitely* one worth watching. Congrats, Bea, and keep shining!

❧

IS BEA SCHUMACHER
A TERRIBLE ROLE MODEL FOR WOMEN AND GIRLS?
by Kiki Zaretsky, healthywomen.com

Plus-size blogger Bea Schumacher is the new star of *Main Squeeze,* and while a lot of people are celebrating, this mom is concerned. Childhood obesity affects more than one-fifth of American teenagers—it's a health crisis that has been a cause célèbre for notable figures from Beyoncé to Michelle Obama. While it's never okay to bully anyone because of the way they look, we do need to have a serious conversation about whether so-called "body positivity" is actually promoting unhealthy behavior among our children.

Let's look at the facts: Bea Schumacher is obese, and obesity is scientifically linked to more than 60 diseases. At a time when our healthcare system is already overburdened, we should be encouraging Americans to eat *healthier* and exercise *more.* When we tell fat people that they're beautiful exactly the way they are, we're essentially giving up on their health—and while they might be okay with that, I'm certainly not!

It's one thing for ABS to cast a more diverse group of people on its shows (I was all for the first Latino Main Squeeze last year!), but it's quite another for a television show with millions of viewers to tell its audience that it's okay to put your physical health in danger. ABS should immediately reconsider casting Bea Schumacher as the next Main Squeeze and recommit itself to promoting a healthy future for our children.

❧

BEA SCHUMACHER
IS SETTING FEMINISM BACK FIFTY YEARS
by Jess Tilovi, jezebel.com

This week, it seems no corner of the Internet is safe from consternation and adulation over the casting of Bea Schumacher as the next star of garbage reality show *Main Squeeze*.

Seriously? We're *seriously* treating this like PROGRESS?

For decades upon decades, the women's movement has begged, cajoled, and insisted on viewing women as full human beings (not just sex objects), and we're finally making some progress: For the first time, more than 100 members of the House of Representatives are women. In the wake of the #MeToo movement, women are reclaiming our personhood and bodily autonomy. Fat activists face enormous prejudice in seeking vital human rights—like unbiased medical care—for the plus-size community.

But Bea Schumacher isn't about any of that. She's about reinforcing the same, tired narrative about who women are and what we should be:

1) She's a fashion blogger who thinks women should spend our time and money beautifying ourselves to conform with the male gaze. (Sorry, just because she's plus-size does NOT make this in any way subversive.)
2) She's going on a show that insists that the entire point of a woman's existence is to find a husband and bear his children. Hard pass!

Let the rest of the Internet try to convince itself that this is a step forward for women. I'll keep calling it exactly what it is: the same old patriarchal bullshit served in a brand-new plus-size box.

THE FATPOCALYPSE IS UPON US

by Anders Bernard, mondaymorningqb.com

In retrospect, we should have seen it coming.

The first horseman of the fatpocalypse was Ashley Graham on the cover of *Sports Illustrated*. And we thought, okay—so she's big. I'd still hit it. Her body's in proportion, just a Kardashian with padding. We never dreamed it was the beginning of the end.

Then Rihanna got fat. So did Taylor Swift. That chick from *This Is Us* got nominated for an Emmy—that was the moment we switched from horsemen to actual horses. The message to women was clear: You don't need to go to the gym, just eat a sandwich instead! It's easier, and who needs a bikini body when you can buy a bikini in a size 40? Who cares that you'll be dead by the time you're sixty when you can carb it up right now?

Now, "plus-size blogger" Bea Schumacher is going to be the next star of *Main Squeeze*. If you've never seen her, picture a barnyard animal that gave up on itself at birth and still thinks it can wear a crop top. And we, the television viewers of America, are supposed to believe that 25 men are going to compete to *marry* this thing. "Reality" TV? Not even close. There's not a single man in America drunk enough to bang this woman, let alone propose to her—and unless ABS found a chub-chasing cult from some backwoods swamp, there certainly aren't 25.

I know what you're thinking: Men don't watch this show, so who cares what this bitch looks like? Here's my point: Telling women they can look like this and still expect guys to drool all over them is a dangerous lie. It's not good for them, it's not good for us, and if we're not careful, the fatpocalypse is going to ruin our lives.

"You *have* to call Chris Evans! He has the best ass in America, like, canonically," Marin insisted through a mouthful of sad turkey sandwich in a sad L.A. satellite studio on the ABS lot. Lauren had allowed Bea one last meal with her best friend before she went on complete blackout for filming, for which Bea was eternally grateful—even if the meal itself left something to be desired.

"You're ridiculous." Bea laughed. "How would I even get his number?"

"Slide into his DMs, then burrow into his heart. It's like you're not even a Millennial."

"Great plan, but it'll have to wait until I get my phone back."

"Ugh," Marin sighed, and sprawled extravagantly across the folding chair where she was sitting. At barely five feet tall with a wiry frame and chic little pixie cut, Marin hardly cut an intimidating figure, but woe betide anyone who crossed her (or anyone who crossed Bea, for that matter). "I can't believe you've been phoneless for three days already. Do you feel like a pioneer on the Oregon Trail? Do you have typhoid? Have you been eaten by a bear?"

"Very nearly," Bea deadpanned—but there was an element of truth to the joke. After three straight days of wall-to-wall interviews, she was absolutely exhausted, and she had to wonder how much worse it was going to get once filming actually began.

"So?" Marin clocked the somber note in Bea's mood. "How are you feeling? Any regrets?"

Bea shook her head. "No, not really. I guess . . . so much of the last six weeks was focused on getting ready for this publicity blitz, and now that it's over, it's like, wow. I haven't even really given much thought to the actual thing I'm about to do, you know?"

"Yeah, but the actual thing is the exciting part! God, Bea, you could be meeting your husband tomorrow night. Isn't that crazy??"

"Yes, Marin." Bea shook her head. "It is crazy. And it absolutely isn't going to happen."

Marin gave Bea a knowing smile. "You say that now, but I just bet when you meet these men, you're going to see how silly you're being. You're going to remember how badly you want to fall in love."

"Doubtful." Bea rolled her eyes. "I know you don't approve, but trust me—Lauren and I have this all worked out. We have a plan. I'm ready."

Marin burst out laughing. "Sorry, but you're going to date twenty-five men on television. How could anyone possibly be ready for what's about to happen to you?"

EPISODE 1

"SHOWTIME"

(25 men left)

*Shot and aired live on location
in Malibu, California*

TRANSCRIPT OF *BOOB TUBE* PODCAST EPISODE #049

Cat: Hey, this is Cat!

Ruby: And this is Ruby.

Cat: And this is *Boob Tube,* the podcast where we take a weekly look at how women are represented on television.

Ruby: This week, we are so excited to talk with our guest Ane Crabtree, who does the incredible costumes on *The Handmaid's Tale.* We're going to talk with Ane about the female form and how it's depicted in a society that's both ultra-conservative and, in its own way, hypersexualized.

Cat: It's a great conversation, so stay tuned, but first: I have a confession to make.

Ruby: It's a juicy one.

Cat: You wonderful listeners know my tastes can run a little highbrow and a little lowbrow.

Ruby: You do love anything that veers toward British royal fanfic.

Cat: It's my British kryptonite! Bryptonite?

Ruby: No.

Cat: Okay. But you may not know that I am a longtime fan and avid viewer of the reality dating show *Main Squeeze*.

Ruby: I believe you've actually taken part in several betting pools surrounding this show.

Cat: If by "taken part" you mean "won," then yes, I absolutely have.

Ruby: And yet we've never discussed any of this on our podcast!

Cat: Well, I'm sure it will shock all of you listening to hear this, but the *Main Squeeze* franchise is not typically a bastion of interesting representation of women on television.

Ruby: Gasp!

Cat: I know. But tonight is the premiere of a new season, and this year, *Main Squeeze* is tackling some of the most thought-provoking questions about body image I think we've ever seen on TV. And maybe doing so in a completely unethical way? Because this year, for the first time, a plus-size woman is going to be the star of *Main Squeeze*.

Ruby: Whoa. Daring.

Cat: Right, as if the idea that a woman who isn't a stick figure deserves a shot at love is somehow controversial. So this woman is named Bea Schumacher, and she's one of the more popular plus-size style bloggers out there. Even though Bea looks how a lot of American women look, for a viewing audience, it's really unusual to see someone who looks like her at all, and it's almost nonexistent to see someone who looks like her portrayed as a romantic lead instead of a sidekick or best friend or mom.

Ruby: Right, and that's where the so-called controversy comes in—if Bea were just the main girl's best friend on this show coming in to give advice or whatever, no one would care at all.

Cat: Well, people would still be terrible to her on the Internet, because a lot of people find the existence of a fat woman something to get worked up about.

Ruby: Sure, in the immortal words of Taylor Swift, haters gonna hate—

Cat: I don't think she coined that.

Ruby: Okay, you're proving my point.

Cat: Anyway, another question is how gendered the discourse around this season is going to be, because we don't know yet whether Bea's suitors will be plus-size too.

Ruby: Oh, that's interesting! Do you even call men "plus-size," is that a thing?

Cat: Technically, you do, but it's not a phrase you hear a lot—society doesn't really feel the need to divide men according to their body size the way we do with women. The point being, there are a LOT of outstanding questions about how this season is going to play out, and I, for one, am really excited to watch, but also kind of dreading what the producers might have planned.

Ruby: Right, because on the one hand, we have the potential for this very mainstream show to do something really subversive, but on the other hand, we're talking about a reality show! Do we think they're actually going to do something feminist and empowering, or do we think they're going to exploit and humiliate this woman for ratings? Which option sounds more likely?

Cat: The only way to find out is to watch the live season premiere tonight on ABS, which I'm certainly going to do. Ruby, have I convinced you to give it a shot?

Ruby: Well, I'm feeling pretty invested now, so I think I am going to watch tonight to see what happens. And speaking of investments, it's time for us to hear from our sponsor for this episode, LadyVest, which is not a purveyor of '90s lesbian fashions. No, LadyVest is an online service that helps women learn how to invest their money to secure their financial independence, which the women of *The Handmaid's Tale* can tell you is a really smart move. Go to LadyVest.com/boob—that's slash B-O-O-B—to get a free consultation and learn more about their services. We'll be back right after this.

——Forwarded Message——

FROM: Beth Malone <btmalone@gmail.com>
TO: Squeeze Main-iacs <main-iacs@googlegroups.com>
SUBJECT: TONIGHT'S THE NIGHT!

Hi, everyone! As you know, tonight is the premiere of the new season of *Main Squeeze,* so for those of you who haven't created your brackets yet, PLEASE DO SO NOW or you will not be able to participate in the league this year. Colin, you've been saying for three years that you want to join the league, but you never fill out your bracket in time, so if you don't do it this year, I'm going to remove you from this email list, okay?

For those who are new to the group (hi, Jenna!), here's how it works: First, you create your bracket on MainSqueeze Bracket.com before 8pm ET tonight—just click the league invitation I sent last week to log in, pick a username, and you're good to go. Then, you'll have until NEXT Monday at 8pm ET to fill in your picks for the WHOLE SEASON. So watch tonight, get to know the men, and then make your predictions for who gets cut each week and who wins it all! The brackets all LOCK before episode 2 airs, so again, Colin, if you don't fill in your brackets by next week, you won't be able to participate all season. I can't even change that as league commissioner, that's just the way the website works, okay?

Okay! Hope you're all as excited as I am for the new season!

xx, Beth

P.S. Did you guys hear Cat talk about our league on her podcast today?? We're famous!

——Forwarded Message——

FROM: Colin Whitman <cwhit7784@gmail.com>
TO: Beth Malone <btmalone@gmail.com>
SUBJECT: Re: TONIGHT'S THE NIGHT!

Jesus Beth, I made a bracket, are you happy? You're the one who cares about this idiotic show, not me.

——Forwarded Message——

FROM: Beth Malone <btmalone@gmail.com>
TO: Colin Whitman <cwhit7784@gmail.com>
SUBJECT: Re: TONIGHT'S THE NIGHT!

Yes, Colin, I *am* happy. Thank you!

——Forwarded Message——

FROM: Ray Moretti <rmoretti@gmail.com>
TO: Bea Schumacher <bea@ombea.com>
SUBJECT: wow

Hey, so, you're on the cover of People magazine. And you're going on TV, to find a husband? Bea, what's happening?

I know I haven't responded to your emails. I'm sorry, that's on me. It's just, I've been trying so hard not to think about you, which is impossible enough on its own, but now with your face staring out at me from all over the internet, and TV, and even the grocery checkout line . . . I don't know. I don't know what to do.

You look incredible, by the way. You should know that. I hope you know that. When I see these assholes talking about you, I want to fucking kill them.

I'm sorry, I know I'm not being articulate here. You're one of the most important people in my life, Bea. When my mom got sick, you're the one who got me through it. Every good thing in my life, every bad thing, you're always the person I want to tell. I love Sarah, I really do. I want to marry her. Or, I don't know, I thought I did. But seeing your face every-where . . . I don't know. Can we talk, Bea? I really want to talk.

——Forwarded Message——

FROM: Bea Schumacher <<u>bea@ombea.com</u>>
TO: Ray Moretti <<u>rmoretti@gmail.com</u>>
SUBJECT: AUTOMATIC RESPONSE re: wow

Hi there! This is a weird thing to say, but I'm off filming a television show right now and have no access to my phone, email, or social media (or daylight, probably). If this is business-related, you can reach my agent, Olivia Smythson, at smythson.olivia@theagency.com. If this is personal (or a hideous death threat!!), I look forward to digging through my inbox and getting back to you once the shoot wraps at the end of April. Have a great day!

"What do you think?"

Bea was standing before an oversized mirror in the wardrobe room, where Alison had placed her in a navy Zac Posen jumpsuit with long sleeves, flowing legs, a ruffled collar, and a plunging neckline, all woven through with sparkling thread that gleamed copper and silver and gold, making Bea shimmer like a galaxy. With her makeup soft and romantic (and caked on thick enough to withstand hot lights and high-def cameras) and her hair in glossy waves, Bea almost felt like the television star she was about to become.

"I think you're a magician," she said breathlessly, and Alison beamed.

"Okay!" Lauren clapped her hands as she strode into the room. "Let's see our Main Squeeze."

Bea did a little twirl for Lauren, who grinned with approval. "This is perfect!"

Lauren herself looked game-day ready in her uniform of skinny jeans with a white tee, black blazer, and heels, her auburn hair pulled back in a perfect ponytail.

"You good to go?" she asked Bea. "Time to head to set!"

"What happens if I say no?" Bea's heart started pounding as it sank in that this was really happening. Had she been completely insane to say yes? What if the whole adventure was an unmitigated disaster?

"It's gonna be a piece of cake," Lauren assured Bea as she guided her toward the makeshift studio the crew had constructed on the mansion's front lawn. "I know it's your first time doing anything like this, but this is my fifth season running this show, and Johnny could host a *Main Squeeze* premiere in his sleep."

The host of *Main Squeeze,* Johnny Ducey, was an erstwhile teen heartthrob (he'd famously mauled hearts in the fantasy Shakespeare crossover *Whither the Werewolf?*). After several public bouts with addiction and subsequent stints in rehab, he'd settled into his lucrative and unchallenging work on *Main Squeeze,* where, it was rumored, he'd slept with female contestants more than once. After so many years watching him conduct earnest interviews with assorted reality stars, it was wild for Bea to contemplate that, in a matter of minutes, she'd be the one sitting opposite him.

"Let's run down the schedule one more time," Lauren continued. "Act 1 is the video package introducing you to America, then your interview with Johnny—that's eight minutes total. Then we cut to commercial—"

"And then we intro the first five men," Bea broke in, reciting the call sheet she'd memorized by rote. "Another break, another five men, another break, and so on until I've met all twenty-five of them. Then they all put on noise-canceling headphones while I give my impressions of them, then I put on noise-canceling headphones while they give their impressions of me."

Bea paused here as she tried to stave off a wave of nausea—why exactly had she agreed to let a bunch of strange men judge her on live television?

"You're sure these men are what I asked for?" she asked Lauren. "Diverse, smart, open-minded?"

"Bea, *absolutely*." Lauren gave Bea's arm a squeeze. "There are a couple of villains in the mix—we're still making a television show—but I don't want you to worry. You're going to love spending time with these guys."

"But what if they don't love spending time with me?" Bea hated herself for letting her insecurities creep in like this, but the closer they got to air, the more she could feel her anxiety taking hold. "What if they hate me, and the audience does too?"

"I promise, that's not going to happen," Lauren reassured her. "I have a plan for tonight specifically to guarantee that everyone in America will be rooting for you."

"Plan?" Bea was skeptical. "What kind of plan? Why don't I know about it?"

"Because I need your reactions on camera to be genuine!" Lauren grinned. "So don't worry, okay? I've got your back, Bea. We all do."

"If you say so," Bea grumbled, but she still found it difficult to believe that everything was really going to work out as perfectly as Lauren insisted.

They'd arrived in the mansion's entryway: Just outside the front door, the lawn had been transformed into a makeshift studio, complete with a stage, a barrage of light and camera setups, and a live audience of a hundred *Main Squeeze* super-fans, all of whom had won an Instagram contest for the privilege of being there, and whose feverish chatter Bea could hear through the door over the whir of the enormous generators powering the whole operation.

"Hey, Bea." Mack, a bushy-bearded sound guy in his fifties, arrived to mic Bea up. "You ready?"

Bea nodded, feeling less and less sure that she actually was.

"Where are the men now?" she asked Lauren as Mack placed a microphone pack in a specially molded pocket Alison had affixed to the back of Bea's jumpsuit.

"In a trailer outside." Lauren paused, hearing something come through on her headset. "Okay, Bea, we're five out from air—I've got to get to the control room. How do you feel? Are you good?"

Bea opened her mouth to say something—anything—but she couldn't find the words. Lauren laughed.

"Yeah, I know, it's a lot. You're going to kick ass, okay? Just go out there and be brazen and bold and unapologetically yourself. Failing that, just smile and say you're ready for love."

Bea forced herself to nod, and then Lauren was gone.

"Bea, can you say something for me? I need to test your level."

"What should I say?" she asked Mack. He smiled kindly.

"Tell me what you're most excited about for tonight."

Bea knew what she was supposed to say: that she was excited to potentially meet her future husband. But she didn't believe that, and she didn't really want to lie about it—not when there weren't any cameras to pretend for.

"I'm excited for all the little girls who are going to watch this and think, *She looks like me.*"

Mack gave Bea a warm smile, and in the next instant, a producer was tugging on Bea's sleeve, leading her out the front door, down the wide stone steps, and into the living rooms of several million Americans.

TWITTER THREAD FROM USER @REALI-TEA

@Reali-Tea Okay shippers & sippers, time for the season premiere of Main Squeeze! Let's see if a lady of largesse can find love on our teevees. Ready?!

@Reali-Tea . . . but first, one million corporate sponsors. Bea uses Lucky Lippies Lipstick in her everyday life? WHAT A COINCIDENCE, they're also advertisers on ABS!

@Reali-Tea Ok ok ok, Bea's doing her live interview with Johnny, she's excited to meet her men, FRANKLY SAME. WHERE ARE THEY?

@Reali-Tea Ah, well. Time for a commercial break. Hiya, Lucky Lippies!

@Reali-Tea HERE WE GO, the first guy is about to walk onstage! Bea looks nervous but maybe a little amped? Go get 'em, sister. We're with you.

@Reali-Tea Oh no. Oh no. Oh no.

@Reali-Tea I don't know if I can actually watch this.

It only took a few seconds for Bea to get used to the lights. In a way, they were helpful; she couldn't see the audience or the crew, only what was happening onstage a few feet in front of her. For her first several minutes on camera, that was restricted to Johnny Ducey's crookedly attractive face, made somehow stranger and blurrier by a combination of Botox and the uppers Bea was quite sure he hadn't kicked, as if he were now a wax model of the movie star he used to be.

Johnny asked Bea all the softball questions Lauren had prepped her for, and Bea delivered all her scripted answers, eliciting the appropriate laughter, empathy, and applause from the studio audience. By the time they broke for the first commercial, Bea was feeling much calmer. This wasn't a massive first date on live TV where it actually mattered what the men across the table thought of her—it was the highly scripted opening act of a story with a preordained ending. This was just the requisite meet-cute that would lead to romantic dates and declarations of love and, eventually, a picture-perfect engagement. Lauren had a plan—all Bea had to do was follow it.

When the commercial break was over, Bea stood at her mark at center stage. Behind the mansion, the sun was setting over the Pacific, and the whole set was bathed in a soothing pink glow, accentuated by the warm lights.

Bea smiled placidly as her first suitor walked toward her.

He was backlit at first, but as he came into focus, Bea took in his broad shoulders and narrow waist, his muscles rippling beneath the perfectly fitted fabric of his Italian wool suit, his thick golden hair, warm brown eyes. He was looking at her with distaste—or maybe, worse, disgust.

"Hi," he said tentatively, well mannered but clearly perplexed. "Are you . . . Bea?"

"Yes, hi, I'm Bea." She struggled to maintain composure even though her heart was pounding. "What's your name?"

"Brian," he replied. "So, you're the person we're going to be dating? Sorry, I'm just a little surprised."

That makes two of us, buddy, Bea thought—this guy didn't bring a new look to the show in any way whatsoever. She smiled wider.

"Yep, that's me! I guess you should head over there, and we'll talk later?"

Bea nodded toward the risers behind her where the men were meant to stand and wait as the rest of them filed onstage. Brian wandered off, looking dazed—Bea felt the same way. Was this just ratings bait, throwing out a stunning Adonis before Bea got to meet the diverse range of men who might actually look like they had any interest in dating her? That must be it. Of course that was it. Bea squared her shoulders and mentally prepared herself to meet the next man, someone she could sell to the world as her Prince Charming. She could do this. She was ready.

Then the second man appeared.

He was imposing and Latino with powerful arms and pillowy lips, like a young Javier Bardem with a mischievous smile. He wore fitted jeans and a button-down, but the ten-gallon Stetson made the outfit.

"Well, howdy," he greeted her warmly with a thick Texas accent, and Bea was momentarily so captivated that she forgot to be horrified.

"Hi, I'm Bea."

"Bea? Jaime. It's a damn pleasure to meet you." He kissed her hand. "Can I say damn? I don't know the rules."

"Who cares about rules?" Bea blurted, and Jaime let out a full laugh, a great laugh—the audience appreciatively joined in.

"Talk more soon, I hope." He gave her hand a squeeze and headed off—Bea didn't bother not to stare at his ass as he left. Talk about *damn.*

Except—wait. That was two men who could just as easily

have been Calvin Klein models as contestants on this show. But before Bea could think too much about what was happening, the third man walked onstage: He was young and Black with a broad, muscular frame, a thick mustache, and a dazzling smile, the spitting image of Michael B. Jordan. No. This wasn't happening. These were all the same men you always saw on *Main Squeeze*—more diverse by skin color, sure, but so far, Bea thought these men looked far more likely to give advice on weight-lifting technique than give her the time of day.

Bea needed to talk to Lauren—crap, they were on live television—could she maybe signal a producer? Get someone's attention? She turned to see who might be around, which of course was the exact moment the third man extended his arms to give Bea a hug hello, and poked her directly in the stomach instead. Bea closed her eyes and imagined the moment replayed in slow motion on YouTube, an unflattering GIF of her mid-section shimmying up the list of trending topics on Twitter.

"Oh no, I'm so sorry, I was trying to hug you—"

But Bea didn't care what Mustache Man had to say, she just needed to get through this, needed to get to the next break so she could talk to Lauren.

"It's *fine*," she insisted through gritted teeth. She willed her facial muscles to relax. "I'm Bea. What's your name?"

"Uh—Sam," he sputtered, thrown off by her bizarre behavior.

"Great!" She tried to sound normal, but her panic was bleeding through. "See you soon, Sam!" She gestured toward the risers, and off he went.

Two more until commercial, she thought. *Keep it together. Two more.*

The next man was already walking toward her, a laid-back guy with a golden tan.

"Hey, am I in the right place?" he joked. A few audience members laughed uncomfortably.

"I hope so!" Bea smiled. "I'm Bea, and you are?"

"Confused," he retorted. "This is *Main Squeeze,* right? I'm on television right now?"

"If you're not, I'm not totally sure what all the cameras are doing here." Bea fought to maintain a light tone. This guy needed to move the hell along.

"Cool. Um. I think I'm gonna go?"

Bea's heart stopped, and all the noise of the set—the hum of the generators, the grind of the cameras, the whispers of the audience—fell suddenly silent.

"What?"

"Yeah, I gotta—it was nice to meet you, though."

And with that, he turned and walked offstage, passing man number five on his way. Bea closed her eyes, seized by a sudden compulsion to burst out laughing. What kind of a waking nightmare was this? What would happen if she left too? How would Lauren fill the rest of the hour?

"Hello, Bea. I'm Asher."

Oh, the fifth man was here. He was really attractive—Asian American with black glasses and thick salt-and-pepper hair.

"Fantastic. The risers are right over there—or you can just leave now if you prefer?"

"What? Do you *want* me to leave?" Asher looked perplexed.

"Makes no difference to me!" She flashed him a grin that she was sure bordered on deranged, but she was fresh out of fucks to give about who these men were or how they saw her. Asher tentatively backed away and headed over to the riser, and then Johnny was onstage to close out the segment and take them to commercial, saying something about this dramatic season being off and running while Bea smiled and gazed blankly ahead.

"And we're out!" a producer called as they cut to commercial. "Back in a hundred and twenty!"

A hundred and twenty seconds—Bea didn't know what Lauren was going to say to force her to continue this torment in two minutes flat, but she was already rushing toward her.

"Bea! Bea, what the hell?"

"Are you kidding me?" Bea didn't want to freak out in front of all these people, but she no longer felt above it, not after what had just happened. "These men hate me!"

"Bea, no—shit, shit, shit." Lauren put her hands on her head, looking a little panicked herself. "I told that guy to walk off, okay?"

"*What?*" Bea was flabbergasted. "Why would you do that?"

"Ratings, Bea! People are going to vilify him and *love* you. They're going to think you're the bravest person on the planet, and they're going to be desperately invested in you finding the perfect guy you deserve. But that must have felt awful—you had no way to know it was fake. I'm sorry, I should have told you beforehand."

Something clicked into place in Bea's mind—

"*This* was your plan to make America love me? To humiliate me on TV?"

"I'm seeing the flaws now." Lauren grimaced.

"It was a bad plan!"

"Back in ninety!" the producer called.

"What about the others?" Bea demanded.

"What others?"

"The other men! You saw how they looked at me. Why would you set me up to be mortified?" Bea asked bitterly.

"You're wrong," Lauren insisted. "Jaime, Sam, Asher—they're good guys. You'll see."

"Sixty seconds!"

"I want to walk off this set right now," Bea rasped, her voice breaking.

"Your contract prohibits that pretty expressly," Lauren pleaded, "but even if it didn't, I still believe in this show. In all the lives you're going to change—including yours."

"Thirty out!"

Lauren looked into Bea's eyes, her expression desperate—

"Bea, by the time this is over, you're going to be the most beloved woman in America. But only if you stay and fight. Can you do that? Forget me, forget the show. Think of your career—your future. Think of all the women at home, glued to their televisions, who know if you find love, that means they can too."

Bea pressed her lips together and nodded. Lauren sprinted offstage as the producer counted them back to air in five, four, three, two, one.

"Welcome back, everyone!" Johnny said brightly, as if completely disconnected from the mess that had recently played out before him. "What do you say, Bea, are you ready to meet your next five suitors?"

Bea lifted her chin and did her best to put on a good-natured expression.

"We'll see, Johnny. If they keep walking out, maybe they'll save me the trouble of having to hold the first kiss-off ceremony!"

Johnny looked rather like a deer in the headlights as he

faked a laugh at Bea's joke. "Okay, then! Up next, please meet Wyatt."

Bea turned to the edge of the stage, where the next man was walking toward her. If Lauren had called Central Casting and asked for an all-American football hero, Bea didn't think they could have done any better. Tall and muscled with blond hair, Wyatt wore jeans and boots and a charcoal flannel shirt buttoned smartly, as if this were a cozy business meeting instead of an appearance on live television. Ducking his head shyly, he looked even more nervous than Bea felt, and she warmed to him immediately.

"Hey—um, hey. Hey, Bea." His voice shook, but he brought her into a hug that was kind and sure.

"Hi, Wyatt." Bea felt her temper melting away. "It's nice to meet you."

Wyatt stepped back to meet her eyes. "What that guy did before, walking away like that. I don't think that was right. Not right at all."

"Me neither," Bea said softly.

"I really like your dress." He smiled. "Actually, I guess it's pants. Is it pants?"

Bea laughed. "It's a jumpsuit."

"Well, whatever it is, it looks beautiful on you."

Bea suddenly felt tears behind her eyes—totally disarmed by this small act of kindness, this show of support. Wyatt looked at her with concern.

"Are you okay?"

Bea nodded. "I think so."

"Good." He leaned in to kiss her cheek, and as the shadow of his tall frame blocked the hot lights for just a moment, Bea closed her eyes and exhaled. This was possible. All she had to do was keep going.

After Wyatt, the second group of men was pretty similar to the first: a parade of athletic men with bulging arms and narrow waistlines, perfectly symmetrical faces that soured with displeasure as they laid eyes on Bea. The second man in the group stopped short when he walked onstage, but recovered with relatively little awkwardness.

The third veered toward incredulity: "Uh . . . seriously?"

The fourth said "Wow" over and over again. "Wow. Wow. Wow."

"Wow?" Bea ventured.

"Wow," he parroted back.

"Who are you?" asked the fifth man.

"I'm Bea," she replied.

"No, but I mean, who are you, like, on this show?"

"I'm the woman you're here to meet. That's why you're meeting me."

"I don't understand."

She told him they'd talk more soon, then attempted to take deep, cleansing breaths during the commercial break.

The third group included a grungy blond surfer named Cooper, a thickly muscled trainer named Kumal, a chilled-out stockbroker named Trevor, and a political consultant named Marco who burst into a broad smile when he saw Bea.

"Gorgeous," he whispered.

"I'm sorry?" Bea wasn't sure how to react to being greeted this way at all, let alone on live TV by a man with dark hair and olive skin who looked like he ought to be lounging on a beach in Capri, his muscles glistening in the Mediterranean sunlight.

"No, I'm sorry." He took her hand and grinned, showing off his blinding white smile. "It's just—you're so beautiful."

"Okay, um, thanks? I guess?" She laughed uncomfortably. Bea didn't know if Marco was putting on an act, but she doubted very much that she could figure it out during his allotted thirty seconds of airtime, so she made polite chitchat and sent him on his way.

She turned to greet the final man in the third group, who turned out to be the first man of the night who wasn't trim and handsome: Jefferson Derting, a Missourian with a roundly protruding belly and bushy ginger beard. In dark jeans and a gray button-down topped with an orange tie and tweedy vest, he put Bea in mind of a hipster bartender who would insist on being called a mixologist. Physically, though, his body type was much closer to most of the men Bea had dated in the past—and to Bea herself—and she felt a sense of relief as he approached her.

"Salutations, little lady." His smile seemed friendly enough, but Bea couldn't tell whether this was his usual mode of greeting or a barb at her expense.

"Fancy meeting a gent like you in a place like this," Bea replied in kind. If he was just doing a bit, she didn't want to ruin it with undue paranoia.

"Seriously, though, I think it's awesome that you're going to be the star of the show this year. About damn time they cast a gal who looks like you." He raised his hand for a high-five, which Bea awkwardly returned. "See you soon, I hope?"

Bea nodded and smiled. "Definitely."

As Jefferson took a walk toward the riser and Johnny took them to commercial, Bea took a moment to steady herself: more than halfway through now. *You can do this.*

"Bea, we have a special surprise with your fourth group of suitors," Johnny gushed when they came back on air.

"Are you sure I haven't had quite enough surprises?" Bea joked weakly.

"In this next group"—Johnny lowered his voice dramatically—"every single one of the men . . ."

Is an astronaut? Is a nice, kind, normal dude? Is a time-traveling wizard possessed of the power to make this night be over?

". . . is named Ben."

"What?" Bea asked, unsure why this merited mention, let alone a grand pronouncement.

"Yes!" Johnny clapped his hands. "Meet the five Bens!"

And so she did: Ben G., a Birkenstock-clad kindergarten teacher who brought his guitar and forced Bea to join him in his class's good-morning song (on. live. television.); Ben F., a personal trainer; Ben K., a personal fitness coach ("So, like a trainer?" Bea had asked, and apparently this was very much the wrong thing to say); Ben Q., a dental student; and finally, Ben Z., who, at six-foot-six, was known by the group as "Big Ben," and whose occupation remained a mystery—there seemed to have been a collective decision that his height was information enough.

Once the parade of Bens ended, they cut to commercial and Alison rushed over—theoretically to check Bea's wardrobe, but really to give her a quick hug.

"Just one more group," Alison whispered in Bea's ear. "You're doing great."

As Alison hurried away and Johnny announced the arrival of the final group, Bea finally started to relax—there was light at the end of the tunnel. It didn't matter whether these men really liked her, didn't matter that this last group seemed the most indifferent yet, didn't even matter that the second-to-last man presented her with a cupcake that he'd scavenged from Craft Services upon hearing that Bea was, quote, "a larger lady." As if Bea hadn't endured thousands of judgmental stares eating sweets (or burgers, or fries) in regular old restaurants, let alone on television. As if her fatness were the essence of her personality, butter and sugar paving the pathways to her heart.

"Thanks," she said curtly to the cupcake-bearer, a smarmy property broker named Nash who struck Bea as a locker-room bully, "but I think I'm going to leave this with you. A snack for the riser!"

She faked a smile as he walked away, then turned to meet her final man, taking a deep breath and insisting to herself once more that it didn't matter who he was or how he reacted to her.

Which was a lot tougher to believe when she realized he was the most attractive man she'd ever seen in her life.

Plenty of the other men were conventionally handsome, but this man was absolutely devastating: dark hair long enough to brush his neck, crooked nose, full lips, crinkly brown eyes, incredibly strategic stubble, geometric tattoos peeking out beneath his shirtsleeves along his muscled forearms.

And he spoke with a throaty French accent. Because of fucking course he did.

"You do not 'ave a sweet tooth?" he asked as he approached—a reference to the cupcake she'd just refused.

"I've been known to indulge," she murmured, "under the right circumstances."

He took her hand as if to shake it, or kiss it, but instead he just held it, his thumb tracing deliberate circles inside her palm, turning her insides molten.

"Well, I am a chef," he quipped, "so perhaps I will discover the sweetness you desire."

"I think I might like that." Her face warmed with a genuine smile, this dazzling man temporarily erasing her ability to feel self-conscious.

"Pardon me if I am forward, Bea." He dropped his voice and looked directly at her. "But I think you should have everything you want."

"What's your name?" she asked, the words little more than breath escaping her body.

He smiled and finally raised her hand to his mouth, brushing his lips against it.

"I am Luc," he answered. "*Enchanté.*"

The moment should have been cheesy, but it was the opposite, somehow—it felt almost too intimate to be shown on camera. The barest touch of Luc's lips on her skin was pure sex, and in that moment, all Bea wanted in the world was to leave the set with him and make everyone else disappear.

"And that's the ball game!" Johnny interjected, reminding Bea her fantasy was impossible—and probably unwise. "When we come back, we'll find out what Bea thinks of these men—and what they think about her—so stick around!"

Bea reluctantly let go of Luc's hand, and PAs descended upon the stage to organize a semicircle of chairs and dole out enormous noise-canceling headphones to all twenty-five men—well, twenty-four, since one had made an untimely exit. For this next segment, Johnny would interview Bea about her impressions of the men while they sat directly behind her, listening to loud music and unable to hear a word she said. For the following segment, though, the dynamic would be reversed, and Bea would be forced to sit in ignorance while the whole group talked about her.

"So, Bea." Johnny leaned in conspiratorially after shouting a few childish insults at the men to make sure they couldn't hear him. "We're all dying to hear what you think of these men! Pretty amazing group, am I right?"

The audience clapped appreciatively, and Bea understood

the game: There was only one way a fat woman was supposed to feel when a trim man paid her attention.

"I'm so grateful," she effused. "I mean seriously, how lucky am I that these incredible men were all willing to spend time away from their jobs, their families, their lives, just for the chance to meet me? It's overwhelming."

The applause level rose, and Bea knew she was playing her part correctly.

"It wasn't all smooth sailing, though, was it?" Johnny's face was lined with faux concern. "That was the first time in *Main Squeeze* history that a suitor walked off the show before the end of the season premiere."

And that's the headline Lauren's PR machine will be pitching the second this episode is over, Bea thought bitterly.

"How did you feel when he walked away?"

"Well," Bea answered frankly, "it's not like that was the first time that's happened to me."

She heard a few gasps and some titters from the audience— perhaps she'd been a little too honest.

"Really?" Johnny pressed. "You've had a man walk out on you that way?"

"What can I say?" Bea did her best to put on a brave face, knowing that's what Lauren wanted. "A lot of men really care whether a woman is thin. For some men, that's the only thing they care about. As if our entire worth can be measured in the inches of our waistlines."

Johnny shook his head. "We'll have to hope the rest of the men aren't like that."

Bea nodded, reassuring herself internally that it hardly mattered if they were.

"Okay, Bea, one last question, and I know all of America

is waiting for the answer to this one: Of all the men you met tonight, who did you like the best?"

Luc sprang instantly to mind—Bea hadn't been that attracted to any man since Ray. But she knew that wasn't the right answer to give in this moment; Luc was too sexy, too volatile, definitely not the choice of a woman earnestly seeking her soulmate. She considered picking Jefferson, but something inside her rebelled against the idea of admitting so publicly what she privately feared: that he was the only man here who might honestly find Bea attractive. She thought back to Lauren's advice—her job was to sell a fairy tale. It was her duty to find a Prince Charming, handsome and noble and, most important of all, capable of graciously sitting by her side for interviews for the duration of their pretend engagement. If those were the criteria, Bea knew exactly who she'd choose.

"Wyatt," she said with a confident voice. "The way he comforted me when I was feeling down? If that's not husband material, I don't know what is."

The audience applauded appreciatively, Johnny thanked Bea for her time, and they broke for commercial. Mack came to fit Bea with her giant headphones, a sad smile on his face.

"Sorry about this," he groused as he got the earphones nice and snug.

"Come on, Mack. We've all got jobs to do."

His smile faded a bit, and he clicked the headphones into noise-canceling mode. As the lights got hot and the men all around her started talking, the sounds of the set dissolved, and Bea felt the stress of the night fade into a nocturne by Chopin.

**SELECTED TRANSCRIPTS OF JOHNNY DUCEY INTERVIEWS
WITH *MAIN SQUEEZE* SUITORS:
Season 14, Night 1**

Johnny: So, what was your reaction when you saw Bea?

Ben K.: I was surprised. I don't mind telling you I was surprised.

Johnny: Like, a good surprised?

Ben K.: Like, a *very* surprised.

Kumal: She seems cool.

Johnny: In what way cool?

Kumal: I don't know, she probably learned a lot in school.

Johnny: What makes you think that?

Kumal: [. . .]

Johnny: How do you think the night is going so far?

Brian: I think beauty comes in all shapes and sizes.

Johnny: . . . okay?

Brian: Yeah. You can't judge a book by its cover.

Johnny: How do you think it went when you met Bea?

Sam: Dude, did you *see* what happened? I poked her in the side! Oh my God, I made a fool of myself on TV. My grandma's going to laugh forever.

Johnny: Have you ever dated a plus-size woman before?

Jaime: That depends on your definition of "dated."

Johnny: Are you worried Bea might send you home at tonight's elimination ceremony?

Nash: [laughs]

Johnny: So, are you?

Nash: Oh, you were asking for real? I hope she does! I'll look like a total asshole if I just leave like that other guy.

Johnny: Do you want to leave?

Nash: I don't know, man . . . do you know what the travel schedule is this year? We going anywhere good?

At first, it was almost novel, peacefully listening to one of her favorite composers on live TV, knowing the spotlight was off her for just a moment while the men had their say. And as for what it was they were saying, well . . . that didn't really matter, did it? If it was slightly bittersweet that all of the romance Bea experienced on the show would be concocted, then it was enormously relieving that whatever heartbreak she experienced would be too.

Say she started "dating" one of these men, jetting to exotic locales, "falling in love," only to discover he'd called her a gluttonous pig on the first night of filming—right now, in fact, as the audience laughed. That would be fine, because she never would have had feelings for him in the first place! He'd be no different from the Internet trolls who taunted her every day, except unlike those trolls, these men would help set her up for future success. Lauren was right: The more obstacles Bea faced, the more America would root for her.

And if some tiny part of her had hoped that maybe Marin

was right, that she might meet someone special tonight . . . well. That was gone. No matter; now it would be easier to keep things professional, to stay focused on her own success. Besides, it was an enormous comfort that none of these men could possibly hurt her as badly as Ray did.

Was he watching tonight? Curled up at this very moment on his living-room couch with Sarah, laughing along at whatever joke someone had just made that had the audience completely in stitches? What *was* that joke? Who even was talking? Bea was seated off to the side, so there was no way for her to see which man was speaking without turning to look—which she was strictly forbidden from doing.

She could see the first few rows of the audience, though: rail-thin Influencers giggling unkindly, whispering to one another, pointing at the various men, typing fervently on their phones. Was Lauren crazy to think that women like this could ever be on Bea's side? Was sisterhood really so universal, or would these girls rather die than, for even one second, identify with Bea—no matter how saccharinely they praised her body positivity online?

Bea wondered if these women saw her as alien.

If these men did.

If Ray did.

When that man walked out on her earlier, had Ray felt a pang of guilt for having done the same—twice—or was he relieved to know that someone else shared the impulse?

Bea had started the night feeling so beautiful, but the men had worked to change that. And now she saw herself through Ray's eyes—not his treasure, but his shame. The audience was laughing again. She closed her eyes and waited for Johnny to take them to commercial.

Each episode of *Main Squeeze* concluded with a "kiss-off ceremony," where Bea would send home the men in whom she was no longer interested. This season, it was being underwritten by a lipstick company called Lucky Lippies—meaning that Bea would be made to put on some preselected shade of lipstick, and after she announced the name of each man she intended to keep, he'd walk up to her, present his cheek, and she would kiss it, marking him for another week together. Bea thought the whole ordeal was tackier than pairing a slide sandal with a ball gown, but her agent had told her Lucky Lippies was on the hunt for a plus-size spokesmodel, so Bea wasn't about to piss them off by objecting.

This was the biggest cut of the season: seven men gone in one fell swoop (including the one who'd left of his own accord—or Lauren's). When Lauren approached Bea during the final commercial break of the night with her list of proposed men to cut, Bea told her she didn't care who stayed—that Lauren could choose to cut anyone she wanted, anyone the producers thought didn't look right on camera.

"Great!" Lauren handed the list over to Bea with a smile. "See? I told you this would be easy."

"Sure." Bea nodded. "Easy."

Back onstage, the guys assembled on their risers, descending one by one as Bea read out the names of the men she'd "decided" to keep. She kissed their cheeks, breathed in the smell of whiskey and overdone cologne. When she called Luc's name, he walked toward her deliberately, his eyes fixed on hers.

"Will you stay, Luc?" she asked him, just as she'd asked each of the men before.

"Of course I will stay. I will go anywhere you ask."

When she kissed his cheek, she tasted salt and smelled something herbaceous, like soap and thyme. He put a hand on her waist, and she felt Ray pressed against her, his weight on top of her, his mouth hot on her skin. He was gone. This was nothing. Bea smiled for the camera and called out the next stranger's name.

EPISODE 2

"BARE"

(18 men left)

Shot on location in Malibu, California

MAIN SQUEEZE SEES UPTICK IN SPRING PREMIERE
by Emmy Benson, variety.com

The new season of *Main Squeeze* has been swathed in controversy—but it seems to be proving that all publicity is good publicity, with ABS easily winning the 8pm and 9pm hours last night. The premiere averaged a gargantuan 4.2 rating among adults 18–49, with 12.8 million viewers overall. That's a sizable increase from the reality staple's last premiere, and just a hair shy of its best opener ever when former fighter pilot Jack Stanwell was discovered to have been sleeping with a major pop star just days before his season premiered.

The premiere came with its own batch of turmoil: Response online was fast and furious after it was revealed that only one of the men competing for plus-size blogger Bea Schumacher's affections was plus-size himself. The hashtag #BrawnIsBeautiful trended for several hours—a reference to the burgeoning "brawn" modeling industry for larger men. Several prominent writers even called for a boycott of the show, and of Schumacher herself. It remains to be seen whether the show's more morally questionable tactics will backfire, but for the time being, ABS has to be very happy with the numbers they're seeing—the question is whether they'll hold up.

TRANSCRIPT OF CHAT FROM #SQUEEZE-MAINIACS SLACK CHANNEL

Beth.Malone: Hey guys, just a friendly reminder that the deadline is TONIGHT at 8pm to submit your picks for your brackets!

Colin7784: Wait, there's a deadline tonight? I didn't know— did you send an email about this??

Beth.Malone: 🫤

Colin7784: Jkjkjk I SUBMITTED MINE BETH GOD

KeyboardCat: Who did everyone pick?? Wyatt and Luc are the obvious choices, but idk, I kind of liked that Asher guy?

NickiG: Seriously, Cat? He was barely onscreen! I think the champ is losing her touch.

Beth.Malone: Guys, we really shouldn't be discussing our picks until everyone's brackets are in.

Colin7784: Sure, wouldn't want to impugn the integrity of our Main Squeeze pool. Hasn't the fabric of our society been torn enough?

Beth.Malone: 🫤

Colin7784: You're going to kick me out of the league, aren't you?

Beth.Malone: I'm strongly considering it.

Enna-Jay: This is a weird question, but do you have to pick someone? Like is there an option where she chooses none of these guys?

KeyboardCat: Since you're new to this show, I can see where you'd think "wow, every single one of these guys is terrible," but don't worry—halfway through the season you always change to, like, NO HOW CAN SHE CUT ANY OF THESE MEN THEIR LOVE IS ALL SO PURE!

NickiG: Is it size-ist to pick Jefferson? Should I not assume she's going to pick the chubbiest dude?

Enna-Jay: How can their love be pure when the couples always break up?

KeyboardCat: Not always!!!! That firefighter in Oregon!

Beth.Malone: Colorado

KeyboardCat: RIGHT

Colin7784: Is it weird that I feel stressed about what's gonna happen tonight? What's gonna happen tonight????

NickiG: Bea's going to go on a group date, she's going to get her first kiss, and there's going to be D-R-A-M-A!

Colin7784: Wow that's a very specific prediction.

NickiG: I know. I'm psychic. (And that's what always happens during week 2.)

Beth.Malone: Seriously guys, you have six minutes left to turn in your brackets.

"Well!" Lauren clapped her hands. "I think that went *great*."

"I don't understand how that could possibly be your take-away." Bea pulled on a robe and mumbled through her pre-caffeinated haze. Lauren had burst into her bedroom at 8 A.M. bearing the overnight ratings report—but no coffee.

"Four point two in the demo!" Lauren exclaimed. "Our last finale was a *two point nine*. Do you even know how big a difference that is?"

"One point three?" Bea ventured, wishing this talk of high ratings and outperforming expectations would soothe the knot currently forming in her chest. She'd hoped that, after the premiere, her nerves would settle and this would get easier—after all, that was the last time she'd have to appear on live television until the reunion show, after the whole thing was done and she was already engaged. The rest of the season would be filmed in advance and edited together each weekend before the episodes aired on Monday nights—that had to be less stressful, right? If something went wrong, they could always take it again.

But as Bea listened to Lauren prattle on about ratings and demographics and watched the Pacific roll and crash in the gray, gloomy morning, she felt a twist in her gut. Last night, she'd only *met* these men. Starting today, she was going to have to *date* them.

"So talk to me," Lauren was saying. "We've got eighteen men left, but only ten of them can go on your date today. Luc and Wyatt are already on everyone's radar, so I need to bench them for the moment—don't worry, you'll do one-on-one dates with them in the next week or two. They're gonna be great frontrunners, by the way—one good guy, one bad, I think we can set up a nice triangle."

"Sounds great," Bea agreed, without any real sense of what it meant.

"What about the rest of the guys? Anyone you want to

spend more time with? We need to pick someone for your first kiss!"

"Honestly, I probably couldn't pick most of them out of a lineup," Bea muttered.

"Come on," Lauren needled. "There's not a single one who sticks out to you? Think back—or I can pull up some head-shots if that would help?"

"Lauren." Bea sighed. "We have to talk about the men you chose."

Lauren frowned. "What about them?"

"The fact that you ignored everything I asked for? You promised me a really diverse range of men."

Lauren looked bewildered. "This is the most diverse cast we've had in the history of the show!"

"Not by body type." Bea's throat was tight. "It's one thing to keep the romance pretend, but being trapped onstage with a bunch of men who would never actually date me? I was humiliated. It felt like my body was a plot twist, or a joke."

"Bea, I'm so sorry—I swear, that wasn't my intention." Lauren came over and sat beside Bea on the bed. "We talked about making this a fairy tale—I thought I was giving you a parade of handsome princes. And seeing all of them compete for you? We're giving women a fantasy, right?"

"Sure, but if they don't *actually* compete for me, the fantasy kind of falls apart."

Lauren met Bea's eye, the whole situation suddenly clicking into focus.

"The guy who walked out." Lauren put a hand on Bea's knee. "Again, I'm so sorry about that, but that was me, not him. I promise you that no other man will do that, that the rest of them are here until *you* decide to get rid of them. Well, until we decide together."

Bea raised her eyebrows, and Lauren laughed. "Look, this season is going to have villains just like every other, but don't forget that I'm the one running the show, okay? When our villains are assholes to you, I'll always make sure that you look like a hero and they look like pure evil."

"And you're sure I'll look like a hero and not the fat girl no one asked to prom?"

"My hand to God, the whole country will see you as the prom queen before this thing is done," she promised. "Now. Can we go through the rest of the men you have here, so you can pick which one gets to be your first kiss? Maybe Jefferson would be a good choice, help you ease into things?"

"Because he's the only one who isn't thin?" Bea shot Lauren a pointed look.

"Bea, you're the one who seems uncomfortable with the rest of the men, not me. If you'd rather kiss one of them, I'd be thrilled."

Bea thought back to the men from last night, tried to imagine kissing them—the ones she remembered anyway. She flashed on one man: black hair, olive skin, green eyes.

"There was a guy who worked in politics? I couldn't tell if he was genuine, but he seemed happy to meet me, at least?"

"Marco." Lauren's eyes lit up. "He's really smart and so handsome—I think he's a great first kiss. You feel good about him?"

"As good as I feel about any of them, I guess," Bea demurred.

"Great! Then I'd better get going." Lauren hopped up and headed for the door.

"Where to?"

"To talk to him, obviously." She grinned. "I'm your producer, Bea. I'm the one who makes everything happen."

As Lauren left the room, Bea took a moment to process what she'd just agreed to do: Today, on camera, she was going to kiss a man for the first time since last summer with Ray. She felt a wave of disloyalty, or maybe even guilt, which was ridiculous—she wasn't with Ray. He was *with* his fiancée.

So why couldn't Bea shake the feeling that this was a truly terrible idea?

.

Once she'd thrown on sweats and had some coffee, Bea made her way down to wardrobe, where Alison was waiting with a gorgeous Reem Acra caftan fabricated in sumptuous red silk. Bea couldn't fathom why her stylists had loaded her up with so much hairspray, but once a camera crew escorted her to the back of the house, she understood: A little speedboat was waiting to ferry her to an opulent yacht anchored a few hundred yards offshore, where she'd meet ten men for her first official date.

"Holy crap." Bea laughed with amazement, taking in the yacht that gleamed pearl white against the vividly blue Pacific, finding it difficult to believe it was actually there for her. On her brief speedboat ride, with two cameras trained on her face, Bea breathed in the salt and spray and allowed herself to relax. Filming this show wasn't just going to be the pressure of interacting with all these men; it was also going to be staggering luxury and once-in-a-lifetime experiences. She needed to be grateful and enjoy them.

She was grateful, too, that the men were already on deck, so none of them were around to witness her awkward embarkation up the yacht's ladder from the little speedboat. Once aboard, though, the yacht was as spectacular as Bea had hoped: The spacious cabins belowdecks were plush and comfortable, outfitted with thick carpets, mirrored dressers, marble bathrooms, and cushy beds.

"I could get used to this," Bea cooed as Lauren showed her to the cabin that had been set up as her private dressing space.

"I'm glad you're happy." Lauren rubbed Bea's shoulder, and Bea felt a surge of affection for her producer, who really was doing her best to make this whole adventure feel special.

"Okay," Lauren went on, "the guys are all waiting on deck; we'll give you some privacy to change your clothes and then you'll head up to meet them?"

"Change? What's wrong with the dress I'm wearing?"

"Nothing! But you can hardly wear a dress to a hot-tub party, can you?"

Bea felt her stomach drop. "Hot-tub party?"

"Yes! For your first date, I wanted to go full luxury: a hot tub on the deck of a yacht on the Pacific. Wow, right?"

"Wow. Right."

"Great! So we laid out some swimsuits for you to choose from—"

"Lauren, no. I'm not wearing a bathing suit on TV. Just—no."

"I'm confused—you said it was really important to show America that you're proud of your body. And you post bikini selfies on your blog all the time!"

Bea closed her eyes. "That's different."

"Why? Help me understand."

"Because it's *my blog*. I'm the one in control: I get to approve the photos, I'm the one choosing to publish them, and I feel proud of every single image. With this—it's video, and it's high def. If I wear a swimsuit on this show, hideous trolls are going to find the least flattering shots of me and turn them into memes and GIFs, they're going to say disgusting things about me and tweet them at me every day."

Bea's breath was shallow, and her palms were sweating. *Stay calm,* she willed herself. *Don't panic.*

"But Bea," Lauren said softly, "don't you think you have a better chance of fighting those trolls if you go out there with your head held high, if you show them that it doesn't matter what they think? Don't you think that's the best way to shut them down?"

Bea laughed bitterly. "The only way to shut them down is not to feed them. Believe me, they're going to make a meal out of this."

"Well—then what about not letting them win? Not letting them control what you do with your body?"

"Sure, if they were stopping me from doing something I actually *wanted* to do, but I don't want to do this! Please, Lauren—can't we just do a regular cocktail party and nix the hot-tub thing? I don't understand why this is such a big deal."

Lauren shook her head. "The guys all wore their swimsuits here—they don't have changes of clothes. If I send them all back to the compound and bring them back out here, it'll take too much time; we'll lose the light. We don't have a lighting setup to shoot here after dark, and we only have the boat for today."

"Okay, so they can wear their suits, and I can wear this dress. It's beachy, right?"

"Bea, if you want to wear the dress, that's your prerogative, but . . ."

"But?" Bea prompted.

"If they're all in swimsuits, and you're in regular clothes— it'll just look ridiculous, you know? It'll seem like you're ashamed of your body, and I know that's not the message you want to project."

Bea wished there were some way to make Lauren understand what she was asking, to help her see how hard Bea had to fight to maintain control over who saw her body and how: carefully choosing outfits that made her feel great about herself, shopping almost exclusively online to avoid the indignity of pitying salespeople explaining that they simply don't stock her size, finally buying her own personal seatbelt extender for air travel so she'd never have to endure the snide looks of another flight attendant or fellow passenger when she was forced to request one. And now, with millions of people tuned in, more people than had ever looked at her in her life, Lauren wanted to obliterate her ability to exert any power over how she was seen. She wished she saw a way around it—but Lauren was right. They were out of options.

"If I do this," Bea said with resignation, "will you promise not to use it as a storyline for the episode?"

"I'm not sure I know what you mean."

Bea narrowed her eyes. "Yes, you do. The way you had that man walk off last night to create sympathy for me—do *not* do that with this bathing suit, with my body. Do not film the men saying wretched things about me to make America like me better. If I'm going to treat this situation as normal and nothing to be ashamed of, then they should too."

"You're right, Bea." Lauren met her gaze. "I promise."

Bea waited for Lauren and the other crew members to leave and shut the door before she closed her eyes and took several deep breaths. Bea modeled on her blog, but she wasn't a model by any means. Her figure wasn't perfectly proportional; her round belly gave her more of an apple shape, and she'd worked for years to overcome her insecurities about the puckering dimples in the skin of her arms and thighs. She knew these parts of her were deeply normal, but all the same, she usually kept them covered or minimized with an army of fashion tricks.

"Well," she sighed, "not today!"

The one saving grace of the situation was that Alison had picked some gorgeous suits for Bea; she settled on an electric violet Chromat bikini with a high-waisted brief and snug halter top that accentuated her cleavage. As she tied a matching sarong artfully around her waist, she rationalized that at least her thighs were covered. It really wasn't so much worse than wearing a skirt and a crop top, which she'd done plenty of times in public—just not on television.

As Bea made her way onto the deck of the yacht and saw the half dozen camera operators (and attendant sound ops and PAs) swarming through the space, poised to capture her every move, she felt a rush of exhilaration despite all her anxiety. Yes, it was terrifying to hand over control of her image to Lauren and the crew, but there was a sliver of excitement too. Bea loved the thrill of selecting that perfect photo of herself, of posting it on Insta and her blog and watching the likes and adoring comments roll in. These people were professionals, and Lauren wanted America to see Bea as a princess. Wasn't it possible that this date could be as glamorous and sexy as Lauren promised?

Lauren had the group of men—all in their swimsuits, all with their toned bodies (except for Jefferson, who was a welcome sight)—arranged in a semicircle awaiting Bea's arrival, which was terrific to really maximize the awkwardness of the situation, especially since Bea realized she only knew half their names. There was Jefferson; Jaime the hot Texan bartender; Ben the kindergarten teacher (who was still, Bea noted, wearing Birkenstocks); the Asian American guy with the black glasses and salt-and-pepper hair (Aslan? No, that was the lion from Narnia); Nash the real estate broker with the nasty look in his eye (Nasty Nash! Now, that was a functional mnemonic); several others Bea couldn't name to save her life; and one whose name had been rattling around in her mind all day: Marco, the politico Bea had chosen for her first kiss. When they made eye contact, briefly, his smile was knowing.

"Hey, Lauren?" Bea grabbed her producer. "This is embarrassing, but can we just run down everyone's names before I have to actually, you know, make conversation?"

"Sure." Lauren looked up from her phone, which was a constant thrum of texts on something called "Producer Thread." "Who don't you know?"

"I know Jefferson, Jaime, Nash, and Ben. And Marco, obviously." Bea's stomach gave an involuntary flip as she said the name—a staged kiss was still an actual kiss, and she was starting to feel actually nervous.

"Which Ben do you know?"

"Kindergarten Ben."

"Personal trainer Ben is here too—in the red swim shorts?"

"I thought personal trainer Ben didn't get a date this week?"

"No, that's personal trainer Ben F. Personal trainer Ben K. is here."

"Ben K.?"

"Ooh—sorry, he prefers 'fitness coach.' "

"Right. That guy."

"And the other trainer is Kumal."

"Got it. And the finance guy is . . . Trent?"

"Trevor. He's a stockbroker. The surfer next to him is Cooper."

"Great. And that just leaves . . ."

"Asher. He's a history professor in Vermont."

"I knew it wasn't Aslan!"

Lauren gave Bea an affectionate pat on the arm and escorted her over to the circle of men to begin filming.

"Just ignore the cameras," Lauren reminded her, and Bea nodded—though it was easier said than done with three of them pointed right at her.

"Welcome, everyone!" Bea delivered the speech the show's poor underpaid writer had scripted for her. "Take a look at this yacht—pretty amazing, right? I just hope our date will be *smooth sailing*—we wouldn't want to make anyone *walk the plank*!"

This sort of wordplay—if, indeed, it could even be called that—was something of a *Main Squeeze* staple; Bea hoped she delivered the lines with enough of a wink to give everyone at home a good laugh. But the men right in front of her stared back rather blankly, and Bea wondered how sternly Lauren had admonished them not to react to anything at all. As she finished the speech and the group splintered off to explore the various yacht activities (shuffleboard, blackout drinking, et cetera), Bea readied herself to mingle.

"Who do you want to talk to first?" Lauren asked.

"Whoever's nearest the bar, I think."

"Attagirl. That would be Trevor."

Bea headed toward him—surely a glass of wine would help lubricate the several hours of looming small talk. But before she could make it there, Ben K. headed her off at the pass to ask if she had a minute to talk, a somber expression on his face and a camera operator standing right behind him.

"Sure, Ben. What's going on?"

He led her to the railing near the front of the yacht, which made Bea wonder if he intended to reenact *Titanic*—

particularly when he took her hands and looked deep into her eyes.

"Bea, I want you to know how seriously I'm taking this."

He paused, which led Bea to believe that she was meant to respond.

"Okay! That's great, because—"

"For too many years, I have spent my nights alone," he proclaimed. "I have yearned for someone special, someone to become my other half. My wife. I am here to seek her."

Is this actually happening? Bea did her best to nod understandingly.

"Bea, if you'll have me, I'd like to put my hat in the ring to become *your* other half. Your husband. And so I am bringing you this gift."

At this, a PA materialized with a wrapped present—it was square and nearly flat.

"Oh wow, thank you," Bea said, completely mystified.

"Aren't you going to open it?"

So Bea did—it was a framed etching of a fedora inside a circle.

"Do you get it?" he asked. "It's a hat. In a—"

"In a ring, yes, I see that. This is, wow. So thoughtful, Ben. I really appreciate this."

Ben K. broke into a wide smile. "I was worried you wouldn't get it."

Bea nodded. "Oh?"

"Yeah, you know. It's kind of a subtle message."

She gave him a quick, uncomfortable hug, then hurried away as politely as possible.

Making her way back toward the bar, Bea caught a glimpse of a few of the men—Jaime, Kindergarten Ben, Nash, and Cooper—chatting in a circle: Jaime seemed to be miming the act of having sex with a larger woman, Nash and Cooper were snickering, and Kindergarten Ben nodded earnestly, eagerly absorbing any tips Jaime had to offer.

Bea felt a wave of nausea that had nothing to do with sea-sickness, but she swallowed hard and walked up to the bar, where Trevor the stockbroker was talking tequila with the middle-aged bartender for the benefit of the camera next to him.

"Bea! How's it going?"

He clapped her on the back in a friendly sort of way—nothing romantic about it, but at least he was pleasant.

"Better now that I'm at the bar," she quipped.

"Woman after my own heart. What are we drinking?"

"Sounds like we're in a tequila state of mind."

"I was gonna do shots, you want in?"

Bea considered the wisdom of impairing her motor skills, judgment, and inhibitions—frankly, she thought the risk of falling on a slippery deck (not insubstantial under the best of circumstances) was worth the potential reward of feeling marginally less stressed about this entire situation. She turned to Trevor with a wicked grin.

"Lay 'em down, Trevor."

"Bro, nice!"

The tequila was cool and smooth, and after two shots, Bea felt the liquid worming its way into her system, loosening the folds in her brain.

"You want one more?" Trevor asked, holding up his own.

"Nah." Bea giggled. "I'm good."

She pushed herself up from her barstool, feeling more re-laxed than she had all afternoon, and warmed a bit by the alcohol. It was chilly on the boat—March in L.A. is hardly tropical—and of all the men, Asher the history professor was the only one who was covered up: He'd thought to bring an L.L.Bean anorak, and consequently looked much more comfortable than anyone else at the party. He was sitting far from the rest of the group at a little table near the edge of the yacht, buried in a book—somehow carving out the sort of peaceful afternoon Bea might really enjoy if she weren't so busy starring in a television show. He seemed to sense her gaze, because he looked up and locked eyes with her for a moment, but she looked quickly away. When she glanced back a few seconds later, he'd already gone back to reading.

Before Bea could decide where to go next, Nash and Cooper arrived—though whether they were deliberately seeking out Bea's company or simply running into her en route to the bar, it was hard to say.

"Hey guys! Having fun?" Bea asked brightly, the tequila having significantly improved her spirits.

"Absolutely," Nash drawled, choking back a laugh, exchanging a knowing glance with Cooper. "We can't get enough of whale watching."

Bea gritted her teeth, willing herself not to flush with anger and shame.

"I hope you find one." Bea forced her lips into a cool smile. "I'm sure it would be thrilling to see a creature whose intelligence so far surpasses your own."

She turned on her heel without waiting for a response, ready to find Lauren and insist the footage of that exchange never see the light of day, but she nearly smacked straight into Jefferson.

"Whoa! Watch your step, Bumble Bee."

He flashed her a warm smile, and Bea felt her Nash-and-Cooper-induced rage start to ebb a bit.

"Wow," she joked, "we're already on a nickname basis?"

"I thought I'd try it." Jefferson grinned. "How'd I do?"

"Hmm, I'd say five for originality, but a solid seven for pluck."

Jefferson laughed, big and hearty. "I'll take it. Now, let me ask you a question—is there anything to eat on this boat? I've been having serious barbecue withdrawal ever since I left home and I could definitely crush some ribs right now."

"You're from . . . Kentucky?" Bea tried to remember, but Jefferson's good-natured eye roll told her she'd missed the mark.

"Kansas City—that's in Missouri."

"Also Kansas," Bea retorted.

"But the barbecue is in Missouri." Jefferson rubbed his belly, which was covered in curly red hair and hung over the waistband of his Hawaiian-patterned board shorts. "The secret's in the smoking—you do a long, slow smoke, preferably over at least four different kinds of wood."

"Sounds delicious," Bea agreed, "but probably not super safe for a boat."

"Just another reason I prefer dry land." Jefferson laughed. "I installed a killer smoker in my backyard last year—maybe if things work out you'll get to see it?"

His expression was so sweet, almost hopeful, that Bea wondered if she should have listened to Lauren and picked this guy for her first kiss after all.

"What about you?" he prodded. "What's your favorite kind of food?"

Bea opened her mouth to answer what should have been an easy question—Thai food, burgers, chocolate cake—before considering the wave of "*If you love to eat so much, you deserve every health problem that overburdens our insurance system*" ire such a response might prompt.

"We have access to such amazing produce in California,"

she said truthfully, but smiling wider than she otherwise might have. "I absolutely love to swing by the farmers' market to see what's in season."

"You'll have to teach me your mysterious coastal ways." Jefferson laughed and patted his belly. "I'm obviously more of a meat-and-potatoes guy."

There was something so appealing about Jefferson's confidence. Sure, some of it was that he was a man, and therefore not automatically subjected to the same kind of judgment as Bea about his body—but there was something deeper there, an inner ease that Bea hoped might rub off on her if she spent a little more time with him.

That would have to wait, though, because Lauren was approaching to get her ready for her next setup.

"We only have a couple hours of light left," she explained. "You ready to film your conversation with Marco?"

Bea smiled tightly and followed Lauren over to the stunningly beautiful hot tub, which was built into a raised part of the deck, allowing for a 360-degree view from the coast to the horizon. Thick steam rose up in sheets, someone had set out an ice bucket of Prosecco and several glasses, and in the tub itself was Marco, his dark hair and olive skin slick with condensation. Bea felt another churn in her stomach with the realization that he was waiting here with the sole and express purpose of kissing her.

"Okay, kids," Lauren teased, "have fun!"

She backed off to give them the impression of privacy (despite three nearby cameras), and Marco looked up at Bea expectantly.

"I've been hoping you would come over to hang with me," he flirted. "What good is a hot tub without a hot girl?"

Bea laughed. "You're really leaning in to that signature *Main Squeeze* wordplay, huh?"

"Oh yeah." Marco grinned. "Are you getting in? I promise, it feels amazing."

Bea was self-conscious for a moment as she removed her sarong, but between her tequila bravery and the goosebumps on her bare skin, she stepped out of it as quickly as possible and slid into the delicious heat of the water.

"Oh my *God,* that's good." Bea exhaled heavily as she let the water rise up to her chest. "I'm already so mad about how cold it's going to be when we get out."

"I don't know about you," Marco said conspiratorially, "but I don't plan on getting out anytime soon."

He scooted closer to Bea, whose face flushed with nerves and heat—he wasn't wasting any time, was he? Lauren hadn't been kidding when she said she would take care of everything. But now that she had, Bea wasn't sure she liked it; it was all too arranged, a speeding train she couldn't exit even if she wanted to.

"So"—she cleared her throat—"you work in politics?"

"I do." He smiled. "I work for a messaging firm."

"Does that mean, like, you do slogans for campaigns?"

"Sure, sometimes. We conduct polls, figure out what ideas resonate with voters, and help candidates adjust their message accordingly."

"So you're the reason people get labeled 'inauthentic.'"

Marco raised an eyebrow, taking in Bea with his sparkling green eyes. "No one is just one thing. We help candidates understand how to put their best feet forward."

"Like taking a picture from your best angle?"

"Exactly." Marco leaned closer. "Except you don't have any bad angles."

She could kiss him now, she knew she could—but something was holding her back.

"If you're such an expert," she said softly, "in peddling these polished versions of the truth, how can I know if you're being honest with me?"

"I'm not bullshitting you." He dropped his voice. "I've thought about this before. A lot."

"Thought about what?" Bea asked lightly.

"For years, I've wondered what it would be like with someone like you."

Bea's whole body went tense.

"Someone . . . like me?"

His breath was hot against her earlobe, her neck.

"Those arms, those lips, that body," he murmured. "God, Bea, you're so big. I bet I could just disappear into you."

He cupped her face in his hands, and he was so handsome, and her heart was pounding, and she felt so horribly ugly, she could taste bile as she remembered Ray's touch, she missed him so much she could scream, but Marco just kept moving closer—

"I really want to kiss you."

No, roared a voice inside her, *not like this.*

His mouth was almost on hers, but Bea stood up so fast she sent water sloshing everywhere, knocking over one of the flutes of Prosecco and shattering it on the deck.

"Can I get a towel?" she shouted at a PA, who came rushing over with one that Bea prayed would be large enough to wrap around her body.

"What the hell?" Marco rose, wiping water out of his eyes.

"I'm sorry," Bea said, hating herself for apologizing to this asshole who'd made her feel like a freak, an oddity. "I'm just not interested."

Bea turned her back on Marco, hoping he wouldn't see how badly he'd upset her. All she wanted was to get back to her dressing room to find a cozy robe, but she was interrupted by Kumal, one of the personal trainers on this date.

"Hey, there you are!"

"Here . . . I am!" After the shock of her interaction with Marco, Bea was so not in the mood for small talk—especially not while soaking wet and wrapped in a towel.

"I've been looking for you."

"Well, there are ten of you and just one of me, so . . ."

"I know, but it's such a big boat."

Bea nodded. That it was.

"Anyway, I've been wanting to tell you, I think it's so cool you're here. I've wanted to meet you for a while, even before I knew we were going to be doing this show together."

"Really? You knew who I was?" Bea peered at this sculpted man—he didn't seem the type to follow plus-size fashion bloggers on Instagram.

"Yeah! I had this client who wanted to show me how big she used to be, except she couldn't find any old pictures on her phone, so she pulled up your feed! And I was like, *Wow, I could really help that girl.* So it's wild that now I actually get to meet you."

Bea's expression went dark. "Help me how, exactly?"

"I mean, obviously you don't *want* to look like that, right? There's so much we could do together! Diet, exercise regimen, but like, really holistic stuff, mind-body wellness—it wouldn't be about changing your looks, per se. It's more about helping you be healthy."

Bea could hear her heart pounding in her ears. She could deal with Ben K.'s absurdity and Nash and Cooper's insults and Marco's fetishizing, but this was a step too fucking far.

"Tell me, Kumal," she said, her voice low, "what exactly do you know about my health? Have you seen my blood sugar? My heart rate? My cholesterol?"

Kumal looked completely baffled. "No?"

"No, you haven't. Yet you assume I'm 'unhealthy' because of my weight. Is that right?"

The conflict had attracted the attention of a few of the other men: The two Bens, Jaime, Nash, and Cooper approached to see what was going down.

"I just think that you can change," Kumal insisted.

"No," Bea countered, "you just think that I *should* change, because you can't imagine I could possibly be happy and healthy and fat all at the same time. You're presenting yourself as some great guy who's just concerned for my health, but you and I both know you aren't. You're concerned with getting some camera time, and with telling everyone at home that it's not okay to be fat and that you're not attracted to me. All of which you've now done. Congratulations!"

"You're seriously overreacting," Kumal said with a conde-scending laugh. "I was trying to help, but hey, if you want to die at thirty, that's your business."

"Well, I don't turn thirty-one until September, so I guess there's still time." Bea smiled. "And if you really want to help me, I know how you can: by leaving this show right now."

A stillness fell over the group. Kumal looked like he couldn't quite believe it.

"Don't be upset, Kumal." Bea smirked. "You don't want to date me. And now you don't have to."

She spun around and marched back toward the bar—she'd broken her glass of Prosecco getting away from Marco, and after those two interactions, she damn well deserved a fresh one.

The men were still talking among themselves near the hot tub, so the bar was blissfully empty, save for the camera that never left Bea's side. After a moment, though, Asher sidled up and took a seat next to her—it was the first time all day he'd left his book and his little table, far from the action of the rest of the group.

Bea looked at him expectantly, but he didn't say anything—just watched her drink, as if he were a field scientist and she were a rare breed of puffin.

"What?" Bea asked curtly, pleased with how good it felt to stop giving a shit what any of these men thought of her.

"Nothing," he mused. "I'm just trying to figure out what you're doing here."

"What's that supposed to mean?" Bea turned to face him, taking in the angled slopes of his frame, his jaw, his cheekbones.

"Exactly what I said," he clarified. "I was roped into watching a few earlier episodes of this series, and it's my impression that usually, the leads come here looking for love. They spend every minute telling every suitor they can find how eager they are to fall in love—but from what I've observed, you haven't done that once. In fact, you don't seem eager to talk to us at all. So I'm trying to figure out what you're doing here."

"Excuse me?" Bea was at a total loss for what this man wanted from her.

"Maybe you came here to prove a point. Or to improve your career? Both of which are fair objectives. But you can understand how my participation under those circumstances would seem like a waste of time." He took a sip of his beer; having made his logical point, he awaited her logical response.

But Bea didn't feel logical. She felt exhausted. She felt hopeless. She felt exposed—as a fraud, and worse, a failure.

"Why don't you tell me how you want me to behave," she pleaded, her voice scratchy with emotion, "after I spend the day being mocked, and manhandled, and insulted. Do you want me to be flirty and coquettish? A tough vixen? A doe-eyed ingénue? Just tell me, Asher. Tell me how to be the woman you thought you came here to meet, tell me how *you* would handle it if every person you encountered found a new sadistic way to make you feel terrible about yourself and your body, and I'll do whatever I can to stop being such a monumental disappointment."

Bea saw the pain in her expression mirrored in Asher's face—he clearly hadn't intended to hurt her. It was all much too much, this man and this place and her wet body and stringy hair and the awful things these men had said to and about her—nothing, she was sure, compared to the awful things America would say to and about her when this episode aired next week. Bea excused herself and went down to her cabin, and she wouldn't come out again until Lauren promised that the little speedboat was waiting to take her home.

When Bea finally made it back to her apartment at the compound, it was dark outside, and she wanted nothing more than to curl up and sob. She put on the comfiest clothes she could find, silently blessing Alison for leaving out some cashmere sweats. Cocooned in layers of softness, Bea turned on some music and tried to forget the sound of Asher's words, echoing over and over in her brain.

I'm trying to figure out what you're doing here.

After the events of this day, Bea was no longer sure she knew.

She decided her best option was to go to bed and try again tomorrow, but instead, she heard a knock on her door.

"Fucking Lauren," she muttered under her breath, "can I not get one damn moment of peace without—"

She swung the door open—it wasn't Lauren.

It was Luc, the devastatingly handsome Frenchman she'd met at the premiere, with a metal bowl full of ingredients in his arms and a camera crew at his back.

"Bea, hello."

"Luc, um, hi? I wasn't expecting you."

"I hope I am not disturbing you, it is just, I heard you had a difficult day, and I thought, perhaps, I could keep my promise to make you something sweet?"

He held up the bowl hopefully, and Bea caught a glimpse of eggs and vanilla. He was completely right—this was exactly what she needed.

"Sure." She opened the door wider. "Come in."

As it turned out, Luc had come to prepare one of the desserts from his restaurant, a lavender-honey crème brûlée.

"This way," he said as he went through her kitchen in search of a whisk, "if you are angry at a man here, you can beat the sugar with the spoon and pretend you are cracking open his head." He tapped Bea's forehead gently with a silver spoon. "You see?"

Bea laughed. "It's very cathartic."

"Good! So you sit, relax, and I will bake."

"No, you have to let me help! I can be your sous chef."

"Ah, so you want to work under me? But this is a coveted position. I only hire the best."

"I think you'd be very happy with me under you," Bea teased, wondering how it was possible this obscenely handsome stranger made her comfortable enough to flirt this brazenly.

"Do you know how to separate the egg yolks?" he asked softly.

"I know the gist."

"Here." He put his hands over hers. "I'll show you."

So together they cracked the eggs and gently tossed the yolks from palm to palm, letting the slippery whites run through their fingers.

"You are a woman of hidden talents." Luc chuckled as Bea deposited the final yolk in a bowl.

"She blogs, she bakes, what can't she do?" Bea laughed.

"Tell me. You must have some weakness."

"Besides my obvious weakness for desserts?"

She handed him the bowl of yolks, and he caught her arm for just a moment, running his thumb inside her wrist.

"It is no weakness to enjoy something sweet."

It turned out the most time-consuming aspect of preparing crème brûlée was waiting for it to cool—for an hour or more—after it had been baked. The camera guys were on overtime, so Luc had premade a couple of dishes of cream that were already cool so they could skip ahead to the fun part: burning the sugar.

"But wait," Bea said, "when did you hear I'd had a bad day? I just got back an hour ago, when did you have time to make these?"

Luc looked to the camera guys, who just kept rolling.

"I don't know if I am supposed to tell you this, but Lauren called another producer earlier to come talk to me. Something about a swimsuit? She felt really terrible. She asked if I could think of a way to make your day better."

"Oh." Bea looked down, the reality of the situation seeping in. This wasn't a man who genuinely liked her—this was another staged scenario of Lauren's, a backup plan to make sure the week wouldn't end without Bea getting her first kiss.

Well. If that was what Lauren wanted, it was Bea's job to deliver. She forced her face into yet another smile, and readied herself for her final performance of the day.

"I guess you'd better show me how to burn some sugar!"

Luc showed Bea how to use the brûlée torch, and it really was fun to make the brittle crust and crack it gently with a spoon. The dessert was thick and sweet; they ate it sitting on the carpet in front of a roaring fire some PAs had surreptitiously built while they were baking.

"The fire, the ocean, the homemade dessert . . . this is a lot," Bea observed.

"Yes, it's a bit excessive, no? And I am French, so my tolerance for romance is very high."

"So that's what this is? Romance?"

"Is that what you want?"

He leaned into her, his body just inches away. Maybe he really did like her—or maybe he was acting. Maybe it didn't make a difference.

"Luc, can I tell you a secret?" she murmured.

His voice was barely above a breath. "Tell me."

"I don't know what I want."

He ran a finger along her jaw, and she nodded, yes. He kissed her softly, playfully, searchingly, and she thought of Lauren, and she thought of Asher, and she thought of Ray, and finally she leaned into him until there was nothing left to think about except Luc and the taste of sugar and cream.

EPISODE 3

"IMPRESSIONS"

(14 men left)

Shot on location in Malibu, Anaheim, and Los Angeles, California

MAIN SQUEEZE RECAP: IS BEA SCHUMACHER THE WORST MAIN SQUEEZE EVER?

by Nichole Sessuber, vanityfair.com

When plus-size blogger Bea Schumacher was announced as the star of this season of *Main Squeeze*, I was over the moon: Was it possible that, after all these years, my guilty little pleasure was going to be interesting, and even—forgive me for saying it—*woke?*

The answer is no.

Or it might be yes.

Or it might not even matter!

Because here's the thing: Right now, the show is *bad.*

Last night's episode was one of the most painful I've seen—even worse than the one where they forced the racist guy and the black guy into a hot-dog-eating contest. Because while that was disgusting, it was also absolutely entertaining.

Not so, last night's horrific adventure on the high seas, where Bea was forced to wear a bikini (at least, I assume she was forced—she certainly looked unhappy about it), endure the snide taunts of men with the emotional maturity of Lindsey Graham, fend off one man who sought to fetishize her body, and finally capitulate for some light frenching with a Frenchie who couldn't be more obviously vying for camera time. (To be clear, ABS, I will absolutely watch whatever hot-chef Luc spin-off you decide to make; you don't need to force Bea to make out with him to get me on board!)

The only moment of last night's episode where Bea seemed at all happy—well, not happy, exactly, but at least like an actual person—was when she was telling off Kumal, the trainer she kicked off the show for insulting her body to her face. It was nice to see Bea stand up for herself, but the show can't keep going back to that well. It will get too boring too quickly, and we're not watching this show for a seminar on body image; we're in this for the romance! For the drama! For the *fantasy* of it all!

But there's nothing fantastic about what we're seeing now. This part of the season is always a little awkward: We don't yet know the suitors well enough to be particularly attached to any of them, so we're dependent on our connection to the Main Squeeze to stay invested in the season. I've spent the last two weeks ready to stan Bea harder than I've ever stanned before, but even beyond the show's terrible one-liners, she just seems stilted and uncomfortable—and frankly, it's hard to watch, let alone root for her. Understandable? Definitely. Enjoyable? Not in a million years.

It's not clear whether the problem is Bea's negative attitude (as Asher contended last night) or if the entire setup of this season is simply an exercise in schadenfreude at this poor woman's expense. But there's one thing I'm sure of: If next week's episode is as grim as this week's, it will be the last one I watch this year.

"Hey guys, can I have the room for a second? I need to chat with Bea."

Lauren's tone was casual, but her voice definitely had a haggard edge. The various wardrobe, hair, and makeup people scurried quickly out of the room where Bea was readying for her next segment: a rundown with Johnny about the dates she'd be going on this week.

"Is everything okay?" Bea asked carefully. She wasn't even sure what to be afraid of—was she going to be fully nude this week?—but whatever was going on, it didn't seem good.

Lauren sat down next to Bea and exhaled deeply.

"Our ratings took a hit last night."

Bea felt a surge of relief—she nearly burst out laughing. "Is that all?"

"Bea, this is serious. If this is just a blip, it's no problem— but if we see a steady decline, well."

"If we see a steady decline, what?"

"Let's just say it won't be good for either of our careers."

Bea's expression hardened. "Okay. What do you want me to do about it?"

"The truth is, there's been some backlash to your perceived attitude toward the show—and toward the men."

"Backlash?"

Lauren sighed. "Bea, it's hard for the audience to believe you could actually fall in love here. And since that's the whole reason they're watching . . ."

Usually, the leads come here looking for love. But you didn't. Asher's words still echoed in Bea's mind, a constant, accusatory thrum threatening to dislodge what little confidence she was clinging to in the wake of the past week.

"What am I supposed to do?" Bea struggled to maintain composure. "The other women who come here are living in a fantasy, but you keep putting me in these nightmare scenarios."

"I literally had you drinking champagne on a luxury yacht off the Malibu coast surrounded by handsome men," Lauren snapped. "If that's not a fantasy, I don't know what is."

"Men who objectified me at best and humiliated me at worst!" Bea shot back. "If you want the audience to buy what we're selling, you have to stop assuming that I'm going to experience these dates the way you would. I don't live in your body. Men don't treat me like they treat you."

"What about Luc, then?" Lauren narrowed her eyes. "He was wonderful to you, but watching the footage back, you seemed like your mind was somewhere else."

Bea closed her eyes and nodded.

"You're right. I don't know, maybe I was still upset about the boat."

"Or maybe," Lauren said shrewdly, "you don't actually have the stomach to pretend to fall in love with someone you don't have feelings for? Because if that's the case, Bea, you and I are both in a lot of trouble."

Bea swallowed hard. "I'll do better this week. I promise."

"Good, then that's all we need to say about it." Lauren's expression softened, and she looked a little pained. "It's pretty unfair that all the good stuff is pretend while the bad stuff is completely real, huh?"

Bea laughed softly. "When you put it that way, I guess it kind of is."

"Keep your eyes on the prize, okay, Bea? *Your* future. *Your* career. You're not doing this for a man. You're doing it for yourself."

TEXT MESSAGE TRANSCRIPT, MARCH 10:
RAY MORETTI & MARIN MENDOZA

Ray [8:34am]: Hi, Marin. This is Bea's friend Ray—we met at her birthday a few years ago? Sorry to bother you, I dug up your number from an old group thread. I've been trying to get in touch with her, but none of my texts or emails seem to be going through? I don't know if you have any way of reaching her while she's filming, but I really need to talk to her. So if it's possible, can you give her the message?

Ray [8:35am]: Thanks. I really appreciate it.

Marin [8:39am]: You have a lot of nerve to text me.

Marin [8:40am]: Please don't do it again. And please leave Bea alone.

Marin [8:40am]: She deserves so much better than you.

Half an hour later, Bea walked onto the lushly dressed garden party of a patio where she'd shoot her rundown with Johnny. But when she stepped outside the mansion, the person she saw literally jumping for joy wasn't her toothy host—it was Marin.

"What the hell?" Bea asked before she could stop herself—Marin was already rushing toward her and clasping her into a vise-grip hug, and it felt so good to get a moment of genuine happiness.

"I'm really here, can you believe it?!"

Bea laughed—part delight, part confusion. "I can't! What is this, what's happening?"

Johnny clearly wanted to get in on a group hug, but as that would have been very weird, he gave a little fist pump instead. "Best friends, reunited!"

Which is when Bea noticed that the cameras were already rolling.

"Oh wow, we're getting right into it, huh?"

Johnny smiled broadly and escorted Bea and Marin to a table set with tea and scones. "Marin and I have some fun surprises cooked up for you this week, Bea—but first, can you tell us about Marin? How did you two meet?"

"We were roommates freshman year at UCLA," Bea answered. "We were completely different—she was always out partying, and I just wanted to stay home to study and watch old movies."

"It was so sad," Marin piped in good-naturedly.

"Marin, do we have you to thank for getting Bea out of her shell and turning her into a star?"

"Nah, she did that on her own." Marin smiled proudly. "I just dragged her to idiotic frat parties on occasion."

"They were the *worst*," Bea groaned.

"Listen, no one's saying frat parties are good, but the frat guys wanted girls to make out with other girls, and *I* wanted to make out with other girls, so our interests were temporarily and powerfully aligned," Marin explained as Bea cracked up.

"Speaking of making out," Johnny said, reaching for a segue, "Marin, do you want to tell Bea what you're doing here?"

"YEAH, I do!" Marin beamed. "Okay, so actually, I first came here three days ago, but we kept it secret from you."

"What! Where was I?"

"I don't know, filming your confessionals or trying on gowns or however you spend your time here."

Bea nodded—none of that was wrong.

"While you were doing that, *I* was meeting your suitors."

"Excuse me?"

"I know! I got to grill them about who they are and what they want in life and, best of all, what they think about you." Marin sat back in her chair with a satisfied smile, while Bea felt increasingly anxious. Had the guys been honest with Marin? Did they say terrible things behind her back—and on camera?

"How, um. How did the conversations go?" Bea stuttered.

"Really well," Marin reassured her. "I felt like I got a great sense of who the guys are. And that's why I'm so excited that I got to choose which two guys are going on your one-on-one dates this week!"

"Wow." Bea's eyes widened. "You finally found a way to be in charge of my love life."

"It's like when you let me swipe your Bumble, but on TV." Marin grinned.

"So Bea," Johnny said, his voice low and dramatic, "are you ready to find out who you'll be dating this week?"

"Do it to it, Johnny." Bea matched his movie-trailer tone, and Marin snorted.

One of the PAs scurried over with two small pieces of poster board, which Marin placed facedown on the table before delivering a speech Bea was sure she'd rehearsed with Lauren.

"Bea, I think you have a lot of terrific guys here, but two of them really stood out to me as perfect matches for you. The first guy I chose is sweet, funny, and has a great attitude about life in general and this show in particular. You should have seen how excited he was when I told him I'd chosen him for a date with you—I hope you'll be just as excited. Your first date this week is . . . Sam!"

Marin flipped over the poster board to reveal Sam's face. Other than the fact that he was the youngest guy in the house and that he'd accidentally poked her during the premiere, Bea knew absolutely nothing about him. He was definitely attractive—and if Marin liked him, he must be fun to spend time with. Bea chalked this up as a win.

"Are you excited?" Marin looked at Bea expectantly.

"Totally!" Bea enthused. "Great pick!"

"Okay, Marin," Johnny went on, "who gets to join Bea for her second date this week?"

"This guy and Bea have a lot in common—they're both super smart, both keep up with the news, both a little bit argumentative, but in a really charming way."

Hmm, this didn't sound like any of the guys Bea had met. Had Marin unearthed a gem?

"Of all the guys in the house, this is the one I could most see you ending up with, and I'm hoping you'll come to agree with me on that. So I really hope you're excited for your date . . . with Asher!"

Marin turned over the second poster, and Asher's smug face stared back at Bea, looking like he saw right through her even in two dimensions.

"Bea, you and Asher had a little bit of a disagreement last week," Johnny goaded. "Do you think Marin made a good choice here?"

"I—um." Bea didn't want to embarrass Marin; she figured it was best to err toward tact. "I haven't spent much time with Asher. It will be interesting to get to know him better."

After they finished filming their segment, Bea and Marin

had a few minutes to chat before Bea needed to film producer interviews to discuss her thoughts on her upcoming dates, so they holed up in the empty wardrobe room, where Marin immediately made herself comfortable on a green velvet sofa.

"So, you having fun on the show so far?"

She gave Bea a pointed glance, and Bea sighed. It was no use faking anything with Marin.

"I know, okay? I already had a whole talk with Lauren this morning—I'm gonna try harder to seem happy this week."

"Try harder to *seem* happy? You're kidding, right?"

"No?"

Marin exhaled in frustration. "Bea, I know that doing this show is about your career, but if you spend this entire time avoiding making connections with really great men who came here specifically to meet you . . . that would be pretty colossally self-sabotaging, even for you."

"Wow, have you been talking to my mother?"

"I've got to tell you, I'm with Sue on this one." Marin grabbed Bea's hand and pulled her down onto the sofa beside her. "Babe, why should millions of Americans care about your 'journey to find love' if you don't?"

Bea sank down into the sofa as Marin put her arms around her, realizing how grotesque this whole experience had made her feel, how much it stung to put on a happy face around all these men while steeped in the knowledge, every waking minute of every single day, that none of them were remotely attracted to her.

"I don't know," she said. "I thought pretending would be easier."

"Don't you see?" Marin snuggled up against Bea. "It's *good* that it's not easy. If it were easy, that would mean you didn't care about finding love. But I know that's not true, Bea. I know how badly you want this. And I know how close you came to having it."

Bea closed her eyes, pained and relieved to be with someone who knew the real reason why she couldn't feel happy when she was kissing Luc.

Marin squeezed Bea's arm. "Bea, do you think it's possible that you don't want to date any of these other men for real because you're still hoping that somehow you might end up with Ray?"

"It's not like I can just force myself to fall out of love with him," Bea protested.

"I know. But you can try to move on—particularly since, you know, you're currently starring on a show where they've literally flown in handpicked men from all over the country to date you?"

"Men who despise me."

"That's not true! I met them all, and a lot of them really like you—especially Sam and Asher."

"Sam is a child, and Asher is a jerk."

"Sam's more mature than you'd think—you'll see when you spend time with him. And Asher is totally your type."

"He's a smug know-it-all!"

"Correct! Your type! You act like I wasn't present for all fifty of your professor crushes."

"Sure, in *college*."

"What about that editor you met at that book party two years ago? You wouldn't shut up for weeks about how hot he was."

"No one's saying Asher isn't hot—"

"Aha!" Marin's eyes lit up. "So you *are* interested in him."

"What does it matter if I am?" Bea huffed. "You saw him on the boat. He publicly accused me of coming here for the wrong reasons, of wasting his time."

"And I agree, his methods left something to be desired," Marin concurred. "But was anything he said actually, you know, untrue?"

Bea sighed. She absolutely hated to admit that it wasn't. But none of these men seemed to understand just how much it could cost her to be open with them.

"I know what happens when I fall in love," she said quietly. "And I can't—last year was so bad, Mar. I don't know if I can live through that again."

Marin smoothed Bea's hair out of her eyes. "You can live a long life never being hurt—and never quite being happy. If that's what you want."

Bea shook her head—it wasn't.

"So try, Bea. Okay? You don't have to get engaged, you don't have to give anyone your heart. But at the very least, just promise me you'll try."

After a long moment, Bea nodded.

"I promise."

HIGHLIGHTS FROM SAM COX'S *MAIN SQUEEZE* APPLICANT SURVEY, AS POSTED ON ABS.COM

Name: Sam Cox

Occupation: Volunteer basketball coach

Hometown: Short Hills, New Jersey

Favorite place you've traveled? Cambodia

Favorite ice cream? Mint chip. No, fudge ripple. Or peanut butter! Also Cherry Garcia. And Phish Food. Wow, I have a thing for jam band ice cream flavors, but I hate their music. What do you think it means?

Who is your role model? My mom, Claudette, is the chief cardiac surgeon at Mountainside Hospital. She's brave enough to hold people's lives in her hands, and strong enough to live up to the responsibility.

If you could accomplish just one thing in your life, what would it be? Okay, *Main Squeeze,* getting deep with it. Respect. Oh, you want an answer? I have no idea.

The next morning, Bea had to get up at an ungodly hour for her date with Sam. Alison dressed her in artfully tattered boyfriend jeans, a whisper-thin Monrow tee, a men's soft leather bomber with the sleeves pushed up to Bea's elbows, and vintage Nikes, so Bea knew they were going somewhere casual, but she had no idea where. And Lauren insisted that the surprise not be spoiled—so Bea and Sam were going to be blindfolded for their limo ride to their date.

"Seriously?" Bea asked when a PA produced two black satin blindfolds emblazoned with rhinestones that formed the *Main Squeeze* logo.

Sam looked skeptical, too, but Lauren was having none of it.

"I promise," she assured them, "you're going to be more upset than I am if we lose time at your destination, so can you put on the blindfolds so we can get moving?"

And that's how Bea and Sam came to be blindfolded, led into a limousine with two cameras trained on their every move, and driven clear across Los Angeles at six o'clock in the morning.

"Where do you think they're taking us?" he asked.

"Maybe some sort of escape-room scenario?" Bea ventured. "Otherwise I have no idea what's with the blindfolds."

"I gotta say, this is some real *Eyes Wide Shut* nonsense for a first date."

"Oh," Bea deadpanned, "did I not tell you we're going to a secret murder orgy?"

"Way better than a public murder orgy," Sam quipped. "Those always end in jail time."

"Crap, do you think they'll be mad about all our cameras?"

Bea heard a fluster of movement that sounded like Sam was flailing wildly around the limo.

"Guys! Guys! Did you know they don't allow cameras in secret murder orgies? Our date is ruined!"

When the limousine finally rolled to a stop, Bea and Sam stumbled out of the limo together, still blindfolded, and were forced to walk another five minutes or so before they stopped for the official unveiling.

"Bea and Sam, welcome to your very first one-on-one date!"

"Thanks, Johnny!" Bea said brightly.

"Now, tell me," Johnny said smoothly, "do you two have any idea where you are?"

"We drove for about an hour," Bea started, "and without traffic at freeway speeds, that puts us maybe sixty miles from the compound? But it's much sunnier and hotter than it was when we left, so that would mean we drove inland, and probably south, too, and if you account for—"

"Okay," a producer broke in, "that was a rhetorical question. Bea, Sam, can we take that again and have you guys just shake your heads?"

"Damn," Sam whispered, "remind me to take you with me if I ever actually get kidnapped. What are you, a secret agent?"

"Or a superhero whose primary power is having spent half my life in L.A. traffic," Bea whispered back as they both shook their heads solemnly, per the producer's instructions.

"All right," said Johnny grandly, "on the count of three, go ahead and remove your blindfolds. In three, two, one—"

"Holy shit!" Sam blurted in the same second Bea shouted out, "We're at Disneyland!"

"I can't believe this!" Sam guffawed.

"Right?" Bea laughed. "Happiest Place on Earth!"

"You can say that again." Sam grinned as he wrapped Bea in a tight hug and gently kissed her cheek.

"Worth getting up for a date so early in the morning?"

"Bea, I'd hang out with you anytime. But is the park even open?"

"Technically," Johnny explained energetically, "the park won't open to the public for another three hours. But you two get to go in now."

Sam cheered and hugged Bea again. She couldn't tell whether he was genuinely into her or just swept up in the thrill of the moment, but Marin's voice echoed in her mind: *Try.*

Okay, Mar, she thought. *It's just one date. I can do this.*

The first hour inside the park was a mad rush from one attraction to another—Bea and Sam could have quiet conversations in tucked-away corners of the park once other visitors were allowed in, but this private time was the producers' only opportunity to capture footage of Bea and Sam on the bigger rides, and they weren't going to squander it. They screamed their faces off on Space Mountain and made spooky noises in the Haunted Mansion—Bea shrieked when Sam aimed a well-timed poke at her middle just as an animatronic ghost appeared beside them.

"I can't believe you poked me again!"

"Too soon?"

Bea laughed, and Sam threaded his fingers through hers. It was the first time she'd held hands with a man since Ray grabbed her hand in the Lyft home last summer, and she was surprised by how easy and uncomplicated it felt, by how carefree the vibe was on this entire date. After they'd been on a few more of the big rides (and narrowly averted catastrophe when Bea's mic pack got stuck in the safety bar of Big Thunder Mountain Railroad), they went to the Jungle Cruise to slow the pace down a bit and build in some time for conversation.

"Have you ever been to Disneyland before?" Bea asked as they drifted past a bamboo forest.

"Just the one in Florida. I grew up in New Jersey, so that was closer."

"New Jersey, really? You don't have an accent."

Sam raised an eyebrow at Bea. "When's the last time you heard a Black guy talk like Snooki?"

Bea laughed. "Touché."

"Nah, my parents were really into the whole prep-school thing, not a lot of kids with accents where I'm from."

"Really? Like you wore a blazer to school every day, the whole bit?"

"Oh, big-time. The blazer, the polo shirt, the *loafers*."

"No."

"Yes. When I finally got to college, I was so happy I didn't even know what to do with myself. People wearing sweatpants! To class! All my dreams were coming true."

"And, um, when did you graduate from college?"

Sam laughed. "Okay, I see you. Yes, I am the youngest guy in the house. I graduated from college two years ago."

"Which makes you . . ."

"Twenty-four. Six years younger than you, right? Is that so much?"

Bea shook her head, but truthfully, she wasn't sure.

"And what have you been doing for the past couple years?"

"I went right to Teach for America after college, I taught fifth-grade math and coached the girls' basketball team, which was basically the best thing ever. So I finished that up last summer, and now I'm figuring out what comes next."

"And you think what comes next might be a wedding? A family?"

Sam shrugged. "My whole life, my attitude has been to say yes to everything. In college, a professor of mine recommended me for an internship teaching English in Cambodia, and it turned out to be the best summer of my life. That's what made me decide to apply for Teach for America. A few months ago, I was walking through a mall when I saw they were recruiting guys for *Main Squeeze*. My buddy told me I should apply, and I was like, 'Sure, why not?' I thought it would be funny. Now here I am. Maybe the universe is trying to tell me something."

"That you were meant to be on reality TV?"

"No, not that."

He held Bea's gaze—and part of her wanted to lean in and kiss him, to let herself believe that this sweet, incredibly attractive man was actually into her. But something in her gut told her not to, that this wasn't the time, that maybe he was pretending. Like Luc, like Ray, like her. So she pointed out a fake tiger in the fake jungle on their fake adventure, and they let the moment pass. But Sam brought the conversation up again a few minutes later as they poked around the Mad Hatter's Haberdashery, trying on increasingly large and ridiculous hats.

"What about you?" he asked. "You're ready for marriage, kids, that whole bit?"

Bea pulled on a huge stuffed clownfish hat that was at least twice as tall as her head. "Marriage, yes, I think so. Kids, for sure eventually, but probably not right away. With my career, I'm lucky to travel all the time—London, Paris, New York. So I'd probably want to wait a few years."

"Hmm, sounds like our timelines might not be so different," Sam said. "Now, tell me what you think. This is the one, right?"

He was wearing a humongous Goofy head that dipped so low it covered half his face—Bea burst out laughing.

"If your goal was to make me take you more seriously, I'm not sure this is doing the trick."

He reached out his arms and stumbled blindly toward the sound of her voice.

"What if my goal was just to make you happy?"

In the end, they went with the classic mouse-ear hats: Mickey for him, Minnie for her. As they stood in front of Sleeping Beauty's Castle to film their last few shots before the park opened to the public, Sam pulled her close to him, near enough to feel the contours of his muscled body against her. This didn't feel as straightforward as holding hands—it felt risky and exciting and decidedly un-platonic. Was it what she wanted? Was it way too much? Or was it even real?

Bea closed her eyes. "Do you think you'd like me if we were somewhere else? Instead of on TV?"

"If someone said, Hey Sam, here's this hot boss career lady

who works in fashion so her looks are always on point, she loves roller coasters and drives a convertible and wants to figure out how to balance family with trips to London and Paris? Um, yeah, I'm pretty sure I'd be interested."

She looked up at his handsome, youthful face, his silly mustache that somehow worked on him, his Mickey ears and goofy smile.

"And you?" he prompted. "You think you'd like some guy who's two years out of college and lives with his parents and has no idea what he wants to do with his life? You think I'm such a catch?"

"Wow, you live with your parents, huh?"

"Yeah, I left that part out earlier."

"You really know how to charm a girl."

"Nah, I don't know. But I'm trying to figure it out." He dipped his head, leaning his forehead against hers. "I really want to kiss you right now."

"I don't know," she said, her voice uncharacteristically small.

"What's holding you back?" He wasn't defensive, just genuinely inquisitive.

Bea's chest felt tight with emotion, with some deeply buried feeling struggling to exorcise itself. She wanted to say something eloquent, but failing that, she said something honest: "I'm afraid."

"Of what?"

"Of making a fool of myself. Or believing in the wrong person. Or getting hurt."

"And a kiss could lead to all that?"

Bea nodded, her eyes wet. She hated herself for not being able to do this simple thing that came so easily to so many people.

"Okay, then." Sam took a step back, then dropped dramatically to one knee and kissed her hand. "That'll have to do for today."

Bea laughed through her tears. "What the hell are you doing?"

"We're in front of a castle, Bea! You gotta let me do the Prince Charming bit."

"And that's enough for you?"

Sam stood up and stepped close to Bea.

"If time is what you need, I can give you that. If reassurance is what you need, I can give you that too."

Bea threw her arms around Sam's neck and hugged him tightly.

"Thank you," she whispered.

The sun was bright and warm, and Bea heard the distant shouts of children. The park was finally open, reminding Bea that this moment that had been just theirs would soon belong to everyone.

MAIN SQUEEZE FAN LAUNCHES PETITION
TO BAN NASH & COOPER FROM SPIN-OFFS
by Amanda Tillman, vulture.com

Avid viewers of *Main Squeeze* know that aside from getting engaged and living happily ever after, there are two prizes that contestants on the show are hoping to win:

The first is more Instagram followers, which leads to more #SponCon (that's *sponsored content,* wherein advertisers pay ~influencers~ up to $10,000 per post, depending how many followers they have). The second is more camera time (which translates to more fame, which translates to, you guessed it, more Instagram followers)—and, if you're really lucky, a coveted spot on one of *Main Squeeze's* many spin-off series, such as perennial favorite *Main Squeeze Mansion,* where twenty castoffs from previous seasons spend the summer in the mansion looking for love.

These spots are usually reserved for fan favorites, but a couple always go to notorious villains—and this year, Nash and Cooper are in the clear lead for that title. The duo have become completely inseparable, spending seemingly every waking moment calling Bea a whale, a cow, a hippo, a hog, a heifer (which is another word for cow, for those keeping track at home!), and, perhaps most memorably of all, a baconwrapped ball of squishy lard.

Nash and Cooper might think these antics will increase their chances of being cast in a spin-off, but one *Main Squeeze* fan, Lilia Jamm from Helena, Montana, wants to make sure Nash and Cooper never bathe in the bright lights of the *Main Squeeze* cameras again.

"Nash and Cooper are bullies," Jamm wrote in her petition on the website change.biz to ban the pair from all future *Main Squeeze* spin-offs. "They are MEAN, pure and simple, and they should not be rewarded for their rude behavior. What does a bully want? ATTENTION!!!!! So let's not give it to them!!!!!!"

Jamm isn't the only fan who feels this way—at the time of this article's posting, her petition already had more than 20,000 signatures. It remains to be seen whether the *Main Squeeze* producers will listen, but one thing's for sure: All of us watching this season are waiting on tenterhooks for Nash and Cooper to face some serious consequences for their constant belittling of Bea.

During the month before they started filming, Lauren had asked Bea if she had any particular dream dates, either in L.A. or around the world. In Los Angeles (aside from a free meal at any truly great restaurant, or In-N-Out, frankly), Bea had only one answer: She'd always fantasized about having the Los Angeles County Museum of Art all to herself.

LACMA was Bea's sanctuary in L.A., the place where she felt most comfortable. When she left her home in suburban Ohio to start college at UCLA, one of the first things Bea did was get on a bus to visit this museum. She wandered through the galleries for hours, lost in the vivid colors, the ancient artifacts, the outsized sculptures that made her feel like a tiny person at home with giants, her favorite childhood story come to life.

Bea had dreamed of being alone in a museum since she was a kid reading *From the Mixed-Up Files of Mrs. Basil E. Frankweiler* with a flashlight under the covers. So when Lauren told her she'd be doing just that for her date with Asher, she felt a mix of trepidation and elation. Of all the men in the house, Asher seemed the most averse to self-indulgent fantasies—so it made Bea a little uncomfortable that he was about to join in for hers.

Alison had a host of outfit options, but all of them felt wrong to Bea—a sequined Sachin & Babi cocktail dress was too fancy (it was just a museum, not a gala), but a pair of slacks and a sleek button-down from Roland Mouret seemed too businesslike. They finally settled on a Sally LaPointe silk pajama–inspired outfit in sapphire blue that matched Bea's eyes almost exactly: easy, flowing pants and a matching blouse with an asymmetrical hemline, paired with nude strappy Prada sandals.

"Classy and sexy at the same time," Alison said, but Bea struggled to feel either as the hair and makeup people gave her a fresh face and tousled waves.

As the production van made its way through West Hollywood's crowded streets toward LACMA, Bea's nerves seemed to coil more and more tightly, wondering if the night with Asher would be congenial, or if he had more accusations to levy—accusations she still had absolutely no idea how to answer.

She didn't relax until the rows of lanterns outside LACMA came into view—the iconic sculpture where so many tourists snapped their selfies without ever bothering to venture into the museum beyond. There were no tourists tonight, though; the entire LACMA complex was blocked off for filming.

The lantern sculpture was called *Urban Light,* and it consisted of 202 immaculately restored antique streetlamps placed in careful rows of ascending height. The producers had Asher waiting in one of the middle rows, leaning against a lantern with his tall, easy posture, his lanky frame cast in warm light and blue shadow. With his gray jeans and a button-down shirt and backlit silhouette, Bea could almost imagine he was Ray as she approached him.

"Bea. Nice to see you. You look great." His tone was awkward, stilted, like this was a real date. The thought made Bea smile—if this was a "real" date, what were all the others?

"Thanks." She gestured toward the museum entrance. "Shall we?"

Asher nodded, and they walked off in silence. *This is going to be some really compelling TV,* Bea thought, and nearly laughed again as they walked inside.

"I always start at this one gallery on the third floor," she explained. "Do you mind if we go there first?"

"Lead the way."

They rode the elevator up, and Bea guided them through a maze of galleries to one you'd hardly know existed unless you were looking for it—or got lucky. Tucked in a corner past rooms full of modernist masterpieces was the museum's sole impressionist gallery: precious Cézannes, scant Renoirs, and even a few Monets. Bea walked over to her favorite painting in the room, the bridge at Giverny at sunrise, Asher following in her wake.

"Hey." Asher moved beside her, his arm brushing against hers. "I owe you an apology."

Bea kept her gaze trained on the painting, tried to keep her tone casual. "Oh?"

He turned to face her. "This isn't the way I want to say this, but I hope you'll understand why I have to."

She furrowed her brow. "What isn't the way you want to say it?"

"Fuck." Asher exhaled.

"No cursing!" a producer piped in.

"Yeah, I know," he said. "Bea, from my vantage point on that fucking boat, it seemed like you were goddamn pretending with every man you fucking encountered. I didn't realize until much shit piss later how awful the other men fucking were to you that day. If I had, I never would have fucking confronted you the way I did. You have every fucking right to be angry with me, and I apologize for my goddamn behavior. I was feeling annoyed and insecure, and I fucking took it out on you. Which was, you know."

"Fucking shitty?" Bea chimed in with a small smile.

Asher nodded. "Exactly goddamn right."

"Asher, come on." The producer shoved his way past the cameras and into their setup. "You know we can't use any of that. We need to take the whole apology again."

"I'm afraid that's not possible." Asher folded his arms. "The point is to assure Bea my apology is genuine. If I give you something that would air on television to make me look like a great guy, how is she supposed to know if I'm serving my interests or hers?"

Bea felt her whole heart lift—for the first time since this show started, she finally had a way to know that a man was telling her the truth. Bea was half-convinced Lauren would find a way to use this footage to make Asher into a joke on the show, but at this particular moment, she couldn't find it in herself to care.

"Can I ask"—Bea took a step toward him—"if you felt like I wasn't the person you came here to meet, why didn't you leave?"

"I made a promise that I would really try to make this work."

Bea smiled. "That's funny."

"Is it? Why?"

"I made the same promise. As recently as two days ago, in fact."

"Yeah? And how's that going for you?"

Bea looked up at him long enough for it to get uncomfortable—except it didn't.

"I don't know yet."

Asher smiled at her. "Is it cliché if I ask if we can start over?"

Bea laughed. "Absolutely, it definitely is."

"So I shouldn't do the thing where I reach out my hand to shake yours and say, 'Hi, I'm Asher.'"

"Not unless you want me to kick you off the show right here and now."

"Ah, an escape hatch! Good to know."

"Hey!" Bea faked being offended, but they were both still beaming.

"Do you want to go downstairs and see some modern stuff?" she asked.

He nodded, and without another word about it, they walked down the museum's wide central staircase side by side.

The more time they spent ambling through the museum's dozens of galleries, surrounded by Rothkos and Picassos, the more Bea found herself enjoying Asher's company. He listened attentively while she talked about Picasso's use of hats to add levity to paintings of his depressed friend, the photographer Dora Maar. She'd written her art history thesis in college about Picasso's reduction of a fellow artist to her clothes and her emotions, as if that were the truth of her.

"Well," he asked, "how do you find the truth of someone, then?"

"If not through their hats?"

"I'm serious." He nudged her. "Tell me something true."

Bea opened her mouth, then closed it again, her heart suddenly pounding.

"It's okay," Asher encouraged her. "I'm listening."

"I'm afraid that at the end of all this, I'll be alone. And all the people who've said horrible things about my body will say, 'See? We were right about her. We were right about all of it.'"

"And if you never really take a risk, you'll never have the chance to find out if they were?" Asher asked pointedly.

"You're going to have to stop doing that." Bea blushed.

"Doing what?"

"Seeing past my tough exterior."

"I like your tough exterior." Asher's lips quirked in a small smile. "When I look at you, I like everything I see."

When they walked out of the museum into the crisp spring night, Bea wasn't ready to leave. The producers told her they had time for one more stop, so Bea led Asher to the cavernous Resnick Pavilion, which had a new exhibit showcasing some of the museum's more controversial works of the last sixty years.

"This looks remarkably like a pot I made at summer camp," Asher said, pointing to a lumpy brown sculpture.

"It's a Claes Oldenburg—a baked potato."

"I should have said mine was a baked potato. It looked like one."

"You did pottery at summer camp?"

"You're surprised I wasn't out playing soccer? I would have sat all day by myself with a book if they'd let me."

"Sounds like we were pretty alike as kids," she said.

"I'm glad one of us grew out of it." He rested a hand on her shoulder. After all the semi-intentional arm brushes and leg nudges of the evening thus far, the warm weight of his palm felt full, somehow, or even heavy—and she loved it. She wanted more.

The sound of 1940s swing music floated toward them from the back of the pavilion, and they wandered toward it to discover the source. It turned out to be a life-size sculpture of a 1938 Dodge Coupe, placed on a plot of fake grass strewn with empty beer bottles. The door was open to reveal two figures in the backseat—a woman lying back with one knee propped up, and a man on top of her fabricated in chicken wire, completely transparent except for his left hand, opaque and white, prone between her thighs. The music was part of the exhibit, the soundtrack of the couple's lovemaking.

Bea read from the description mounted near the sculpture.

"They exhibited this in the 1960s, and the County Board of Supervisors tried to make them remove it. They called it pornography. But the museum refused—so they had to keep the car door closed if children were present."

Asher smiled at her. "Pretty sexy stuff."

"Did you just say 'sexy' to me?"

He laughed and extended his arm. "Do you want to dance?"

"Are you serious?"

He nodded, and Bea let him pull her in, his hand on the small of her back, his Old Spice scent near enough to inhale. He was a remarkably good dancer—strong frame, sure step— and his hands felt amazing sliding over the smooth silk of her blouse.

"How can you dance like this?" She gazed at him with wonder.

"I was raised going to temple because my dad is Jewish, but my mom is Chinese—she'd never been to a bar mitzvah. When I started getting invitations, she was sure all the other kids would know how to dance and I'd look like an idiot. So she made me take ballroom lessons at the senior center."

"You're kidding."

"Nope. I was the twelve-year-old Fred Astaire of Tarrytown, and I spent my Tuesday afternoons dancing with old ladies. Between that and the pottery, I was a *pretty* popular kid."

They laughed, and Bea felt him bring her a little closer. Her breath got quicker, and he gently squeezed her waist. The music stopped—the song was over, and there was a pause before the next one began. Bea knew what would happen if this were actually a real date, if they were somewhere else, if he were braver, or if she were, if—

He dropped his hands abruptly, jerked back and left her

moored in infinite space, the cameras jutting through, black and claustrophobic as she felt the blood rush to her face, her breathing fast and shallow.

"I'm sorry," he said dumbly. Bea stood stock-still, trying to ward off whatever she was feeling until she was anywhere else, wishing Marin could be here to witness this moment so she would never shove Bea off a cliff into abject humiliation ever again.

"Okay!" said a producer. "Let's take that again, get you dancing to the next song, then we can slow it down for the end-of-date kiss—you guys ready to go?"

Asher looked pained. "I can't. I'm sorry." He turned to Bea. "I'm sorry."

Bea kept her face impassive, her tone deadened. "It's no problem. Let's call it a night."

@Reali-Tea Ok y'all, time for this week's kiss-off ceremony: Bea's rocking a purple lip (shade: "You're turning violet, Violet!") and presumably dismissing some Barneys who've barely gotten camera time. Let's see who gets the ax!

@Reali-Tea First kiss goes to Sam—no surprise there, how cute was their date?? Tho she really should have kissed him imo BEA IF YOU CAN HEAR ME, MAKE OUT WITH HOT MEN IN DISNEYLAND, OK?

@Reali-Tea Next up is football hero Wyatt, looking so cute in his sweater! Build me a fire, Wyatt! Bea looks so happy to see him and hug him, I seriously need these two to get their one-on-one next week. @MainSqueezeABS pls make this happen???

@Reali-Tea Third kiss goes to Luc, and if he thinks we didn't all see him cop a feel when Bea leaned in to kiss him, HE IS SORELY MISTAKEN. (oh god she's so lucky truly how soon until overnight dates????)

@Reali-Tea Kisses for Jefferson, Trevor, Jaime, and Kindergarten Ben. Snooze! Jefferson seems like he has potential, but he'd better make an impression soon, or he's gonna get swept off with the rest of these also-rans.

@Reali-Tea Kisses, inexplicably, to Nash and Cooper???? Does Bea seriously not see that these two are GARBAGE, or is this blatant producer manipulation? Main Squeeze Nation, let us bow our heads and pray for the imminent removal of this human refuse. 🙏🏻 🙏🏻 🙏🏻

@Reali-Tea Wait, is Bea kicking off Asher?? I know she was blindsided when he wouldn't kiss her (same tbqh!!!!!!!!), but it seemed like she liked him so much?? Hard to say now, though—he looks miserable, and so does she.

@Reali-Tea Phew! Asher gets the final kiss!!!! I have a feeling there's more to come for these two—and I can't wait to find out what it is.

EPISODE 4

"HOMECOMING"

(10 men left)

Shot on location in Cheshire, Ohio

SCRIPT OF *MAIN SQUEEZE* PROMOTIONAL AD
released 24 hours in advance of Season 14, Episode 4

OVER FOOTAGE OF A BLACK, STARRY SKY IN OUTER
SPACE, WE HEAR A VOICE—

> VOICEOVER
> This week, on a brand-new episode of *Main Squeeze,*
> we'll go boldly where no boyfriend of Bea's has gone
> before . . .

ZOOM THROUGH HYPERSPEED TO . . . A QUAINT
SUBURBAN HOUSE

> VOICEOVER
> Her parents' house.

SFX: DOORBELL *(ding-dong!)*

> VOICEOVER
> We'll find out what Bea was like as a child.

INSERT FOOTAGE: INTERVIEW WITH BEA'S PARENTS

BEA'S MOM, SUE

Beatrice never brought home any boys. We even thought for a while she might be gay, didn't we, Bob?

VOICEOVER

We'll see what her family thinks about her suitors.

INSERT FOOTAGE: INTERVIEW WITH BEA'S BROTHERS

BEA'S BROTHER TIM

I've never trusted a Frenchman in my life, and I'm not about to start.

VOICEOVER

And we'll find out the *real* reason Asher wouldn't kiss Bea on their last date—the answer will shock you.

INSERT FOOTAGE: BEA AND ASHER IN HER FAMILY'S BACKYARD

ASHER

Bea, I need to tell you, about that night . . .

INSERT FOOTAGE: BEA'S SISTER-IN-LAW TINA GASPS DRAMATICALLY.

VOICEOVER

Don't miss a moment of the *Main Squeeze* family feud, this Monday at eight, only on ABS.

TRANSCRIPT OF *BOOB TUBE* PODCAST
EPISODE #052

Cat: Hey, this is Cat!
Ruby: And this is Ruby.

Cat: And this is *Boob Tube*. This week, we have a really exciting episode—we're doing a deep dive into the feminine archetypes on *Buffy the Vampire Slayer* and deciding which modern characters best carry those torches.

Ruby: I'm still waiting for another Willow.

Cat: So say we all. But before we get into that, we need to return to the land of reality TV, because *one* of us is having a lot of feelings and opinions about this week's episode of *Main Squeeze*.

Ruby: Someone needs to speak the truth about how Asher is the WORST.

Cat: You're wrong—he's so smart and cute with his big glasses!

Ruby: He's every Brooklyn intellectual fuckboy who holds women to impossible standards but considers it beneath him to pick up the phone and schedule a second date.

Cat: Noooo, Asher is legit!

Ruby: Then why didn't he kiss Bea at the museum?

Cat: He's old-fashioned! He's a gentleman who wants to know it's real before he lets things get physical.

Ruby: That interpretation is generous bordering on delusional— I think he has a secret girlfriend.

Cat: What?! Asher would never.

Ruby: He's definitely hiding something—and, if I may be so bold, your defense of him is obviously grounded in the fact that you personally want to bone him.

Cat: How DARE you.

Ruby: Am I wrong?

Cat: No, of course not. Okay, since I'm clearly biased, who's your pick for Bea?

Ruby: TEAM SAM, BITCHES!

Cat: Seriously? He's a child!

Ruby: He's smart and handsome and full of joie de vivre.

Cat: He's unemployed and lives with his parents.

Ruby: He likes Bea for who she is and doesn't drag her into his bullshit.

Cat: Does Sam have any bullshit? Does he have any anything? He's twenty-four, what does he know about life?

Ruby: Wow.

Cat: What?

Ruby: I've just never heard you sound that old before.

Cat: Okay, okay, so we've clearly drawn some lines in the sand. I'm with Asher, you're with Sam. But what say you about Luc?

Ruby: Ugh, I hate myself for how much I want to kiss him.

Cat: Right?? He's so cheesy, why do I like him so much?

Ruby: There's something really appealing about how self-aware he is. Like, sure, I'm a cartoonishly handsome French guy seducing you with food, but aren't you enjoying it? And I'm like, yeah, Luc, you know what? I *am* enjoying it.

Cat: I'm really looking forward to him and Bea getting to spend more time together now that she seems to have found a little more confidence.

Ruby: Wait—I have a question. Whatever happened to Wyatt? Bea was so into him the first night—is she gonna go out with him or what?

Cat: This is actually a pretty typical move on shows like this—when there's an instant connection between two people, the producers often keep them apart for as long as possible to try and give the other contestants a chance to catch up. But I'd be very surprised if we don't see some quality time for Bea and Wyatt in the next episode or two.

Ruby: Oooh, a new player on the board. I'm into it.

Cat: So Ruby, we know from the promos that this week Bea is bringing her ten remaining suitors home to meet her family in Ohio—that's a pretty serious step. It begs the question: Is there a legit chance Bea will marry one of these guys?

Ruby: I don't know about that. Doesn't she strike you as not totally even wanting to get married? She doesn't seem like the dead-eyed Pinterest girls who treat weddings like the end-all goal of one's existence.

Cat: Absolutely—I think that's why I like her so much. But at the same time it's like, hey, you know you came on this show to find a husband, right? Don't let me down, Bea!

Ruby: Exactly! Sacrifice your future at the altar of my enjoyment!

Cat: She just walks down the aisle to marry some horrible jerk, sobbing, "Are you not entertained?"

Ruby: Man, I'd watch the shit out of that.

Cat: A thousand percent agree. And speaking of shit-watching, are you worried about what your pet is doing in your home all day while you're at work? PupperCam is the service that allows you to watch your pet, say hi to them over a speaker, and even distribute treats to let them know you're there with them, even when you're gone.

Ruby: Wow, just like my nana said she would be right before she died.

Cat: If PupperCam worked from the afterlife, I'm sure it would be your nana's preferred means to send you treats from heaven.

Ruby: Thanks, Nana! We'll be back right after this.

Bea was a senior in high school when her oldest brother, Jon, got engaged. Carol was his high school sweetheart; she followed him and his football scholarship to Kent State. Bea remembered the Thanksgiving when they told the family they were getting married—the whole group exploded into shouts and hugs and Bob dug a dusty bottle of whiskey out of a very tall cabinet and everyone did celebratory shots, even Bea.

Tim's college girlfriend, Tina, was there, and Bea saw her eyes flash with envy while Carol and Jon posed for pictures, Carol laughing and showing off her ring. Bea hoped her own jealousy was better concealed. Seeing Jon and Carol together, their blinding smiles, the way they held hands under the table during dinner, made Bea so heartsick it caused her physical pain. She wanted that feeling so profoundly, and was nearly equally certain she'd never have it. Less than a year later, Tim and Tina were engaged too. If Carol ever thought that Tina was deliberately trying to steal her thunder (as Bea certainly did), she was too gracious to say so. Bea was a bridesmaid in both weddings, navy satin and peach chiffon, a cacophony of unflattering cuts and unforgiving fabrics that caused Bea to vow never to have bridesmaids of her own.

For years at Easter and Thanksgiving and Christmas, Bea and her youngest brother, Duncan, were a team, rolling their eyes at the familial antics of their older siblings and their wives—and, soon after, babies.

"Truly kill me if that's ever my life," Duncan whispered during an unbearably loud Easter brunch that featured the colicky screams of one infant, the biblical spit-up of another, and the full-tilt meltdown of a toddler.

"Same," Bea agreed, deeply thankful to have at least one

ally at family gatherings where she increasingly felt like a stranger.

In their mid-twenties, though, Duncan met Julia—another designer at the firm in Columbus where they both worked. The first time Bea met her, she knew it was all over. With Julia's long brown hair and cat-eye glasses and red lipstick, she was so funny and smart and effortlessly cool, and Duncan had changed so much—where before he was detached and sardonic, now he was alert and attentive.

Duncan and Julia got married three years later, and they had their first baby in December; Bea met their newborn daughter this past Christmas, the first family gathering where all three of her brothers had children.

That Christmas morning, fewer than three months ago, while everyone gathered in pajamas to open presents, Bea had closed her eyes and let herself imagine Ray beside her, gently rubbing her back as the assorted kids ran around in total mayhem. She traveled back in time and superimposed him into every family memory: Ray laughing at her terrible dresses at Jon's and Tim's weddings, murmuring in her ear that he couldn't wait to rip them off her; Ray holding her and gently swaying during Duncan and Julia's first dance; a teenage Ray, five years younger than she'd ever known him, squeezing her hand while Jon and Carol posed for happy photos, saying, *Don't worry, Bea. Someday, that'll be us.*

It was the worst Christmas Bea could remember.

And now, twelve weeks later, never having brought a boyfriend home in her life, Bea was on a plane to Columbus accompanied by ten men, a mobile production crew, a literal truckload of gear, and, soon enough, the prying eyes of several million Americans.

She wasn't worried about her family being tough on her

suitors—frankly, she'd probably find it satisfying if they were. But if her mother actually liked any of these guys, Bea would never hear the end of it. "Why couldn't you make things work with that nice Frenchman? Or what about that professor? He was so charming, so smart!"

Yes, Mom, I was unbelievably charmed when the thought of kissing me so disgusted him that he physically jerked away from me. What a long and happy life we'll have together.

It still stung to think of Asher at the museum, how stupidly caught up in the moment she'd been, how much she'd believed that he was legitimately interested in her, and vice versa. He was probably trying to convince himself he was evolved enough to be attracted to a fat woman, but when the moment arrived, he couldn't actually bring himself to kiss her. Bea had met this type plenty of times, sat through any number of Tinder dates with some guy who was obviously mentally weighing how badly he wanted to get laid (this type of man assumed, just as Marco had, that a woman who looked like Bea would say yes and be grateful for any sex they offered). These dates always ended the same way: a strained expression, a stilted handshake or hug or peck on the cheek, an immovable sense on Bea's part that what *she* felt hadn't mattered at all.

Except, an annoying little voice contradicted, when she danced with Asher, it certainly didn't seem like he was brushing her off. The way he wrapped his arms around her, pulled her close—he was reveling in her body, not repulsed by it. But maybe that was just wishful thinking. Or maybe he'd cut the night short for some other reason. She didn't want to know. She agreed to keep him around for another week at Lauren's insistence, but on one condition: that he stay the hell away from her. Bea couldn't imagine that would be a problem. He'd made it clear that that was what he wanted.

TRANSCRIPT OF PRODUCER INTERVIEW
WITH BEA'S MOTHER AND STEPFATHER
Conducted prior to cast arrival

Producer: What was Bea like as a kid?

Sue: Oh, Bea was a *dream* of a child! So serious, so focused on her books, from the time she was a toddler, isn't that right, Bob? She didn't mind at all that she had so few friends; she was always really committed to her studies.

Producer: So she didn't have a lot of friends?

Sue: Well, you know how girls are when they're young, so cliquish. Bea was terribly shy, so she had a hard time making impressions on the other children. By the time she made it to high school, I think she was just more comfortable on her own. I always said that Bea was a late bloomer, that she'd find herself when she went off to college. Didn't I always say that, Bob? And that is exactly what happened.

Producer: What about boyfriends? Did Bea have a high school sweetheart?

Sue: Oh no, the boys always brought their girlfriends around the house, but Beatrice never brought home any boys. She's always been very private—we even thought for a while she might be gay, didn't we, Bob? Remember, when she joined the theater crew and wore all that black? We thought we might have a lesbian on our hands, which would have been fine, we just wanted her to feel *supported,* that was always the main thing!

Bob: The theater crew wears black so they can move things around onstage without the audience seeing.

Sue: That's true, it's very practical—and black can be very slimming. You know, we didn't have many options for Bea's clothes while she was growing up. With her size and our budget, we mostly shopped at Target. When she was younger, she would wear the most darling things, flowery dresses and the like, but then in high school she just wanted to wear black. These baggy T-shirts—not flattering.

Bob: You got the sense she didn't want to draw attention.

Producer: Why do you think that was?

Bob: The kids here never bullied Bea—not overtly. Sue and I are both teachers at the elementary school, so we could keep an eye on her when she was there. As she got older, the other kids started to leave her out, not invite her to parties, that sort of thing. The longer that went on, the more she saw it as a kind of safety. If the other kids just didn't pay her any mind, that meant they weren't being cruel, either. But being ignored is its own kind of hurtful.

Producer: When did you notice a change in Bea? In her personality, her appearance?

Bob: After Paris.

Sue: Paris, that's right. She went abroad for her junior year, and when she came home, she was a changed person. She wore the strangest clothes, she had this one velvet cape she never took off—it was like she was a character in *Batman*! None of us knew what to make of it, but it made her so happy, and she was so much louder than she'd ever been. It was a real joy—it felt like we were meeting our daughter all over again.

Producer: Are you surprised she's starring on a TV show, given how shy she used to be?

Sue: We were certainly surprised when she told us—she'd never expressed interest in doing anything like this!

Bob: But it makes sense. She has her videos she does on Instagram, and all her fans who love her so much.

Producer: Do you watch her videos?

Bob: We both do, we watch every single one. In an emergency, I think I could do a very competent French tuck.

Producer: What kind of man would you like to see Bea end up with?

Sue: Someone who wants children!

Producer: You're ready for some grandkids, huh?

Bob: We have six, we see them every Sunday.

Sue: But it's different with Bea. She's my only daughter, and she's so far away—oh, I would just love for her to have a baby and come home a little more. And a wedding! With all her style, wouldn't that be a treat? Bob, we could do it at the church, and Ernesto's could cater.

Bob: Let's meet the men she's dating before we start planning the reception, okay?

Sue: If she gets engaged on the show, do you think they'd get married this year? A fall wedding would be so romantic with all the leaves.

Bob: We want Bea to be happy. That's the main thing. We really want her to be happy.

HIGHLIGHTS FROM WYATT AMES'S *MAIN SQUEEZE* APPLICANT SURVEY, AS POSTED ON ABS.COM

Name: Wyatt Ames

Occupation: Wheat farmer

Hometown: Boone, Oklahoma

Where would you most like to travel? Maybe Finland, or Alaska? I'd love to see the Northern Lights.

If you could have any career, what would you do? I love working with my family. But if that weren't a factor, I might like to work with horses, or maybe in an animal hospital.

Do you have any tattoos? My sister and I both got our dad's initials on our shoulders after he passed. We took his truck and snuck up to Tulsa to get them. When we got home, our mom was waiting up for us—we thought she was going to be so mad. But the next day, she drove us back to the parlor so she could get one too.

"Okay," Alison tittered, "open your eyes!"

"What the hell is this?" Bea blurted before she could stop herself. She was in the designated hair/makeup/wardrobe conference room at the Econo Lodge where they were staying, and she was positively surrounded by long, sparkling dresses.

"They're for your date with Wyatt," Alison clarified, as if this explained anything at all.

"In Cheshire, Ohio?" Bea was incredulous. "The only time I've ever even *seen* anyone in town dress this formally is—wait. No. Alison, no."

Alison laughed with unbridled glee. "It's prom night, baby!"

And so it was that Bea ended up in a slinky Badgley Mischka gown embroidered with ombré sequins that shifted in the light from navy blue to deep turquoise. With sky-high heels and her hair pinned back in glossy curls, Bea felt like she was finally getting the glamorous pre-prom experience she'd yearned for in high school.

"See?" Alison reassured her. "Not a disco ball at all."

"More like that sparkly dress Ariel wears when she comes out of the water at the end of *The Little Mermaid*."

"Oh my God, a forever look," Alison exclaimed. "My little mermaid finally has her legs."

"Changing her body to please a man, just like everyone," Bea quipped.

"Not you." Alison draped her arms around Bea affectionately.

"Yeah, well. Couldn't if I wanted to!"

Bea thought back to her adolescence in this place, the years of fad diets and attempted starvation that never resulted in a loss of more than five or ten pounds (always immediately regained the second she ate a normal meal). No matter what she did, Bea was always the fattest girl in school, and maybe also the quietest, doing whatever she could to escape unwanted attention. As she rode in a limousine toward the small park in the center of town where she was meeting Wyatt—towering oak trees, a picturesque gazebo strung with fairy lights, and a small crowd of people cheering and waving posters, waiting to welcome home their town's most famous daughter—she had the sense that if she wasn't quite rewriting history tonight, she was, at least in some small way, righting it.

It was all a little surreal, but as Bea emerged from the limo, she thought the craziest part of all might just be the man who was waiting for her: Tall, broad, and golden, Wyatt looked every inch the football hero Bea remembered—except, in a perfectly fitted tuxedo, he was no longer the casual farmer in boots and jeans.

Tonight, he was the prom king.

"You look so pretty." He smiled shyly as she approached him, leaning down to kiss her cheek.

"You too," she sputtered, suddenly very aware of the on-lookers surrounding them.

"I got this for you." He held out a plastic box, and Bea felt like they were reenacting a memory she didn't have as she held out her wrist and he slipped on the red rose corsage. "Well, the producers did. It's nice, though, don't you think?"

Bea kissed his cheek and agreed that it was.

"Aren't you chivalrous," Bea joked as he held open the limo door, and he blushed bright red. Even though Wyatt was ruggedly handsome, the total picture of idealized Marlboro Man masculinity, there was something fragile about him—something Bea couldn't explain but instinctively felt she needed to protect. It was a bizarre sensation, particularly since the rest of the men in the house could seem like a many-headed Hydra, different faces of one monster ready to attack.

"What was your prom like?" Bea asked when they were in the limo and en route to her old high school, two cameras rolling to capture their conversation.

"I don't know," Wyatt admitted. "I stayed home."

"Really?" Bea was taken aback. "But you were on the foot-ball team, right? In our school, those guys were like kings."

"I wasn't really part of that," Wyatt demurred. "The other guys—we got along and everything, but we didn't really spend time together outside practice."

"Why not?" Bea was genuinely curious.

Wyatt shrugged. "Different interests."

"Oh," Bea replied, wanting to know more, but not about to pry.

"What about you?" He nudged her knee. "I'll bet you were the best-dressed girl at your prom."

Bea shook her head. "I didn't go either."

"How come?"

"No one to go with." Bea sighed. "I was friends with the theater tech kids; we were kind of antisocial. School dances were so not their scene."

"But you wanted to go, didn't you?"

Bea felt her chest tighten. She didn't just want to go—she'd been absolutely desperate.

"I made my stepdad tape *Pretty in Pink* off cable, and I watched it over and over," Bea confessed. "I thought Andie was so brave, going to prom alone. But she was beautiful, and all these guys secretly loved her. If I went to prom alone, everyone would have laughed."

"Why did you think that?" Wyatt coaxed gently. "Were people at your school mean to you?"

Bea thought back to another football player—blond and tall, like Wyatt, but where Wyatt was gentle, he'd been rough. Where Wyatt was warm and inquisitive, he'd been cold and indifferent, his existence a daily punishment for Bea having had the audacity to have feelings for him.

"No." Bea smiled as she lied. "They were fine."

Cheshire High's real prom wasn't until late May—that would be a rubbery chicken dinner at a local banquet venue with ostentatious carpets and faux gilt chandeliers. This "prom," staged for the purpose of this week's episode, was a bonus dance funded by the *Main Squeeze* production. The Cheshire High School gym, scene of many of Bea's athletic humiliations and faked period cramps to avoid the same, was decked out with streamers, balloons, and swirls of rainbow-colored spotlights, and filled to the brim with high school kids in off-brand formalwear dancing to the music of some band no one had heard of (whose label had surely paid for this opportunity to get them on TV). The band—which was actually pretty good, Bea noted, punky women in black lipstick and torn fishnets—was playing on a makeshift stage the crew had constructed under one of the basketball nets, illuminated by heavy production lights.

Bea and Wyatt waited to make their big entrance in a far less glamorous location: the gym's equipment closet, lined with smelly pinnies and stacks of basketballs.

"Are you nervous?" Wyatt asked her.

"A little," Bea admitted. "Teenagers are terrifying."

Wyatt looked wan; Bea realized he was considerably more tense than she was. The band finished its song, and Bea and Wyatt's field producer ushered them into place for their entrance. They heard thunderous applause as Johnny took the stage and shouted, "Cheshire High, how are you doing tonight?"

The kids cheered gamely, and in a matter of moments, the producer was shoving Bea and Wyatt through the door and into the gym, where they pushed toward the stage despite a blinding spotlight and what felt like a throng of screaming fans, light and noise pressing in on them from every angle.

"Give it up for Cheshire's own Bea Schumacher!" Johnny shouted as Bea and Wyatt ascended the stairs to the little stage, and the kids applauded. "So, Bea, I understand you never went to a dance when you were in high school. What do you think of your very first prom?"

Bea heard some snarky murmurs from the kids—terrific, one more moment of feeling like a loser in the Cheshire High gym.

"So far, so good." She forced a smile.

"Well, what would you say if I told you that you and Wyatt had been voted prom king and queen?"

Bea eyed Johnny skeptically. "I would say the voting was

pretty well rigged, since none of these people have ever met me?"

The kids laughed appreciatively, as did Johnny. "You've got us there, Bea. As a matter of fact, the students chose their own prom king and queen as well—let's welcome Cort and Tara to the stage!"

The kids started screaming and cheering again as two teenagers bounded up to join Bea and Wyatt—a guy in a rented tux who was tall and handsome and absolutely a basketball player (or maybe a football player? or maybe both?) and a girl who was blond and teensy in her lacy pink dress.

"Okay, you four," Johnny said conspiratorially, "since there can only be one *true* prom king and queen, what do you say we have a little competition to see who wins the crown? It's time to play the prom date game!"

Bea had no idea what that meant, but it turned out the "prom date game" was a barely reimagined version of *The Newlywed Game,* wherein Bea and Wyatt would compete against Cort and Tara to see how well they knew their respective prom dates. This didn't seem quite fair to Bea, considering that Cort and Tara had presumably spent more than ten minutes in each other's company prior to tonight, but it was no use protesting. A PA handed them all squares of poster board and thick black markers, and they wrote down responses to a list of questions before Johnny publicly grilled them to reveal their answers. Five rounds into the seven-round game, Cort and Tara had, predictably, won every single time.

"What," Johnny asked dramatically to begin round six, "is your prom date's favorite condiment?"

Bea guessed Wyatt's correctly ("She's right, I *do* love ketchup"), and revealed her own proclivity for sour cream ("It goes with every kind of potato!"), before Cort was forced to admit he'd misread the question when he flipped over a placard that read "Trojans."

"It's mustard, Cort." Tara shook her head disdainfully. "He knows how much I love mustard."

Cort hung his head in shame as Bea and Wyatt grinned at each other, pleased to have finally won a round of the game—but their victory was to be short-lived.

"Okay, guys, we saved the best for last," Johnny effused. "What is the craziest place your prom date has ever had sex? Or, Cort and Tara, the craziest place they've ever been kissed, in your case?"

Cort and Tara exchanged a knowing look, and Tara giggled. "Whatever you say, Johnny."

The teens were answering first this round, and it was clear there was no question as to whether they'd guessed correctly: They were both holding back uncontrollable laughter as they shouted "Mr. Asalone's classroom!" in unison, which was met with a roar of cheers and applause from the rest of the kids. Cort and Tara high-fived, and while Bea was happy for the teens' sex-positive attitude, it certainly didn't make her feel better about the answer she was about to give.

"Over to you, Wyatt and Bea," said Johnny. "Bea, what's the craziest place you've ever had sex?"

Bea sighed and figured if she was going to be ridiculed for her answer no matter what, she might as well tell the truth. "Get ready to be really shocked, everyone," she said with what she hoped was a good-natured laugh. "My answer is, in bed!"

The crowd was silent, and Bea saw some of the kids frown and tilt their heads with apparent pity. But she felt a surge of affection for Wyatt when he turned over his placard and she saw that he'd written "FASHION SHOW."

"Wow." Bea laughed. "Looks like we really stereotyped each other."

She flipped over her own placard to show him she'd written "BARN," but instead of laughing along, Wyatt flushed deep pink.

"Wyatt?" Johnny prompted him. "Did Bea guess right?"

Wyatt looked at the floor. "No," he said quietly.

"It's okay," Bea said gently. "I mean, you heard my answer, right? Whatever yours is, it's fine."

He looked up to meet her gaze. "The answer is nowhere."

Bea was puzzled for a second—but then she realized what he meant.

"So you've never . . . ?"

He shook his head.

The gym was completely silent except for the sound of whirring generators. "That concludes our game!" Johnny said grandly, pushing through the sense of awkwardness that had settled over the crowd. "Bea and Wyatt, you were worthy competitors, but it looks like this year's crowns will go to Cort and Tara!"

Everyone clapped halfheartedly as the two teens donned their sparkly plastic headgear, and Johnny moved them quickly to the next portion of the night: the dancing. The kids poured onto the floor as the band kicked back up, and Bea and Wyatt grabbed some punch and went to sit on the bleachers. Bea was grateful for a chance for a more private conversation with Wyatt—even if they were still being filmed.

"That took a lot of courage," she told him.

He shrugged. "Didn't have much of a choice, I guess."

"That's not true," Bea argued. "You could have lied."

"With this poker face?" A small smile played on his lips. "You would have seen right through me."

Bea laughed warmly, and he threaded his fingers through hers.

"Does it freak you out?" he asked. "That I'm . . . you know."

"No." Bea shook her head. "It's kind of a relief, actually."

Wyatt tilted his head. "Really? Why?"

"I guess I just assumed I was the least experienced person here, because I've never been in a long-term relationship," Bea said quietly. "It's been really intimidating, feeling like—I don't know. Like all of you would judge me, or not take me seriously. It makes me feel young, somehow."

Wyatt's face lit up with recognition.

"That's it exactly," he agreed. "There's this part of me that feels stuck. Not quite grown-up."

"And being here, in my hometown—in this high school, even—it's so acute, you know? Like I'm a teenager again, alone on prom night, feeling like a fool. Just some loser who'd only ever been kissed one time, who had no hope of ever finding a real boyfriend."

"At least you kissed someone," Wyatt looked wistful. "I never kissed anyone in high school."

"Really?" Bea had no idea how to square the way this man looked with the things he was telling her. "Can I ask why not?"

"I don't know, really," he mumbled. "I was pretty shy."

"I'm sorry," Bea said. "I don't mean to be nosy."

"No." He looked at her intensely. "You're trying to get to know me. I want that, Bea."

"You do?"

He squeezed her hand. "I really do."

"I'm glad." Bea smiled, thrown off guard by how different he seemed from the guys like him she'd known when she lived here. Or maybe that was the point—maybe those guys weren't like him at all.

"Let's change the subject." He smiled kindly. "Why don't you tell the story of your first kiss?"

Bea's stomach clenched at the memory—the warm, flat beer, the smell of the woods, the scratches on her face from the branches that scraped her as she ran. The shame she'd felt when her brothers found her waiting by the car and asked if she'd had fun at the party.

Wyatt clocked the ashen expression on Bea's face.

"I'm sorry—you don't have to tell me," he assured her.

Part of Bea didn't want to tell the story—didn't want to relive the humiliation, and certainly didn't want her brothers to find out what had really happened after all these years. But another part of her was moved by Wyatt's bravery, by the way that everything about him subverted her expectations. By her own desire—one she couldn't quite explain—to trust him.

"Growing up, my brothers all played sports," she started shakily. "Their friends were always around the house, and I mostly hid in my room, but sometimes they would be sweet to me, or joke around—make me feel like the kid sister in a movie, you know? They were loud and immature for the most part, but they had this one friend James who was really quiet. He was tall, and had this thick blond hair—he was on the football team with my brother Tim."

"You liked him?" Wyatt asked.

"Yeah." Bea felt her face flush, feeling so silly that even now, more than a decade later, while she was starring on a television show and James was who-knows-where, it still made her feel so small to admit she'd had a crush on a boy.

"I thought the fact that he was quiet meant that he was shy, or secretly really deep." She laughed uncomfortably. "I imagined that he wanted to have these intense conversations, that he would love having them with me. I thought it was some big secret that I liked him, but my brothers knew—Tim said something about it at dinner once, and I was so embarrassed. I left the table in tears."

"It's okay that you're sensitive," Wyatt said softly. "You shouldn't be ashamed of that."

"I wish he'd been more like you," Bea said. "You're the version of him that I actually wanted."

"What happened when he kissed you?" Wyatt asked.

"Um," Bea took a deep breath, "there was a party in the woods, a couple of weeks into my freshman year. Tim and Duncan brought me along, and at first it was so cool, you know? Talking with their friends, and the girls were so nice to me, making me feel like I belonged. But then . . . um. Then James asked if I wanted to go for a walk."

"And of course, you did."

"Of course I did! It seemed like a miracle, like somehow this secret wish I'd held for so long was becoming real." Bea paused, a wave of nausea washing over her as she realized she'd used nearly the same words to describe her first kiss with Ray.

"Anyway," she went on, "he took me a little ways into the woods, away from everyone else. I thought maybe we would talk or something, but he was just on me, kissing me, shoving his hands under my dress. He was really rough with me. And I just—I didn't want it. I was so afraid, and so confused because I'd imagined being with him for so long, but the reality was awful and terrifying and nothing like I'd hoped. After a couple of minutes I couldn't take it, I started crying and begging him to get off me."

"Did he listen?" Wyatt asked carefully.

"Yes," Bea said firmly. "Thank God, he did. But he looked so disgusted with me. He said he only kissed me because my brothers asked him to. That no one else would want me, and

I should be grateful. I said I was sorry—can you imagine? I apologized to *him*."

"Jeez." Wyatt shook his head. "What happened then?"

"Nothing. He went back to the party, and I hid by Tim's car until it was time to leave. I was too ashamed to tell my brothers what happened. I assume James never told them either—or if he did, they never said anything about it to me."

Wyatt sighed heavily, like he was absorbing some of the weight of Bea's past, lifting it off her shoulders and carrying it on his.

"Bea," he asked, "would it be okay if I hugged you?"

"Very okay," she whispered, and it felt so good to settle into Wyatt's strong arms.

"Do you think about James much?"

"Not really." She exhaled as she leaned comfortably against his chest. "But I guess there's something about men who look like him—who look like you, who look like all the men here, if I'm honest. Some part of me that still feels like I should be grateful for any attention you show me, even if it's nothing close to the way I want to be loved."

"What would happen if one of us proved you wrong?" Wyatt touched Bea's hair gently, tipping her face up toward his. "What would you think then?"

"I guess I'd have to reassess." She smiled, and Wyatt leaned down to kiss her.

It was a slow kiss, and quiet—a kiss that drew Bea in and spread warmth all through her body, a kiss that broke her heart a little as she realized the same sense of longing she'd felt as a teenager (for romance, for passion—hell, even for prom) was still screaming inside her. And the more she tried to push it down, to tell herself it didn't matter, that she was fine being single, that she didn't need any of this, the more it roared to the surface, threatening to dislodge everything she thought she believed.

As they pulled apart, a few of the kids hooted and cheered, and Bea laughed for joy, for awkwardness, for absurdity. It was, she realized later, only the second time she'd ever been kissed in her hometown.

TEXT MESSAGE TRANSCRIPT, MARCH 21: JON, TIM, AND DUNCAN SCHUMACHER

Jon [11:18am]: What are you guys wearing to this thing? Is there a dress code?

Tim [11:20am]: It's just a cookout at Mom's, we can wear anything

Duncan [11:21am]: No, guys—no prints, no letters, no visible brands, remember? They laid it all out in the email from the producers

Tim [11:22am]: ICE CREAM ICE CREAM ICE CREAM

Jon [11:22am]: ??

Tim [11:23am]: Sorry, Amy got my phone

Tim [11:24am]: We've got to present a united front, let these guys know they can't mess with our sister

Tim [11:24am]: We need to wear something that shows them we mean business

Duncan [11:25am]: Like . . . business suits?

Jon [11:25am]: If I wear a suit, Carol will want to change what she's wearing, and I'm not getting into that again

Tim [11:26am]: So what then?

Duncan [11:27am]: Maybe we all wear gym clothes. Sweatpants, t-shirts with really big arm holes cut out, let these guys know we're ready to GO if the circumstances dictate

Jon [11:28am]: YES. That's the move. We're doing it.

Tim [11:29am]: Really? Carol would let you wear sweatpants to be on TV?

Jon [11:29am]: Man, who's in charge in your marriage? I'm in, Duncan's in. Are you in?

Tim [11:30am]: Yeah, fuck it. I'm in.

Tim [1:17pm]: You guys are fucking assholes

Jon [1:17pm]: Hahahahahahahhaahhaahah

Jon [1:17pm]: Dude, you look so stupid

Tim [1:18pm]: You think this is funny? Tina spent all morning getting her hair done. She wants to murder me.

Duncan [1:19pm]: Well, I wouldn't advise her to try, you look like a serial killer

Tim [1:19pm]: This is bullshit. I'm getting some ribs.

Duncan [1:20pm]: As long as you didn't remove them from one of your victims

Jon [1:20pm]: I can't believe you're going to be on television looking like a gym rat

Tim [1:21pm]: Is Bea mad?

Jon [1:21pm]: No, she thinks it's classic

Jon [1:22pm]: Ugh that kindergarten teacher is coming to talk to me

Jon [1:22pm]: He has his guitar

Jon [1:22pm]: Help

Tim [1:23pm]: I will not help

Tim [1:23pm]: You deserve this

Tim [1:24pm]: Enjoy itsy-bitsy spider, bitch

Duncan [1:24pm]: Wow Tim, is that what you say right before you commit murder? Creepy tagline!

Tim [1:25pm]: YOU GUYS SUCK

Jon [1:58pm]: Okay, time to divide and conquer. Who's talking to which guy?

Duncan [1:58pm]: I've got Asher

Tim [1:59pm]: Which one is that?

Duncan [1:59pm]: The professor who ditched Bea at the museum!

Jon [1:59pm]: Oh right, Carol was FURIOUS about that.

Duncan [2:00pm]: Same. I need to figure out his angle

Jon [2:00pm]: Cool. I'm gonna check on Luc

Jon [2:00pm]: That guy is way too smooth

Duncan [2:01pm]: Tim, you ready to do your thing with Nash and Cooper?

Tim [2:01pm]: Hell yeah. I just need to go find Mom.

"Hey, Bea—you haven't seen Nash and Cooper, have you?"

Lauren's tone was casual, but Bea could see she was somewhat frantic.

"Sorry, I haven't." Bea shook her head. "Did you check around the side of the house, where the maple grove is? The property extends further than you think over there, maybe they went for a walk?"

"I'll check that out—thanks!"

Lauren headed that way, and Bea closed her eyes. Great. As if it weren't stressful enough bringing ten men home to meet her family, now two of them had taken off entirely? And unlike the first night, this wasn't Lauren's doing; this was just Nash and Cooper deciding they'd had enough of even pretending to be interested in dating Bea. Not that she was remotely interested in either of them, obviously—but it still stung to know their disappearance (and the producers' subsequent search for them) would certainly be yet one more humiliating plotline on this week's episode.

Add it to the list, Bea thought, mentally ticking them off: The man who walked off on the first night. All the men who didn't, but who were shocked and horrified to meet her. The myriad horrors of the boat. And worst of all, Asher lulling her into believing, just for a second, that any of this could be real.

But what about Sam? a small voice fired back. *What about Wyatt?*

Bea scanned the yard and saw that Sam and Wyatt were both embroiled in a high-stakes game of capture the flag along with a couple other guys and several of the older kids. Sam broke into a grin and waved to Bea when he saw her watching—she felt a pang in her gut as she waved back. She wanted so badly to believe that this was possible for her, that she could have a husband and children and easy Sunday gatherings like this one.

But everything inside her told her that she couldn't.

"Bea, may I steal you for a moment?"

Per usual, Bea felt an involuntary lurch of attraction when

she saw Luc, who looked perfect in strategically rumpled slacks and a white button-down. He had two glasses of rosé in hand—the man knew how to make an entrance.

"Of course." Bea smiled, trying to shove aside her stormy thoughts and enjoy her time with a man who might not be genuinely interested in her, but who at least seemed to genuinely take pleasure in her company.

Bea hadn't spent any one-on-one time with Luc since the night of the crème brûlée and their kiss—she remembered how comfortable she felt with him as they walked over to a patio area near a tall oak tree, where they sat on an outdoor loveseat. Bea's fuchsia Mara Hoffman sweater dress was warm and soft, the wine was cool and fresh, and everything felt tactile as Luc slid his arm around her waist.

"I have missed you," he said softly. "Is that ridiculous to say? I know it hasn't been long."

"It feels like it's been a long time."

"Ah, but for you it feels long because you have seen so many men, done so many things. For me it feels long because I have thought only of you."

Bea rolled her eyes. "Come on, that's not true."

He leaned in to kiss her on the cheek, his lips lingering near her ear. "You have no idea how dull it was in that house."

"Hey! How's it going?" Bea's brother Jon broke the moment as he plopped down in a chair across from them.

"Good." Bea cleared her throat. "This is Luc—Luc, meet my oldest brother, Jon. Luc is a chef from France."

The two men shook hands. "France, huh? Hope you're not too bored here in unglamorous Ohio."

"Where I come from, in Normandy, is not so different from this."

"Is that true?" Bea asked. "You come from the countryside?"

"Yes, I grew up near a city called Rouen, north of Paris, not far from the coast? You may know it as the city where Joan of Arc was burned at the stake."

"Oh, so you guys have cool progressive ideas about women."

"*Exactement.*" Luc laughed, and Jon looked brightly from him to Bea.

"You two seem to be getting along. You like each other?"

Bea flushed red and shot her brother a dirty look.

"I cannot speak for Bea," Luc replied, "but yes, I like her very much."

"What do you like about her?"

"Jon!"

"What?"

"That's a ridiculous question!"

"What's a ridiculous question?" Tim ambled over in his truly ridiculous sweatpants.

"Luc just said he likes Bea, and I was asking why," Jon explained as Tim helped himself to a seat. "He's French," Jon added with rather more distaste than necessary.

"Ugh, guys, can we not?" Bea protested.

"Are you embarrassed by this?" Luc turned to Bea.

"Yes, obviously."

"Why should you be? I am not embarrassed to say that I like very much your wit, and your company, and the way you get warm in your face anytime you're annoyed, like you are with me now." He ran a finger along her cheek, and she laughed and sighed in exasperation. Luc turned back to Jon and Tim.

"I also like that she is beautiful. And a very good kisser."

"Come on, man."

"She's our sister!"

Bea laughed, and Luc kissed her to prove his point— just a quick kiss, but something about the effortlessness of it knocked Bea over. After all the years of watching her brothers with their girlfriends and then their wives, all the hundreds of meaningless, easy, casual kisses, this was the first time any man had kissed Bea in front of her family.

The moment lingered in Bea's mind as a producer escorted her to the drinks table to film a conversation with Jefferson— he'd apparently raided Bob and Sue's meager liquor cabinet, and was mixing himself some sort of elaborate cocktail.

"Hey, there she is!" He broke into a wide smile as Bea approached. "Can I fix you a classic gin fizz?"

"I don't understand how you found all these ingredients in my parents' house," Bea marveled as Jefferson handed her a frothy lemon-tinged drink in one of Sue's antique glasses.

"Just gin, lemon, sugar, soda, and egg white," Jefferson ticked off the ingredients.

"What'd you do with the yolk?" Bea asked, remembering the feel of eggs slipping through her fingers as Luc stood behind her.

"I tossed the yolk in a flower bed." Jefferson grinned. "The nutrients are good for the plants."

"Wow, so you're a bartender and a gardener." Bea smiled, thinking how much Bob would enjoy that particular fun fact. "If my parents find out, they'll want you to stay forever."

"Really? You think so?" Jefferson's voice trailed off and he looked away from her, his eyes scanning across the yard, a faint smile on his face. Bea couldn't tell what he was thinking—but then he turned back toward her, and he looked emotional.

"You know, it's been really cool to be here, meet everyone," he said. "Because all this—the house, the yard, the kids, everybody getting together and just having a good time? That's exactly what I want, you know? And I guess—what I want to know is if you want it too."

Bea felt a pang in her gut: *Yes,* she wanted to scream, *I want this more than you could possibly imagine.* But the idea of saying that out loud—in this place, surrounded by these men, under the judgmental stares of millions of eyes—felt terrifying. Like giving voice to this secret piece of herself would allow everyone in the world to tell her just how foolish she was for wanting something so laughably out of reach.

"Hey." Jefferson stepped toward her, his voice low. "Is something wrong?"

"No," Bea murmured, shaking her head. "It's just—I love my family so much, you know? It makes me really happy that you like it here."

Jefferson reached for Bea's hand and gave her a reassuring squeeze.

"I really want to kiss you right now," he murmured.

Bea looked up at him, confused. "You do?"

"Yeah." He laughed gently. "That surprises you?"

"I guess it does, a little," she admitted.

"Well, then that's on me for not making my intentions more clear."

"Your intentions?"

"Bea"—he leaned in—"I think you're awesome."

For a second she thought he was going to kiss her, but he laughed again instead.

"I'm sorry, I feel super weird about our first kiss being in front of your entire family and all these kids."

"Yeah, understandably." Bea laughed too.

"But next week?" He gazed into her eyes. "I hope?"

"That's really what you want?"

"It is," he asserted. "I hope you believe me."

Bea honestly couldn't tell whether she was lying or not when she assured him that she did.

Feeling dazed and overwhelmed, Bea wasn't sure where to go next. She saw her parents hanging out by the food, but the idea of enduring her mother's earnest questions about which of these men she planned to marry was more than she could bear. So she wandered toward the capture-the-flag game instead, where two of her sisters-in-law, Carol and Tina, were watching by the sidelines. But she stopped short as she approached and heard what they were discussing.

"I *certainly* don't know what Asher was playing at," Tina quipped, "leading Bea on and then pulling away."

"She seemed so upset, poor thing," Carol said kindly.

"Wouldn't you be?" Tina took a big drink of wine. "She finally goes out on a limb for one of these guys and he just leaves her there alone! I would have quit the show then and there."

You and me both, Bea thought bitterly. She took a step back—and nearly slammed right into her third sister-in-law, Julia, who looked chic as always in a black boatneck sweater, cropped jeans, and her signature red lipstick. She was carrying her baby, Alice, who was bundled in a soft blanket and sleeping like a perfect angel.

"Oh crap!" Bea exclaimed as quietly as she could so as not to wake the baby. "I'm so sorry, I didn't see you there."

"Moms with sleeping infants are real ninjas that way." Julia winked. "You want to walk with me? The movement keeps her calm."

"I'd love that," Bea agreed, grateful to have an uncomplicated feeling for the first time all day—and equally grateful that their camera crew was filming them from ten feet away to give them at least the illusion of privacy. "How's it going with her? Are you guys getting any sleep?"

"Believe it or not, I'm getting more than Duncan," Julia

confided. "He's working so hard to keep the house in order so that I can focus on the baby, so protective of my time and energy."

"Duncan?" Bea raised an eyebrow. "My *brother* Duncan?"

Julia laughed. "He's come a long way since the days of railing against the anthropological farce of the American nuclear family."

"Oh my God." Bea rolled her eyes. "Honestly, who let him go to college?"

"No good came of it, that's for sure." Julia grinned. "It's funny now, but at the beginning of our relationship, I was sure we'd never be long-term because he was so closed off and defensive, all his anti-marriage shtick."

"Seriously?" Bea was incredulous. "It was obvious to me how crazy he was about you from day one."

"Maybe," Julia said with a shrug, "but he was also terrified of being vulnerable, of letting me in to the point where I could really hurt him. Anytime I tried to have a conversation with him about something real, he would make it into a joke or change the subject. It finally got so intolerable that I broke up with him."

"*What?*" Bea was aghast. "How is it possible I never knew about this?"

"He came around pretty quickly," Julia explained, "once he realized that he was only hurting himself preemptively, denying himself a relationship that could make him really happy. And I wonder . . . Bea, I hope you won't get upset with me for saying this, but watching you, these past few weeks, I have to wonder if you aren't going through something similar."

"What do you mean?" Bea was genuinely puzzled. "If anything, the problem here is that none of these men wants me."

"Okay, first of all, that's definitely not true. What about Luc and Sam? And Asher, most of all?"

"I think Asher made it abundantly clear that he's not attracted to me." Bea sniffed.

"Yes he is." Julia was thunderstruck. "I saw the look on his face when you were dancing. Whatever the reason he pulled away—I promise you, Bea, it isn't that."

"Then . . ." Bea looked at Julia, full of confusion. "Then why?"

"I honestly don't know," Julia answered. "But I think that question misses the point."

"What do you mean?"

"On this show, *you're* the one in charge. For three weeks, we've watched you freaking out that these men might not want you, when the entire show is structured around your decision of whether you want them. All this misery and self-effacement, I'm sorry, Bea, but it's this version of you that Duncan and I don't even recognize. You're so poised, and self-possessed, and completely wonderful—how is it possible that these men you don't even know are able to unmoor you in this way?"

Bea's throat felt suddenly tight, and she struggled to find words—some words, any words. She stared blankly across the yard, when she saw Duncan talking with Asher, seemingly deep in conversation. A screen door slammed, and Asher looked up—he caught Bea's eye as she was staring right at him, and her stomach jolted as she quickly looked away. After a moment, she looked back, and Asher was still there, gazing at her. He lifted a hand in greeting. Bea could barely make herself nod in return.

"Bea," Julia said gently, "what do you want? Is it really such a scary question to answer?"

Bea's head was swimming. She'd been so sure that staying

professional on this show had been the right decision—to prioritize her goals for her career, just as she'd always done before. But when she thought of all the nights lying alone, longing for Ray, when she thought of the vicious lie that had been swirling in the recesses of her brain since high school, that she was too fat and too ugly ever to have the kind of love that seemed to come so easily to her family and friends, when she thought of how badly she'd wanted Asher to kiss her in that museum, and how terrified she felt that admitting her desires could only compound her humiliation, but, on the other hand, that *not* admitting them could seal her fate of being alone forever . . . It suddenly felt like she was only fighting against herself, and there was no possible way to win.

"I think I need to—excuse me." She backed away from Julia. "I'm sorry, I have to go."

She told a producer she needed to use the bathroom, then took off toward the home she'd loved since childhood. After Bob and Sue got married, they'd taken on a new project every year, fixing up the shabby original house and eventually putting on multiple additions. Now, decades later, the place had a hodgepodge feel to it—a strange, cozy, mismatched maze that was always filled with family.

Bea ducked through the kitchen, warm and woodsy and packed with production staff and caterers, then slipped past the powder room and down one of the house's crooked hallways. Two turns later, she opened a door still hung with a simple wooden sign that read *Bea*.

Bea's room had been the same since childhood, lavender walls and a soft white carpet, a little twin bed and a whole wall covered in books.

Bea sat on the floor and drew her knees to her chest,

breathing in the smell of the place. She closed her eyes, and she was crawling into bed at four o'clock in the morning after James kissed her, shoving her torn sundress in the wastepaper basket under her small white desk. She was here on senior prom night, reading another romance and dreaming of something more. Here again last Christmas, silently crying and missing Ray so much she thought it might kill her, wondering if there'd ever be a time in her life when she would visit her parents and need more than this one twin bed.

What would seventeen-year-old Bea think if she could see her future as a TV star with dozens of handsome suitors? And would her awestruck opinion shatter if she knew it was all a sham?

Bea buried her face in her knees and tried to breathe—just slowly, just anything—until she heard a soft knock on the door.

"Beatrice? Are you in there?"

She thought about keeping silent, but she figured the longer she stayed hidden, the more it would throw production into a tizzy, and the worse it would be when she eventually emerged.

"Yeah, Mom. I'm here."

The door cracked open, and Bea saw Bob and Sue, their faces full of worry.

"Oh, *Beatrice*." Sue flew into the room and knelt on the floor beside Bea, wrapping her arms around her daughter. "It's been a terribly long day."

Bea smiled through the tears she hadn't even noticed were running down her face. "Yeah, Mom. A really long day."

Bob stepped in quickly after Sue and shut the door behind him.

"No cameras?" Bea asked hopefully. Bob grinned.

"Nah, kiddo. We gave them the slip."

"Darling," Sue said delicately, "how are you feeling?"

"I'm . . ." Bea wanted to crack a joke to defuse the tension, to reassure her parents that she was really fine. But she couldn't. Because she wasn't.

"It's a lot on your shoulders, this whole endeavor," Bob said. "Must be a lot of pressure."

Bea nodded—it was.

"We met a lot of nice young men today," Sue offered.

"Yeah?" Bea tried to smile. "Who did you like, Mom?"

"I liked that Sam very much. Didn't we like him, Bob?"

Bob nodded; they did.

"He's so young," Sue went on, "but then, that'll be why he's so optimistic, isn't it? It was nice, talking with someone so hopeful. And that Wyatt was sweet. And so handsome! Of course, we heard from your brothers all about that Frenchman of yours. Is he the one you think you'll marry?"

"Sue." Bob's voice had a warning note.

"Bob, she's supposed to get engaged, that's the point, it's why she's doing this! If I'm not allowed to ask about this now, when am I?"

"It's okay, Mom. I know this is something you want, and I want it too. I hate that I keep letting you down."

Sue opened her mouth to speak, but Bob jumped in first. "Now wait, wait a minute, Bea. Do you think your mother and I are upset with you for being single?"

"Not upset." Bea's voice cracked on the second syllable. "Just, disappointed, obviously. The guys all have their wives, and kids, and I've just never been able to . . . I don't know. It hasn't been in the cards for me. And I'm so proud of my career, of everything I've accomplished."

"So are we!" Sue protested.

"I know, Mom. I know you are. But when I come here,

and I see all of you together—I want this so much. And it just feels impossible. Like you're all living on this island, this place where people know how to love each other, and no matter what I do, I can't figure out how to get there."

"What happens when you try?" Bob asked gently.

Bea shook her head, crying in earnest now. "I drown, Bop. Every single time. I drown."

Bob nodded tightly, tears in his eyes too. Sue smoothed back Bea's hair.

"Safer to stay where you are then, isn't it?" she coaxed. "Even if where you are makes you miserable."

"What do I do, Mom?" Bea pleaded, feeling incredibly young. "I don't know what to do."

"You know," Sue's voice was raspy, absent her usual affected cheer, "when your father left—not Bob, your biological father—I thought I was done. A woman alone with four kids, no savings, this run-down house. I thought, *Who could possibly want me?*"

"*Mom.*" Bea exhaled. In her entire life, Bea could count the number of times she'd heard her mother talk about her biological father on one hand.

"The night he called to say he wasn't coming home was the worst of my life," Sue went on. "All you kids were asleep, or I thought you were, but then I heard you crying. So I went into your room, and you were standing in your crib, and you said, 'Up me, Mama.' That's what you used to say, 'Up me.' So I picked you up, my sweet girl, and you were crying, and so was I. And I was so afraid, Bea. I didn't know what I was going to do. If you think you're hopeless, well, I was so far past that point, I was completely shut down. Until I met Bob."

"And he made you believe again?"

Bob laughed. "Hell, no. Your mother didn't want a damn thing to do with me."

"Wait, really?"

Sue shook her head. "Between working and raising all you kids, I was completely in survival mode, focused on whatever was in front of me—I couldn't possibly consider adding another person into the mix! Bob saw I was running myself ragged, and he offered to help. That first time he came to the house, that was when things started to change."

"Because of you, Bean." Bob rubbed Bea's knee affectionately.

"Me?" Bea was bewildered. "How? Wasn't I only five?"

"Four," Bob corrected. "When I came over here, the whole place was chaos. Your brothers were running around the yard, your mother was trying to get dinner on the table, and I didn't know how to help with any of it. Then you came running over to me, and you were about the cutest thing I'd ever seen. You had this big book of fairy tales, you remember? You never went anywhere without it."

Bea pointed to the bottom shelf, where the tattered book in question still rested.

"That one there?"

Bob smiled. "The very one. You held it out to me, and you said, 'Story?' Bean, I don't know how any man could say no to you, but I sure as hell never could. You were so trusting, you plopped right in my lap and we sat there and read for hours."

"That was it." Sue was choked up. "I saw you two together, and I thought, *Oh. She's going to have a father.*"

"You make it sound so easy," Bea whispered.

"No"—Sue grabbed Bea's hand—"no, Beatrice, it's the hardest thing in the world. To have been that hurt, to feel that afraid, and to know that the only way you can be really, fully happy is to risk going through it all again? It's a terrifying choice to make. But if you want to let someone be that close to you, it's the only way."

"That's it!" Bob lit up like he always did when someone hit on a new insight. "It's about choice. A lot of people live their lives by default, walking through the doors in front of them because it seems expedient. That's one way to have a family. But us? We chose each other. And that's what you're doing here, Bean—that's why it feels so scary. Because it is. You're choosing your family."

"And what if I can't?" Bea wiped the tears out of her eyes. "What if there's something inside me that's just—I don't know, incapable?"

"Not possible." Bob smiled, his whole face warm and crinkled. "Bean, everyone in this family knows how much love you have inside you. We're together because of you. Your good heart was the key that unlocked our whole lives."

"I don't know what to do, Bop. I want to be brave, like you two, but I just—I don't know what to do."

"It starts with the choice, just like your mom said. Here in this room, it seems to me you have a sense that you might want one of these fellas to be your family. If you want that, you can have it. But first, you have to tell them that's what you want. Bean, you have to choose."

Bea was worried Lauren would be furious when she came back outside, but there was so much going on that her twenty-minute absence appeared to have escaped unnoticed.

Bea scanned the busy yard looking for Asher—he was chatting with Duncan and Julia, all three of them laughing. Asher was holding baby Alice, booping her nose and puffing out his cheeks to make her smile. It was obvious that he was wonderful with children, and Bea wondered how he could be so natural with this little baby and yet so stilted with her. Duncan had an arm around Julia's waist, and she leaned comfortably into her husband, the two of them easy in a way that sent a twist of pain through Bea's chest. She wanted this. And if she kept on like she was, she would never, ever have it.

Bea didn't know if it was possible that she could fall in love on this show, but if she was going to try—really try—she knew this step had to come first, even if she was about to plunge headlong into utter humiliation.

"Hey," she said to Asher as she approached their group. "Can we talk for a second?"

"Oh." He looked apprehensive. "Sure. Of course."

He handed baby Alice back to Julia, and together they walked over to a quartet of Japanese maples Bob had planted when Bea was little—one for each of the four kids. The trees had been saplings then, but they were nearly twenty feet tall now, their branches long and twisted, leaves flashing crimson in the orange light before sunset.

"Are you all right?" Asher looked concerned. "I didn't think—I mean, I'm surprised you want to talk to me."

"Me too." Bea laughed a little, mostly from nerves—but, she was amazed to discover, a little bit from joy. "I wanted to apologize, actually."

Now Asher looked downright wary. "What for?"

"What you said on the boat," Bea fumbled the words, "that you didn't think I was here to fall in love. I was angry at you for saying it on camera, and for saying it at the end of such an awful day. But mostly, I was angry because you were right."

Understanding dawned on Asher's face, and his expression softened.

"When I came here, I was still, um, getting over someone. Who really hurt me, and—and I didn't know if I was ready to meet someone new. Then on the first night, seeing all of you for the first time, that sealed it. I thought there was no way any of you could possibly have feelings for me, so why would I risk my heart for you? It didn't seem worth it. Then at the museum, I thought maybe I was wrong, but then at the end of the night, when you . . . well."

Asher took a step toward her. "Bea, I need to tell you, about that night—"

"Please," she stopped him, "just let me get this out, okay? I need to say this."

He nodded. Her heart was pounding, and she thought for a second about changing her mind—but she knew, from somewhere deep, that she had to go on.

"I don't know why you didn't want to kiss me," she said quietly. "Maybe you're not attracted to me, or maybe you sensed me holding back, or—I don't know, something else. But I want to tell you, um. That I think you're great. And I really like you. And if you can—I mean, if you want to—I want to try. That's what I wanted to say."

Asher took another step forward, and for a moment she thought he was going to wrap his arms around her—he didn't.

But God, she wanted him to.

"Bea, the reason I didn't kiss you at the museum is because I have two children."

Bea gaped in disbelief. "I'm sorry. You what?"

"I know." He smiled sadly. "I should have told you. My son is the one who submitted me for this show; I never would have come here if it hadn't meant so much to him. I thought there was no way I'd actually be interested in a woman I met on reality television of all places, that I'd be here for a week or two at most and come home with nothing more than a funny story to tell my students. But then I met you, and you were . . . nothing like I expected."

Bea felt anxious. "In a bad way?"

"No." Asher laughed. "In *every* way. You were so quick-witted with Johnny and the other men, and kind of mean and over this whole thing in the same way I was. I found myself wanting to spend more time with you, and I was furious you didn't seem to want that too. Do you remember the first thing you said to me?"

Bea flushed with horror at the memory of how cold she'd been to Asher on the night of the premiere, still reeling that the man before him had simply walked offstage.

"I told you to go ahead and leave."

Asher nodded. "I told myself I'd stick around long enough to get to know you, see if there might be an attraction be-tween us. Then, at the museum . . . I can't remember the last time I felt like that. I wanted—well, I think you know what I wanted."

"I didn't, Asher. I thought you were repulsed by me."

His face fell in dismay. "You can't be serious."

She nodded, and he took her hand.

"Bea, I am so sorry."

"Me too," she whispered.

He lifted her hand to his chest so she could feel his heart pounding, leaned down so his face was inches from hers.

"When I walked out of that museum," he said softly, "I thought I was protecting my kids. They know how it feels to be abandoned, and with the way this show is set up, the odds of us actually pursuing a relationship outside of it? The idea of risking their hopes—and mine—seemed indefensible."

Bea's breath was shallow. "And now?"

"Now I think the only indefensible action would be to let you go."

Then his hands were in her hair and he was kissing her, a hard, fast release and there was nothing false about it, nothing pretend and nothing safe, swirling laughter and panic and comfort and free fall and every, every second captured on the whirring cameras, their bodies warm and intertwined against the chill spring air.

It felt like terror. It felt like freedom.

It felt like the beginning.

TRANSCRIPT OF PRODUCER INTERVIEW WITH BEA'S MOTHER, SUE
Time stamp: 3:17pm

Producer: I understand you spoke with Nash and Cooper in the kitchen earlier today. What did you three chat about?

Sue: Oh, the real estate agent! And that surfer, I wish he would wash his hair. We had a lice outbreak in my class this year, and we learned how important it is to check your scalp regularly. If that Cooper doesn't watch himself, he could be absolutely *covered* in lice.

Producer: That's good advice, Sue. Is that what you talked about?

Sue: Yes, as a matter of fact! Oh, and then I asked those nice boys if they would run out and get some ice cream for the group. I thought the kids would love that. I certainly would have picked some up if I'd been allowed to cater this affair.

Producer: Sue, we've been all through this, the production uses outside catering for our events. We can't have you cooking all day, we need you free to talk to us, like you're doing now!

Sue: That's fine, but *I* would have picked up some ice cream.

Producer: So you sent Nash and Cooper to the grocery store?

Sue: Heavens, no! We only buy from the nice dairy farm up the road. It's the most marvelous place, you can see all the cows, and they make the ice cream fresh every day! I sent them there with Tim.

Producer: But Tim is here, playing capture the flag. And Nash and Cooper aren't back.

Sue: Well, that's ridiculous. They went together. If Tim's back, they're all back. Maybe you should check again.

TRANSCRIPT OF PRODUCER INTERVIEW
WITH CONTESTANTS NASH AND COOPER
Time stamp: 6:41pm

Producer: When did you have a sense that something might be wrong?

Nash: It seemed weird that they wanted us to go get food. Like, aren't there assistants for that? We're *on the show*.

Producer: So why did you go?

Cooper: I don't know, man. Bea's brother was there, and he's so fucking creepy. He was waving the truck keys at us. We just got in.

Producer: What happened then?

Nash: He said the place was just up the road, but he didn't mention it was this long, winding backcountry dirt road with maybe fifteen turnoffs. And when we got there . . . the smell.

Cooper: I've never seen so many cows in my life. The stench, the manure . . . it was so much.

Producer: So did you get the ice cream?

Cooper: No, man! Tim dropped us off at some random gate, said we just had to walk through the cows and the ice cream shop was right there, that he was gonna go park. Then he fucking took off! We had to wade through a literal field of shit. A field. Of. Shit.

Producer: (laughs)

Nash: Hey, fuck you, man. It was *not* funny.

Producer: Come on, guys. It's kind of funny.

Nash: We were in the middle of nowhere, with no humans, no directions, no phones—

Producer: No cameras.

Cooper: Exactly! It took us, what, three hours to find our way back to civilization?

Producer: And you smell like cows.

Cooper: (turns to Nash) Hey—do you think they did this because you called Bea a cow?

Nash: (realizes) Motherfucker.

EPISODE 5

"DESERTED"

(5 men left)

Shot on location in Marrakesh, Morocco

TRANSCRIPT OF CHAT FROM #SQUEEZE-MAINIACS SLACK CHANNEL

NickiG: Has everyone seen last night's ep yet?? Bc I am ACTUALLY DYING here I don't want to spoil but I need to discuss!!!!

Enna-Jay: Hard same

Beth.Malone: Hey, you guys know we don't spoil any episodes until noon PT on Wednesdays, that's the policy

NickiG: BETH CAN WE MAKE AN EXCEPTION

KeyboardCat: I've watched! Beth, have you?

Beth.Malone: I have, which I guess just leaves Colin. Colin, did you watch yet?

Colin7784: What, like I'm so into the show I watch it immediately, you think I have nothing better to do on a Monday night?

Beth.Malone: 😑

Colin7784: Yeah, I watched

NickiG: GREAT, so Asher has kids?!?! Omg who saw this coming??

Enna-Jay: He was obviously hiding *something*

Enna-Jay: But this is like, so endearing

NickiG: Is it?? Or is he just abandoning his children to be kind of a douche to a nice lady on TV?

KeyboardCat: His son is the one who submitted him in the first place!

NickiG: Please Cat you're a well-documented Asher apologist

KeyboardCat: Maybe I'm just a Bea stan and Asher is lit'rally her only viable option

Beth.Malone: Ummmmmm beg to differ how cute was her kiss with Luc?

KeyboardCat: Wait come on you don't actually think Luc is there ~for the right reasons~ do you?

Beth.Malone: He's the hot French chef we need in these dark times and I stand by him

Colin7784: Does Bea actually want to be an insta-mom tho?

Enna-Jay: She did say she wanted kids eventually

Colin7784: Sure, but eventually is different from like, right now

Beth.Malone: That's actually a really good point

Colin7784: Wow Beth did it hurt you inside to say that

KeyboardCat: But also can I get a hallelujah that Nash and Cooper are finally gone?????

Enna-Jay: I know, how nice is it going to be to watch this show without any villains left? Just guys who ACTUALLY like Bea?

NickiG: What I don't get is it's not like Nash and Cooper were even that hot—they had good bodies and everything but their faces were okay at best

KeyboardCat: Isn't that always the way tho??? It's the not-hot guys who are fucking obsessed with dating the hottest possible women to validate their existences

Colin7784: Okay actually, in men's defense—

Beth.Malone: No. Colin. No.

MAIN SQUEEZE CAST SPOTTED BOARDING FLIGHT TO MARRAKESH
posted on *TMZ.com*

JOHN F. KENNEDY AIRPORT, NEW YORK CITY: The cast and crew of *Main Squeeze* were spotted boarding a flight to Marrakesh at New York's Kennedy Airport. TMZ can exclusively confirm that **Bea Schumacher** was eating a Cinnabon at the flight's gate—guess she really does ignore her critics! *(CLICK THROUGH FOR PHOTOS OF BEA WITH CREAM CHEESE ICING ON HER CHIN.)* If you're reading this from Marrakesh and see the cast and crew around town, send your descriptions and photos to tips@tmz.com.

"So"—Lauren twisted the cap off a bottle of iced tea with a sharp pop—"it seems like you've fully abandoned our plan not to go falling for any of these men."

"I guess that's true." Bea tried to look contrite, but couldn't quite muster it—her lips kept quaking into a smile as she luxuriated in her first-class seat on their transatlantic flight to Morocco. "How were last night's ratings?"

"Huge, obviously." Lauren grinned. "People love that romance shit. But you realize we have a new problem now? If you're going to try to make things work for real with Asher, you need to do the same with the other four men."

"What?" Bea was incredulous. "Why?"

"Because you're a terrible actress!" Lauren hissed, lowering her voice as a flight attendant walked by with warm washcloths. "If you're genuinely falling for Asher, but just pretending to date the rest of the men, all of America will be able to see it. We're only halfway through this season, and if everyone knows from this week on exactly who you plan to end up with, believe me, we will *hemorrhage* viewers. Not good for you—not tenable for me."

"Okay," Bea conceded. "What do you want me to do?"

"I know for a fact that Asher isn't the only guy here who has feelings for you. In fact, I think any of the five guys you have left would be open to a serious relationship."

Bea raised an eyebrow. "Even Luc?"

Lauren laughed. "Okay, well, inasmuch as Luc is capable of having a serious relationship with anyone, I think he'd be down to try with you. He likes you, Bea. How do you feel about him?"

"I mean, I'm obviously super attracted to him, but I just don't know if it could be anything long-term." She glanced toward the back of the plane, though of course she couldn't see Luc, who was somewhere in coach with the other four men and most of their crew. She conjured his image in her mind's eye instead, feeling the firm way he'd raked his fingers through her hair when he kissed her.

"Your chemistry is genuine, and that's a good start," Lauren was saying—Bea jerked her mind back to the present. "I'm gonna give you two a one-on-one this week. It's been overdue since the premiere—you can get to know him better, and if nothing else, we'll get some good making out on camera."

Bea smiled and shook her head. "It's a tough job, but someone has to do it."

"Attagirl. What about Sam? You two got along so well on your date."

It was true; they had—but Bea had a difficult time believing she could build a serious relationship with a guy who was only twenty-four.

"I guess I didn't push myself to see if I could really develop feelings for Sam on our date," Bea considered, "because his age made it easy for me to dismiss him, and at that point I was still trying not to fall for any of the men."

"But the attraction is there?"

"I mean, I have eyes."

"I think you two could have real potential—and Marin thought so too, remember? I'm gonna cook up something special for your date with him this week. Can you do me—and him—the kindness of giving him a real chance?"

"Yes." Bea nodded. "I can do that."

"Great! So that just leaves Wyatt and Jefferson. Thoughts on them?"

"I like them both as people—especially Wyatt."

"The question is who do I send on your third date of the week—you're bringing two guys on that one."

"Does that mean I'll need to eliminate one of those men on the date?" Bea asked with trepidation.

"No. Since you're only eliminating one man this week, we'll save that for the big ceremony with all five of them." Lauren drummed her fingers on the armrest between them.

"You and Wyatt need more time for sure, but I can't really justify giving him another date when you just had one last week. Particularly since I assume you'd like to spend more time with Asher?"

Bea nodded, a flush creeping into her cheeks. She definitely wanted that.

"What about Jefferson, then? Are you interested in him?"

"I mean, when he showed up on the first night, I thought, *Oh thank God, a man who looks like someone I could actually see myself ending up with.*"

Lauren looked up, eyes alert with interest. "You're into him."

Bea shrugged. "A little."

"That's settled, then—he'll go on the third date along with Asher." Lauren grinned at Bea, but her smile faded.

"What is it?" Bea asked. "Is something wrong?"

"Bea, I've been around for a lot of seasons of this show, and I've seen people get really hurt by the way things go down. I think you know how much I like you and respect you—at least, I hope you do."

Bea gave a small nod.

"So before we go ahead with all this, I want to make sure you understand what you're doing," Lauren cautioned. "Before, I was the one manufacturing the show's twists and turns. But the more you invest in these men—and them in you—the more the show will depend on your emotional highs and lows. Your elation. Your heartbreak. I know this process hasn't been easy on you, but I've had this job for five years, and I know how much harder things can get. And I just—I want to make sure you're ready for that."

Bea wasn't remotely convinced that she was, but what was the alternative? Lying to Asher, ignoring the others? Spending a whole life as the only single person at family gatherings and telling herself it didn't make her miserable? Lying alone in bed night after night with the memory of Ray's body beside her instead of the actuality of someone else's?

This thing she had dreamed of so desperately for so long was here, within her grasp—she had to reach for it, even if she might stumble and fail.

"Yeah," she told Lauren, affecting far more confidence than she felt. "I'm ready."

Bea had been dying to visit Marrakesh for years, so she was thrilled to learn that she and her suitors would be spending several days there. The producers had procured a mammoth *riad* in the heart of the city, floor after floor of intricate tile work, sumptuous fabrics in vibrant colors, and finely carved brass lamps spilling radiant patterns of light across every available surface. The whole place was sensuous, and Bea immediately felt more at home than she ever had in the immaculate muteness of the *Main Squeeze* compound, where everything had been shades of white and beige.

Bea only had a couple of hours after they arrived to try to nap and conquer her jet lag. Lying in an elaborately hewn wooden bed spread thick with woven blankets, the prospect of an evening with Sam looming before her, Bea was starting to feel, for the first time since shooting began, an actual sense of the fairy-tale magic *Main Squeeze* sold so hard to its viewers.

Bea woke in the late afternoon, and Lauren had the *riad* staff bring strong Turkish coffee. Then it was on to wardrobe to pick something out for her dinner date with Sam—Alison suggested high-waisted trousers and a crop top.

"Isn't that a little risqué for a country where a lot of women veil?"

"I think . . . you'll be glad to have this option," Alison said carefully.

"Option for what?" Bea pressed, but Alison wouldn't say.

Bea wanted to wear something that made her feel sexy and comfortable, so she chose a draped Cushnie jersey dress that gently hugged her curves and playfully bright Sophia Webster heels. When she met Sam in front of the *riad*, his reaction told her she'd chosen correctly.

"How is it possible you look this good after spending the night on a plane?" His hands wandered down her back for a moment as he hugged her hello, leaving a trail of electricity.

The whole ride to the restaurant, Bea had a feeling that was anxious, unwieldy, almost giddy—this was the first date she'd actually been excited for since Ray. But when they arrived, her excitement turned to dread as it dawned on Bea why Alison had been so opinionated in her wardrobe suggestion.

"*Belly dancers*," Bea muttered under her breath. "Fuck me."

"What's going on?" Sam asked, puzzled by the sudden turn in Bea's mood.

The restaurant was an opulent place, everything draped in damask and velvet, patrons lounging in lushly appointed circular booths built into the walls. And dancers were absolutely everywhere: Swathed in skin-skimming silks and skimpy bra tops that jangled with ornamental bells, curvaceous women gyrated around the dimly lit space, pausing graciously at every table.

"You're not a fan?" Sam asked with a grin.

"They're going to make me dance," Bea said, her face dark. "That's why Alison wanted me to wear a crop top—so that I'd have an option besides those tiny string things the dancers are wearing."

"Wait, what?" Sam paused, incredulous. "If you don't want to dance, they can't make you, can they?"

Bea rolled her eyes. "You weren't there the day they got

me to parade around a yacht in a bikini, pretty much entirely against my will."

"I wasn't there, but I wish I had been."

"Why, you have a fetish for uncomfortable women?"

"No, but I wouldn't have minded seeing you in that bikini."

Bea caught his eye as they followed the maître d' to a table in the center of the restaurant, skirting to avoid two women in the throes of wild undulations.

"You hate this, huh?" Sam rubbed the tense muscles at the base of Bea's neck as he settled into the chair beside her.

"I just feel like I'm in some kind of Turing test where I have to convince the world, over and over, that I really do feel good about my body."

"Do you?" There was no malice in Sam's question, no accusatory tone—without knee-jerk cause to get defensive, Bea considered the question on its merits.

"I've worked hard to, but part of that requires me to have some control over my own circumstances. Like, I would never go to the gym in shorts and a sports bra, even if that's what I'd wear to work out at home."

"And you're saying taking off half your clothes to do a dance you don't know for an audience of millions is . . . worse?"

Sam raised his eyebrows dramatically at Bea, and she laughed appreciatively. "Yeah, just a little."

Before they could continue their conversation, Johnny came over to welcome them and introduce the concept of the date.

"Bea and Sam, welcome to Marrakesh!" He was entirely too enthusiastic—just looking at his gleaming eyes made Bea exhausted. "This country is known for its vibrant culture and incredible food—you'll be sampling both tonight. But first, are you ready for some entertainment?"

At this, Johnny stepped aside and half a dozen belly dancers appeared; traditional music flowed through the speakers and the women executed a flawlessly choreographed dance. As Bea watched these curvaceous women jiggle and pop various parts of their bodies, the dread inside her mounted that she was about to be asked to do the same.

"Okay, Bea," Johnny goaded, "you're not going to let those girls have all the fun, are you? What do you say? Are you up for a little dancing?"

Bea steeled herself for further embarrassment, but before she could say anything, Sam spoke out.

"Actually, I had a different idea. I'm a little tired of Bea getting to have all the fun on these dates—would it be possible for me to do the dancing instead?" He turned to Bea. "If that's okay with you, Bea."

Bea wanted to say something to let Sam know how profoundly she appreciated this gesture, but that felt much too heavy at a moment when his smile was so expectant and so wide.

"I've never had a man dance for me before," she said coyly.

"Well, I think it's high time we rectified that," Sam cooed, leaning over to kiss Bea's cheek. "I'll see you soon."

Without waiting for permission from Johnny, the producers, or anyone else, Sam got up and walked off with the dancers—who, Bea noted with a mild note of chagrin, seemed more than happy to have him.

While Sam rehearsed, Bea enjoyed a gorgeous spread of vegetarian appetizers—roast carrots spiced with cumin, shredded cabbage riddled with crunchy za'atar, and perfectly sour pickled beets. Half an hour later, the lights dimmed, the music grew louder, and Sam emerged from who-knows-where, sporting silky jodhpurs and a tight black T-shirt that, regrettably, was not cropped enough to bare his belly. Bea angled her chair away from the table so Sam could dance directly in front of her.

Sam struck a pose with three other dancers, and the music piped in through the speakers. At first, Bea took the minor melody for a traditional Moroccan song, but something about it was familiar. Sam beamed as the hook kicked in—Bea recognized that the song was Jennifer Lopez's "If You Had My Love," and she laughed and clapped with delight as Sam languidly rolled his torso in time with the other women. If he was having trouble with the choreography, he masked it with pure confidence, popping his hips and shoulders like he'd been doing this for a matter of years instead of minutes.

"*If you had my love and I gave you all my trust, would you comfort me?*" He sang along playfully, then leaned low to whisper in her ear. "Dance with me, Bea."

As she rose to move with him, none of it felt like a joke—it was fun, but not funny, serious, but not self-serious. Bea loved to dance, and as Sam moved behind her, his hands traveling down her arms and waist and hips, Bea swayed against him, allowing herself to imagine where he might put his hands (and what he might do with them) if no one else was watching. Asher's face popped briefly into her mind—was she being disloyal to him? Was it insane that she was already experiencing such an intense attraction to another man so soon after having declared her feelings for him?

This is what you're supposed to be doing here, she reminded herself. *Try to enjoy it.*

When the music ended, everyone in the restaurant burst into applause. Sam took a bow, then held out his hands to encourage the crowd to cheer for Bea, which they did enthusiastically. Her face was flushed—with heat, with energy, with the things she was just thinking about Sam—and as they sat down to enjoy their dinner of spicy merguez sausage and mountains of fluffy couscous, Bea found she was absolutely ravenous.

"I didn't know you could dance like that." Sam gave Bea a mischievous look.

"Yeah, well I didn't know you were so fluent in the lyrics of one Ms. Lopez," Bea countered with a grin of her own. "Were you even born when that song came out?"

"Excuse you, I have two older sisters. The lyrics of everything they listened to in high school are forever ingrained on my soul."

"Wow, so you're the baby! Did they spoil you rotten?"

"Not exactly." Sam broke eye contact with Bea to refill his glass of flinty white wine. "My family isn't as easy as yours."

"What do you mean?"

"My dad is a corporate executive, and my mom is a surgeon—they had pretty high expectations for all of us. My sisters measured up, but . . ."

"You haven't figured things out yet."

"That's not how they'd put it."

"How would they put it?"

He shifted in his seat. "That I'm unmotivated, that I'd rather live off their money than make my own way in the world, that I don't take myself seriously."

"Is that how you see yourself?"

"Everything seemed so easy for my sisters. Ivy League for both of them, now Jessica's a doctor like my mom and Zoe is an engineer. They knew what they wanted, and then they did it. I think I could do the second part no problem—I just haven't figured out the first."

"What about teaching? Did you like that?"

"I loved it. But for the rest of my life? I want to do more things, see more things. I can't imagine myself in a classroom for the next forty years."

Bea pushed a carrot back and forth through a pile of couscous. "Do you think this show was maybe a way for you to put off that decision? Just . . . I don't know. Fill time?"

Sam sighed. "Partly, yeah. Things can get tense around the house—going off to be on TV seemed like a much more fun alternative."

"And are you having fun?"

"Come on." He lowered his voice. "You know I am."

"What—um . . ." Bea wasn't sure how to ask the question. "Is it *just* fun, though?"

"Are you asking if I see this as fun or something more?"

Bea flushed, a little embarrassed. "I guess I am."

"Bea"—he took her hand—"I am really into you. Like—really. Really, really. Okay?"

Bea knew all the reallys were intended to reassure her, but they had the opposite effect—she suddenly felt more nervous than she had before.

"What about you?" Sam nudged. "Where do you think we stand?"

Bea ducked her head, her voice small. "I know you make me smile. And that I want to spend more time with you."

"If that's the case," he smiled slyly, "you're in luck."

He took an envelope out of his jacket pocket and handed it to her.

"What's this?" Bea turned over the blank envelope in her hands, suspicious.

"It's an invitation to a luxury hammam. I'm supposed to ask if you want to go there after dinner; apparently they have a private treatment all set up for us."

"What kind of treatment?" Bea asked, leaning closer. Under the table, Sam's knee touched hers.

"I don't know exactly. But I'm told it involves a series of pools, hot water, different oils and scrubs." He pressed his leg against hers, and Bea felt the flush from their dance creeping back into her system.

"I know you said you didn't like wearing a bathing suit on that yacht," he added, "but since this would be just the two of us . . . and since you did deprive me the last time . . ."

Bea nodded. "Yes. Let's go."

The entry to the hammam was hidden in a maze of winding alleys deep in the Marrakesh medina. The reception room felt much like a traditional spa with its bleached wood floors and shelves of products you could take home to attempt to re-create your time here, desert-salt scrub and orange-blossom shampoo. But once Bea and Sam had checked in, changed into the bathing suits Alison had surreptitiously provided to the producers, and covered up in thin cloth robes, they descended a stone staircase and emerged into what felt like another universe.

The hammam was absolutely cavernous, with smooth gray floors and soaring arched ceilings inlaid with swirls of blue and purple tiles arranged in intricate mosaics. Carved lanterns lined the room's perimeter, surrounding a placid blue pool that was bathed in a thousand points of light. This was the communal bathing area; two of the hammam's workers—a stocky man and a slight woman—led Bea and Sam to a private room for their traditional hammam treatment.

"It is more intimate this way," said the woman, who introduced herself as Rehana.

"Nothing's intimate with these guys around." Bea gestured to the cameras, but Rehana's manner was immovably calm.

"You'll see, you'll be very relaxed," she assured Bea with a smile.

The treatment room was warm and cavelike, lit only with candles, made entirely of the same gray material as the floors in the communal room, with a low, curved ceiling and a steaming tub of water that ran the entire length of the wall opposite the door.

"Your robe?" Rehana held out her hand. Sam handed his robe to his helper, Issam, without hesitation, giving Bea her first glimpse of the rippling muscles that had so far been hidden by his clothes. She felt herself flush red—Sam's face creased with concern.

"We don't have to do this. We can just go back to the *riad*, have a drink by the fire."

"No." Bea swallowed hard. "I want to."

She handed her robe to Rehana, revealing the swimsuit Alison had sent over: a black Cynthia Rowley one-piece with a notched neckline that dipped low between Bea's breasts, tied together with a little bow. She kept her gaze trained on Sam's face, waiting for his expression to betray some hint of disgust. But his pupils dilated as his eyes traveled down her body, and he clenched the towel he was holding.

"Are you ready to begin?" Issam's voice was deep and honeyed. Bea nodded. Issam and Rehana positioned Bea and Sam in the middle of the room, facing each other. They brought over wooden buckets filled with steaming water from the tub, gently ladling the water over Bea's and Sam's arms, legs, torsos, and finally their heads until they were both warm and wet.

Sam reached out and wrapped a lock of Bea's wet hair around his fingers. She had a sudden urge for him to yank her closer, to kiss her hard and shove her against the hot, smooth wall of this dim room where everything was slick with condensation.

"What?" he asked, his lips curving into a smile that matched hers.

"Can you read my mind?"

"I hope so, because I *really* want you to be thinking what I'm thinking."

He had to step back so Issam and Rehana could continue the ritual, first scrubbing them down with rough black soap, then washing it away and soothing their skin with sweet mango butter, and finally massaging their scalps with rose oil. When it was over, Bea and Sam stood close together in the center of the room, hot water cascading over them and rinsing them clean. The air around them felt warm and thick, the tension buzzing between their bodies, the anticipation of touching him so strong Bea couldn't think of anything else.

Once they were dry and back in robes, they made their way back to the communal bathing room—it was empty now except for Bea, Sam, and a couple of camera ops and sound techs. Even the producers had left, probably to lull Sam and Bea into some false sense of privacy. They shed their robes and stepped gingerly into the warm pool, which was perfectly calibrated to match the temperature of the balmy air, and of their bodies. They waded toward the center, where the water was deep enough to reach Bea's chest. After all the noise of the rushing water in the private room, this room seemed incredibly still and quiet, nothing audible above Bea's and Sam's own breath.

"If I don't kiss you right now, I'm going to lose my mind," he rasped.

"We can't have that," Bea responded, and then his hands were on her, grabbing her hips under the water and pulling her close, kissing her firmly, roughly, just like she'd wanted him to—there was nothing tentative about this, no question of faking it. He wanted her, and she wanted him back. He kissed her cheek, and then the spot at the edge of her jawline just below her ear. Bea heard a groan escape her, a guttural sound, and then threw her hands over her mouth.

"What is it?" Sam asked, flustered.

"We're on *television*," Bea squeaked, and then she burst out laughing.

Sam turned and good-naturedly splashed some water at the cameras. "You guys can't give us a break, huh?"

Bea covered her face, somewhere between arousal and mortification and total joyous bliss. Sam lifted her fingers to peek underneath them.

"Hi, Bea."

"Hi, Sam."

"I like you a lot."

Bea's heart pounded so hard she knew Sam could feel it.

"I like you a lot too."

The morning after her hammam escapade, Bea woke feeling—well, if not entirely confident, then at least more comfortable than she'd been throughout filming. She lazed in bed as the *riad* staff brought sweet mint tea, fresh orange juice, and eggs scrambled with herbs and olive oil. She let her mind drift to kissing Asher in Ohio and their intense connection, to Sam last night in the hammam and his electric energy. It wasn't fair to compare those kisses to Ray last Fourth of July—she and Ray had known each other so much longer, the buildup to their night together had been so drawn out and fraught that kissing him had felt like an ocean of clear water after years in endless desert, drinking so quickly and deeply that she went from parched to drowned.

With Asher, and now Sam, it was different—they were finding their path together, all excitement and uncertainty. And then . . . there was Luc. She was looking forward to their date this afternoon—and perhaps to kisses that would feel less agitated and complex than those they shared the night of the yacht and the crème brûlée.

Bea felt that same rush of effortless chemistry when she saw him waiting for her in front of the *riad,* sporting dark jeans, a charcoal sweater, and just the right amount of trans-atlantic scruff.

"Morocco suits you," he murmured as he leaned down to kiss her on the mouth, a soft hello that lingered for a delicious moment.

"You like me in menswear?" Bea teased. She was wearing head-to-toe Veronica Beard today: high-waisted linen trousers in a soft brown clay, a ribbed white shell with a low scoop neck, and a stunning slouchy houndstooth blazer that made her feel like Rosalind Russell circa *His Girl Friday.*

"I like you anywhere." Luc smiled and kissed her again; he tasted like salt and smoke.

"If that's true, then I think you're really going to like me today."

"Oh?" He let his hands settle at her waist, comfortably holding her as they talked. "What adventures do you have planned?"

"I thought we could spice things up a little. Maybe add some flavor to our date."

"You are making cooking jokes, yes?"

"Yes. Cooking puns, technically."

"Ah. And perhaps my English is to blame, or perhaps the puns are bad?"

Bea grinned. "The puns are awful."

They rode in a fancy old car to the Marrakesh spice market, an open square stuffed with dozens of vendors whose glass jars filled with rainbow spices lined shelves that stretched to the roof of each stall like some kind of Wonka-esque dream. Luc's eyes lit up as he took Bea from stall to stall, sharing tastes of hot cayenne and pungent cumin and savory ras el hanout. He held out a strand of golden saffron for Bea to try; she went to take it from his finger, but he shook his head.

"It is too delicate. This way is better." He lifted his finger to her lips, and it felt so much more erotic than kissing as she took it into her mouth, gently letting the intensity of the pure saffron wash over her tongue.

He let his finger rest on her lips for a moment, and she wanted to kiss it, to kiss him, to get the hell away from the crowd of bystanders and the laughing merchants she felt certain were mocking her in Arabic.

Instead she just smiled, and Luc ran his fingers along her jawline. "A pity I need my hands back at all. I'd rather leave them with you."

After the spice market, they went to the home of a squat, exuberant grandmother who offered cooking lessons in her copper-filled kitchen.

"Today, we make chicken with couscous, vegetable, and saffron. You like saffron, yes?"

Luc put his hand on the small of Bea's back. "She loves it."

Luc's tendency to veer over-the-top was one reason Bea couldn't see herself trusting him—was he putting on a romantic performance, or was he just genuinely European? But chopping chicken and vegetables together while Grandma Adilah yelled at them to adjust their form, Luc cursing under his breath in French that she didn't know the first thing about knife work, then laughing when Bea understood well enough to call him out, Bea felt she was starting to get a sense of what a life together might actually look like, how his character might be outside the trappings of all these grand gestures.

"Tell me about your restaurant?" Bea asked, mincing ginger as Luc butchered a chicken, his knife easily finding the magic spaces between the joints.

"It is not *my* restaurant." He sniffed.

"But you're the head chef there, right?"

"Yes, it is my place—but I am cooking someone else's vision. Ultimately, nothing is your own unless you can make your own choices, unless success or failure rests only with you. Like with your work, no? No one tells you what to photograph, what to say. You say what you think, and this is why so many people adore you."

Bea hunched over the ginger so he wouldn't see her blush. "That's kind of you."

Luc shrugged. "It's just the truth, no? This is what I want, to get my own place—many places, if I can."

"In America or Europe?"

He smirked. "And why not both? Would you object to summer in New York and winter in Paris?"

"Spring in L.A., autumn in Rome?"

Luc paused his chopping and leaned in toward Bea. "I think this is an excellent plan." They kissed, and it was all so easy, so attractive. A shared little fantasy where they both were welcome tenants.

Once the cooking was done, they ate their meal in Grandma Adilah's twinkle-lit garden, where warm blankets and space heaters were required to keep them from freezing in the desert night. After dinner, they fed each other slices of orange drizzled with honey, and Bea thought she'd never tasted anything so perfectly sweet in her life.

Back at the *riad,* Luc kissed Bea good night, surrounded by cameras and bathed in artificial light. When Lauren called cut and declared the date was a wrap, Bea said a quick good night to Luc and made her way back to her room. The date had been flirty and enjoyable—time with Luc always was—but Bea didn't feel any more certain about him than she had beforehand. She washed off her makeup and threw on sweatpants and a ratty old T-shirt, then crawled into bed; she was looking forward to a good night's sleep before her day with Asher and Jefferson tomorrow.

She had just turned out the light when she heard a knock on her door.

"Ugh," she groaned, and flipped her bedside light back on. She trudged over to the door and opened it, expecting a producer or PA with some new bit of information about her morning call time.

But instead, there was Luc, wearing chic dark sweats that probably cost more than most men's best suits, carrying a bottle of wine. It was just like his surprise visit the night of the crème brûlée—except this time, there weren't any cameras.

"Luc, what are you doing here?" Bea folded her arms over her chest, wishing she'd put on one of the buttery nightdresses Alison had packed for her, or that she'd bothered to brush her hair instead of throwing it into a crooked bun, crunchy hair spray and all. "Do the producers know you're here?"

Luc grinned mischievously. "We are adults, no? We can choose our own destiny?"

Bea felt a mild panic rising—she barely knew this man. Before, his behavior had always been so predictable: the cheesy flirting, the vying for camera time, for fame. But now he was alone in the doorway of her darkened bedroom—what did he want from her? Did he expect sex? She certainly wasn't ready for that—oh God. What the hell was happening?

"Oh no," he murmured, his expression falling as he read Bea's face. "I thought it would be a little pleasure to see you without the cameras, but now I see I have made you uncomfortable?"

"No," she stammered, trying to figure out the right thing to say and what she actually wanted in the same breath. "I'm just surprised, that's all. Um, I need to go to sleep soon, but one glass of wine would be okay? I guess?"

"You are certain?" He looked unsure. "The last thing I want is to give you troubles."

"It's okay." Bea smiled, heartened that he seemed nervous too. "Please, come in."

She turned on more lamps in the room as he slipped inside and shut the door behind him. She pulled a robe out of her wardrobe to throw on over her PJs.

"No," Luc said with a smile, "but I love you in this T-shirt."

"Really?" Bea laughed. "Maybe I should have worn it on our date today."

Luc produced a small wine key from his pocket and began opening the bottle, a deep Moroccan red.

"Perhaps I am wrong," he said, "but when I see you in your fashions, your makeup, your hair all done, I think this is like your armor, your uniform for war."

"Love is a battlefield?" Bea raised an eyebrow.

"*Non*, Ms. Benatar." He smiled. "There is something about these fashions that feel like—a challenge, I think is the right word. Like you are telling the world the way you want them to see you."

"Doesn't everyone do that?" she asked, feeling a bit self-conscious that this man who seemed so self-involved had seen her so clearly.

"Yes, but not for a living." He grabbed two glasses from a sideboard and poured the wine, then brought them over to the little settee where Bea was sitting. "Now, like this, you are soft. Unguarded. I prefer it."

They clinked glasses and drank; the wine was dark and fruity.

"So." Bea tried for a flirtatious tone, but she was afraid it came out more pointed. "Do you want to tell me what you're really doing here?"

"Here in your room? Whatever you like."

"No." Bea flushed. "Here on this show."

Luc cocked his head. "What do you mean by this?"

"Well," Bea explained, "tonight, for example. When you were telling me about your restaurant, and how you want to own your places. Being famous would help with that, right? Make it easier to get investors?"

Luc looked puzzled. "Yes, of course."

"I mean, that's why you came on this show, isn't it? To raise your profile, to become a celebrity? To help your career?"

"Certainly," Luc admitted. "Is this a problem?"

"No, but—" Bea paused, unsure how to articulate her concern. "I guess I thought that that's why you wanted to spend time with me. Not that we weren't having fun, but just that—I don't know. If we weren't here, on this show, you would never give me a second glance. That's why I don't understand why you're here in my room now, when there aren't any cameras."

Luc put down his wine, his expression darker now. "You are saying you do not have interest in me."

"Luc, come on. I was sure you had no interest in *me.*"

"But why? Why would you assume this?"

"Look at you!" Bea spluttered. "The longer I keep you here, the more fame you get. And if I pick you in the end, it means magazine covers, and TV specials, and interviews, and . . ." Bea felt like an idiot. Of course he was here to increase his own chances of winning, especially now that she was getting closer with Asher and Sam. Of *course.* "I just answered my own question, didn't I?"

Luc frowned. "I do not understand."

"It's fine, Luc. I like you, and we have a good time together. I won't send you home unless there's a reason to, okay? I'm not trying to get in the way of your goals."

She stood and walked toward the door, assuming this was the assurance he wanted, but he looked even more upset as he came to follow her.

"You think I am a liar."

"What? I didn't say that!"

"This is what you are saying right now!" He ran his fingers through his hair in frustration. "You think I am using you for my own gain, that my enjoyment of you is false. Is this really what you think of me? That I would be so cruel?"

"Luc, you have to understand where I'm coming from here."

"Why did you agree to do this show?" he demanded. "You work in an industry where publicity is valuable, like mine— was this a factor in your decision?"

"Of course it was." She exhaled. There was no use in lying to him, even if she did feel like a hypocrite.

"So?" he pressed. "What am I to think? Are you leading me on, pretending to fall in love with me so your audience will fall in love with you?"

"That's not the same!" Bea protested.

"What is different? You think I would pretend to have feelings for you because I am some kind of liar, but you would never do the same to me?"

"I had twenty-five men here, Luc. Why would I single you out and pretend to be interested in you?"

"Perhaps because, for our first week together, I was the only one showing interest in you."

The remark hit Bea in the gut—that awful first night, the catastrophic afternoon on the boat, and Luc, out of everyone, taking time to make her feel beautiful. She didn't feel beautiful now.

"Maybe the fact that you wanted me from the beginning is the reason I don't trust you."

Luc looked genuinely confused. "Why would you say this?"

"Because it makes it seem like you have an agenda! You have a lot to gain by being here, and more to gain the longer you stay. You're one of the most attractive men on this show, one of the most attractive men I've ever met. I don't date men who look like you, and I can only presume you don't date women who look like me. So what am I supposed to think, Luc? That you're some perfect prince come to rescue me from my nightmare of a love life? Or that you came here with a goal, and you didn't waste any time setting out to achieve it?"

"Is that what you thought when you met me?" he asked quietly. "Is it what you thought the first time I kissed you?"

"I thought you were playing me." Bea shrugged. "Maybe I was right."

"And you think this because you believe I cannot be attracted to you. This is how you see yourself?"

Bea wanted to speak, but tears threatened. "It's how men like you see me," she choked out, and Luc's face crumpled, his anger suddenly gone.

"I understand, I understand," he murmured, pulling her close. "You are not so tough after all, my Bea."

"Who ever said I was tough?" she joked, burying her face in his chest.

"I think you are beautiful," he whispered. "Your face, your body, your laugh. Can you believe this?"

Bea looked up at him, trying to read his face. "I don't know."

"Hmm. I think perhaps this is good news for me."

Bea frowned. "How so?"

"Because this means I will have to prove how much I want you."

He rested the pads of his fingers lightly on her cheekbones, gently circling the contours of her face. The gesture was so small, so intimate, that Bea felt shaky—she closed her eyes. He leaned down to kiss her, and with no cameras, no makeup (hell, no bra), it felt like something honest and apart from the artifice of the show, like instead of a luxury *riad* in Morocco, they could be in his apartment in New York, or her place in L.A. Everything was slow, languid; none of it felt urgent or performed. He kissed her for a long time, and then he held her, still standing, breathing slowly.

"I'm glad you came over," she whispered.

He smiled and kissed the crown of her head. "So am I."

⚯

TEXT MESSAGE TRANSCRIPT, MARCH 27:
MAIN SQUEEZE PRODUCER THREAD

Shareeza [6:38am]: Is Bea finished in wardrobe yet? We're supposed to load out in ten

Mike [6:38am]: She is DRAGGING this morning, she's so tired and cranky and everything's taking forever

Mike [6:39am]: Which makes no sense, didn't we wrap her early last night?

Jeannie [6:39am]: One of the PAs ran into Luc in the hall at 4am

Jeannie [6:40am]: Related???

Shareeza [6:41am]: Lauren, are you seeing this? What do you want us to do?

Mike [6:44am]: Bea just rejected outfit #4. Lauren?? Where are you???

Lauren [6:49am]: Was with Luc trying to figure out what went down last night

Lauren [6:49am]: (He went to Bea's room and NO ONE caught it! Come on guys!!!)

Lauren [6:50am]: Reezy, get down to wardrobe and tell Alison we're going right now—we've only got the camels for five hours

Shareeza [6:51am]: Copy! Bea says if someone doesn't get her an iced coffee she's breaking up with everyone

Lauren [6:51am]: Honestly same

Bea was absolutely exhausted after her night with Luc, but once some blessed PA procured her caffeine and the production crew headed out of the city into the fresh air of the mountains, she started to feel a bit better. The Atlas Mountains were stunning—blue and jagged, blanketed in thick green groves on their western side where rain fell, rocky and barren to the east where Morocco abruptly faded into endless sand. Bea journeyed up the side of a mountain in a 4x4 with their guide for the day, Rahim, who had a truly lush beard and a warm, mischievous manner that made Bea laugh—something she sorely needed after all the emotional drama of the night before.

"Riding a camel is basically like riding a horse," Rahim explained over the whip of the mountain winds, "but the meat is much gamier."

"I feel like you switched thoughts there, Rahim."

"If the trek goes south and we need to eat our camels to survive, I just want you to know what you're getting yourself into—a nice, smoky flavor."

They made it to a little plateau near the base of the mountain, where Asher, Jefferson, and the camera crew were already set up to film Bea's arrival.

"Hi guys!" She waved, inelegantly dismounting the 4x4—Jefferson rushed over to steady her.

"Take it easy, we're not even on the camels yet." Jefferson let out a big laugh, and Bea was reminded momentarily of that feeling she'd had on the first night when he called her "little lady," when she couldn't quite tell whether he was laughing at her expense. But he flashed a broad grin and kissed her on the cheek, and she dismissed the thought; it was genuinely nice to see him.

"Hello, Bea."

Bea looked up to see that Asher was still several feet away—he made no move to come closer.

"Hey." She walked over to him, noting how wonderfully normal he looked in his faded jeans and woolen sweater: a dad from Vermont. She wanted to hug him, to rest her head on his shoulder and snuggle into his arms—but something about his manner stopped her, made her ill at ease.

"Seems like you've had a good week," he said, an edge in his voice.

"Yes, this country is amazing. I really love it here." Bea was so confused—the last time she saw him, they'd been confessing their feelings and kissing passionately. What had changed?

"Okay!" Rahim's voice broke in. "Riding a camel can be tricky. They spit, all four of their legs can kick in all four directions, and they're frankly not thrilled that you're here. So I need you all to be *careful* when you mount them. They'll sink down to the ground, and you need to lean *back* as they rise up. If you lean forward, there's a not-insignificant chance they throw you over their heads, and we have a lot of cameras here, so even if you don't get injured, your mortification will live forever on YouTube. Okay?"

Bea, Asher, and Jefferson all nodded with trepidation. Bea was starting to think maybe belly dancing wouldn't be the most frightening date option in Morocco after all.

"Great!" Rahim clapped his hands. "Let's get this party started."

The camels were putrid and surly, and Bea said a silent prayer as hers rose to its feet that she wasn't about to be pitched headfirst onto a rocky path. But once the camel stood up and they got going, she was bowled over by the majesty of the experience. The camels were markedly taller than horses, and while riding them wasn't exactly comfortable, their lilting gaits did have something of a hypnotic quality.

For half an hour they rode higher into the mountains,

until they reached a plateau where the producers had arranged a beautiful picnic. Thirty minutes on a camel didn't seem like long, but by the end of the ride, she was more than ready to take a break—thick Moroccan bread with savory roasted lamb was just the ticket.

"What, no camel meat?" Bea joked with Rahim.

"Shhh, they'll hear you!" Rahim looked meaningfully at their camels. "We can't let them know how lean and nutritious they are."

"I think you should consider being the spokesperson for the camel-meat industry."

"Why do you think I agreed to do a camel tour on reality TV? I've got ambitions, baby."

After lunch, the producers had blocked out discrete mini-dates for Jefferson and Asher to give each of them time to talk alone with Bea. First, Bea took a short walk with Jefferson to a magnificent vista that overlooked the entire city of Marrakesh below, the high walls and turrets and palm trees and twisting alleyways gleaming in the afternoon sunlight.

"This is so beautiful," Bea said, feeling grateful to be in this extraordinary place. It reminded her of a road trip with Ray up to Malibu almost ten years ago, a Saturday treat after a terrible week at the agency. The convertible top down, the wind in their hair, walking together over jagged cliffs as they laughed and talked for hours, admiring gorgeous views like this one. Bea realized that she'd barely thought of Ray all week—was it just the ocean between them that made him feel so far away? Or had making room for the possibility of these other men left a little less space for his memory?

"Whatcha thinking about?" Jefferson gave Bea a little nudge, easing her back into the present moment. She looked up at him, cast in golden light and the handsomest she'd seen him.

"Just thinking how profound my time here has felt, even though it's only been five weeks." Bea laughed with a moment of self-awareness. "Wow, I sound like everyone who's ever starred on this show, don't I?"

"It's a good thing, though. I feel the same way." Jefferson sighed and leaned against the stone wall that framed the vista. "I've been saying for years that I'm ready to get married, feeling frustrated that I can't find a woman to be my wife. But being here with you, I'm starting to wonder, was I really ready before? Because this feels . . . so different."

"Really?" Bea didn't mean to sound incredulous, but she and Jefferson had really only shared two conversations—nice ones to be sure, but there was certainly nothing life-altering about them.

Jefferson laughed. "I know, I probably sound insane to you—believe me, it sounds even crazier to me. And maybe I'm just getting swept away with this show, with all the amazing things we've gotten to do. But I don't know, Bea. Watching everything that's been thrown at you for the past month, how gracefully you've handled it all, how you've been vulnerable but kept your sense of humor—yeah. It's been really special. It's taught me more about the kind of person I want to be."

"Wow," Bea said quietly, not really knowing how to react to this. "I really wish you and I would have had more time together before now."

"It's not too late, is it?" He reached for her hand—she noticed his was a little clammy. Was he nervous about this conversation? If so, it was incredibly endearing.

"It's funny," she said, "the way you describe yourself in

Kansas City, with dating, I mean—that's pretty similar to how I've been for the last few years."

"Seriously?" Jefferson looked skeptical.

"Yeah—I know most of the girls on this show are pretty marriage-minded, but that hasn't been me. At all. And as much as I've said I'm ready for marriage, I haven't really given any man the chance to form a real relationship, let alone get engaged."

"Why do you think that is?"

Bea shrugged. "The easy answer is that I've been focused on my career—and that's true, I have."

"And the harder answer?" Jefferson gave her a knowing look.

"I guess . . ." Bea stopped, then pushed herself to go on. If this could be her only chance to figure out whether there might be potential for something real with this man, she owed it to him—and herself—to try to be vulnerable.

"Growing up, I was always wary of boys. When I was little, kids in elementary school were so cruel—even in high school, they treated me like a joke, you know? I didn't really date until college, and guys there were happy to sleep with me—just not to be seen with me in public. After that, I think I really shied away from putting myself out there. I would fall in love with these unavailable people, and tell myself it was my own bad luck, but the truth is, maybe I was just trying to avoid finding something real, because it still scared me so much."

"And now?" Jefferson looked into her eyes. "Are you still afraid?"

"Hell yeah, I am." Bea laughed softly. "This show is the scariest thing I've ever done. But also—I see all this potential, and it's thrilling. Like I'm flying off the side of this mountain and taking it on faith that it'll somehow be okay."

"Maybe you'll land on happily ever after," Jefferson quipped.

"Yeah?" Bea smiled. "What would that look like?"

"Well"—Jefferson draped an arm over her shoulders as they turned to admire the view—"it'd be you and me, a big house with a yard, a dog for sure—you like dogs?"

"I love dogs." Bea grinned.

"Thank *God*." Jefferson faked intense relief. "So us, the house, the dog, a couple of kids, road trips on the weekend to a cool barbecue joint or a national park. Friends coming over for game nights, smoking wings and brisket for football Sundays, getting old, being happy. You know, life."

"That sounds pretty good." Bea leaned against Jefferson's chest, and he pulled her in to face him.

"So since there are no kids or relatives around," he said with a grin, "do you think it'd be okay if I kissed you?"

There was absolutely no reason not to kiss him—but something in Bea still hesitated, still didn't feel quite right.

"It's okay, Bea," Jefferson said gently. "You don't have to stand in your own way anymore. You can let yourself be happy."

Bea nodded yes, and as he leaned in to kiss her—a gentle kiss, respectful and sweet—Bea still wasn't sure if she really saw a future with Jefferson, but she did know that she loved the big, solid certainty of him, the way that when he held her, they just fit.

And it felt really, really nice.

After Bea went back to the main staging area, she climbed into another 4x4 beside Asher, who didn't seem any happier to see Bea than he had that morning. They rode in silence to a spectacular waterfall, water spilling over a jagged cliff and thundering into a deep green pool below, then hiked in equal silence to the edge of a copper-hued rock formation, where soft mist cast in rainbow prisms floated across their bodies. It was one of the most romantic places Bea had ever been, but Asher would barely look at her. She'd spent all week looking forward to being alone with him, reliving their Ohio kiss in her memory, and now he was acting like she'd done something to offend him—only, as she hadn't seen him, she couldn't imagine what that might be.

"Hey!" she shouted over the noise of the falls. "Is everything okay?"

"What do you mean?" he asked, his back still toward her.

She grabbed his arm—he turned in surprise. "Can you at least look at me?"

He did, but his expression was hard, his manner guarded.

"Are you stressed about your kids?" she asked. "Whatever it is, can we please just talk about it?"

Asher's jaw tensed. "Did you sleep with Luc last night?"

"*What?*" Bea felt like she'd been slapped in the face.

"He and I are roommates in the *riad*," Asher said curtly, and Bea's stomach dropped. "He left the room around midnight, and didn't come back until four. When I asked where he'd been, he smiled and said he was with you."

Bea flushed crimson. So not only was Asher furious, now the one private moment she'd had with a man all season long was going to be a major plot point of this week's episode.

"I don't like asking you to air your private business on television," Asher said, "but if you're going to meet my children, I think I have a right to know what happened."

"Really?" Bea pushed back. "Because I'm having trouble seeing how one thing relates to the other."

"Bea, I haven't introduced *anyone* to my kids since their mother left. You think I'd let you meet them if you're not taking this seriously?"

"You think I'd want to? Come on, Asher. I'm not a monster, I don't want to drag your kids into a limelight you don't want them in—I would never ask that of you, period, let alone if I didn't think—"

Her heart was pounding. She couldn't say it.

"What?" he prodded. "If you didn't think what?"

Bea closed her eyes. "If I didn't think I could really fall in love with you."

She looked up at Asher—his expression was pained.

"I hate this," he said finally.

"What do you hate?"

"You, with other men."

"You knew the premise of this show when you agreed to be on it, right?"

"That doesn't mean I have to like it," he sulked.

"No one's asking you to! But I don't see a way for us to make it through this if you shut down during what precious little time we actually get to spend together because you're busy thinking about everyone else."

"I know," he admonished himself. "Believe me, I hate that I'm behaving this way. I couldn't get back to sleep after Luc came back. I kept thinking about the two of you, and wondering . . ."

"What?"

For the first time all day, he looked Bea dead in the eye.

"If you feel as strongly for me as you do for him."

Bea sighed in frustration. As much as she didn't relish sharing this particular detail on television, she had a feeling it was the only thing that would get this date (and this relationship) back on track.

"Asher, I didn't sleep with Luc."

He looked up at her, surprised and a little hopeful. "You didn't?"

Bea shook her head. "Not even close. And I'm sorry he gave you that impression. You know how he is, I'm sure he was just trying to get a rise out of you."

"It's not just him," Asher said softly.

"Oh?"

"Sam was pretty happy when he came home from his date."

Bea exhaled deeply. She'd been so worried about these men hurting her, she hadn't even considered the fact that she could hurt them.

"Come here," she said to Asher, taking his hand and putting it over her heart, just as he'd done in Ohio. "I know how awful it is to see someone you care about with someone else, okay? Believe me, I've been there. But if you can't trust that I'm taking this seriously, you might as well leave now. Is that what you want?"

Asher let out a huge sigh and pulled Bea into a hug.

"That's the opposite of what I want," he mumbled into her hair, and Bea relaxed into his touch. This was what she'd longed for all day, and now that she was here, she finally felt some of the tension in her body unspool.

He pulled back so he could look at her. "Forgive me for being a jealous ass?"

She nodded, then took his hand and led him over to a picnic blanket piled with pillows that the production staff had set out. They settled down to enjoy thermoses full of hot tea as they looked out over the falls.

"So," Bea started, "we have a big decision to make this week."

"Regarding my children?"

Bea nodded. "Will you tell me more about them? How old are they?"

"Gwen is twelve, and Linus is nine."

"Wow, so you were a really young dad."

"Yeah, just twenty-three when Gwen was born."

"What's she like?"

"She's very serious." Asher smiled. "She wants to be a scientist someday; she got very into zoology this year and did a whole research paper about the differences between leopards and cheetahs."

"I love leopard print?" Bea ventured.

"I'm not sure that counts as having something in common." Asher patted Bea's thigh. "Gwen can be a tough nut to crack—she's a lot like me, if I'm honest. Very thoughtful, very critical. Even a bit guarded. She didn't want me to come on this show."

"Really? Why not?"

"She thought it was a waste of time—and as you know, I agreed. But it meant so much to Linus . . . I just couldn't say no to him."

"Will you tell me about Linus?" Bea asked, and Asher's whole expression softened.

"He has this sweetness that can change your whole day. And he's sensitive—he picks up right away if Gwen's in a bad mood, or I am. He just wants everything around him to be filled with joy."

Bea didn't miss the note of pain in Asher's voice. "Hey, what's wrong?"

Asher looked at Bea for a long moment, and then sighed.

"I'm afraid of putting him on television."

"Because he's so young?"

Asher shook his head. "Linus is gender nonconforming. He still uses he/him pronouns, and I don't know how he'll come to identify—for now, I'm following his lead. He loves to wear dresses, tutus, glitter, all of it. He's a human ray of sunshine. But the kids at his school . . ."

"There's been bullying?"

"In the past, yes. His teachers have always been great about working with me to make school a welcoming place for him, and so have the other parents—we're lucky to live in a really inclusive town. But to open him up to the rest of the country, to subject him to all the horrible things people say online?"

"I know something about that," Bea said quietly.

"I know you do." Asher's voice was strained. "So you can understand why I'm so hesitant to bring cameras into our home."

"Maybe this is stupid," Bea murmured, "but do you think this could be a way for you to show Linus that you're not afraid to tell the world how proud you are of him? That you think he's perfect just the way he is?"

"That doesn't sound stupid at all," he said softly. He took Bea's hand, and her heart swelled with affection for this new side of him she was discovering.

"It's funny," Bea said softly, "the way you form impressions of people. When we first talked on the boat, I thought you were such a snob."

"You weren't totally wrong on that one," Asher dead-panned, and Bea laughed.

"Then at the museum, I started getting a better sense of who you are, and I started falling for you," she continued, "but I didn't know this huge thing about you, that you're a dad—and a sole caregiver at that."

Asher looked down. "I should have told you sooner."

"No"—Bea squeezed his hand—"that's not what I'm saying. What I mean is—you keep surprising me. And the more I learn about you, the more I want to learn about you. I know what a big deal it is to meet your kids. And I want to get to know them, to see what they're like. But also, I can't wait to see what *you're* like with them. To get to know another new part of you."

He pulled her closer to him, and she snuggled against his chest as he wrapped his arms around her.

"Are you sure you're ready for this—for me to meet them, I mean?" she asked, pulling away to look him in the eye. "I'll understand if you aren't."

Asher met her gaze, his expression firm. "Bea, my readiness depends on yours. This isn't just about meeting my kids—it's about what comes after. With me, having a family one day isn't some dim hypothetical; it's a present reality. So especially considering what your visit could mean for Linus, the real question for me is, are *you* ready?"

"You're right," Bea agreed. "That is the question."

"And what . . . is the answer?"

Bea shook her head. "I can't know for certain, Asher. Not yet. Believe me, I wish I could."

"I understand. But can I ask something of you?"

"Of course. Anything."

"Give it some thought before the ceremony tonight. And if you think the answer is definitely no—or even probably no—send me home."

"That feels impossible."

"To me too," he said, hugging her close.

She buried her face in his scratchy sweater, breathing his scent, all pine and wool, and he ran his hand along her jaw, tipping up her chin so they could look at each other. He kissed her face, and then her mouth; he pulled her closer and closer until there was no space left between them, until all their questions and doubts were drowned out by the roar of the falls.

By the time they made it back to the *riad,* dusty and drained, Bea wanted nothing more than to eat some couscous, crawl into bed, and go to sleep, but that wasn't in the cards: After a frustratingly brief shower, she had a consult with Alison about which gown to wear to the kiss-off ceremony, another two hours in hair and makeup, and an hour after that of recording direct-to-cameras about how difficult this decision was going to be—all the while genuinely worrying about what she was going to do.

To make her decision even tougher, all five of the men had recorded video messages for her, which she was made to watch on camera to capture her reactions. First was Sam, his jubilance completely infectious, his infatuation with Bea totally obvious.

"Bea! I haven't seen you in two days, which is the worst!" He looked dramatically from side to side, as if to make sure no one was watching him, then leaned in close to the camera. "But I've spent the entire time thinking about kissing you in the hammam, which was the *best.*"

"Marin was right about him," Bea murmured with a little grin.

Next up was Luc, stunningly handsome in a plain white T-shirt, looking straight into the camera with his smoldering eyes.

"My Bea, this week I have seen a new side of you, I think. Thank you for trusting me, for showing me your softness."

He gave her a little smirk, and Bea felt a wave of nausea.

Luc had thought this would be a private reference, but because of his unseemly brags to Asher, every single person watching would know he was talking about their night together. That night had felt like the foundation of a fragile trust between them, but now she found herself doubting every word that came out of his mouth. But the question remained: Was she sure enough that he was lying about his intentions toward her to send him home, despite the fact that she had more chemistry with him than any other man here?

Then came Asher's video, which was perfectly Asher: "Bea, per our discussion, I know what a difficult decision this is for you. I hope you'll decide to continue to pursue our relationship."

It would be easy to write him off as cold or unfeeling, but Bea was starting to learn how to read his subtext, to see all the things he didn't say, to trust in their connection and in him. Letting him go was unthinkable—but she owed it to him (and his children) to think about it all the same.

The fourth video was Jefferson's, and Bea felt a twist of uncertainty when she saw his face.

"Hey beautiful," he said with a grin. "I had so much fun today, and I can't wait to introduce you to my family—and everything you've been missing with that KC BBQ! But on a more serious note, I also want to say, Bea, you and I just make sense together. I felt it from the second I saw you— didn't some part of you feel it too?"

Everything Jefferson was saying was true—sweet, even— so why did it make her uncomfortable? Was she really getting in the way of her own happiness, as Jefferson (and Marin, and her mother) had suggested? Or, on the other hand, was she simply trying to convince herself to have feelings for a man who looked the part of a husband for a woman like Bea?

Maybe she and Jefferson just needed more time together to cement their bond—but if what he wanted was a wife and family in Kansas City, and Bea could hardly see that for her own future, was it even worth the effort?

Then again, Wyatt lived on a farm in Oklahoma, which was even more foreign to Bea—but she couldn't deny the surge of joy she felt when his face appeared onscreen. Her feelings for the other men were so fraught and complex; with Wyatt, she just felt happy.

"I missed you this week." He beamed. "Morocco's very beautiful. Did you know you can eat camel meat? I tried a camel burger. So that was . . . different! Anyway, I hope your week was great, and I hope you decide to come visit my family on our farm. We have a tractor that I think you're really going to love."

Bea still had far more questions than answers about Wyatt: Did he want a relationship at all, let alone one with her? Did she want a relationship with him—and would having one actually mean moving to Oklahoma? But no matter what the answers to any of these questions were, one thing was certain: Of all the men left, Wyatt made Bea feel by far the most safe. And she really, really wasn't ready to give that up.

"So?" Lauren came in after the videos were done playing. "Do you know what you're going to do?"

Bea nodded. "I think so."

"And you feel good about your choice?"

"No! I feel nauseous and exhausted and like it's entirely possible I'm making the wrong decision."

"Good." Lauren smiled. "That means you're right on schedule. Let's roll!"

She led Bea into the *riad*'s living room, where all the furniture had been removed, and her five suitors awaited her in a semicircle.

"Hi, guys." She smiled, pushing through her jitters. "How's your jet lag? You ready to head back home and confuse our bodies all over again?"

The guys laughed amenably, and Bea was struck by how few of them there were. This week's lip color was Don't Wine About It, so Bea readied herself to leave a deep berry stain on the cheeks of four men to whom, against all odds, she'd grown very attached.

"Sam?" she called, and he strode toward her with a brilliant smile. Bea had some input as to which men would stay, but Lauren always determined the order in which she called them. After their night in the hammam, it was no surprise that Sam had rocketed to frontrunner status.

After Sam came Luc, who rested his arm possessively at Bea's waist as she kissed him on the cheek. Bea bristled at this—she hated the idea that Luc was actively trying to make the other men jealous, but at the moment, there wasn't much she could do about it. It would be easier next week, she reasoned, when the men were all in their separate hometowns, not cooped up together in one house day after day.

"Wyatt," Bea said next, and she felt a rush of reassurance as he broke into a soft, easy smile and stepped forward to give her a huge hug.

"I'm so happy you're coming home with me."

"Me too," she assured him after she kissed his cheek.

Once Wyatt stepped aside to join Luc and Sam, that left Asher and Jefferson. Bea looked from one man to the other and took a deep breath.

"Asher and Jefferson," she said, "I want to thank both of

you for how open you were with me today in the mountains. You've both made me think about the role of family in my life, about what I want that to look like, and what I'm ready to take on. This wasn't an easy decision."

She looked over to Johnny, who took his cue to give his regular speech before the final name was called.

"Okay, guys, Bea is about to choose her final suitor. If your name isn't called, you must immediately leave the *riad*. Bea, whenever you're ready."

Bea inhaled—she wasn't sure she was ready at all. But either way, it was time.

"Asher," she said, and the relief that washed over his face was palpable.

"You scared me," he whispered after she kissed his cheek.

"Back at you," she said, and he hugged her tightly. The truth was, Bea wasn't totally sure she was ready to be a mother—but she knew she absolutely wasn't ready to say goodbye to this man.

"That's it for this week's ceremony," Johnny pronounced. "Jefferson, take a minute to say your goodbyes."

"I'm sorry, Jefferson." Bea delivered the speech she'd rehearsed with Lauren in what she hoped was a consoling manner and not a condescending one. "I really appreciated our time together today, and I'm so happy I got a chance to know you better. I just think our visions for our futures are pretty different—but I know you're going to make an amazing husband for whatever woman is lucky enough to become your wife."

She hated the awkwardness of dismissing only him, especially since he'd been so sweet to her. But she couldn't deny how much closer she felt with the other four men.

"Can I walk you out?" she asked, conforming to Lauren's

dictates. She was meant to accompany Jefferson to the *riad's* entrance, say a brief—and hopefully emotional!—farewell, then see him off as he got into a car that would take him to the airport and out of Bea's life forever (or, at least, until the reunion show).

But Jefferson didn't seem very interested in acting according to plan. He was shaking slightly—maybe with laughter?—his eyes hard and narrow.

"Are you kidding? You think you can do better than me? Trust me, Bea, I've never had a problem getting a girlfriend—and none of them have ever looked like you."

Bea shook her head in confusion. "No, I—Jefferson, it's not a matter of better, it's about what I want for my future—"

"And what you want is to go live on a farm in Oklahoma? That's your dream? Please, Bea. You're a fat hypocrite—I guess that's half a revelation."

Bea stopped cold. "I'm sorry, what?"

"You heard me." He stalked toward her, taking his time, savoring that all eyes were on him. "Now that I'm out of the competition, I guess I can finally be honest with you—good thing, too, since no one else has been."

"What are you talking about?" she asked, her voice unsteady.

"What I'm talking about, Bea, is the fact that none of the men in this room is remotely interested in you. Least of all me."

Bea shot a glance over at the other men, but Jefferson kept going.

"Sure, they talk a good game, but you've never seen them without the cameras rolling. You have no idea the horrible jokes they make about you, the way they laugh at your expense. How could you? You're so desperate for love that you'll believe any nice thing a man says to you. It's sad, Bea. And it's probably pretty great television. But at some point, you've got to wake up and face the fact that you are the only person on this show who actually believes that any of these men could fall in love with you."

"You're lying." Bea felt the first tears coming. "If none of you were interested in me, why would you even stay on this show?"

Jefferson laughed. "Are you stupid? The longer we stick around, the more likely it is that one of us will be the next Main Squeeze! Don't you think it's worth it, pretending to like you for a few hours a week to increase our odds of having twenty-five women compete for us? And you made it so easy, Bea, you really did. Honestly, you bought that I didn't want to kiss you last week because there were *kids* around? How gullible can you be? I was just putting off getting physical with you for as long as possible."

"Stop"—Bea was shaking—"please stop."

"I think in time you'll come to see that I'm doing you a favor. No one in your life is honest with you—that's how you ended up on this show in the first place, got tricked into being a national laughingstock. So take it from me: You're not single because you're focused on your career, or because you're pining after unavailable men, or subconsciously trying to protect your heart because some kids made fun of you in elementary school, or whatever bullshit you tell yourself. You know why no man wants to be seen with you in public? It's not that hard to figure out. You know what's standing between you and marriage? About eighty pounds."

Bea didn't know what to do, where to go. She stepped backward and nearly tripped on the hem of her dress, wobbling in her high heels.

"Bea," Wyatt stepped forward, "don't listen to him, it's not true—"

"No," Bea yelped, and Jefferson laughed. She hated herself for crying in front of these men she'd finally started to trust, but who could just as easily be using her, same as Jefferson, same as Ray, same as always. She couldn't be here, couldn't take this. Couldn't spend one more second on this set where her existence was one big joke, the setup her fatness and the punch line her loneliness.

"Excuse me, I—excuse me." She choked out the words and left the living room as fast as her high heels could carry her, then blindly stumbled up the stairs back to her room and slammed the door.

EPISODE 6

"DECLARATION"

(4 men left)

*Shot on location in New York, New York,
Boone, Oklahoma,
Middlebury, Vermont,
Newark & Short Hills, New Jersey*

TRANSCRIPT OF CHAT FROM #SQUEEZE-MAINIACS SLACK CHANNEL

NickiG: I WANT JEFFERSON TO DIE

Beth.Malone: He will eventually

NickiG: NOT SOON ENOUGH

Enna-Jay: Has anything like this ever happened before?? That was . . . awful

KeyboardCat: I mean, there's never been a plus-size person on this show before, so no, not really.

Enna-Jay: Can Bea just leave? SHOULD she?

KeyboardCat: No!! She still has good guys left!!

Beth.Malone: That's a hot take, Cat

KeyboardCat: I believe!! #TeamAsher

Beth.Malone: 🙄

Colin7784: jeez, you guys have been right this whole time

Beth.Malone: Yes definitely. About what?

Colin7784: men are trash

@AndersMMQB You all gave me shit when I said they shouldn't put a fat woman on Main Squeeze, but look what happened!
@AndersMMQB This isn't the UN, dummies. It's reality TV. If you put a fat cow on there, people are going to call her one. It's not Jefferson's fault for speaking the truth. It's Bea's fault for expecting anything different.

In the hour after Jefferson's outburst and Bea's dramatic exit, her greatest source of comfort was the lock on her bedroom door. The door itself was heavy and wood, stained dark and engraved with intricate latticework. The key was old-fashioned, thick and brass, and the lock emitted a satisfying click when Bea shut out the entire mess of her life.

Bea paced the floor beside the little settee where, just the night before, Luc had held her and assured her she was beautiful. What an idiot she'd been to believe he was telling the truth.

What did she know about these men, really? Luc was a player, Wyatt was lovely but a bit of a mystery, Sam was an exuberant kid, and Asher . . . Asher. Maybe he was just fooling himself. Maybe she was too.

It was after midnight now—their flight back to America departed in seven hours.

"I should pack," Bea said to no one in particular. But she didn't. She sat on her bed, still in her gown, her face in her hands. One breath in, another out. All those weeks of holding the men at bay, trying not to form attachments—as much as that hurt, it was better than this. She should have listened to Lauren.

She tried to convince herself that this was no big deal—after all, what was she really losing? They were just hopes. They'd been intense, maybe, but she could live without them. Put off her chances at happiness for another few weeks until all this was over, just as she'd done so many times before. Waiting to schedule dates until after she got home from this next trip, after she finished up this project, after she lost a little weight. After, always after, until her romantic life became a kind of stasis, cryogenically suspended in a perpetual state of anticipation.

After this show is over, my life will change. I'll meet so many new people. Maybe I'll find someone then.

And then, a knock on her door.

Go away.

Another knock.

"Bea, are you in there?"

Was that Sam?

"Of course she's there. The producers said as much."

And Asher.

"Dude, I know she's in there, but it's after midnight, I'm trying to be polite."

"Maybe she's sleeping?"

There was Wyatt.

"No, but you see, the light is on."

And Luc.

"Should we knock again?"

"Maybe she doesn't want to talk to us."

Silence, all of them listening. Bea didn't want to hate them.

"I think we should knock again."

But the loud click of the lock gave her away as she opened the big wooden door.

"Hi, guys."

There they were, still in their suits, ties undone, looking shades of relieved and apprehensive—and flanked by cameras and sound guys.

"What is this?" Bea asked, suspicious.

Sam took a tentative step forward. "Can we talk for a minute?"

As the men and the camera crew filtered into the room, Bea sank down onto the bed—Sam and Wyatt sat beside her. Luc lounged on the little settee, and Asher stood uncomfortably, surveying the scene. For a moment, they all looked at one another, totally unclear on who was meant to speak first. Finally, Luc broke the silence.

"Someone must say it. Jefferson was dull and self-important, and none of us liked him."

Wyatt shook his head. "Luc, that's not the point—"

"We cannot allow this, this, what is the word, for one who helps Saint Nicholas?"

"An elf?" Sam offered.

"*Oui, c'est ça,* we cannot let this nasty elf poison Bea's mind against us."

"Bea," Sam added, "what Jefferson said down there . . . it wasn't true, okay?"

Bea swallowed. "So you guys wouldn't be happy to have twenty-five women competing for you?"

"In other circumstances, of course we would." Luc's manner was easy as always. "But Bea, for us this is not winning. Being with you—this is what we want. This is why we are here."

"Jefferson was just angry," Wyatt piped in. "He wanted to hurt you."

"What can we do?" Sam asked. "How can we help you get past this?"

Bea just looked down, willing herself not to cry again. Sam gave her a little nudge, his shoulder against hers. She thought back to the hammam, his hands on her hips—that had been real, hadn't it? Not a trick of her mind, a lie for the cameras? It suddenly seemed impossible to know.

"I'm so sick of questioning everything—especially you guys," she admitted. "Since the first night, it's felt like I've been some kind of detective, always on guard, looking for signs that none of this is real. And now, with so few of you left, with how much I like you . . . it feels unhinged. What Jefferson said—I guess in a way that was easier to believe."

Wyatt looked concerned. "You'd rather believe we're all lying to you than that we all genuinely like you? Why, Bea?"

A tightness was forming in Bea's chest, like some deep and ugly piece of her was being excavated, tearing at her insides as it was dragged to the surface. "If you're lying to me, and the worst things I believe about myself are true, then . . . then I'm safe. Then none of you can really hurt me."

"We don't want to hurt you," Sam said softly.

Bea looked to Asher—of the four of them, he was the only one who had yet to speak.

"What if you do anyway?" she asked him. But he didn't answer—just reached into the pocket of his suit jacket.

"Bea, we don't want you to take our feelings on faith. We have something to ask you."

The rest of the men fumbled in their pockets, too, and Bea was puzzled when she saw what they'd come up with: tubes of ChapStick.

"What the . . . ?"

"You think you're the only one who can kiss cheeks and be all gallant?" Sam asked as they all slicked on their ChapStick. "We can be gallant, Bea."

"I can see that." Bea couldn't help laughing, even as tears leaked out of her eyes.

Then Wyatt stood—he offered Bea his hand and helped her to her feet—and the other men stood as well.

"Bea," Wyatt asked, "will you stay with me another week? I know this week has been exotic and all, but I think you're going to be pretty awed by my family's wheat fields."

Bea smiled. "Yes, I'll stay." Wyatt kissed her cheek. He stepped aside, and Sam approached her.

"Bea, my bea-tific bea-uty," Sam started.

"You're going to win me over with wordplay?"

"Absolutely, I am, because you're the Bea's knees." He grinned, and Bea laughed. "Bea, I love spending time with you, and I want you to meet my family. Will you stay with me another week?"

Bea nodded. "Yes, Sam." Another kiss. Sam moved to make room for Luc.

"Bea, this week for us was special. But I know there is better yet to come."

He took her hand and brought it to his lips—he kissed one finger, just as she had when he'd given her that perfect taste of saffron. She couldn't help but glance at Asher as Luc did this—she saw his jaw was set, his face hard. But there was nothing she could do about that now.

"Bea, you will stay with me another week?"

"I will." Luc kissed her cheek too.

And then there was just Asher—his lips tight, his posture rigid. Bea tensed up, wondering if they were about to rehash his jealousy of Luc. But as it turned out, he was upset about something else entirely.

"Do you doubt me?" he said. The room went quiet, and the tension level rose considerably.

"I don't want to," Bea said truthfully.

"Do you believe I would bring cameras into my home and let you meet my children if I wasn't serious about this—about you?"

"No." Bea's voice was barely above a whisper. "I know you wouldn't."

"I hate that men like Jefferson want to hurt you. Bea, I was so angry down there. But I will never give you a reason to believe him. I want you to meet my family. I want you, period. Stay with me, Bea. Okay? Stay."

Bea couldn't find words, but she nodded, and Asher wrapped her in a hug and kissed her on the cheek. In his arms, she closed her eyes, allowing herself to forget for just a moment about the other men in the room, the cameras watching them, and all her doubts.

——Forwarded Message——

FROM: Jefferson Derting <j.derting@gmail.com>
TO: MoroccanAir Baggage Retrieval Service<baggage @wegomorocco.com>
SUBJECT: RE: RE: RE: Lost baggage

Hello. After several emails and one two-hour phone call, I am *STILL WAITING* to hear what happened to my baggage. I flew back to the U.S. five days ago, and you people don't seem to have any idea what happened to my stuff. I was on *TELEVISION* for a month, so *ALL MY CLOTHES* were in that bag, in addition to a *VERY EXPENSIVE VINTAGE BE-SPOKE BEARD MAINTENANCE KIT* which I purchased *AT AUCTION*. Can you help me or not? I don't want to have to Yelp about this, so get back to me, comprende?

—Forwarded Message—

FROM: MoroccanAir Baggage Retrieval Service<baggage
@wegomorocco.com>
TO: Jefferson Derting <j.derting@gmail.com>
SUBJECT: RE: RE: RE: RE: Lost baggage

Dear Mr. Derting,

As best as we can surmise, the mix-up occurred during your
transfer in Madrid, at which time you boarded a flight bound
for the United States. Your baggage, however, continued on to
London, then Crete, then Bucharest, and finally Bratislava. At
that point, an associate identified it and had it flown to our
One Globe baggage retrieval center in Frankfurt. However,
due to a storm system in the area, I'm afraid that is where our
trail runs cold. It's possible your bag was received and logged
in Frankfurt, but the electrical blackout caused that record to
be deleted within our system; or it may simply never have arrived. We're working on that information and will report back
as soon as we can. We thank you very much for your patience,
and we would like to offer you complimentary beverages on
your next MoroccanAir flight. Have a pleasant day!

Our very best,
R.M.

R.M. Nostam
Baggage Retrieval Specialist
MoroccanAir Airlines
A Partner of the One Globe Alliance
One globe. One you. One planet.

⚮

I WENT TO THAT HOT *MAIN SQUEEZE* CHEF'S RESTAURANT SO YOU DON'T HAVE TO

by Leslie Curtin, eater.com

After last week's episode of *Main Squeeze*, no corner of the Internet was safe from discussion of one topic: French chef (slash International Hot Dude) Luc Dupond and his illicit night with Bea in Morocco. Did they sleep together, or did they *sleep* together? Is he on the show for the right reasons? And, most importantly—can the guy actually cook? This reporter braved the Snap-happy crowds at his restaurant, Canard Chanceux (that's French for "lucky duck"), to find out.

Spoiler alert? The answer is no.

If you're opening up a restaurant in downtown Manhattan, you're facing steep rent and stiff competition, which means you have one of two choices: Either you can cook outrageously good food that keeps the crowds coming back, or you can put out plates that look really, really, really good on Instagram. You want to take a wild guess which thing Canard Chanceux is doing?

And yes, I'll admit, it's fun to see your lamb lollipops ascend a spiral staircase made of freeze-dried frites while a column of foie-infused smoke (reader, I wish I was making that up) shoots up the middle. But you know what's more fun? *Eating food that tastes good.*

In Luc's defense, this isn't his restaurant, nor his concept (he was hired by the owners to replace the previous chef after a much-publicized embezzlement scandal). Who knows how well he would do if he were to achieve his dream of opening up his own place—a dream that's within reach now that he's become a quasi-celebrity. But one thing's unfortunately for sure: His fame will no doubt draw even greater hordes to a restaurant where everyone should photograph the food, but nobody, least of all you, should eat it.

Hometown week was the craziest shooting schedule of the season—four cities across America in just six days. Since there was neither time nor budget to go to Normandy to meet Luc's family this week, Bea was spending an afternoon with Luc in New York City to meet his friends and eat at his restaurant. Still smarting from his behavior in Morocco and questioning his motives, Bea told Alison she wanted to feel tough on this date—like a hot bitch you don't mess with. They settled on skintight Veda leather leggings paired with a silky black blouse (several buttons undone to reveal the lacy low-cut cami Bea wore underneath), spiky McQueen heels, and a luxe dark Baja East trench coat slung around her shoulders. They finished the look with bombshell waves, smoky eyes, big lashes, and soft, pouty lips—Bea thought it was the sexiest she'd looked all season.

As she stepped into the sleek mirrored foyer of the restaurant, Bea saw that Luc agreed with her assessment. He slipped the coat from her shoulders, letting his hands linger at her waist and slide down over her hips as he kissed her hello on the cheek.

"My God." His voice was throaty in her ear. "I wish today you were the meal."

"Then what would I eat?" Bea smiled and swept into the restaurant, leaving Luc to trail behind her.

The dining room was inky and angular, the chairs hard, the ceilings low, the surfaces dark and lacquered. The whole place had a sultry, subterranean feel—it made perfect sense to Bea

that this was the sort of restaurant where see-and-be-seen trad-
ers and club kids came to drop $1,000 on a Tuesday. At the
back of the room, a smoked glass wall gave a murky view of
the restaurant's kitchen, where prep for the evening was well
under way; they were filming this meal at 2 P.M. so as not to
interfere with that night's dinner service. Bea was so distracted
by the motion, energy, and chaotic order of the chefs and the
line cooks going through their routines, and the realization
that all these people reported to Luc, that she barely noticed
the table of his friends waiting to meet her.

"Everyone, this is Bea," Luc announced, and three of the
most attractive people Bea had ever seen turned to appraise her.

"Bea, I'm Stefania." A towering brunette with creamy ala-
baster skin and a crisp English accent rose to kiss Bea's cheek
and clasp her hands as if they were already old friends. "Luc
has been telling us about you."

"All good things, I hope?"

"Of course! He's absolutely smitten by you. But that's Luc,
isn't it? Never denies himself a pleasure."

"I've noticed that too." Bea threw Luc a little look, and he
grinned impishly back.

"And this is my partner, Isabeau."

Isabeau was a Black woman from Paris, and so chic Bea
thought she'd be right at home in the fashion world; her flowing silk pants hung low on her hips, and her hair was arranged
in swirls of Bantu knots.

"*Enchantée*—love your blouse." Isabeau kissed Bea's cheeks
as well.

"Thank you. Your slacks are fantastic."

"What, these?" Isabeau waved her hand dismissively. "I
made them in an afternoon."

"You're a designer?" Bea's eyes lit up.

"No, she's in marketing, of all things." Stefania rolled her eyes. "Just much more beautiful and talented than the rest of us."

"Not more than you, *chérie*." Isabeau grinned and kissed Stefania—Bea liked them both immediately.

The final member of their party was Boaz, who was Israeli and a chef as well. He and Luc came up together at "some shit fusion concept in Flatbush, all pretension, no flavor" (Boaz's words), but now he co-owned his own restaurant in Cobble Hill, a fact Luc noted with palpable envy.

"You too, soon enough," Boaz said to Luc, draping an arm about his shoulders and massaging his neck.

"Yes, but you have said this for years," Luc groused.

"But now you're a big TV star, eh?" Boaz winked at Bea. "You're making all his dreams come true."

Bea pressed her lips together—that was exactly why she was worried.

There was no time to say more about it, though, as servers arrived bearing platters of flaky white fish grilled with lemon and tomatoes, bowls of fresh greens in sour mustard dressing, and an overflowing pot of mouthwatering cassoulet.

"You see?" Boaz said to Luc. "This is what I've been telling you. For your place, forget all that Instagram shit. *This* is your food."

"This food isn't on your menu?" Bea asked.

"*Non*," Luc explained. "For you I wanted to make something more traditional, like what my mother would prepare if she were here."

"You should see the stuff he cooks here." Boaz laughed. "Everything a tower, tiny little portions stacked up high. He lets the presentation talk instead of the taste."

"*Mais non*, it's not my menu," Luc protested.

"Sure." Bea gave Luc a knowing look. "But even if you're

working at someone else's restaurant, wouldn't you rather be somewhere where you can make your own food? Don't you get tired of always pretending to be someone you're not?"

"I am not always pretending," he said softly. An awkward silence fell over the group.

"The fish is scrumptious." Stefania broke the tension. "Luc, do you remember when we went to that little place in Calais, what was it called?"

"Angelie Sur la Mer," Luc answered.

"Yes, Angelie by the sea!" she said, translating. "It was the quaintest little place, with a view of the cliffs, and the *fish*." She groaned with pleasure at the memory. "You could barely get Luc and me to leave our room, we hardly saw daylight, but when it was time for dinner, it was on with our things and out the door so fast your head would spin."

"This guy." Boaz laughed. "The only thing he loves more than sex is food."

Bea sighed. Of course Luc had slept with Stefania—of course.

"This depends on the food—and the sex." Luc grinned and kissed Bea's cheek, and the rest of the table laughed amiably when she blushed crimson. She was mortified. How many times was this man going to imply she'd slept with him when she hadn't?

"This poses an interesting question," Isabeau mused. "If you ask any of us which we prefer, the best meal of our lives or the best night of lovemaking, I am hard-pressed to think of anyone who'd choose the meal."

"I don't know," Bea countered. "I think I might."

"Really?" Isabeau looked intrigued.

"The memory of the sex is so much more subjective. If the person you had the wonderful sex with doesn't turn out to be so wonderful, the memory can become a source of pain." Bea shrugged. "But a really great cheeseburger is still a really great cheeseburger, no matter who was across from you when you ate it."

"This is your best meal?" Luc teased. "A cheeseburger? So American."

"Sorry to disappoint you." Bea met his eyes, only half-joking.

"Never," Luc responded. "But I am curious to know about this amazing night that has caused you so much pain."

Bea shook her head. "That's my point exactly. Some nights, you'd just as soon forget."

Luc raised his glass. "Then we must toast to nights we are glad to remember. And to people we are glad to have beside us, even if we are eating a cheeseburger."

The others raised their glasses in turn, and Luc leaned over to kiss Bea softly. As he pulled away, she searched his eyes, wondering how she could have spent so many hours with him and still feel she didn't know him at all.

After dinner and goodbyes, it was still light out—just after 5 p.m.—so Lauren decided that Bea and Luc should take a stroll along the High Line. It was a chilly day, so the promenade was fairly empty, but of the few joggers and tourists about, several gawked at Bea and Luc and their camera crew, and a few even paused to take photos. A harsh wind blew and the sun was beginning to set over New Jersey as Luc and Bea walked side by side.

"So," Luc said, breaking the silence, "did you enjoy the dinner? And the company?"

"The food and the people were lovely," Bea replied.

"Then why are you upset?"

"I'm not upset," Bea snapped.

Luc shot her a pointed look. "Upset and lying about it."

Bea exhaled. "I take it you and Stefania used to date."

"Yes, what of it?"

"I just didn't know I was going to meet someone you slept with today."

"Two people, *en fait.*"

Bea frowned. "Isabeau too?"

"*Non.*" Luc grinned at Bea, who couldn't help blushing as she took his meaning. "Does this bother you?"

"I just think you could have warned me that you were planning to introduce me to a string of your gorgeous exes."

"This is why you are unhappy? *Non,* but you were in a bad mood even before you met them, so this cannot be the reason."

"I was not in a bad mood." Bea scowled.

Luc smirked at her—totally not buying it. He took her by the shoulders.

"Come, say what you think. You are still upset about Jefferson?"

"No." Bea was so frustrated. "Maybe! I don't know."

"You think I am not being honest with you? Bea, we discussed all this in Morocco."

"When you came to my room in the middle of the night, you mean?"

Luc gestured meaningfully toward the cameras. "Perhaps we should not mention this?"

"Oh, come off it, the whole world knows. You made sure of that when you bragged about it to Asher, when you let him think we'd slept together. That was fun for me to deal with."

Luc closed his eyes—finally, the answer he was looking for.

"This is why you are angry."

"For starters," Bea fumed.

"Okay, good," he encouraged her. "*Dites-moi.* You tell me."

"You did the same thing today! All that talk of sex, letting your friends think I was another addition to their little club. You say this isn't a game to you, but you're treating it like one, Luc—like I'm a chess piece instead of a human being."

"Yes, of course! You are a prize, and I must have you." He grinned and tugged her hand, pulling her close—she shoved him away.

"You're not listening!" She exhaled in exasperation.

"Bea, yes I am." He pulled her back in. "I am sorry I made Asher jealous. After Ohio, he walked around every day with his little smirk, like you are his already. So I let him know, he is not the only one who has your affection. I did not think he would cry to you about it."

"Don't blame this on him," Bea chided. "He was really upset."

"*Alors,* perhaps I was too."

Bea frowned at him. "What did you have to be upset about?"

"Now who is not listening?" Luc asked.

Bea regarded him skeptically. "You were jealous of Asher? Seriously?"

"In Ohio, I met your family, we talked with your brothers, I am thinking, *Wow, this is good,* yeah? Then I see you in tears, you are running off to the woods with Asher, you are more passionate with him than you have ever been with me."

"And you wanted to get back at him." Bea shook her head, understanding. "But Luc, why would you do it by revealing something that could make me look bad? Especially since you were the one who came to my room to talk—I didn't invite you there."

He took her hands in his, lifted them so he could kiss them. "For this, I am really sorry, Bea. I did not think he would say something to you, let alone in front of the cameras. That was a little cruel, no?"

Bea sighed—she hated to admit that Luc had a point.

"And today?" Bea asked. "You weren't trying to make me feel—I don't know. Envious, or inferior, introducing me to those beautiful people you'd slept with?"

"Bea, these are just my friends," Luc entreated. He put her hands behind his neck, bringing her body to press against his. "I promise, they are not who I was imagining in my bed today."

"Oh?" Bea felt her body warm as his lips brushed her cheekbone, her hair. "And what makes you think I'd get in your bed after the way you've behaved?"

"Mm," Luc murmured. "If I've behaved badly, perhaps you should punish me."

"What?" Bea looked up at him, not sure what he was getting at.

"You are angry," he intoned. "With me, with Jefferson, with others, maybe. You feel we have all the power. The control. But in this show, Bea, you are the one controlling me—controlling all of us."

Bea shook her head. "It doesn't feel that way to me."

"Really?" Luc looked surprised. "You do not think of us, sitting in that mansion, or the hotel in Ohio, or the *riad* in Morocco, hours on end, dying with boredom, always talking about you, thinking about you, waiting to hear the next time we will see you? And then after we do, it is excruciating, replaying every moment, wondering what could have happened differently, if you will decide to let us stay or send us home. We are all enthralled to you, my Bea. And what is worse—I find that very much, I like it."

Bea laughed uncomfortably. "Luc, be serious."

He pulled her closer, and she pushed him back, but he pulled her in again, stronger—the struggle sparked with an erotic charge.

"I *am* serious." His eyes bored into hers. "It is so frustrating, watching you push this power away. I want to shout at you to take it, to feel it, to *use it*. To remember that you're the one in control."

"How?" she asked, her voice small. "How do you want me to use it?"

He held her gaze for a long moment, then took her right hand and brought it to his cheek, slowly moving his face against her palm so she could feel the heat of his skin, the rough scratch of his whiskers.

"Hit me," he whispered.

"What?!" Bea yanked her hand back. "You're insane."

"You have never done this before? A little slap?"

"Um, no, Luc. I haven't."

His eyes flashed. "A virgin."

"You're being ridiculous."

"And you are afraid." He stepped closer. "When Jefferson said these awful things about you, you said it was easier to believe him because if he is right, and we do not care about you, then you can't really be hurt. But this is not the real reason you believed him."

"What do you mean?" Bea asked, not sure she wanted to know.

"The truth is, you believed him because this is how you see yourself. But it is not how I see you. And I want you to know how it feels to be this woman I see."

His breath was hot, his hands were strong, always pulling at her, always pushing.

"I don't want to be a joke," she whispered.

"You aren't one." He nipped at her ear. "I promise."

She looked up at him—this was crazy.

"What if I hurt you?"

"We are only human," he urged. "We hurt each other all the time."

Adrenaline coursed through her as she took a step back, never breaking eye contact with Luc. "You're sure?"

He gave her the barest grin. "*Oui, mademoiselle.*"

Bea smiled. "Okay, then."

She brought back her hand and let it fly.

TRANSCRIPT OF CHAT FROM #SQUEEZE-MAINIACS SLACK CHANNEL

Colin7784: HOLY SHIT, SHE SLAPPED HIM

Beth.Malone: COLIN, NO SPOILERS THE EPISODE ISN'T EVEN OVER YET

Colin7784: Sorry sorry holy shit

NickiG: What the hell just happened

KeyboardCat: I am so turned on right now

Enna-Jay: HE'S KISSING HER HE'S KISSING HER AGAINST A WALL

NickiG: This is the best television of my life

Beth.Malone: Guys, come on, PLEASE NO SPOILERS

Colin7784: We're literally all here watching right now, who would we even be spoiling?

Beth.Malone: The rules are important! They have to mean something!

NickiG: Lol ok Mistress Beth

Beth.Malone: Oh my god, please never call me that again

Colin7784: Or what? Will you punish us, Mistress Beth?

Beth.Malone:

Colin7784: 😈

Enna-Jay: 🔗

NickiG: 👠

Beth.Malone: 🙄

KeyboardCat: 😼

FLYER POSTED IN THE BOONE, OKLAHOMA, FARM SUPPLY MART

TOMORROW: TRACTOR PARADE
HIGHWAY 47-12PM
WELCOME HOME WYATT
FROM MAIN SQUEEZE!!!!

BRING FOOD
IF YOU WANT

Wyatt had promised Bea a tractor if she visited his family's farm, but when she met him at the main street in the center of Boone, she found he'd done her one better: There was a parade of a *dozen* tractors flanked by hundreds of onlookers—it seemed the whole town had shown up to wish Wyatt well and meet the girl he'd brought home.

"Oh my gosh." Bea laughed as he helped her climb into the gleaming red tractor beside him. "This is unbelievable!"

"There are farms where you're from—no one's ever taken you to a tractor parade?"

"No one." Bea threaded her arm through his. "You're my first."

Bea hadn't meant the line to be a double entendre, but from the way Wyatt blushed and looked away, she worried she'd embarrassed him. They still hadn't really talked about his virginity, about why he hadn't had sex or what that might mean for their potential relationship. But given how much faster things were progressing with the other three men in that department (particularly in light of the incredibly sexy afternoon she'd spent making out with Luc pressed up against a brick building on the Chelsea High Line), Bea knew they'd have to discuss it today—just hopefully not in front of Wyatt's family.

Bea and Wyatt leaned out of their respective tractor windows and waved to the crowd, who cheered and even shouted their names. After they'd made their loop on the tractor, Wyatt helped Bea down so they could mingle with the crowd and enjoy some lemonade.

"You can't eat any of that potluck, though," Wyatt told Bea. "There'll be hell to pay with my mom if we don't come home hungry."

The group at the tractor parade was warm and unpretentious, and it was such a relief to be seen as normal, to *feel* normal, even in the midst of a parade thrown in her honor.

Back at the farm for lunch, though, the pressure was a little higher as Bea met Wyatt's mother, Hattie, his sister, Peg, her husband, Miguel, and their two kids.

"Have you tried the bread yet?" asked Hattie. "We make it with the wheat we grow right here on the farm."

"It's amazing." Bea could barely speak through the mouthful of warm, fresh brown bread. Maybe she'd given farm living short shrift after all.

"That recipe has been in our family for four generations,"

Hattie explained. "Now, what about you, Bea—do you bake? I know you can eat!"

Hattie laughed good-naturedly—she was no small woman herself.

"Mom," Wyatt warned, but Bea put a hand on his arm.

"No, Mrs. Ames, I'm not much for baking. I'm more of a cook than a baker—and not much of a cook either, I'm afraid."

"What about your mother, then? Didn't she cook?"

"My mom made a lot of casseroles, pasta, burgers, things like that. I have three older brothers, so we went through a lot of food. On two teachers' salaries, we had to be economical."

Hattie nodded her approval. "That's one thing Bill and I always tried to teach our kids. No sense spending what you haven't got—that's a quick way to hand your life over to the bank."

"Will you tell me more about Bill?" Bea asked. She knew from Wyatt that his dad had died nearly a decade ago after a sudden stroke.

"He was a good man." Hattie smiled, her eyes misting slightly. "I know we always say that about the dead, but with Bill, it was true. You know the Bible commands farmers to leave the corners of their fields to feed the hungry?"

"Old Testament, right?"

"That's right, good girl," Hattie approved. "Most farmers around here would never take that literally—times are tight, and what good does it do anyone to leave your crops untended? What are the hungry supposed to do, come chew on your wheat? But Bill, he measured out the corners of our farm, just as the Bible commands, and every year, he took whatever money we made from the wheat in those four corners and gave it straight to the food bank. Can you imagine?"

"That's a beautiful tradition," Bea said gently.

"Bill always wanted to see Wyatt get married and have some babies. He got to walk Peg down the aisle, and we'll always be grateful for that. But for a father, seeing his only son start a family of his own? Well, that's something special. I know he'd be very happy about this today, Bea. Yes, I do know that."

Bea thought it was a lovely sentiment, but out of the corner of her eye, she noticed Wyatt's face was ashen.

After lunch was finished, Bea and Wyatt split up with the two camera teams so everyone could discuss their impressions of one another: Wyatt and Hattie sat on the front porch, and Wyatt's sister, Peg, took Bea for a walk in her vegetable garden.

"Those are little gems, and that's kale," Peg said, pointing out her various greens.

"I live in Los Angeles, we know a lot about kale," Bea joked.

"Mm." Peg's droll manner was impossible to read. "So how are things going, with you and my brother?"

"Wyatt's really wonderful." Bea smiled. "With the other men, I feel so vulnerable, but he just makes me feel—I don't know. Protected, somehow."

Peg knelt down to pull up some fresh radishes. "Did you know that Wyatt has never brought a girl home before?"

Bea frowned. "No, I didn't know that."

"Mm. He's a private person, doesn't like to talk about who he's dating. You understand we were pretty surprised when he told us he was going off to date a stranger on TV."

"Sure," Bea agreed, not certain where this was going.

"I guess my point is, back when he told us he was going on the show, we weren't sure why. Now here we are, all these weeks later, watching him on TV every Monday—and I'm still not sure. Are you?"

"He's here to find love," Bea insisted. "Same as I am."

Peg shrugged. "If you say so."

As Bea and Peg made their way back to the house, Bea thought back to all her interactions with Wyatt: his kindness the first night of shooting, the way he helped her open up at the prom by bravely opening up himself, their easy manner together, the sweet way he kissed her. Their connection was real, wasn't it? And it was romantic . . . wasn't it?

Bea had thought that Wyatt's virginity was his biggest secret. But after this day, and these conversations, she was starting to realize that maybe it wasn't.

The sun would be setting soon, so the producers took Bea and Wyatt out into the fields for their final shot of the day: a passionate goodbye kiss. After that, they'd fly back to New York to spend the night, then get up at the crack of dawn to do the whole thing again with Asher in Vermont tomorrow. It was a punishing schedule—Bea was jealous that Lauren had opted to skip this day and leave the Oklahoma shoot in the hands of some junior producers. Bea knew she'd probably spent the entire time editing, but still, the notion of a day off from filming sounded like heaven.

"How you holding up?" Wyatt asked as the camera guys made what seemed like the millionth adjustment to their lighting gear.

"I'm okay." Bea nodded wearily. "You?"

He nodded back, but there was something strained in his smile.

"All right," one of the camera guys shouted, "we are ready to GO!"

Which, of course, was when the generator blew and the whole field went dark. Producers and crew scurried in every direction screaming about backup gennys and how quickly this could get fixed—the delay was annoying, but Bea realized almost immediately what it meant: For the first time, she could have a conversation with Wyatt that wouldn't be overheard.

"Hey," she said softly, "why didn't you tell me you'd never brought a girl home before?"

"I didn't want to put any more pressure on you," he replied. "Everyone asks so much from you here. I never wanted that to be me."

Bea felt a surge of affection for him, how he always went out of his way to be so kind to her. But there was still a question she knew she needed to ask, however painful the answer might be.

"Wyatt, I know we haven't really talked about, um, why you've chosen not to sleep with anyone yet. And obviously that's personal and entirely your choice. But I do need to know, I guess, whether that's something you want? With me?"

Wyatt looked down, and Bea felt her stomach clench. She knew he wasn't like Jefferson, wasn't leading her on for his own selfish purposes—but if he didn't want her, while these other three men seemingly did, then she had to know the truth.

"It's okay," she assured him. "If you don't feel that way about me, you can just tell me."

"It isn't that," Wyatt said quickly.

"Then what?" Bea pressed. "Are you worried about having sex for some reason? Believe me, I've been there—you know how afraid I've been with men. We can work through that together, if that's what you want."

"No." Wyatt shook his head. "I'm not afraid."

Wyatt had shown her, again and again, that he was her true friend. Bea thought of his mother at lunch, how happy she'd seemed to think her son had finally found love—how upset Wyatt had looked in that moment. And suddenly, it clicked into place: what Wyatt was doing here, why he'd never brought a girl home, why she was so comfortable with him in a way she wasn't with any of the other men.

"Wyatt, are you gay?"

He looked up in surprise.

"Oh my God, I'm so sorry," she blurted. "I don't know why I thought it was okay to just say that, I'm being so inappropriate—"

"No, no"—he took her hand—"Bea, I'm not gay."

"Oh." Bea nodded. "Oh, okay."

He sighed and looked out at the fields for a long moment.

"I've thought about it. I mean, I always thought, one day, I would meet a girl I'd want to date. And when I never met her, not in high school or college, I thought, okay, well, maybe I like guys? But I never met a guy I wanted to date either. So I figured, when I met the right person one day, I would know. But I never did."

"And that's why you came on the show?" Bea prompted. "To see if you could find that person?"

Wyatt nodded. "I watched the show a couple times, and it seemed like romance was just *everywhere*, you know? Like this was a story about knights and princesses, but in real life—and I thought, I don't know. Like how sometimes if you're trying not to get a cold, you take a really big dose of Vitamin C? I thought coming here would be a really big dose of romance, something to jump-start feelings I was sure must be buried inside me. And if I could go on these fairy-tale dates with a girl like you, maybe then I would finally understand this thing that comes so natural for everyone else."

Bea looked at him sadly. "But you haven't, have you?"

"No." He exhaled deeply. "I think I finally have to be honest with myself and admit that all this romance stuff—and sex, and kissing, even—it's just not for me. When I kissed you, I thought, she's so pretty, and I like her so much, but this isn't the way I want to be with her—or with anyone. You know? It just wasn't the right way."

He was shaky with nerves, and Bea thought he might even be close to tears.

"All these years," he said, his voice hoarse, "I've felt like I was half a person. Like this part of me that should be there just . . . wasn't."

"Hey." Bea squeezed his arm. "I don't think that makes you half a person, not at *all*. You're one of the best people I've ever met, and this is just a piece of who you are, you know? A piece I feel really honored you shared with me, for the record."

"I just don't want to disappoint my family," he sighed. "You saw how much my mom wants me to get married. It kills me that I can't give that to her."

"I know our situations are different, but I feel a version of that with my family too," Bea said softly. "My parents say they're not disappointed in me, and I believe them, but I know how much they want this for me. And not just them—all my fans, everyone watching this show. I'm terrified I'm going to end up alone and disappoint every single person who's invested in me finding love. Even though of course I know you can live a totally full life without a relationship—Wyatt, you're proof of that."

Wyatt pulled back to look at her, a curious expression on his face.

"What if you and I did find love?"

Bea peered at him, not understanding. "I'm not sure what you mean?"

"Listen," Wyatt said, his voice urgent, "this would be only if you want, but you could keep me around—on the show, I mean. And then, if you want to be with one of the other men, then that's great, Bea. But if you don't, then I could propose, and you could be with me. Not forever—not really. But for the end of the show, and a little while after."

"My happy ending," Bea murmured.

"Exactly."

"But Wyatt, I don't want you to lie about who you are. Besides, don't you think it would hurt your mom even more to see you get engaged and then have it not work out?"

Wyatt shook his head. "If we got engaged, and my mom got to see it—I think that'd make her happy, at least for a little while. And if it was a kindness I could do for you? That would make me happy too."

Bea thought back to her first night on the show, her gut instinct that Wyatt could be her perfect Prince Charming. Now, all these weeks later, here he was, offering her everything she'd come into this experience to find: a kind, honest, gorgeous man to hold her hand and walk together through the treacherous waters of trolls and critics and make the world see her as beautiful. As beloved.

When the generator finally came back online, Bea had no trouble at all kissing Wyatt passionately as the sunset turned the whole field incandescent. It might not be true love, but here, in this approximation of reality, maybe it was close enough.

✺

EXCERPTS FROM RATEMYPROFESSOR.COM: ASHER CHANG-REITMAN

RobF19: DO NOT BE LATE WITH PAPERS FOR ACR. He doesn't care about your dog, or your cold, or whatever crisis got in the way last-minute. He gives you lots of lead-time for the assignments, so if you don't get started early enough, he doesn't give a fuuuuuuuuuuck. No excuses for this dude. Believe me, I have *tried*.

AliS18: Hottest prof in the history department for sure. Won't flirt though, which is lame.

MarcusT17: Have you seen him on TV? Maybe he just won't flirt with YOU.

YahelC19: Or with any students???? Bc that's disgusting????????

AliS18: Nothing he does could ever be disgusting

MarcusT17: Ugh but you are

AliS18: Shut up Marcus you're just jealous.

Bea was incredibly nervous to meet Asher's children, but first, it was time to meet his students: She was sitting in on a meeting of his upper-level seminar on the history of Asian immigration to the United States from 1850 to 1900. The class was in a snug room with a walnut conference table and big picture windows overlooking the trees outside; Bea's heart jumped as she walked in and saw Asher in his jeans and button-down, looking even more handsome than she remembered.

"What, no tweed blazer?" she joked. "You're ruining my hot-professor fantasy."

He grinned as he came toward her, wrapping her in a huge

hug—she was thrilled and relieved that he seemed much more at ease than he had in Morocco.

"Guess you'll have to settle for an average-looking-professor reality," he quipped.

Bea took her seat at the conference table as a handful of junior and senior history majors filtered in, all of whom seemed largely unfazed by the interloping cameras in their midst.

"Okay." Asher clapped his hands to begin class. "I'm sure you've all missed me dearly over the last month, but I trust Professor LaBruyere has been an able substitute?"

The kids mumbled a halfhearted assent, and Asher laughed.

"Damning by faint praise—and on television, no less. You guys are brutal."

The kids settled in, and Asher began his lecture on the little-known involvement of Asian American soldiers in the Civil War, detailing firsthand accounts he'd read from diaries and military transcripts to piece together the movements of a particular unit in the Union Army that had been led by a Chinese corporal.

"Did any Asian soldiers fight for the Confederacy?" one kid asked.

"What do you think?" Asher turned the question back on the class. "How would that have worked?"

"It wouldn't have," said one girl with flowing blond hair and a navy-blue fleece. "The Confederacy had a law against nonwhite soldiers."

"Yeah, until 1865, when they were about to lose," countered another girl—she was Black and wore horn-rimmed glasses. "But Asian people weren't legally categorized as a race back then. So that made it trickier."

"That's exactly right," Asher confirmed. "Have any of you heard of Chang and Eng Bunker?"

The students looked back blankly, but Bea smiled; finally, she knew an answer.

Asher didn't miss her look—he never missed anything.

"Bea?" he asked, a smile twitching on his lips.

"They were conjoined twins from Thailand who came to America to tour in freak shows," she responded, remembering watercolor and charcoal portraits of the pair she'd studied in one of her own college classes a decade prior. "They're the reason we use the phrase 'Siamese twins.'"

Asher beamed with pride. "Precisely. After they finished touring, Chang and Eng settled in North Carolina, where they married local sisters, fathered twenty-one children, and? What else do you think they did, being rich men in North Carolina in the 1850s?"

The blond girl shook her head. "They bought slaves."

"Yes." Asher nodded. "In the Civil War, two of Chang and Eng's sons, Christopher and Stephen, fought to protect their fathers' rights to retain slave ownership. They were two of five Asian soldiers we know of who fought for the Confederacy."

Bea was awed. Ever since she'd met him, she'd thought of Asher's manner as tense and halting, but maybe that was just his discomfort in being so far out of his element. Seeing him here, so relaxed and charismatic, she felt an even stronger pull toward him—and that much more nervous for how the rest of their day would play out.

After the class wrapped up, they took a walk through the bucolic Middlebury campus, colonial buildings nestled among dense lawns and evergreen trees.

"You seem really at home here," she told him.

"It's been the perfect place for me," he said, taking her hand. "When I finished my PhD, I was on my own with two small kids, and I didn't have time to take on a tenure-track position. The lecture job here was a perfect compromise. I get to do what I love, but still have time to be a dad."

"That's wonderful." Bea squeezed his hand. "Do you think you're here for the long haul?"

Asher stopped walking—Bea turned to look at him.

"No, actually."

"Oh?"

"I wasn't sure when to tell you this," he said, "but I guess now's as good a time as any. Now that my kids are older, I've been thinking it's time to go for tenure. There aren't any open positions here, so we'll be moving in the fall."

"Do you know where?"

"I have offers in hand from Michigan and Columbia." He paused. "And USC."

"As in . . . ?"

"L.A."

"Oh," Bea breathed.

"Obviously, I have a lot of factors to consider. What's good for my career, for the kids—and I know my parents would be really happy to have me in New York; they're still in Westchester."

"Of course," Bea agreed. "That all makes sense."

He took her hands. "But I'm thinking about it. Okay?"

Bea nodded. "Okay."

During the afternoon break from filming, as she changed into form-fitting jeans and a burgundy Marc Jacobs cashmere sweater with a V-neck just low enough to reveal the barest hint of cleavage ("Very hot mom," Alison observed), Bea tried to convince herself that tonight's dinner was just another in a long series of dates on this show. But standing on Asher's stoop with wrapped gifts in tow and cameras at her back, Bea felt the weight of this night bearing down on her—not only what could happen if it didn't go well, but what it might mean if it did.

She'd barely touched the doorbell before she heard a scream of "I'LL GET IT I'LL GET IT" and a stampede of feet from inside the house—the door swung open and there was Linus wearing big glasses, a Spider-Man sweatshirt, dark leggings, and an absolutely lavish tutu.

"Are you Bea?" he asked, not standing aside to let her in.

"Yes." She matched his solemn tone. "Are you Linus?"

He nodded.

"I really like your tutu," Bea said, and he brightened immediately.

"It's blue, for boys! Come in, we're having CHICKEN," he screamed, and ran inside, leaving the door wide open in his wake.

"Hi, hi, I'm so sorry." Asher rushed to the door, wearing an apron and oven mitts. "I was just getting the chicken out of the oven. Can I take your coat?"

"With those things on your hands?" Bea laughed. "I'm good—just point me to the closet."

Bea had pictured Asher's abode as a neatly organized modernist palace—clean lines, little clutter—but of course, that wasn't a realistic notion of any home with children. In reality, the house was bright and chockablock, stuffed with books and knickknacks and sporting equipment, not to mention rogue dress-up costumes and dance outfits. Leon Bridges played on a vintage turntable, and Linus twirled around the living room while Asher finished making dinner in the open galley kitchen.

"Can I get you some wine?" he offered.

"Please," Bea responded, just as Linus called to her, "Bea, come dance with me!"

Asher threw an apologetic look to Bea. "Buddy, Bea just got here, what if we let her sit down for a minute?"

"I love dancing." Bea made her way past a cameraman to join Linus, but a loud throat-clearing stopped her.

"*Ahem.*"

Bea turned to see a twelve-year-old standing on the stairs, and she was indeed Asher in miniature: same rigid posture, same black glasses, same vaguely contemptuous expression. If it hadn't been for her glossy chin-length hair and fringe of dark, thick bangs, Bea could easily have mistaken Gwen for a younger version of her father.

"How soon is dinner?" Gwen asked curtly, looking only at Asher, and deliberately avoiding any eye contact with Bea.

"I'm just finishing up," Asher said. "Do you want to come down here and join us?"

"No thanks, I have homework." Gwen turned and retreated up the stairs. "Tell me when it's ready."

"Will do," Asher called after her, but her bedroom door was already shut.

"So, that was Gwen." Asher smiled as he made his way over to Bea, glass of wine in hand—she gladly took a drink.

"I think she liked me," Bea joked nervously, hoping this night wasn't ruined before it had even begun.

Asher kissed her cheek. "Don't worry. She'll come around."

Bea leaned against him and tried to relax. If Asher wasn't freaking out, she certainly didn't need to. But a few minutes later, when the table was set and ready to go, Gwen still hadn't come downstairs. Asher shouted for her for the third time, his annoyance starting to show.

"Gwen, come *on*. We're eating!"

"I had a worksheet to finish," she said matter-of-factly as she walked downstairs, but she paused when she hit the ground-floor landing. "What are those?"

She nodded toward the gifts Bea had left on the table in the entryway—Bea got up to retrieve them.

"They're for us?" Gwen asked.

Linus gasped. "*Presents,*" he whispered, his eyes growing wide behind his giant glasses.

"I was going to wait until after dinner, but . . ." Bea made eye contact with Asher, who nodded.

"You can open them now, but quickly. Aren't you guys as hungry as I am?"

"No!" Linus exclaimed as he tore through the paper on his gift—but Gwen just held hers in silence as she took her seat at the table, making no move to unwrap it.

"Richard Ave-don," Linus sounded out the name. "Who's that?"

"It's pronounced Ah-ve-don," Bea said gently, opening the oversized book of photos she'd bought for him. "He's one of the most famous fashion photographers ever. Some of his pictures are even in museums."

"No way." Linus turned the pages delicately. "Like the museum you went to with Dad?"

"Exactly." Bea grinned and caught Asher's eye. "Your dad told me you really like clothes, like I do. These were some of my favorite pictures when I was your age, so I thought you might like them too."

Linus gave Bea a tight hug—well, as tight as his tutu would allow—and she closed her eyes, feeling the weight of his small frame nestled against her. When she looked up, she saw that Asher was watching them, his eyes full of emotion.

But across the table, Gwen regarded Bea with distaste.

"Did you think this was all you needed to do?" she asked. "You bring us presents, we'll want you to be our new mother?"

"Gwen!" Asher exclaimed.

"What?" Gwen's tone was impassive. "It's true, isn't it?"

"It's not," Bea interjected softly. "Obviously, I don't expect you to set your opinion about me based on gifts. We're supposed to be spending time getting to know each other—that's what tonight is for."

"Why did you bring the gifts, then?"

"To make a good impression." Bea smiled. "And you see? My plan worked flawlessly."

There was a moment of stillness as Gwen looked at Bea, appraising her. Bea held her gaze . . . and then Gwen unwrapped her gift: a DVD of the 1938 classic movie *Bringing Up Baby*.

"It's one of my all-time favorites," Bea explained, "and I thought you might like it too."

"Why would you think that?" Gwen wrinkled her nose. "It looks like a romance."

"It is," Bea admitted, "but Baby is a leopard—the leopard is Katharine Hepburn's pet, and it gets loose, so there's a whole thing about that, and your dad, um. He told me you like leopards? Cary Grant plays a museum director, and there's a dog who steals a dinosaur bone, so . . ."

Bea looked to Asher for help, but he shrugged apologetically. "I've never seen it."

"So Dad told you about my research project." Gwen turned over the DVD in her hands. "I take it you two talk a lot about Linus and me?"

"Of course we do," Bea replied. "He's really proud of you guys."

"But in Morocco, you told him you didn't know if you were ready to be a mom."

"Gwen," Asher warned, "that's between Bea and me, okay?"

"No, it isn't," Gwen corrected him sharply. "It was on TV—everyone knows. And it concerns us, Dad. What if Bea decides to walk out on us like Mom did?"

Bea drew in a sharp breath—this was the most she'd heard about the circumstances of Asher's divorce, and in truth, she was dying to know more.

"This is neither the time nor the place to discuss that." Asher's tone was terse, and Bea noticed a flush of anger creeping into his skin.

"Then when is?" Gwen demanded. "This is our only time to meet Bea, and we're supposed to say 'Oh goody, can't wait for her to move in' by the end of dinner?"

Asher moved to respond, but Bea put a hand on his arm to stop him.

"Hey," she said to Gwen and Linus, "did you guys know my biological father left our family when I was a baby?"

The two kids turned to look at her, Linus's eyes wide, Gwen's narrow.

"That wasn't your dad in Ohio?" Linus asked.

"That was my stepdad," Bea explained. "He and my mom got together when I was four, so as far as I'm concerned, he's my real dad. They didn't show this on TV, but that day at my parents' house, I got really sad—I went and hid in my room, and my parents came to find me. I told them I was scared that I would never fall in love, that I would always be alone."

Asher looked at her, his expression pained.

"What did they say?" Linus asked.

"My stepdad told me that if I wanted to get married, I couldn't just fall in love. He said I had to choose someone to be my family, and that they had to choose me back. He said that was how it felt with our family—that we didn't just happen. We chose each other. Do you know what I did right after that?"

Gwen looked up at Bea, piecing it together. "You went to talk to Dad."

"Yeah." Bea swallowed hard. "That was when I told him how I felt about him, and it was when he told me about you guys."

"I didn't know that," Asher said quietly. She turned to him, hoping she could convey with her expression how much that moment had meant to her—and how much this one did.

"I know what a big deal this is for you, Gwen, I promise," Bea assured her. "But I want you to know that, for me, this is about us deciding if we all want to choose each other. Not just me, and not just your dad, but both of you too. All of us have to choose together. I can't speak for your dad, but I know I would never feel comfortable joining your family if all four of us didn't agree it was the right thing to do. Okay?"

Gwen looked at Bea for a long moment . . . then nodded. "Okay."

"Do you have any other questions?" Bea asked. "I'll do my best to answer everything."

"Hey guys," Asher said gently, "do you think we can stop grilling Bea for a minute so we can eat? The food is getting cold."

The kids nodded, and for a few moments, the only sound was forks and knives scraping on plates as they all started eating. Then Gwen looked up at Asher.

"You're home tomorrow, right?"

Asher nodded. "I leave for New York on Saturday."

"Can we watch Bea's movie tomorrow night, then? So you can tell her whether we liked it next time you see her."

"That sounds like a great plan," Asher agreed. He looked up and caught Bea's eye across the table. With the smallest of smiles, he mouthed the words, *I told you.*

"Cool," Gwen said, then went back to her chicken and mashed potatoes like nothing big had just happened, like this hadn't suddenly become one of the best nights of Bea's entire life.

Bea couldn't believe she was only two weeks away from this whole insane experience being over; she also couldn't believe how, well, *okay* everything seemed considering how shaken she'd been by the Jefferson meltdown just a week ago. Bea's spirits were high as she pulled up to meet Sam on the steps of Shirley Chisholm Elementary in downtown Newark, where he'd spent two years teaching, and where he still volunteered coaching the girls' basketball team.

"Hey, beautiful." He wrapped Bea in a tight hug. "I missed you this week."

"I missed you too." She realized the words were true as she kissed him hello.

"I don't want to bring us down right away, but I do have some bad news I need to share."

"Yeah? What's up?"

"On our last date, at the hammam, I took off my clothes to impress you—"

"Oh, is that what happened?"

"Yeah, and it worked too." Sam grinned.

"Okay," Bea teased, "confidence, I like that. So what's the bad news?"

"Well"—Sam affected a hushed, serious tone—"this is a place of *learning*. For *children*. So I think it behooves us both to keep our clothes on."

"Maybe we should just go back to Morocco." Bea leaned close to him.

"I think that's a really good idea," he whispered, then pulled her in for a kiss. "We just gotta do something first."

"Oh?" Bea raised an eyebrow, and Sam took her hand and led her through mural-covered hallways toward the school gym. She expected he might introduce her to the basketball team, but when he opened the door, she saw the room was absolutely packed with people—dozens of adults and kids sitting in rows of folding chairs with a long aisle spaced out in the middle—and they all started clapping and shouting as Bea and Sam walked in.

"You guys doing all right?" Sam shouted, to general assent.

"Sam, what is this?" Bea asked as he escorted her to a seat in the front row.

Sam stood in front of the audience, and spoke into a handheld microphone. "Bea, when I told the girls on the basketball team I coach that you were coming to visit, and suggested that maybe we could do something special to welcome you, they said, 'Coach Sam, tell us about Bea. Who is she? What does she like?'"

The whole audience turned toward Bea as if to divine this information by looking at her, but Sam kept going.

"And I told them, 'Bea is a very beautiful, very funny, very smart lady. And she loves fashion—she writes about fashion for her job.' The kids loved that. So they wanted to know if they could welcome you to our town with their very own fashion show."

On cue, the lights changed in the gym, Lizzo started blaring over the gym's loudspeakers, and the aisle between the rows of chairs turned into a makeshift catwalk.

"Oh my God!" Bea cheered and applauded as each little girl strutted her stuff down the aisle, all while Sam served as emcee.

"Keria is wearing a hand-draped outfit, that's her nod to traditional Grecian dresswear," he explained as a little girl with a very fierce attitude worked her bedsheet creation.

"Keria, that looks *excellent*," Bea shouted, and Keria tossed her hair and spun in a perfectly timed pivot when she hit the end of the runway.

"Sam, where did you learn about Grecian draping?" Bea called to him.

"I read about it on a very informative blog," he answered, and Bea flushed with pride.

When the show was over, the kids and their families all crowded around for pizza and juice, and Sam introduced Bea to his many adoring former students and colleagues.

"It's a good thing Sam found some ten-year-old girls to play ball with, because he cannot hold his own on the court," one middle-aged teacher ribbed.

"Easy now, I've got some game," Sam retorted.

"Oh yeah? What do you think, Bea? Does Sam have game?" The teacher winked in Bea's direction, and she turned to Sam and grinned.

"I don't know, Sam. Maybe you should show me this supposed game of yours."

"You want to see my game?" Sam called out. "What do you guys think, should I show Bea I've got some game?"

The crowd cheered, and Bea thought he was going to go off and find a basketball, but she was absolutely shocked when he took her in his arms and kissed her instead. It wasn't a quick peck either—it was a long, sexy kiss while he dipped Bea backward like they were old-time Hollywood stars and this was the grand finale. The crowd whooped and whistled, and Bea could feel herself blushing bright red, but she also reveled in the moment, how good it felt to kiss Sam.

"So, what do you think?" he asked softly as he lifted her to her feet.

"I concede it." Bea kissed him again, gently. "You've got game."

That night, Bea was meeting Sam's family for dinner at their home in Short Hills. Though just twenty minutes away, the wealthy town was a far cry from the crowded, vibrant streets of downtown Newark. These avenues were wide and tree-lined, and the colossal houses were set so far back that Bea could barely make them out in the lingering daylight.

"Holy shit," Bea gasped as they went through the gate and up the long driveway of Sam's family's house—it was a gorgeous whitewashed brick colonial with dark shutters and a copper roof that had faded to a deep, rich patina.

"You're judging me a little less for crashing with my parents now, aren't you?" Sam laughed as he met Bea on the porch.

Walking into the lavish home filled with sculpted ceilings, wood-paneled walls, generously proportioned furniture, and a staggering art collection, Bea was thankful she'd changed her clothes for dinner. Jeans were fine for a tour of an elementary school, but now Sam was wearing trim charcoal slacks and a dark silk sweater, and Bea was glad to look equally presentable in wide-cut raspberry pink Prabal Gurung trousers paired with a crisp red shirt.

"You look like Valentine's Day." Sam kissed Bea on the cheek.

"Does that mean you're going to be mine?" Bea teased.

"I hope so." Sam was all bravado as usual, but Bea couldn't help but notice how full of anxious energy he seemed as he led her into the formal dining room, where his family was waiting.

Sam introduced Bea to his father, Steve, a vice president of a big Wall Street brokerage firm, and his mother, Claudette, who was the chief cardiac surgeon at Mountainside Hospital. His sisters, Zoe and Jessica, had joined as well. They were an imposing group: razor-sharp, impeccably dressed, each more accomplished than the next. Bea understood how living with these people could give you an inferiority complex—she felt a sudden rush of appreciation for her own family and their simple, unyielding support for one another.

Steve and Claudette employed a cook, who'd prepared a gorgeous spread of salmon roasted with oranges, asparagus, and scalloped potatoes. They ate at an antique Queen Anne table and drank Sancerre from balloon glasses made of crystal. Bea enjoyed it all as much as she possibly could while praying, quite fervently, that she wouldn't spill.

"So, Bea, where were you at school?" Steve asked as he helped himself to another glass of wine.

"UCLA," Bea answered. "I studied art history there and at the Sorbonne my junior year—Paris is still my favorite city."

"You go back often?" Jessica asked.

"I do, for work."

"Bea writes about fashion," Sam said proudly.

"Really?" Claudette looked mildly impressed. "For one of the magazines?"

"No, I have my own site."

"Very entrepreneurial of you," Steve commended her. "You'll have to lend Sam some of your industrious spirit."

"Dad," Sam objected, but Steve rolled on.

"Tell us, Bea, if you hadn't made a career for yourself, do you think your parents would have supported you indefinitely? When do you think it's right to shove a chick out of the nest?"

Bea looked to Sam for guidance, but his eyes were downcast, his expression stony.

"Come on, Dad," Zoe cajoled her father. "Let's have a nice dinner, okay?"

"I just have some skepticism—as does your mother—about what's actually happening here. Bea seems like a competent woman with a thriving career, whereas our son has been unemployed for the better part of a year, has turned down the various positions and internships I've procured for him—"

"Because I don't want to work on Wall Street." Sam scowled.

"And his best idea for his future is to go on reality television."

"I'm so thankful he did," Bea interrupted, unable to stay silent any longer.

"Oh?" Steve asked, an edge to his voice. "Enlighten us."

"Well . . ." Bea looked to Sam, but his face was inscrutable. "I don't know how much of the show you've watched, but it hasn't been the easiest experience. Some of the men I've met were really cruel to me."

"I'm sorry to hear that," Claudette said sincerely.

"There were times when it got so bad, I even thought about quitting. But right from our first date, Sam has been such a source of joy and compassion. Obviously he's incredibly smart, but he never rubs your nose in it. He always finds a way to make me laugh, no matter how awful I'm feeling. He's been patient, and caring, and never rushes me when I need to take things slowly—which is kind of an alarmingly rare trait in men."

"And it doesn't bother you that he's unemployed, living at home?" Steve prodded. "If you two get engaged at the end of this ridiculous exercise, you're planning to support him financially?"

"I mean, I don't know how happy he'd be if we had to make things work on my salary." Bea laughed. "But I have faith in him. He'd figure it out. We both would."

Sam looked over at her with a pained, hard-to-read expression, and she reached under the table to squeeze his hand. The rest of the meal was polite, but reserved—and Sam barely said a word, leaving Bea to wonder if perhaps she'd done something horribly wrong by sticking her nose in the middle of a family squabble.

At the end of the evening, Sam walked Bea outside to where the production van was waiting to drive her back to New York—they'd shoot the kiss-off ceremony there tomorrow.

"Bea," Sam said, taking her hands, "I need to say something to you."

Suddenly, Bea's heart was thumping—was everything okay?

"I don't know if you really meant everything you said to my dad in there, or if you were just trying to stick up for me, but either way, it meant a lot."

Bea looked up to meet his gaze—he seemed shifty, nervous, so unlike himself.

"And I know that some of these other guys you've got here, they can offer you a lot more than I can. They've got careers, got their lives together. And as you saw today, I really don't."

"Sam," Bea broke in, but he put a hand on her shoulder to stop her.

"I've liked you from the beginning," he said. "I've never met anyone who could be so tough and so sweet at the same time. You never let anyone tell you what to think—not the idiots we met on the show, not the producers, not even my dad. And tonight, watching you stand up to him, all I could think was, *Sam, you idiot. You're in love with this girl. And you have to tell her.*"

Bea's breath caught in her throat. "What?"

"I'm in love with you, Bea." He wrapped his arms around her and pulled her close. "I love you."

An amazed grin crept across Bea's face. Her first impulse was to doubt Sam, to tell him he didn't know what he was feeling, that it couldn't possibly be love. But as they kissed and held each other, Bea had another, more powerful—and, frankly, much more terrifying—thought: What if this was working?

What if this was real?

@Reali-Tea Okay team, we ready for a kiss-off ceremony?? Bea looks HAWT in that bronze dress, here's hoping whoever she sends home this week doesn't turn into a raging monster.

@Reali-Tea This is the most difficult ceremony yet, blah blah blah, all these men mean so much to her, WHO CARES BEA, GET TO THE GOOD STUFF!

@Reali-Tea Here we go! First name called is Asher, obvi. Ugh those two are so sweet together, and how much did you love Bea with his KIDS???

@Reali-Tea Next is Sam, no surprises there—hard to get sent home after you drop the L-bomb. Awww, he looks *so* happy, nicely done!

@Reali-Tea Meep, that just leaves Luc and Wyatt! HMMM. Who will it be????

Bea stood in her artfully draped Maria Cornejo gown, which she'd selected as a nod to Keria's creation from the day before, wearing this week's shade of lipstick (Ain't Life Peachy?), looking from Luc to Wyatt, Wyatt to Luc.

She had no fucking idea what to do.

This was the first kiss-off ceremony she'd gone into without a clear plan, which Lauren hadn't liked at all.

"Bea, I need to know where to point the cameras *before* you make your decision," Lauren explained for what felt like the billionth time.

"I don't know what to say." Bea threw up her hands in frustration. "You're telling me we're an hour behind schedule, and I'm telling you I don't know yet."

Lauren pinched the bridge of her nose between her fingers and closed her eyes.

"Keeping Wyatt is the smart play," she said. "You've said it from night one, and your conversation in Oklahoma confirmed it. He's the one you can be sure will stand by your side at the end. No fuss, no drama."

"And you don't think it would be the same old problem?" Bea pressed. "People disbelieving our relationship, saying I look miserable?"

"Bea, when you're with Wyatt, you *don't* look miserable. You look totally at ease, like you've finally found a man who lets you be yourself. Trust me, with the big swelling music and the gorgeous light at sunset, you two are the picture of fairy-tale romance—exactly the kind of couple I've been selling to the public for years."

"I guess that's the whole point of fairy tales." Bea's tone was sour. "They aren't real."

Lauren approached Bea and put a hand on her arm, eyes full of concern. "I know that you've come to believe you can find love on this show, and I hope it works out for you, I really do. But you and I are the only two people who know just how fragile these relationships are, and if they fall apart in the next two weeks? I don't want to film a season finale where you end up alone. I don't want that for the show, and I don't want it for you."

Bea nodded—she knew that Lauren was right, that it would be insane to cast aside her picture-perfect safety net. But she couldn't say goodbye to Sam, not after he'd told her he loved her, and ending things with Asher was a complete non-starter. Which meant she had to choose between Luc and Wyatt—both of whom were staring at her now with apprehension, and she was still no closer to making her choice than she'd been with Lauren half an hour before.

"Bea?" Johnny urged. "Bea, we're going to need a decision."

Looking at Luc, his anxiety plainly evident on a face that was usually so self-assured, Bea honestly couldn't tell whether he was nervous about leaving the show or losing her—and since the two outcomes were hopelessly intertwined, there was no easy way to parse them.

Wyatt, by comparison, looked calm and steady, same as always. Usually, just looking at him helped Bea feel more calm too—but not tonight. Tonight, her insides roiled, and absolutely nothing could make them stop.

"Bea?" Johnny tried again.

Everyone was looking at her—the crew was getting restless. She just had to choose. Lauren raised her eyebrows expectantly: *You know what to do.*

She did. She knew the right thing to do. The only thing left was to do it.

"Wyatt," Bea said out loud, then closed her eyes. She couldn't look at Wyatt coming toward her. Couldn't possibly look past him to find out how badly she'd hurt Luc.

"Hey." Wyatt was there, taking her hand, smiling down at her in his warm, reassuring way.

"Wyatt." Bea's voice sounded hollow. "Will you stay another week?"

"Of course." He beamed, leaning down so she could kiss his cheek. That was it, decision made. All that remained was to say goodbye to Luc.

Luc.

She looked past Wyatt's shoulder, and there he was. He looked shocked. He looked wrecked.

Wyatt took her hand and squeezed it, gave her a jolt of encouragement.

"It's okay, Bea," he said, his voice low. "We'll keep each other safe."

Was this safe? Was safety sending away a man for whom she had real feelings, choosing a façade instead? Was standing next to Wyatt and pretending to love him the safe choice, or was she just proving Jefferson right—selling a lie, telling every person who admired her that she still, after all of this, didn't actually believe that she was capable of finding real love?

She looked over at Luc again—she had to. She had to walk him out to say goodbye.

"My Bea." He looked devastated. "I do not know what to say."

"Luc, I . . ." Bea shook her head; she felt numb. Wyatt had taken his place with Sam and Asher. No. This was wrong.

"I'm sorry, wait," she said, but no one seemed to hear her—there was too much happening. She raised her voice. "Can everyone please wait just one second?"

All the buzz and activity in the room stopped instantly—it was pin-drop silent now.

"Wyatt, I—I'm sorry. I'm *so* sorry. Can we talk for a minute?"

Wyatt looked totally bewildered—even if he didn't have feelings for her, the viewers at home wouldn't know that. Bea absolutely hated herself for humiliating him like this.

As he walked back toward her, she inhaled deeply. She couldn't break down while she did this—it wouldn't be fair.

"Bea, what's going on?"

"Just now," she began, "when you said to me that you would keep me safe. It was a perfect thing to say, because that's how you've made me feel this whole time, you know? I could always count on you to listen to me, to comfort me. And you helped me come out of my shell, Wyatt. In Ohio, especially— you helped me see how different the men here were than the men in my past, and that I had a chance here to actually be happy. But only if I was willing to risk getting hurt.

"So now I think—I think I have to take your advice. Even if what I really want is to make this safe choice of spending more time with you, of knowing how easy it would be, be- cause we've become such close friends. And maybe this is self- ish of me, but Wyatt, I really hope we can stay friends, even if this is the end of our road on this show."

"Bea," Wyatt broke in, "I can't let you do this."

"What?" Bea was shocked. "What do you mean?"

"I can't let you come off like you're the villain here, when the truth is that I—no." He shook his head. "You're being brave, and I need to be brave too."

Johnny stepped toward them. "Wyatt? Is there something you'd like to say?"

"Yes, actually. Um, I want to say that Bea and I have become very close friends, like she says. We love spending time together, but the connection between us—it's not romantic. And that's because . . . Well, it's because I'm not a person who has romantic feelings for other people. That's just not who I am. Bea's the first person I ever told about that, and she was so good to me about it. But it's not fair for me to stay here when she has a chance of finding something real with one of you three." He turned to Asher, Sam, and Luc. "I hope it works out with one of you guys. I really do."

Bea stepped forward and took Wyatt's hand, and he pulled her into a tight hug.

"I'm gonna miss you," he murmured into her hair.

"Not as much as I'm gonna miss you."

He kissed her forehead, and with a small wave, he turned and walked out of the room.

"Wow." Johnny guffawed, trying for levity. "That was a first."

But no one laughed—the room was still in a state of stunned silence.

"Well, Bea," he went on, "I guess that leaves us with one order of unfinished business."

"Oh," Bea said, realizing. "Right."

She turned to Luc, suddenly filled with trepidation. She'd just rejected him on television—would he even want to stay another week, after all that?

"Luc, I owe you an apology," she said softly as he approached her.

His expression was something she hadn't seen from him before, a mix of his usual mischief with something earthier, more sad.

"You see?" he said, taking her hand and kissing it. "I told you that you were the one in control, but you did not believe me. Perhaps now you understand?"

"So you'll stay?" she whispered. He nodded, and she threw her arms around him, unable to fathom that just a few minutes ago, she'd been ready to send him away. Yet here he was—not punishing her, not sulking. Just rubbing her back. Just making her feel loved.

"Why are you so good to me?" she intoned, burying her face in his chest.

"You know why," he murmured.

She kissed his cheek, and he went to stand beside Sam and Asher so Johnny could bid them farewell and they could finally wrap this shoot. Looking at her three remaining men, Bea felt good, felt *right*. This was what she was supposed to do, this was how she pushed herself to find something real, to overcome the loneliness that she had mislabeled, for so many years, as safety. For the first time all day, Bea started to relax.

It was almost enough to ignore the dark look that briefly crossed Asher's face as Luc took his place beside him.

EPISODE 7

"REVELATION"

(3 men left)

Shot on location in Épernay, Moustiers-Sainte-Marie, and Amboise, France

Everyone on Earth has a happy place. For Beatrice Schumacher, that place was France.

Bea couldn't quite trace the origins of her Francophilia, though she had a shameful suspicion it had something to do with childhood viewings of the movie *Sabrina* (and the remake at that) on cable TV. *Paris is always a good idea,* she'd repeat, emulating the titular character and imagining herself being swept away along the banks of the Seine. She thought the story was so romantic—a shy duckling who grows up to be a sophisticated swan, changing from someone you don't even see into a woman you can't stop staring at, with handsome men battling one another for her affections, breaking her heart over and over in the process.

As the *Main Squeeze* crew touched down in Paris for Bea's week of three overnight dates, Bea found herself wishing that perhaps her *Sabrina* fantasies hadn't turned out quite so literally.

Juggling relationships with three men was one thing when

Lauren and the other producers were supervising every moment, but this week was set to be something else entirely: For the first time (save Luc's little Moroccan escapade), Bea would have the option to share a hotel room with each of her remaining suitors. Away from the cameras. With the expectation that if they were serious about their relationship, they'd have sex. Bea hadn't spent the night with a man since Ray, and on one hand, she was buzzing with excitement—but on the other, she was terrified to be completely vulnerable with three men who still had the capacity to hurt her so much, and so publicly.

Bea thought again of Wyatt, how courageous he'd been to share the truth about himself with an audience of millions, even if it meant risking alienation from his family. There was so much Bea hadn't told Asher, Sam, and Luc for fear of being judged or rejected. But she knew that if she had any hope of finding a real relationship with one of these men, she needed to follow Wyatt's example.

Her first date of the week was with Sam in Épernay, at the heart of the Champagne region of northeastern France. They met at the Avenue de Champagne, the grand boulevard in the center of town. Set against rolling, vine-covered hills, the avenue was upright and stately, but not overly stuffy. Gray paving stones were arranged in graceful arches, and the road was lined with beautiful brick buildings with gated courtyards, all perfectly painted and landscaped, showing the pride these houses took in their centuries of tradition.

"*Bonjour, Sam!*" She waved when she saw him, and he rushed up to greet her.

"*Enchanté, chérie.*" He bowed dramatically.

"Wow, your accent is so bad."

"Wow yourself, I was trying to be *romantic.*"

Bea laughed and walked with him into the house of Moët

& Chandon, where they were to have a private tour of the cellars. A deadpan young woman led them through a vast system of caves where thousands of bottles of champagne lay in various stages of the aging process.

"Do not touch these," she said, casually waving toward a wall full of bottles.

"Why not?" Bea asked.

"If you were to drop one during this stage of fermentation, it would explode with the force of a small bomb. Glass would be everywhere, very messy." She clicked her tongue and kept walking.

Bea shot Sam a dramatic look behind their tour guide's back, and he laughed and kissed her; ever since he'd told her he loved her, his energy was even more buoyant than usual.

At the end of the tour, they visited the house tasting room, where everything was furnished and painted in lustrous shades of gold. Bea and Sam sipped coupes of grand vintage champagne, those special bottles created when the vintner deemed it a particularly good harvest, as opposed to the house's usual bottles, which were blended from two years' worth of grapes to create a consistent taste from year to year. The sommelier was exuberant—they chatted about their favorite wines and Bea fell in love with a coppery rosé champagne with a lovely dryness; he gifted her with a bottle to bring back to her hotel.

"Or perhaps you two will share it?" He smiled knowingly at Bea and Sam.

"That's up to her." Sam kissed Bea's cheek.

"We'll see." She tried for a playfully sexy tone, but the words came out as more of a high-strung squeak. Sam gave her hand a reassuring sort of pat.

After the tasting was done, it was off to their next activity: a sunset hot-air-balloon ride over the vine-covered hills of Champagne. Their balloon operator was a rotund, jovial, mustachioed fellow named Albert who wore a tan three-piece suit and a top hat, like he'd arrived for the tour by way of the turn of the twentieth century.

"This will be a beautiful tour, a spectacular tour, for two spectacular lovebirds!" He spread his arms grandly, waiting for Bea and Sam to mirror his excitement.

"I think I need to say something." Sam looked a bit wan. "I don't . . . feel terrific about heights?"

"Oh my God." Bea shot the producers an accusatory stare. "Did you guys know this? Sam, I'm so sorry, we don't have to do this."

"No." He shook his head. "No, this is our romantic adventure, and I'm not going to ruin it. You're sure that thing is safe?"

He pointed to the balloon silhouetted in the distance, and Albert nodded vigorously.

"But of course, monsieur, the balloon is extraordinarily safe! You will see, it is as gentle and as graceful as a cloud."

"A graceful cloud. Yeah. I can do that." Sam sounded like he was psyching himself up.

"Are you sure?" Bea asked. "Really, we can skip it—just head back to the hotel and drink our wine."

Sam nodded. "Let's do this."

"*Alors, allons-y!*" Albert cheered, and led them over to their balloon, which was absolutely gorgeous: It was made of nylon, but treated to look like old-fashioned canvas, ivory with a pattern of vines and flowers in tones of sepia and muted rose.

The fire was whooshing into the balloon's opening, and Bea expected the launch to be filled with jerks and bumps, like an airplane taking off, but it wasn't at all—when Albert's support staff untied the ropes that had been tethering the balloon to the ground, they simply floated off into the air. Bea also assumed it would be loud, but it was nearly silent, just the sounds of the fire and the soft wind as they drifted past countless vineyards, where thousands of grapevines were showing their first hint of green.

"This is breathtaking," Bea said reverently, not wanting to break the spell. She turned to Sam. "You doing okay?"

He nodded. "A graceful cloud."

"That's us," Bea agreed.

"Maybe if you hugged me a little? Help steady me?"

"You're shameless." Bea laughed, but she nuzzled into his arms all the same, and it felt so good to hold him, the countryside spread below them like a picnic.

"So, what do you think?" Sam asked her.

"I think it's amazing," Bea replied.

"No, I was asking—what I said to you in New Jersey. We haven't really talked about it."

"Oh." Bea looked up at him. "What do you want to talk about?"

"Was it too much? Too soon? I've been nervous."

"No, not at all. In fact, I actually . . ."

"What?" Sam urged, tipping up Bea's chin.

"I should tell you—God, this is embarrassing." She felt her face flush.

"I'm a grown man afraid of a hot-air balloon, so whatever it is, I think I can handle it."

Bea tried to smile, but her heart was suddenly pounding. "What you said to me, um. No one's ever told me that before. In a romantic context."

Sam frowned. "Are you serious?"

Bea nodded. "I know I've made a whole thing about how young you are, but sometimes I feel like I'm the young one."

"Have you ever said it to anyone?"

Bea shook her head. "I haven't."

She'd wanted to say it to Ray—at least, she thought she had—but he'd never given her the chance.

"Okay." Sam nodded, taking this in. "How did it make you feel to hear that I love you?"

"Exhilarated." Bea smiled. "Really, really happy—and also terrified."

"Sounds serious." Sam was only half-joking. "Can you tell me why you felt scared?"

"I can try," Bea said quietly, taking a moment to feel the sun on her face, the breeze in her hair, the strange steadiness of this good man standing beside her in the sky.

"I've spent a lot of time falling for people who weren't really available," she said carefully. "Which means, sad as it sounds, that a lot of my romantic life has taken place in my own imagination. Picturing what it would be like if we were together, extrapolating meaning from subtext, from things left unspoken. But then you go and tell me that you love me, and . . ."

"And what?"

"It's like, all of a sudden, I'm confronted with what I've been missing. Like, do other people actually live this way? They just fall in love, and they tell each other, and they never have to be ashamed, or embarrassed, or certain the other person doesn't feel the same? And then—if you're in love with me, and if I could really fall in love with you, does that mean I have to learn how to need you? To depend on you? What happens when you disappear on me like everyone else always has?"

"There's always the other option," Sam said pointedly. "The one where I stick around."

"And that doesn't scare *you*?" Bea prodded.

Sam's face changed. "Bea, no, not at all. Before, in my other relationships, it's always been like, I knew there was a timeline for a natural endpoint, when we'd graduate college or leave a certain job or whatever. I *needed* to know there was a timeline so I could be comfortable. With you, it's the opposite. I don't want to think about a timeline for this ending, because I don't want this to end."

"But Sam, you're only twenty-four! I don't know, don't you want to live in Japan for a year, or join the circus or whatever?"

"First of all, clowns are terrifying, and I'm already dealing with one fear right now, you know, high above the Earth, so I'll thank you not to compound things."

"Sorry, sorry."

"But to answer your question—you make me feel like a whole different person. Not in a bad way. It's like I've spent my entire life in a building, but just on one floor. And I'm like, *Cool, I've got this ranch house, it's got everything I need, I could live here forever*. But then I meet you, and you show me this thing has an elevator, and we're going all the way to the top. It turns out that I've been living in a skyscraper this whole time."

"That makes your fear of heights pretty ironic," Bea whispered.

"Haven't you noticed?" He leaned in to kiss her. "When I'm with you, I'm not afraid."

It was dark by the time they made it to their hotel, a beautifully converted eighteenth-century manor with a face of carved white stone. Bea and Sam's last scheduled shot of the night would be of them entering their shared room, a lavish suite, no doubt. The cameras would leave them alone for eight uninterrupted hours as soon as they hung the Do Not

Disturb sign on the door—or, since this was France, *Ne pas déranger.*

But before they got to that part, Bea had to officially invite Sam to spend the night together, and he had to accept. This part of the evening was basically a formality: On *Main Squeeze,* couples didn't always have sex, but they always, always spent the night.

At least, that's what Bea was telling herself to calm her nerves as she and Sam stood on the hotel's grand front steps, bathed in artificial light.

"Sam, I had a great time with you today."

"Me too—despite the persistent fear of death."

"What can I say? I bring out the best in people."

He laughed, and she held out a clunky brass key tied to a red ribbon. It wasn't the actual key to any room in this hotel—it was the same symbolic prop that had been used for dozens of similar invitations throughout *Main Squeeze* history.

"Sam, I've loved getting to know you, and I think we're ready to take the next step. Would you like to spend the night together?"

Sam opened his mouth, then closed it. "Actually, I've been thinking. I know that in the past, men have treated you like you weren't worthy of a real relationship. And I know you're concerned about me—as young as I am, whether I'm ready for a commitment. Bea, I want to prove to you that I'm taking this seriously. I'm not just here to have fun, I'm not feeding you some line so you'll sleep with me. Let me show you that I'm ready for this, for us. Let's wait."

Bea's stomach dropped, and her body felt suddenly cold. She understood his rationale—in Sam's mind, he was showing her (and all of America) that he really was grown-up. She didn't know how to tell him, here, with the cameras rolling, that no one watching this show would think he was declining to sleep with her out of some sense of chivalry. They'd simply think he didn't want her.

Maybe he doesn't, a voice in her head rang out.

Bea shook this off—of course he wanted her. Hadn't he made that clear in the hammam? She assured herself that this decision wasn't a matter of Bea's insecurity, but Sam's immaturity. He and Bea hadn't had a single moment together off camera, and here, with the possibility of a whole night to get to know each other better—hell, just to be alone in a room together for the very first time—he was saying "no thanks" for the sake of an ill-thought gesture. Was this really a man who was ready for a serious relationship, let alone marriage?

She told him she understood, and he kissed her passionately, as if to erase her doubts, but something about it felt wrong, felt like performance. Before they parted ways, he hugged her one last time and whispered into her ear.

"I love you, Bea. Okay? I love you."

But this time, Bea found it was harder to believe.

When Bea learned she'd be traveling to France for her overnight dates, she knew exactly where she wanted to go with Asher, and she was thrilled when Lauren agreed: Moustiers-Sainte-Marie, her favorite village in Provence. Moustiers was just east of the plateau Valensole, where in summer every hectare burst with blooming lavender and sunflowers and the thick, hot air was densely perfumed with sweet honey. But now, in spring, the region was much more quiet, scattered only with wildflowers and the occasional tourist, a far cry from the droves who would soon descend.

Lauren had originally proposed that Bea and Asher take a kayaking adventure near Moustiers, but Bea had swiftly vetoed this; there was absolutely no chance of her agreeing to wedge herself into a kayak on camera. Instead, a compromise was struck where the two would go pedal boating on the Lac de Sainte-Croix, right near the opening of the Gorges du Verdon.

"You're here." Asher stood smiling on the dock where they were meeting, the outrageously turquoise lake shimmering behind him in the midday sunlight.

"Hey, you." Bea ran into his arms, and after all the uncertainty Sam had instilled in her, it felt so simple to kiss Asher in the plain, bright light of day.

Getting outfitted in life jackets (Bea was forced to wear a men's XXL, which was comically long on her) and into the pedal boat was something of a production, but once they were off on the lake, surrounded by canoes full of camera operators, Asher and Bea pedaled through the green waters into the mouth of the gorge, where limestone cliffs towered over them.

"So, my kids loved you," Asher said, unable to suppress a grin.

"Excuse me?" Bea was skeptical. "Gwen tolerated me at best."

"Nope," Asher corrected. "Last night she emailed me an *article* she thought you might enjoy about the handlers who work with animals in Hollywood. That's basically Gwen-speak for 'be my new best friend.'"

Bea was genuinely surprised. "And did they like the movie?"

"Bea, I swear to you, I've heard of little else since you left. Linus wants to know when you can come back to teach him how to contour his cheekbones to look like Katharine Hepburn's."

Bea cracked up. "Do you even know what contouring is?"

Asher looked affronted. "I'll have you know I once spent two hours of my Saturday at a Sephora in Burlington learning exactly what contouring is and how one achieves it. It was terrifying."

"I cannot *believe* you went to a Sephora class."

"Yeah, well. I tried to persuade Linus we'd have more fun at a Revolutionary War reenactment, but he was unconvinced."

"So, tell me, young grasshopper." Bea gathered herself up very seriously. "What did you learn in Sephora school?"

"Well"—Asher traced the lines on Bea's face with his fingers—"when you contour, you want to use bronzer under the cheekbones, here, and along the jaw. To create shadow."

"Don't forget the hairline."

"Yes, of course." Asher pressed his thumbs to the center of Bea's forehead, then ran them down to her temples, massaging her gently. "The hairline."

"Good." Bea relaxed into his touch. "What else?"

"You highlight all the places that draw light—the cheeks, the bridge of the nose, and just above the lips."

He rested a finger on her cupid's bow, and she kissed it softly.

"Did you know you can also contour your décolletage?"

Asher smiled, somewhere between turned-on and incredulous. "Seriously?"

"Seriously. But I can't show you that right now." Bea was holding back laughter too. "Because it would be very dangerous to remove our life jackets."

Asher shook his head and grinned. "Can I please just drop the pretext and kiss you?"

"I swear to God, you'd better."

It was a little too cold to dine outside that night, but Bea insisted—they were eating at one of her favorite restaurants in the world: La Bastide de Moustiers, Alain Ducasse's boutique Provençal property, where they also had rooms for the night. The restaurant's terrace was built into the hillside, and all the tables faced outward so diners could eat while gazing at the beautiful mountains. The waitstaff brought out thick woven blankets to keep them warm, then course after course of the most bright, delicious food she'd ever tasted. They had the whole place to themselves to eat and watch the sunset, the mountains drenched in orange, then pink, then gold.

Once the food had been cleared and the light was almost gone, they nestled together, drinking a champagne toast, the intensity of their connection—how strong her feelings were getting, the fact that his children were now involved—both reassuring Bea and, in its own way, unnerving her.

"I didn't expect this," she murmured, "any of it."

"I know." He leaned in close. "After Vanessa, I thought I was done. For a long time anyway. But now . . ."

"Now?" she urged.

"I'm rethinking things."

He kissed her, and she stayed close to him, caught between her curiosity and her desire to preserve the moment.

"You never talk about her," Bea said quietly.

"Vanessa?"

Bea nodded, and Asher sighed.

"I keep expecting that one day I'll wake up and it won't hurt anymore. That I'll finally understand what happened, and I'll be past it. It's been seven years, and still. No such luck."

"I know the feeling."

"Do you?" Asher looked at her. "The guy who hurt you last year?"

"Of course it's not the same," Bea said quickly. "I would never compare the two, she left her children. But waking up every morning, not wanting to think about it, but not being able to help it? That part I know really well."

"I thought that meeting someone new would help," Asher admitted. "And in some ways it has—to be with you, to feel so hopeful for the first time in years. But in other ways, I find I'm thinking about her even more. With every milestone you and I cross, I think back to what it was like with her. I don't mean to compare you, and I hate that I've been thinking of her so frequently."

Bea exhaled. "Asher, it's only natural that we're comparing this experience to past ones. How could we not? Especially if we're looking for warning signs to make sure we won't be hurt again."

"I suppose we could will ourselves to forget them, focus on moving forward."

"That doesn't really sound realistic, does it?"

He took a sip of wine. "Perhaps not."

"So, um. How did you meet her?" Bea asked, hoping this question was small enough to draw him out.

"In college," Asher started. "She had this brilliant energy, and I was enamored. There was this shop near campus where we'd order tea rolls and Nepalese chai, and we would sit there for hours, arguing about moral determinism and the nature of humanity. I was so in love with her—and I was hardly the only one, men always fell all over themselves around her. But she told me she loved how reliable I was. How I never let her down."

Bea tried to imagine him, this young, earnest person who hadn't yet become untrusting. She grieved a little for what he'd lost—and what she had.

"Senior year, we started talking about whether to stay together after graduation. She wanted to travel, but I was accepted into a PhD program. We didn't want to break up, but we thought we had to. Then we found out she was pregnant."

"Oh wow." Bea exhaled. "Did you consider an abortion?"

"Of course. But we were taken in by the romance of the situation. She said it would be a new adventure, and we would be homesteaders, raising our little family. It was a sign, she said. We were meant to be together. I couldn't believe I was so lucky that she wanted to be connected to me for the rest of her life."

"What happened after you moved?"

A dark expression came over Asher's face. "We didn't have any idea how hard it would be. We had no money and this tiny grad-student apartment, I was working all the time, it was freezing cold in Ithaca and she was cooped up all winter long with only an infant for company. I made friends through my program, but whenever I tried to include her, she would make some excuse, say she couldn't leave Gwen. I didn't understand how depressed she was."

"That must have been so hard for both of you."

"It did get better," Asher asserted, "for a while anyway. When Gwen got old enough for daycare, Vanessa got a job in town, working at the local co-op. She started working on their farm, making all these friends. We finally moved into our own house, and she seemed happy again. She was always cooking some exotic new vegetable, bringing people over, hosting dinners, music circles in the yard."

"Music circles?" Bea raised an eyebrow. "Doesn't really sound like you."

"It wasn't," he conceded with a laugh, "but I was so happy that she was happy. When we found out she was pregnant with Linus, I thought, *This time will be different. This time, we'll be the family we were always supposed to be.*"

"And was it? Different?"

Asher shook his head. "It was worse—much worse. After Linus was born, Vanessa was angry all the time. She would fly into rages over the smallest things, me bringing home the wrong brand of milk, whatever; storm out of the house and not come back for days. She refused to be around the kids, spent all her time at the farm. I started to feel like I was keeping the love of my life in a cage, and she despised me for it."

"So what happened?"

"I guess I should have known," he clipped. "All that time she spent away from home, you'd think it would have been obvious. But I was still devastated when I found out she was cheating."

"*What?*" Bea gasped. It hadn't been obvious to her. Asher nodded sadly.

"I went to the co-op one day to pick her up, and there she was, kissing another man in broad daylight. Not just a peck on the lips, either." Asher shook his head, as if trying to rid himself of the memory. "She said she forgot I was coming, but I think the truth is she wanted me to see. Maybe she'd wanted me to see for a long time, but I refused to look. I couldn't take it. I knew we were unhappy, but to see her, to actually see her with someone else—I just lost it. I felt my whole life collapsing on top of me. I kept hearing that word in my head, 'reliable'—thinking, Is this who I am? Is my character defined by my capacity to be used and punished again and again by someone who thinks so little of other people's feelings?"

"That's not true," Bea protested. "You deserved so much better than that."

"I didn't think so." He looked pained. "I wish I could tell you that I screamed at her, that I stood up for myself at all. But I did the opposite. I sat on our couch sobbing, begging her to stay. After everything, how angry I was, how much I hated her by then, how much I knew she hated me, I still couldn't let her go. It didn't matter. She left anyway."

"Asher," Bea whispered, and she pulled him into her arms, unable to hold back any longer. He tensed at first, but then he exhaled and let her hold him.

"Where is she now?" Bea asked, gently smoothing his hair. "Do the kids ever see her?"

"Last I heard, she was working as a diving instructor in Thailand, but we've barely talked since the divorce was finalized. I used to send her these emails, begging her to come home and see the kids, or at least call on their birthdays. Now I think it's better that she doesn't. It only gets their hopes up— it's not fair to them."

"Or to you," Bea added.

"I only hope—" His voice broke. "I hope Gwen and Linus will be able to forgive me."

"Hey, hey, no, for what?" Bea's heart was cracking open. "You stayed, okay? You didn't leave them. There was nothing you could do to control Vanessa, she made her own choices. You do everything you can for your kids, you came on this show for them, and I promise you, they know that. They adore you."

Asher looked into Bea's eyes; there was something desperate in his expression.

"Was this too much?" he asked. "Should I not have told you?"

"No," Bea said fervently. "I'm so glad you did—it helps me understand you so much better."

Asher looked at her sheepishly. "Like why I had a meltdown when I thought you'd spent the night with Luc?"

"Yeah, for one." Bea laughed kindly. "And why you're so fiercely protective. Of your heart, of your kids. Of me."

"I wish I could protect you from ever getting hurt," Asher said, his voice tinged with emotion. "If you want to talk about—what happened to you last year, I mean. You can. I'm listening."

Bea sighed; she'd barely talked about this at all, let alone on television. But Asher had been so vulnerable with her, and she knew she owed him the same honesty. The same bravery.

"I've never had much luck with dating," she started, her heart beating quickly. "Sometimes I tell myself that's about my size, but of course I know that's ridiculous, there are plenty of women who look like me in wonderful relationships. That's just never been the case for me.

"But then there was—a man," Bea stopped herself before she said his name. She couldn't do that on camera; it wouldn't be fair to Sarah. "We were best friends for years; he had this way of making me feel like I was the smartest, funniest, most interesting person in the room. And even though we were just friends, even after he moved across the country, I was so in love with him. He was kind of my escape, you know? A place where I retreated from how terrified I was of dating anyone else. For years, I compared every new man I met to him, which wasn't fair to anyone. I had no real reason to believe it could actually work out between us, but I just kept holding out hope. Anyway, it's not like anyone else was beating down my door for a chance to be with me. It's not like I gave anyone the chance."

Bea exhaled deeply, and Asher rubbed her palm with the inside of his thumb.

"Last summer, he came to visit me, and I don't know why, but everything was different. It was like we were together, like we had always been together, like it was suddenly so obvious that there was nothing platonic about us. We had this one perfect night, and it felt like my whole life made sense. Like all the years of loneliness were finally going to be over. Except."

Asher squeezed her hand. "Except what?"

"He left. He left before I even woke up, and then he was just gone. He wouldn't respond to my texts or emails, ignored my calls. He wasn't my friend anymore, he wasn't my anything. I was despondent. I felt so weak that one night could destroy me like that, but to have dreamed my whole life of finding love, to experience it for a few hours only to have it snatched away . . ."

"Why did he disappear like that?" Asher demanded. "You two had all this history, how could he just abandon you without an explanation?"

He didn't need to explain—he was engaged to someone else. But she couldn't tell Asher that, not right after he'd told her how devastated he'd been by Vanessa cheating on him. So Bea shrugged.

"He never told me," she said. "I guess I wasn't what he wanted."

"He didn't deserve you." Asher pulled Bea close, and she felt so good to be with him, so relieved to have told him about Ray, so guilty not to have revealed the whole truth about his engagement. But, Bea reasoned, disclosing too many specific details with the cameras rolling would be as bad as saying Ray's name outright—it was only right that she should keep the story vague.

"So what do you think?" Asher asked. "Can we move past our ghosts?"

Bea looked up at him—was he asking her to spend the night together? She felt a surge of hope, and of certainty.

"I should tell you," she said, "I haven't been with anyone since him, since last summer. But I want to—I mean, we don't have to actually—I'm sorry, I'm so flustered. What I'm saying is, I want us to share a room tonight, if you do."

To Bea's horror, Asher's whole expression changed—he looked embarrassed and awkward, like he had no idea what to say.

"Oh God," Bea mumbled. "How did I read this so wrong?"

"Bea," Asher sputtered, "I want to spend the night with you; believe me, I want that. Do you believe me?"

Bea forced a nod, but she felt sick.

"I have to think about my kids. This is going to be on TV in a few days, and they *just* met you—it's too fast. I can't throw caution to the wind. I have to show them I'm being more careful than that with their future. I'm so sorry, I should have brought it up much sooner that sharing a room was never an option for me."

"But . . ." Bea couldn't get a clean breath. "I thought it went so well with them."

"It *did*," Asher entreated. "Bea, it was better than I could have hoped. But we have time, right? We don't have to do this tonight. We have all the time in the world."

He hugged her tightly, and she wanted to feel comfort, but the gnawing, ragged emptiness tore through her, like a whisper: *First Sam, now Asher. He doesn't love you. None of them do.*

After they wrapped their shoot, Bea had to walk alone across the entire property to her secluded, romantic suite, the one where she and Asher had been meant to stay together. Asher had offered to walk with her, but somehow, that felt worse. When she got to the room, she closed the door and turned off all the lights, hoping that, if she could make the space quiet enough, the voices in her head would stop screaming.

For so long, Bea's recollection of her night with Ray had felt like a movie on loop, playing over and over in her mind's eye, more vivid and alive than any other memory she had—the colors more intense, the sensations more acute. These past few weeks, though, Bea had started to feel the movie fading—after all these months, it was like she finally had the ability to change the channel. Tonight, though, after hours of tossing, restless and alone, Bea gave in. She let the movie wash over her, bright and gripping, and imagined Ray beside her, subsisting for one more night on the memory of how it had felt to fall asleep in his arms.

Bea woke feeling groggy, her head pounding with exhaustion and dehydration and general wretchedness. She wanted to be excited for her final date of the week—a day with Luc at her favorite château—but after all the pain and rejection of her nights with Sam and Asher, she found herself wishing she'd kept Wyatt around after all. She just wanted some part of this to feel easy.

"Hey." Lauren approached her on the little propeller plane they'd chartered. "This seat taken?"

"All yours," Bea said glumly, and Lauren strapped in beside her.

"Shitty week, huh?" Lauren looked like she genuinely felt for Bea.

"Not the greatest," Bea said quietly. "Any chance I can skip today and just go home?"

"Sadly, no," Lauren sighed. "I wish I could tell you that this was all for show, that I'm the one who made the guys decide to spend the night on their own for ratings, for a twist. I told you this would get a lot harder if real feelings got involved."

"Congrats." Bea rolled her eyes. "You nailed it."

"No, come on, Bea, that's not what I mean."

"What, then?"

"A couple of things, because I know you're going through hell right now, and I have a lot of information you don't—I'm the one interviewing these guys ad infinitum when you're not in the room, okay?"

Bea looked up at Lauren. "What do you know?"

"First, that Sam and Asher both really care about you. I know Jefferson got in your head, flared up all the doubts you've been having since day one. And I know how badly it hurt to have two guys in a row refuse to spend the night with you—but neither of them knew the other was going to do that. You've worked so hard to trust them—don't stop now."

"Because it would be bad for the show?"

Lauren exhaled in frustration. "Bea, we've been through this—at this point, what's bad for the show is also bad for you. You want to spend your last two weeks here moping and feeling sorry for yourself and end up alone? Have at it. But I also want to remind you that there's an exceptionally attractive man waiting for you in Amboise, who frankly hasn't fucking shut up for weeks about how badly he wants to get you in bed."

"Really?" Luc had said as much to Bea, but somehow hearing it from Lauren made it seem like it could actually be true.

"Yes." Lauren sighed. "Really. So maybe we can put this

week in a different perspective? You had *great dates* with Sam and Asher. You opened up to each other and got closer, and they both told you in no uncertain terms that they want to stick with you for a long time. So you didn't spend the night with them? Fine. You have a fresh start with Luc today—and I have something really special planned for you guys. Don't waste it. Don't let every fear and bad thought you have about yourself stop you from having the fabulous fantasy with him that you deserve."

Bea knew Lauren wanted what was best for the show—to avoid another depressing episode on the order of the boat catastrophe. But she also couldn't help feeling that Lauren had grown attached to her, had begun to root for her success. And she was right, in any case, about their goals at this stage being aligned. It wasn't Luc's fault that Sam and Asher had rejected her—there was no sense in punishing him for it.

"Okay," Bea told Lauren. "I'll do my best."

Bea wasn't sure what Lauren meant by "something special," but when they got to the hotel in Amboise and began filming, she saw Johnny lounging beside a full-on Cinderella horse-drawn carriage. It was painted gold, driven by a man in fancy pantaloons and a white powdered wig, and drawn by four white horses with elaborately curled manes.

"What is all this?" Bea laughed, somewhere between giddiness and horror.

"I have an invitation that explains everything," Johnny pronounced, then handed her a scroll that was tied with red ribbon. Bea unfurled it and read aloud:

"*Dear Bea, you've spent the whole season planning such amazing dates for me and the other men here.*" This was hardly true, she noted internally—Lauren and the producers did most of the planning. But she read on anyway: "*So today, I wanted to plan something special for you. Will you join me for a royal ball at the Château de Chenonceau? I'll see you there when the clock strikes five.* Oh, Jesus," she added despite herself.

"Do you accept the invitation?" Johnny asked.

"Who would say no to a royal ball?" Bea laughed, giving in to the ridiculousness of it all.

"Excellent." Johnny held open the door of the carriage, and Bea climbed in.

When they arrived at the Château de Chenonceau, they couldn't see the castle itself—just a small building for buying tickets and an elaborate tree-lined avenue that ran through the immaculate gardens before it reached the palace beyond. The little ticket building had a space that was usually a gift shop, but today, it had been remade into a dressing area for Bea.

"Just wait until you see." Alison grinned. "Christian Siriano asked if he could make something for you."

She led Bea to a room filled with light, where a spectacular ball gown was waiting on a dress form. The corseted bodice was a rich forest green with a wide portrait neckline and bracelet sleeves, and the full princess skirt was hand embroidered with thousands upon thousands of swirls of crinkled tulle, deepening in an ombré from the palest mint green at the skirt's waistline to a green as dark as the bodice at the hem. This wasn't just a custom gown—this was couture, worthy of the cover of *Vogue,* of any runway in the world. Made personally and especially for Bea.

"I know it's not exactly your style," Alison was saying, "but when Christian called, I knew right away that this would be the perfect occasion. What do you think?"

Bea could barely raise her voice above a whisper. "It's the most beautiful dress I've ever seen."

As Bea's team put the finishing touches on her hair and

makeup, Bea thought back to her interview with *People*—could it really have been just seven weeks ago?—when she'd told the interviewer she'd never heard of a fairy tale featuring a fat princess. Now, here she was, feeling more beautiful than she ever had in her life, on her way to attend a ball with a man handsome enough to be cast as a prince in any movie, a man who'd spent the better part of their time together working to convince her how strongly he felt about her. It was going to be a big, special moment on television—but even more than that, it felt to Bea like she had reached a real turning point in her own life. Last winter, alone and missing Ray so intensely, she'd fervently wished for her life to change; today, she couldn't deny that it had. That she was becoming someone new. That she was believing, despite all the mess of the week so far, that she was on a path toward something better.

"So?" Alison asked. "How do you feel?"

She felt like a dream. She felt like a fraud. She felt like a fucking princess.

"Grateful." She turned to Alison with tears in her eyes. "I feel really, really grateful."

Back outside, climbing into the horse-drawn carriage was considerably more difficult now that Bea was wearing a massive gown, but she was fully committed, and with the help of a couple of intrepid sound guys, they made it work. The carriage drove down the center of the tree-lined avenue to the Château de Chenonceau, the afternoon sunlight dappling through the leaves and making everything look magical.

The Loire valley was home to dozens of magnificent castles that had belonged to one French noble or another, but the Château de Chenonceau was Bea's favorite. The château was built *over* the Loire river instead of beside it, the castle itself becoming a sort of graceful bridge, its piles and arched girders serving as the foundation of the home. As the outline of the magnificent structure came into view, Bea saw that there were people everywhere, all dressed in period garb like the courtiers who would have been here hundreds of years ago.

"This is incredible," Bea laughed with amazement—and then she saw Luc.

He was standing at the castle doorway in an immaculate black tuxedo finished with a crisp white bow tie—of all the people there, they were the only two in modern dress—and he was so handsome, she couldn't humanly believe he was there for her. Luc helped her down from the carriage, then took a moment to admire her.

"Bea, in this dress—you are perfect."

"I'm not complaining about you in that suit either."

She took his arm, and he led her into the palace, through the arched entryway where a butler handed them both glasses of sparkling rosé, and into the grand gallery directly over the river.

The gallery at Chenonceau was different from other castles' ballrooms because of the strange shape of the building, but Bea thought it was all the more special for that. The room was long and narrow, with soaring ceilings, black-and-white stone floors, and rows of tall windows looking out over the river in both directions, giving the space the airy feeling of being suspended in midair. Dozens of men and women in suits and gowns were dancing to the music of a small orchestra, and when Luc asked Bea to join them, she didn't hesitate.

Luc wasn't the strongest dancer, but God they had fun, the cameras rushing to keep up with them as they laughed and swirled around the floor until they had to take a break because Bea felt dizzy.

"What is it? Is everything all right?" He looked at her quizzically, but she just smiled.

"It's nothing." She leaned against him. "Should we get another drink?"

He grabbed two glasses from a passing server and suggested that they take a walk to explore the château.

Upstairs, they wandered through bedrooms where Diane de Poitiers and Catherine de Medici had once slept, admiring the carved fireplaces and ornate tapestries. The sun had set, and stars were starting to appear; Luc led Bea out to the balcony over the castle's entryway to better observe them.

From the balcony, Luc and Bea could see the castle gardens, which were filled with glowing lanterns—the production staff had really outdone themselves tonight. Bea's corset was too tight to eat much (so *that's* how those women stayed so thin, she thought bitterly), but the wine made everything pleasantly wispy and buzzy: the people wandering through the gardens, the orchestra music playing dimly downstairs, Luc's arms grazing her waistline.

"I think about you each night." His throaty voice tickled at her earlobes. He was stronger than he looked, she thought. The tide of his arms was pulling her in, always wanting more. Everyone wanted so many things from her—to believe in herself and see her own true beauty, but not to be conceited, to know her place. Be more than your looks, but never speak out of turn. Don't be defined by love, but remember, you're nothing without it. Be a princess. Find your prince. You don't need a man to complete you. Stand on your own two feet.

It all swam together—this place, this dress, this man, this role she was supposed to play, this person she just wasn't. Princesses don't sleep with engaged men and get rejected twice in two days. She shouldn't be here, this was never supposed to be her, it was just Lauren's brainchild to help their careers. Lauren. Lauren wanted her to have a good night, to have fun with Luc, but how was she supposed to when she felt so confused? But Luc wasn't confused—he was right there, his chest pressed against hers, tasting faintly of smoke as he kissed her—he was kissing her. When had he started kissing her?

"Wait"—she pulled back, gasping for breath—"wait . . . I'm sorry, my head. I'm sorry."

Everything was spinning, and she had to sit down—wasn't there anywhere to sit down?

"I knew something was wrong." Luc helped her to one of the balcony benches, then turned to a field producer. "Can you send someone up here? Bea isn't feeling well."

"No, I'm fine." Bea tried to take a deep breath, but she couldn't. The corset was squeezing her, the air was too thin. "This is silly. I had too much to drink."

"You're not silly. You had perhaps two glasses? Let them check on you, all right?" He was sitting beside her, gently stroking her hair.

In short order, the on-set paramedic arrived and confirmed Bea was exhausted and dehydrated. His prescription: food, water, and since she couldn't eat in her gown, to change into some more comfortable clothes.

"But the ball!" Bea protested and turned to Luc. "I'm ruining our date."

Luc kissed her forehead. "You are just taking us on a new adventure. Let's put on pajamas and have some frites. After all, we are in France, *non*? What is France without some fries?"

An hour later in luxe cashmere sweats, Bea sat beside Luc in the château courtyard, sipping water and admiring how good he looked in his tuxedo pants and white button-down, his undone bowtie hanging loose around his neck. The staff had set up a gorgeous table spread with food for them, surrounded by hundreds of candles.

"How did they do this so quickly?" Bea asked.

"I asked if it was possible, and they said, since I was French, they could, so long as I promised them I was the one you liked best." He dropped his voice to a comedic whisper. "They do not want you to marry an American. They are very invested in us together."

Bea was sure he was joking, but looking around, a lot of the staff had gathered eagerly to watch them enjoy the cheese and charcuterie and warm, crusty baguettes they'd laid out. Luc made sure Bea's plate was never empty and her water glass was always full, shooing the staff away when they tried to do anything, adamant that he'd care for her himself.

Bea thought back on all the little moments when Luc had rescued her throughout filming. The very first night, when she thought she might have a panic attack, he was the one who made her feel beautiful. After the catastrophic group date on the boat, it was Luc who came over with crème brûlée, who kissed away her heartache. He'd let her rail at him in Morocco, spent hours by her side. And in New York, when she'd publicly dismissed him, then changed her mind, he didn't get angry or defensive. All he did was take her in his arms and tell her, again, how much he wanted her.

From the very beginning, Bea had thought Luc was the most attractive man in the house. Was that why she couldn't trust him—why she could never quite believe he might actually like her as much as he said he did? She had grown to believe that Asher had true feelings for her, as did Sam. Was it so impossible that Luc could too? And, more to the immediate point, was she so certain he was a liar that she'd throw away an opportunity for them to spend another night together off camera to find out more?

Luc gazed at her deeply, the candlelight illuminating his five-o'clock shadow that had started to grow in.

"What are you thinking, my Bea?" he asked, lifting a hand to her cheek.

She was thinking of how long she'd been here, of how much she'd changed since that first night of filming. She was thinking of Asher, and of Sam. She was thinking of Ray, how much she still missed him, how far away he seemed.

"I was thinking . . ." Bea formed the words slowly, like if she wasn't careful they might disappear before she could speak them. "Maybe you and I should go back to our hotel?"

Luc's whole beautiful face warmed as his lips spread into a smile. "Together?"

She nodded. "Together."

As they gathered themselves to head back to the vans, Bea saw Lauren standing near the castle entrance, talking with a couple of the camera ops. She looked over at Bea and caught her eye—then gave her an assuring nod. Bea nodded in return, and Lauren smiled.

Sleeping with Luc was nothing like sleeping with Ray.

With Ray, there had been an oppressive urgency, a shared knowledge that whatever the two of them would ever have together could only exist in the space of these few hours, this one night. It was ending as it was beginning, their long-delayed happiness already mingling with their inevitable destruction. They didn't luxuriate in lengthy explorations of their bodies—there wasn't time for that. They consumed each other instead, and when morning came and he was gone, Bea felt chewed over, destroyed.

With Luc, everything was different. The soft way he kissed her, how tenderly he removed her clothes.

"And you're sure you are okay?" He must have asked a dozen times, and every time she laughed and told him she was, and every time he smiled with genuine relief, and every time she let herself fall for him just a little bit more.

"You understand my concern," he said, kissing the edge of her jaw beneath her ear. "At the château, I kissed you, and they had to call the paramedics. I would not want to cause a cardiac arrest."

Bea tried to come up with a rejoinder, but she was having trouble being quippy. Then Luc started kissing her neck and slowly moving his mouth down her body, and she stopped being able to form any thoughts at all.

"You're certain you want this?" he asked a few minutes (or maybe hours) later. He'd gone to find a condom and now was back in bed, lying beside her, his muscled body fully displayed in the lamplight. Bea ran her hands along the dark tattoos on his arms, marveling at how unself-conscious he was—she had pulled a sheet up to her armpits as soon as he'd gotten up.

"I think I do," she said, but her voice was small and unsure.

"Bea," he said, kissing her gently. "It's okay if you're not ready. Tonight, next week, next month. I'm not going anywhere."

She reached for his neck, and he pulled her close to kiss her. "I'm ready."

He slid the sheet down her body, and the light touch of his fingers grazing her torso gave her chills. She leaned over to turn off the bedside light, but he stopped her.

"Why are you doing this?"

Bea blushed. "I just—that's what I usually do."

Luc grinned at her. "But you know the chef eats first with his eyes."

"I'm no expert, but I thought the chef ate pretty well with his mouth."

Luc threw his head back and laughed, then leaned down and kissed her deeply.

"Let me see you," he whispered. And Bea nodded.

"Tell me," he urged. "Tell me what you want."

"I want you," she implored—there was nothing uncertain in her voice now. "I want this."

He lowered himself down, his body hovering above hers. "Do you remember what I said, the first night I met you?"

Bea's eyes searched his—the moments all jumbled together, she couldn't pick out the one he meant. She shook her head, then gasped softly as she felt him move into her. He let his weight press her down, and she loved the feel of him pushing her deeper into the mattress. She twisted her limbs around him, pulling him closer, kissing him harder.

"Tell me," she pleaded, and suddenly she was desperate, she had to know. "Tell me what you said the night you met me."

He moved his fingers down, and she felt everything being pushed out of her body and brain except him and this; the sounds they made were low and primal.

"I said," he rasped, "you should have everything you want."

He moaned her name, and his voice was full of gravel; the stones flooded over her, rough and smooth like the banks of a river, remembering and forgetting, and she was gone.

The next morning, Bea woke in an effervescent mood, despite the audacity of the production staff banging on their hotel room door at some indecently early hour.

"Don't let them in," she whispered to Luc, leaning over to kiss him. "If we're very quiet, I'm sure they'll go away."

"This is a very good strategy," he whispered back, starting to kiss her for real.

"Guys, come on, we've got to get moving!" a producer shouted.

"Okay, okay," she called, fastening her robe. "Come in already!"

The producers had brought coffee as well as fresh-squeezed orange juice and warm pain au chocolat. Bea was famished, and she happily let the cameras get all the obligatory giddy post-coital footage they needed as she and Luc enjoyed their breakfast.

Afterward, she kissed him goodbye and left to get ready for the day. She had an hour or so of direct-to-camera interviews to film, and then it was time for another kiss-off ceremony— the last one of the season, in fact. Which raised an interesting question, actually: Who the hell was Bea going to send home?

Sam was the only man who'd said point-blank that he was in love with Bea—and after last night, Bea could hardly say goodbye to Luc. Even after how badly he'd hurt her when he rejected her in Moustiers, dismissing Asher seemed ludicrous— she couldn't imagine her life without him. At the same time, he'd run so hot and cold this entire season, and given what he'd revealed about his ex, Bea had some doubts that he'd ever truly let himself be vulnerable again.

Bea's heart told her that Asher was the right man for her, but her mind yearned for Sam's kindness and humor—and for the certainty he claimed to offer. And as for her body? Well, that was Luc's. She talked in endless circles about the pros and cons, but by the time her interviews were over, she was no closer to making a decision. And of everyone on set, there was only one person whose opinion she actually wanted to hear.

"Hey," she interrupted a junior producer, "do you know where Lauren is? I'd like to check in with her before the ceremony."

The producer scrunched her face up. "She hasn't been on her walkie, but she's probably in edit bay? I know she was up cutting pretty late last night. They're set up in Room 108."

"Great, thank you!" Bea chirped, and headed down to the first floor. She knocked on the door of Room 108 a couple of times, but there was no response—maybe Lauren had fallen asleep? Bea felt guilty waking her, but after all the millions of times Lauren had invaded her privacy at all hours of the day and night, she decided it was justified. The hotel was a gorgeous old place that had no magnetic keycards, just regular, actual keys—which meant you could leave your door unlocked. So Bea gave the doorknob of Room 108 a try, and she found that it opened right up.

The big room was mostly dark and filled with scattered desks and tables covered in laptops and monitors. Lauren always brought a mobile editing unit so they could cut footage on the fly and upload it for the main edit bay back in L.A.—it was the only way they could cut the episodes quickly enough to be ready for air just days (or sometimes hours) after they finished filming. The room looked empty, but a crack of light was spilling out from the bathroom, whose door was ajar, and Bea heard voices.

She took a tentative step closer, but stopped short when she heard a moan—that was definitely sex, and it was definitely Lauren. *Wow,* Bea thought, *guess everyone's getting lucky today.*

Bea truly didn't mean to spy, but as she turned to leave the room, she caught a glimpse of the bathroom mirror: Lauren was perched on the vanity, her legs wrapped around a man—his face was obscured, but Bea's eyes went directly to the clearly visible tattoos running down his arms.

She took an involuntary step back—and slammed right into one of the editing tables.

"Shit!" she screeched, pain throbbing through her thigh.

"I *said* to give me twenty, who's in here?" Lauren called.

Bea tried to scramble out of the room as quickly and quietly as possible, but she wasn't fast enough—Lauren came out of the bathroom and flipped on the light.

Luc was right behind her.

"Oh fuck, Bea." Lauren stepped toward her, still buttoning her shirt. Luc stood stock-still, looking dumbstruck.

Bea closed her eyes. "This isn't happening. Even my luck can't possibly be this bad."

"Bea, I'm so sorry," Lauren spluttered, "you can't imagine—I'm absolutely humiliated right now."

"Oh, I think I can imagine exactly how humiliated you feel," Bea said coldly.

"Shit." Lauren brought her hands to her temples. "Bea, you have to believe me, I never intended for you to find out about this—"

"And what?" Bea laughed, feeling crazy. "What, it was just totally fine for you to sleep with Luc behind my back as long as I didn't know it? What the hell were you thinking?"

"Clearly, I wasn't!" Lauren pleaded. "We were just talking one night, early in the season, before you were actually trying to date any of these guys, and I know it's cliché—believe me, I know how ridiculous I sound right now. But we'd both been drinking, and, well, you know how Luc is. It just happened."

Bea set her jaw. "It's not early in the season now."

"I know." Lauren agreed. "I know I should have stopped

this the second it started. It's just—you do something once, and then twice, and then it gets easier and easier to justify going on with it. And with how mixed your feelings were for Luc, I never imagined he'd still be here this late in the game. I thought my thing with him would end when you sent him away."

"Is that why you told me to send him home last week?" Bea demanded. "To make this easier for yourself?"

"Partly, maybe," Lauren admitted. "But also because I know you're looking for a committed relationship, and I obviously know that Luc can't give that to you."

Bea turned toward Luc for the first time in the conversation. It hurt just to look at him, to take in the mouth, the arms, the body that had been intertwined with hers only a few hours prior. His eyes were downcast now, his face clouded with guilt and shame.

"Is that what you thought too?" she asked. "That a relationship wasn't possible for us?"

"*Non*," Luc spoke softly. "For me, you are very special."

"How special can I be if you're sleeping with other people?" Bea asked bitterly.

"And you are not?" he countered. "You were with two other men just this week!"

Bea's face burned—she couldn't bring herself to tell him that, as a matter of fact, she wasn't.

"Bea"—he took a step toward her—"you must believe that with us, it is different. With Lauren, with other women—"

"There are others?" Bea interjected.

Luc sighed. "For me, this was just fun, yes? Just a way to pass the time. But with you, the way we talk, the way I feel when I am with you . . . This makes me so happy, my Bea.

Don't you think we could be happy together, after all of this is done?"

"Does that happiness include you sleeping with other people?"

"For me, love is not possessive," he said simply. "I would never ask this of you, and I hope you would not ask it of me."

She looked at him, wondering how it was possible they'd never discussed this. Was she foolish to feel hurt? Did she even have a right to assume some modicum of monogamy while she was openly dating two other people?

"Bea," Lauren broke in, "I need to say again how truly sorry I am."

"I can't," Bea interrupted. "I'm sorry, I just—I need some time, okay?"

Bea willed her body into motion. She walked out of Room 108 and back into the hall, through the lobby, and to the elevator that would take her up to wardrobe. As she waited, she realized with bitter irony that her visit with Lauren had precisely its intended effect: Bea now knew without a doubt exactly who she was going to send home.

Three hours later, Bea was standing in the hotel's lovely courtyard surrounded by marble fountains and intricate topiaries under an overcast sky, wearing a curve-hugging Brandon Maxwell black velvet wrap dress with a low neckline and a high slit, her hair in sleek Veronica Webb waves, lips painted vivid red: *Miss Scarlet in the conservatory with a knife*. Sam, Asher, and Luc were standing in front of her—Sam looking nervous but excited, Asher tight-lipped and tense as he always was at these ceremonies, Luc staring down at the ground.

"Before we get started," Johnny said as the cameras started rolling, "Bea has something she'd like to say. Bea? The floor is yours."

Bea nodded and stepped forward. She felt sick with nerves, the image of Luc and Lauren in the bathroom fresh in her mind, the feeling of Luc's hands etched in her skin, the memory of Sam's and Asher's rejections stinging in her gut. She knew that if she was going to move forward with any of these men, it was time to say out loud what she wanted. Without that, none of them stood a chance.

"This was a really tough week," she started, her voice quivering. "We had a lot of miscommunications, and though I know it wasn't your intention, all three of you hurt me, and badly. And I know that's partly on me, because I haven't been totally clear with you about what I want. So. So I'm going to do that now."

She took a deep breath and looked up at the men, all three of whom were staring at her intently.

"I want to fall in love," Bea's voice broke, "with someone who loves me. Who wants a committed relationship with only me. To figure out if we're right for each other, and, hopefully, to build a life together. And if you don't want that, too, well. Then I want you to tell me. And I want you to leave. Okay?"

The men nodded, everyone looking uneasy, and Johnny gave Bea the cue to begin the ceremony, in the order they had discussed.

"Sam?"

Sam exhaled and walked toward Bea, his expression more serious than she had ever seen it.

"Bea"—he took her hands in his—"I am so, so sorry that I hurt you this week. You know I didn't mean to, but that's on me for making a decision that affected both of us without talking to you to see what you wanted. I hope you can forgive me for that, and I hope you want a future together as much as I do."

Relief mingled with the tension Bea was feeling as Sam leaned down and she pressed her lips against his cheek. She still wasn't remotely sure whether he was ready for a serious relationship, but at every turn, he exceeded her expectations, and she was grateful they'd get to spend another week together.

"Okay, Bea," Johnny prompted. "You can only bring one more man to the finale. Who's it going to be?"

Bea knew who she wanted to bring—she just didn't know if he was ready for this next step. She called Asher's name, and he looked considerably less pleased than Sam as he approached her.

"I don't know why you keep doubting this," he said tensely. "I'm not sure what else I can do."

"Asher, you have to understand," Bea pressed, "this whole time, it's been so hard for me to know what's real. I just—I have to know that we're on the same page, that this isn't me wanting something you're not ready to give."

Bea knew Asher had a right to be frustrated, but the truth was that she was getting pretty aggravated herself. Sam had no problem expressing his devotion to Bea—hell, even his love for her—so why was it so damn difficult for Asher?

He exhaled heavily, like he was reading her thoughts—or maybe just her face.

"I know." Asher smiled. "I know how hard it's been for you. And I want you to know how excited I am for us to live our lives outside of this. No cameras. No pressure. Just us. Okay? That's what I want."

He leaned down so she could kiss his cheek, and she lingered near him, breathing in his assurances, hoping they would steel her for what was coming next.

"Luc, I'm sorry." Johnny affected his most serious tone. "That concludes our ceremony. Please take a moment to say your goodbyes."

Walking toward Bea, Luc looked, if possible, even more handsome than he had that first night of filming. He looked worn now, more tired, more sad. But he wasn't a stranger anymore, Bea thought. She knew him, and he was much more beautiful for that. No matter what he'd done, it was going to be terrible to say goodbye.

"I know I let you down this week," he murmured, "and for this, I cannot forgive myself. You must know that our night together was perfect; for me, this is one of the best nights of my life. I hope you believe it's the truth?"

Bea's throat felt too tight to speak—but she nodded. Luc took her in his arms and hugged her close; over his shoulder, she saw that Asher's face was stony, and her nerves started churning again. Was he thinking of Vanessa? How angry was he to learn she'd spent the night with Luc?

"My Bea," Luc said, brushing a loose curl away from her face. "I still believe you should have everything you want. I am only sorry I cannot be the one who gives this to you. We both know why I must be the one to go today. But I wish I did not have to."

Bea smiled at him sadly. "It should honestly be illegal to be that charming."

Luc laughed softly, his great, throaty laugh, and it hit Bea how much she was going to miss him.

"I have to say goodbye to you now," she whispered.

"Don't say goodbye," Luc teased gently. "Say '*adieu.*'"

"Oh my God." Bea laughed. "You are so fucking French."

"*Mais, bien sûr.*" Luc grinned, and with that perfect familiar glint in his eye, he walked off and disappeared into the hotel.

Bea sighed—that was it, right? The hard part was done; it was time to wrap the ceremony and load the vans to drive to Paris for their final week of filming. But the cameras were still rolling, and everyone held their marks.

"What's going on?" she asked. "Aren't we finished?"

"Not quite," Johnny said, and paused dramatically. "Because we have one more man we need to bring out."

"What?" Bea blurted. "Who?"

Bea looked wildly around, but she didn't see anyone—and Johnny was still talking.

"Bea, all of us at *Main Squeeze* admire how brave you've been in your search for love. We want you to find the right man to be with for the rest of your life, so even though it's unorthodox, when we heard we might be depriving you of a serious option, we felt that bringing this man here was the right thing to do."

Johnny gestured toward the hotel doorway, where Bea saw that a figure was approaching. It wasn't anyone she recognized from the show—but there was something familiar about his height, his gait. As his features slid into focus, an unspeakable dread took hold of Bea.

It was Ray.

Bea's insides seized up and contracted—she couldn't breathe. There he was, walking toward her, the first time she'd seen him since they'd slept together nine months ago, a ghost, a bomb, the shrapnel of him still radiating pain throughout her body.

"Asher, Sam," Johnny was saying, "I apologize for this unusual turn of events. This is Ray, a man from Bea's past, and he believes he may belong in her present."

Bea tried to read Asher's and Sam's expressions—Sam's face was shocked, Asher's frighteningly dark—but then Ray was in front of her, taking her hands.

"Hiya," he said, and she could see that he was a mess too; his hands were shaking.

"What are you doing here?" She fought for breath.

"I was trying to get in touch with you for weeks, but none of my messages went through," he explained. "I finally emailed the producers and told them I had to see you."

"Even though you're engaged?" Bea asked before she could stop herself—shit, she shouldn't have said that on TV. But if Ray was here, then surely . . . She looked into his eyes for confirmation of the thing she'd wanted so much for so many months, the unspoken, fervent wish that had made her feel so disgustingly guilty.

"I broke off the engagement," Ray confessed. "I moved out last week; I should have done that a long time ago. And I know—listen, I know how bad this timing is, it's not how I would want to do this for you, for us. I wish we could have more time. But they told me you could be getting engaged next week, and I just—I couldn't let that happen. I had to come and see you. So, here I am."

He went to hug her, but Bea stepped back, wobbling in her heels.

"Okay!" Johnny clapped his hands. "There will be plenty of time for you two to catch up, but right now, we need to make some decisions. Bea, I need to ask you whether you'd like for Ray to join you on the show, or if you want to send him away right now?"

Bea's head was spinning, but before she could respond, Asher stepped forward.

"No—I'm sorry, no." He turned to Bea. "Is this the guy you told me about?"

Bea nodded, no longer able to stop herself from crying, her body quaking with sobs.

"And you just, what, you forgot to mention he was engaged?"

"Asher—" She started toward him.

"I can't *believe* you," he seethed. "After you met my children, after I told you about Vanessa, after you promised to be honest with me, you lied?"

"No." Bea shook her head. "No, Asher, I didn't—we were on camera, and I thought they were still engaged, I couldn't say what happened on TV, it wouldn't have been right—"

"You're still lying," Asher snapped, "you're lying to me right now. You didn't tell me what happened because you wanted to protect your image, and you wanted me to protect you."

"That's not fair." Bea's voice was ragged. "I made a mistake, Asher, please, it was a long time ago—"

"No," he shot back. "It was two nights ago. To think how bad I felt for not spending the night with you, when this whole time, you've been hiding who you really are."

"Hiding who I am? Are you serious?" Bea cried. "Asher, maybe if we'd had some time together off camera, I could have explained, but you didn't give us that chance."

"I see." He pressed his lips together. "So, I'm responsible for your lies because I made a decision to put my children's interests first? I'm sure you would have preferred I rush right into sharing a room with you, but fortunately for both of us, I'm not Luc."

"Is that what this is about?" Bea was irate. "Tell me, Asher—

and don't you lie to *me*. Are you angry because I withheld one piece of information that I had a right to keep private? Or are you angry that I slept with someone else?"

Asher looked at her coldly, his eyes filled with derision.

"I'm not angry, Bea. I'm grateful I got to see your true colors before this went any further."

And with that, Asher turned on his heel and marched out of the courtyard. Bea thought of running after him, of screaming for him to wait, to come back, but she knew, as surely as she'd ever known anything, that he was gone—and even worse, that he was right. All this time, she'd told herself she was cursed, but maybe that wasn't true at all. Maybe she was just a liar, just a cheat, finally getting exactly what she deserved.

EPISODE 8

"DECISION"

(2 men left)

Shot on location in Paris, France

TMZ BOMBSHELL EXCLUSIVE: *MAIN SQUEEZE* PRODUCER SLEEPS WITH CONTESTANT, PRODUCTION SHUTS DOWN

PARIS, FRANCE: Most dramatic twist ever????? TMZ has learned EXCLUSIVELY that the reason French chef (and fan favorite) **Luc Dupond** departed *Main Squeeze* is that star **Bea Schumacher** wasn't the only woman on the show he'd slept with! Multiple sources confirm that Dupond was having a secret on-set affair with *Main Squeeze* executive producer **Lauren Mathers.** One source contends that Bea caught Dupond and Mathers *in the act,* but TMZ cannot confirm that story conclusively at this time. What we do know—for sure— is that Bea was aware of Dupond's infidelity before the kiss-off ceremony where she dismissed him. Both Dupond and Mathers declined to comment for this piece, but we're hearing Mathers is in hot water with her bosses at ABS—particularly since PRODUCTION HAS HALTED IN FRANCE!

The cast and crew of *Main Squeeze* arrived in Paris last night for their planned final week of filming, but as of yet, no shooting unit has left the hotel. After Bea walked out in the middle of her previous kiss-off ceremony, the company drove from Amboise to Paris on schedule, but today's planned shoots were all canceled. No word yet on when production is expected to recommence or whether next week's season finale will air Monday night as scheduled. We're also still awaiting word on whether attorney **Ray Moretti** will join the cast as one of Schumacher's final two men, or if **Sam Cox** will win this season by default. *(WHO IS RAY MORETTI? CLICK THROUGH FOR SLIDESHOW.)* If you're reading this from Paris or have any inside information to share, send all tips and photos to tips@tmz.com.

TRANSCRIPT OF *BOOB TUBE* PODCAST EPISODE #056

Cat: How are you holding up, Ruby?

Ruby: Cat, as the kids would say, I'm shook.

Cat: The people who make *Main Squeeze* promos are pretty liberal with the phrase "most dramatic ceremony ever," but this time, I think they actually made good on that promise.

Ruby: I feel like you didn't adequately prepare me for just how low this show would stoop to deliver thrills to its viewers.

Cat: There are some lessons you can only learn firsthand.

Ruby: Okay, let's take a minute to process everything that just happened. First, can I just say, we really nailed it with our respective picks for Bea.

Cat: Did we?? I picked Asher, who ABANDONED her at the first sign of trouble, and you picked Sam—

Ruby: Who's the only man left from the original cast. I win!

Cat: Wow, so that was just a backdoor way for you to brag?

Ruby: I am crafty and clever like a reality TV producer.

Cat: SPEAKING. OF. WHICH.

Ruby: Okay yeah—so for those who haven't heard, TMZ broke the news that Luc actually had an affair with the executive producer of the show, which seems absolutely crazy to me. Cat, as our resident *Main Squeeze* expert, can you confirm that it's not normal for one of the contestants to sleep with the showrunner?

Cat: I mean, I have no idea how often it happens, but this is certainly the first time it's been exposed by the national media.

Ruby: Do you think she'll be fired?

Cat: I've got to imagine that's a fireable offense, but who knows? This is reality television, not a symposium on ethics and moral philosophy.

Ruby: Is it wrong that I would watch that?

Cat: Um, it's called *The Good Place,* and it was the best show on TV. But we digress.

Ruby: Okay, so let's recap: We've got Asher, who seemed like a nice grown-up option for Bea, except he quit the show. Do we think he's really gone, or is he coming back?

Cat: We don't know anything for sure, but from what I've read on the *Main Squeeze* sub-Reddit—

Ruby: Oh, Cat.

Cat: Don't judge, you're part of this fandom now too. Anyway, according to the Redditors, this isn't the producers messing with you—Asher really did leave the show.

Ruby: And I presume we're also done with Luc forever?

Cat: Farewell, Luc, you beautiful, beautiful douchenozzle.

Ruby: Do you think he was good in bed?

Cat: Men that good-looking rarely are, but Bea certainly seemed happy the next morning, so I guess maybe?

Ruby: Plus the whole slap/kiss thing in New York was vaguely kinky, I bet he's not totally vanilla.

Cat: Well, hopefully for Bea's sake, she at least got to have some good sex before she got totally blindsided.

Ruby: So the two men she has left are Sam and this other guy, Ray, who's like sort of her ex but also was apparently engaged to another woman until very recently?

Cat: All of Ray's social media feeds have been set to private or deleted entirely, which isn't surprising considering the circumstances of his newfound fame. But some intrepid bloggers dug through his friends' feeds, and they found out that he's an attorney living in Atlanta, that he and Bea worked together in Los Angeles in their early twenties, and there are pictures of him with a perfectly lovely looking woman who we can guess is the recent fiancée in question.

Ruby: Has anything like this ever happened on the show before?

Cat: We've seen exes show up from time to time, but they're usually dismissed pretty quickly, like, "Oh God, Brian, why would you think this was a good idea?" Very occasionally, we've seen men ask to be members of the cast, and sometimes they even get to be, but that usually happens way earlier in the season. To have this guy show up on the precipice of the finale is pretty unprecedented—not to mention that Bea actually walked out of the ceremony before asking him to stay, so we have no idea if she's even going to!

Ruby: So if she doesn't, then what, it's only Sam for the finale and I automatically win everything?

Cat: That's one way of looking at it.

Ruby: It's the way I choose, Cat.

Cat: Speaking of choice, we know that you have lots of options for cook-at-home meal kits, but "Je ne sais quoi" kits offer something special: a secret ingredient to add to every recipe. I've been using the kits at home, and they're super fun—you get a little envelope with a red "X" to add to your meal, and they do always have that extra something special—if you will, that "Je ne sais quoi."

Ruby: Wow, so you literally do not know what . . . is in your food.

Cat: You literally don't! It's just as much of a mystery as next week's *Main Squeeze* finale. We'll be back right after this.

Bea hadn't spoken a word since Ray's arrival and Asher's abrupt departure. Over Johnny's pleas and Lauren's protests, she simply walked out of the courtyard, then holed up with Alison and refused to leave the wardrobe room until the producers gave in: They declared that they were finished filming in Amboise and would drive to Paris the next morning as planned. Bea didn't leave Alison's side for the entire trip, and she ignored anyone else who tried to speak to her.

Once they arrived in Paris and the producers let Bea into her hotel room, she double-locked the door and crawled into bed, fully clothed. She was exhausted from being up most of the previous two nights—first a night of bliss with Luc, then a night of agony tossing and turning and wondering how this all could have gone so wrong. She was grateful that her first day in Paris was a travel day with no scheduled filming so she could finally get some rest, but try as she might, bone-tired as she was, sleep still wouldn't come. Bea thought back to the first night of filming, to that anonymous man who'd taken one look at her and walked away. How ironic that Bea's fears that others would follow in his footsteps never materialized until now—and when a man she truly cared for finally did choose to leave, it wasn't because of Bea's looks, but her lies.

Bea knew on some level that she wasn't the only one to blame—that Asher was jealous and judgmental, that he'd made her feel insecure throughout this process, that he was probably already looking for an excuse to bail in order to have done so that quickly and completely. But here in this lovely hotel room with a view of the Seine, Bea felt hollow without him, like some essential part of her had been scooped out.

The sun rose, and Bea's start time for her day of shooting came and went. The producers called and called, so she turned off the ringer on her hotel phone. Who was she even supposed to see today—Sam or Ray? She hadn't technically said that Ray could stay, but she suspected Lauren would insist: It would be an awfully boring finale if Sam were the only man left. *And besides,* she thought, *Ray broke off his engagement and flew all the way here.* To see her. To try and work things out between them. To stop her from getting engaged to someone else. Someone else like Asher . . . the man she'd thought might really be her husband. And now, because of Ray, he was gone for good. Was that reason enough to dismiss Ray outright?

Or was there a chance, after everything, that they really were meant to be together?

There was too much to think through, too many conflicting emotions to parse with no clean point of entry. Lacking any better ideas, Bea decided her best available option was to take a long, hot bath.

Her suite's bathroom had bleached wooden floors, gleaming slate walls, and a gigantic soaking tub made of smooth white ceramic. Bea piled her hair into a bun and slipped into the steaming water, feeling like some tiny portion of the awfulness of the past twenty-four hours was beginning to leach out of her. Bea closed her eyes and willed herself, for just a moment, to relax.

That's when the knocking started.

"Fucking fuck," Bea muttered, keeping her eyes closed and willing the knocker to leave her alone. She ducked her head under the water, but when she came back up a few seconds later, the knocking was even louder, and was now accompanied by shouted entreaties.

"Bea, come on!" Lauren's voice was muffled from the hallway, yet still had a piercing quality that was completely impossible to ignore. "I'll stand out here and scream all day if I have to, you know I will! We have the whole floor, so there's no one to complain! Come on, Bea! We have a finale to shoot, and you can't hide in there forever! Aren't you hungry? I brought pastries!"

Bea exhaled audibly. The truth was, she was starving. And as much as she wanted to shut herself away in this bathroom until everyone she'd ever met (and the collective consciousness of the Internet) had forgotten she'd ever agreed to do this show, she knew that wasn't entirely tenable. So she dragged herself out of the tub, toweled her hair dry as best she could, and wrapped herself in an all-too-thin cotton robe before opening her door.

"Du Pain et Des Idées is your favorite, right?" Lauren affected an air of nonchalance. "That bakery up in the tenth? I sent a PA to get these for you."

"You think you're going to bring me a pistachio elephant ear and all will be instantly forgiven?" Bea narrowed her eyes, but she took the pastry Lauren held out to her all the same, and couldn't help but utter a small groan of pleasure as she took the first perfect bite. Lauren came into the room and shut the door behind her.

"Bea." Lauren looked contrite—and, Bea noted, a good deal more haggard than normal. She was in leggings and a sweatshirt herself, a far cry from her normally polished attire. "I need to tell you again how sorry I am about Luc."

"What about Ray?" Bea's voice was soft, but firm. "Are you sorry about him too? And Asher?"

"I had no idea Asher would walk out on you." Lauren shook her head. "I mean, really, he couldn't stick around to have a conversation? Couldn't even wait to see if you would let Ray stay? I expected him to handle Ray's arrival more maturely—didn't you?"

"Maybe if you had warned me," Bea argued, "I could have done something differently, or at least told him first about Ray being engaged."

"Bea, come on. I'm still making a TV show here, I can't just give you a quick heads-up about the biggest twist of the season."

"But why do it!" Bea demanded. "Why bring Ray here at all?"

"Because I thought it was the right thing to do!" Lauren looked genuinely confused. "You decided that you wanted to find love on this show, and from everything he told me, the guy is genuinely in love with you—and he seemed to believe that you felt the same way. He insisted that you wouldn't want to get engaged to someone else without knowing how he felt about you first, and I believed him. Yes, I orchestrated his arrival for maximum drama, but I never, ever thought you'd be so upset about it—and honestly, I'm still not totally sure why you are."

"Because he hurt me," Bea said quietly. "He hurt me more than anyone else in my life ever has."

"And don't you think," Lauren asked gently, "that the reason he was able to hurt you so badly is because you care about him so much?"

Bea buried her face in her hands, knowing that of course Lauren was absolutely right, but desperately fearing what it could mean, after all this time, to open her heart back up to a man who had treated her so callously.

"I don't know," she rasped. "I honestly don't know if I can do this."

"Bea, I know you're in pain. How could you not be? Yesterday morning, you thought you had Luc and Asher, and now you don't have either of them. Of course you're reeling; it would be insane if you weren't. But I also need you to see the good in your situation. You're in Paris. Sam is here, and he loves you. Ray is here, and he broke off his engagement for you. Millions of people are rooting for you to find love, and they think Asher and Luc are jerks. They want you to be happy. The question is whether you want that too."

"And if what I really want, more than anything, is to walk off this set, buy a plane ticket, and go home?" Bea asked.

Lauren sighed. "Is that actually what you want? To shut yourself off from these men, to deny yourself the chance to find out whether you could really be with one of them? If you'd told me that when I first met you, Bea, I would have believed you. But after everything that's happened, and how much you've changed? I don't believe it now."

"Even if that's true," Bea conceded, "I don't know what to say to Sam, and I *really* don't know what to say to Ray, and I—"

Bea's voice broke. She'd never experienced this many intense emotions in her life, and she was starting to feel extremely ready to shove them all in a box to be shut in an attic and never seen again.

Lauren looked at her with sympathy. "Would it help if you talked to Marin?"

"Really?" Bea felt a small lurch of hope. "How?"

"Magic!" Lauren joked. "No, Skype, obviously. The camera guys will bring a laptop with a line to Marin, and you can video chat."

"I'm really looking forward to the day when everything I do won't be documented for an audience of millions." Bea sighed.

"I'm getting a taste of that myself this week," Lauren groused. Bea shot her a puzzled look.

Lauren picked up her phone and handed it over to Bea, who frowned.

"I'm not allowed to see a phone."

"And I'm not allowed to sleep with a cast member, but here we are. Just look. It'll make you feel better."

Bea looked down—Lauren's phone was open to an article on TMZ revealing, in big bold letters, that Lauren had slept with Luc.

"Holy shit," Bea muttered.

"See?" Lauren prodded. "And you thought you were the only one having the week from hell."

"One might argue you brought this on yourself," Bea countered.

"Yeah, well."

"Is this true?" Bea looked up from the article. "They really might fire you?"

"I'd like to see them try," Lauren scoffed, but Bea could sense a chink in her usually steadfast confidence. "Last night was the highest-rated episode seven in franchise history."

"Really?" Bea put down the phone. "Even higher than the time those two women ditched the Main Squeeze to run away together?"

"Yes!" Lauren beamed. "What did I tell you, Bea? People love you! Also, that lesbian plot was totally fake, but Farmer Greg was so boring, I had to do *something,* you know?"

Bea closed her eyes and smiled, happy to have any absurd situation to think about other than her own.

Lauren left her to get dressed, and a few minutes later, a camera crew arrived with a laptop, as promised.

"Babe!" Marin yelped from her window on the shiny screen. "What's happening? Are you okay? They wouldn't tell me anything, they just said you needed to talk."

"Ray's here," Bea said, the gravity of the situation seeping back in as she spoke the words aloud.

"I saw that—what the hell is going on?? They just cut to black at the end of the episode, after you walked out of the kiss-off ceremony. What's happened since? Have you heard from Asher?"

Bea shook her head. "I think he's really gone, Mar."

"Bea, no." Marin covered her mouth. "He's crazy about you, I know he is."

"Not anymore." Bea exhaled heavily. "You heard what he said."

"He was just hurt," Marin consoled her. "And insecure, and definitely jealous—you were totally right about that. But let's come back to him. What's happening with Sam? And Ray?"

"I haven't seen either of them since the ceremony."

"OUTSTANDING! Send Ray home immediately!"

"Without even talking to him? Mar, he broke up with Sarah and came all the way here—"

"He came all the way there when *he* wanted, to suit *his* needs, without a thought in the world for how it would affect you. He heard you might be getting engaged, and did he think, *Wow, maybe Bea finally has a shot at being happy with someone else?* No. He thought, *Hey, I'm Ray, I need to get on an airplane and make a mess of Bea's life, because that's my signature move.* And when his actions caused a really great guy to walk out on you, he was probably cheering internally that he managed to improve his odds. He's a selfish asshole, Bea. That's who he's always been, and it's who he's always going to be. Send him home."

Bea took a breath. "Asher didn't leave because Ray showed up. He left because I lied to him."

Marin rolled her eyes. "You have a right not to tell the world on television that you slept with someone engaged, okay? Wouldn't you have discussed it privately with Asher at some point if Ray hadn't shown up and forced your hand?"

"I don't know. I guess it doesn't matter now."

"It does matter, Bea. It matters a lot whether you allow this man who has hurt you so much to hurt you even more."

"I only have two men left," Bea argued.

"Yeah, and one of them is a nice, sweet guy who's head-over-heels in love with you, and the other has been doing his level best to make you miserable for the better part of a decade."

"Well—doesn't that mean something?" Bea pushed back, her anger rising. "That I've loved him for so long, that I've wanted to be with him all this time, and now, finally, here he is, saying he wants the same thing. How crazy would I have to be to throw that away?"

"Not as crazy as you'd have to be to waste another second on him. Do you want to turn back into the person you were last year? Breaking plans, crying every day, refusing to go on a single date? You were unglued. Why would you *ever* let him back into your life?"

"You don't know what it's like." Bea felt bitterness creeping into her voice. "To think about someone so much for so many years, to dream about him and picture your life together. You've never felt that way about anyone."

"Don't do that, Bea. Don't deflect. This isn't about me, it's about him. This is exactly why I told him to stop trying to contact you."

Bea's face went dark. "When did you do that?"

Marin opened her mouth, and then closed it.

"At the beginning of filming," Marin admitted. "He texted me to tell you he'd been trying to reach you, but that none of his messages were going through . . ."

"Was this before or after you came to set to see me?"

Marin looked down. "It was before."

"And you didn't tell me?" Bea was horrified. "After all the months I spent begging for him to talk to me, you lied and kept it from me when he finally did?"

"Bea, I liked the guys I met so much, and I didn't want Ray to ruin things with them—which, by the way, is exactly what he did."

"It's not Ray's fault the producers orchestrated things so Asher would be totally blindsided!" Bea shot back. "Maybe you don't always know best about my life, Marin. Maybe sometimes I get to make my own decisions—even if you'd rather I stay single like you forever."

Marin shook her head. "You're going to feel like a real idiot when this is on television and you hear how spiteful you sound."

Bea turned to the camera operators. "I'm done with this conversation. Can we be done now?"

But they didn't say anything—they just kept rolling.

"This isn't you, Bea," Marin pleaded. "He brings out the worst in you, because he makes you think he's all you deserve."

Bea couldn't take it anymore. She slammed the laptop shut, then stormed back into the bathroom and closed the door.

——Forwarded Message——

FROM: Ray Moretti <<u>rmoretti@gmail.com</u>>
TO: Kiss Off Entertainment <<u>info@kissoff.com</u>>
SUBJECT: I'm the man from Bea's past

Hi, whoever's reading this. I don't know exactly what to say here, but on last night's episode in Ohio, Bea said that when she started the show, she was still getting over someone. I believe the person she was talking about was me. And the truth is, I'm not over her. Not even close. I know you're already halfway through your season, and maybe I'm too late. But if there's any way that I could see her, or even talk to her, I'll go anywhere, I'll buy a plane ticket, I'll do whatever it takes. So, if there's even the slightest chance here, I hope you'll get in touch. Please. I'm just not ready to lose her.

On some level, Bea was enticed by Marin's suggestion to send Ray away without so much as a conversation—after all, it would be easier than confronting him, than admitting to him (and to the world) exactly how badly he'd hurt her. But even if talking to him was a terrible idea, Bea had to know, finally, the truth of what had happened between them, whether he had ever loved her the way that she loved him. She told Lauren she'd see Ray that afternoon, but that she didn't want a planned date—just to go for a walk through her favorite city with a man who was once her best friend. Lauren agreed quickly, sounding frankly relieved that Bea was consenting to see him at all.

Part of Bea wanted to spend hours in hair and makeup and wardrobe before she spent time with Ray, to transform into a powerful, sexy TV goddess—her "armor," as Luc had described it. But tempting as that was, she put on her own jeans and an old flannel shirt instead, some mascara and sheer red lipstick. She knew she'd look a mess on camera, but at least she felt like herself. It didn't make sense to be *Main Squeeze* Bea with Ray, all glamour and glitz. All the artifice of the show, the lavish romantic fantasies—none of that was them. They were just two old friends with too much history, too much pain.

When he opened the door of his hotel room, he said, "Hi."

He looked wrecked, like he hadn't slept either, maybe in days.

So she said, "Do you want to take a walk by the river?"

And he said, "Maybe north to the canal?"

"I love the canal."

"Bea." He smiled sadly. "I remember."

They barely spoke on the walk—it was as if they were acclimating, remembering how it felt to be in each other's presence. It was chilly and gray by the Seine, the water churning, tourists stopping to ogle the *Main Squeeze* camera crew. But as they made their way out of the center, the crowds thinned, and Bea began to feel the same sense of ease she remembered from the months when she lived in this neighborhood ten years prior.

Once they reached the canal, Bea ducked into a wine shop and bought a bottle with her own euros. Bea and Ray sat on the steps of one of the canal's dozens of bridges, drinking their paper-cup red, two cameras pointed at their faces, a boom mic over their heads. All of it so alien, but being with each other the pinnacle of normal.

"I didn't think I'd see you again," he said, his voice that same come-hither mumble, the one you had to lean close to hear.

"When? After last summer?"

"No, the ceremony. I've never seen you that upset."

"Well, sure," Bea said drily, "you usually take off before you have the chance."

"Usually?" Ray looked apprehensive. "How many instances have there been?"

"Um, countless?" Bea was surprised to hear the anger in her voice. "Last July, for starters. The night we kissed at Chateau Marmont. The millions of times we were curled up talking in some bar and you ditched me for one of your L.A. girls."

"Come on, Bea." Ray flushed with embarrassment. "You know I never cared about any of them the way I cared about you."

Bea sat up straighter, took a drink of wine. "Then why didn't you act like it?"

"I did," Ray protested. "I spent every free minute I had with you."

"No—that's not what I'm asking. Ray, you flew to Paris to tell me you left your fiancée for me. And I just, I'm having trouble understanding why you need to make this grand gesture now, all these years later, when you never even went on a single date with me when we lived in the same place, when I was completely in love with you."

"I didn't know." He hung his head. "Bea, I swear, I didn't."

"Didn't know that I was in love with you? Or didn't know how you felt about me?"

"Either one. I was a mess back then. You remember what I was like, going out every night, hungover every morning."

"Calling me to bring you a vanilla shake and a McChicken with sweet n' sour sauce for the fries?"

"Oh my God," Ray moaned. "When you would show up at my door with that bag, it was like someone opened the gates of heaven."

"Yeah, and when I'd walk into your apartment and it was completely obvious that some other girl had just been there, I felt like I was in hell."

Bea shook her head, blinking back the first prickle of tears. "Ray, last summer—"

"I know," he cut in. "I know how badly I fucked up."

"No." She stopped him. "You don't, because you weren't there. I loved you for so long, and then during the biggest crisis of our relationship, you just disappear, like I never meant anything to you? We're not twenty-two anymore. You can't keep saying you're a mess and letting that excuse your behavior."

"Bea," Ray implored her, "I was so fucking confused. I felt like such an asshole for cheating on Sarah, and I thought staying with her was the right thing to do, but whenever I talked to you . . . I wanted to leave. Not talking to you felt like the only choice I had."

"You could have said that to me! You could have taken five minutes of your life to explain why you wanted to end our friendship and never speak to me again."

"I kept thinking, *Maybe I'll wake up tomorrow and it'll be okay. I'll be able to talk to Bea, and I won't love her, and she won't hate me.*" Ray took a drink. "But every day, I woke up, and I still loved you. And I was still so sure you hated me."

Bea was taken aback. "Ray, you've never said that to me."

"That I love you? I've said it a million times."

"I know, but—the way you said it just now, you made it sound like. You know."

Ray met her gaze, his face a mix of sadness and hope. "Like I was *in* love with you?"

"Well?" Bea's heart was pounding. "Are you?"

He took her hands. "Yeah, Beatrice Eleanor Schumacher, of course I am. I am completely, inescapably in love with you."

Bea closed her eyes. It was the sentence she'd wanted to hear for eight years, the sentence she'd imagined him saying millions of times.

But now, after everything she'd been through, Bea found that it wasn't enough.

"You still haven't told me why."

"Why I'm in love with you? You want me to do one of those rom-com things where I enumerate the reasons? I mean, I can—"

"No, Ray. You haven't told me why this took so long. Why we never got together when we lived in L.A. Why you kissed me once, then moved away and never said another word about it. Why sleeping with me freaked you out so badly that you had to cut me out of your life."

"I told you, with Sarah—"

"But why did you get engaged to Sarah in the first place? You always said you wanted to come back to L.A., so why did you follow her to Atlanta instead? Why didn't you come home to be with me?"

Ray shook his head in frustration. "I don't know what you want me to say."

Bea didn't know if there was even a point to pushing him on this, whether she was accomplishing anything more than pouring salt in her own wounds. But she needed the truth. If she was ever going to move on—either with him or away from him—she had to know.

"I read this article once," she said, "about this scientific researcher who analyzed people's porn searches."

"I'm sorry, you what?" If Ray looked confused before, now he was downright bewildered.

"Yeah, so, he got access to all this data, and he compared it to a survey of what people said they were looking for in a romantic partner, to try and figure out what people say they want versus what they actually want. And he found that some huge number of men, I forget the percentage, but it was really high, was looking online for porn of fat women. But when you ask men what kind of body type they want in a partner, almost none of them said they wanted someone fat."

Ray's face clouded with emotion as he started to understand what Bea was getting at.

"So the researcher talked about how this plays out," Bea continued, "how all these women are trying to lose weight because they think that's what men want, and all these men are trying to date thin women because they think that's what they're supposed to want. Do you know what he called it?"

Ray didn't answer—he just looked down.

"He said it was inefficient. A waste of time."

Ray blinked rapidly. "I know I wasted your time, Bea. Years."

"But *why?*" Bea pleaded. "Ray, I can't forgive you if you won't say what you did."

"Back then I ruined things with every woman I slept with, and I couldn't do that with you. I needed you too much." He shook his head. "I thought I was protecting us."

"By my count, the last two women you slept with were me and Sarah, and you ruined those pretty well too."

He took a long drink of wine, and Bea saw his hands were shaking.

"When we were in L.A., I knew I loved spending time with you. I knew how important you were to me. And I knew— fuck, Bea. I knew I wanted you."

"Is that really so hard for you to say?" Bea's voice was cold and quiet.

"Yes, but not for the reason you think. It's hard because I'm ashamed of how small-minded I was. Back then, when I tried to picture the two of us together—really together—I just couldn't. It didn't make sense to me. When I met Sarah, I thought, *Okay, this makes sense.* I moved in with her because it made sense, proposed because it made sense. It wasn't until last July that I realized what an idiot I'd been, how much I'd fucked up my own life—and yours, and hers—but by then I felt like it was too late. I couldn't see a way out of it."

"And now?" Bea pressed. "Now—what? You saw me on TV and suddenly the clouds parted and your true path was lit from above? Ray, how am I supposed to believe you've changed? After everything? How can I believe it?"

"Because I'm here." He put his hands on her knees, and she felt the warmth of him spreading through her, the same way she had on the Fourth of July. "Because I stole Sarah's copy of *People* and stared at you in that gown for hours. I bought every single magazine you've been in, by the way. I started reading all the blogs, all the rumors, desperate for any information about you, about these guys who were trying to take you away from me."

Bea was so nervous she was trembling. "They weren't trying to take me, Ray. You didn't want me."

"You're wrong." Ray wrapped his hands around Bea's wrists. "When I walked into that courtyard yesterday and saw you in that dress, I wanted you more than I have ever wanted anything in my life. I wanted to kiss you so hard you'd forget those other men existed. To make you remember you wanted me first."

He slid his hands up to her elbows, their forearms clasping, the movement bringing him closer.

"It was never a question of wanting you," she whispered.

"Then what is it?" He was inches away now, and she remembered the taste of him, and he smelled of musk and spicy clove, just like she knew he would, the same as always.

"The way you hurt me . . . I don't know. I don't know if I can trust you. If I even should."

"Let me make it up to you. I'm here, Bea. I'm in love with you. Let me show you. Let me show you for the rest of our lives."

Then he was kissing her, and it was all so strange and so familiar, to be cloaked in comfort and panic and the immutable weight of him, and something deep inside her clicked into place, the question finally answered of whether she would ever feel his lips on hers again.

She didn't know how long it went on like that, them making out on the bridge, their legs tangled together like a couple of insufferable teenagers. Eventually, a producer broke in to tell them they were losing the light; the crew needed to be let go for the day, and it was time to go back to their hotel.

In the van on the ride back down toward the Seine, Ray asked Bea if they could spend the night together. A voice in her head screamed, *Yes, please, yes,* but she shoved it downward and told him she wasn't ready, that she needed more time.

"You have all my time, Bea." He draped his arms around her, pulled her in, like she was his. "Every minute I have left is yours."

That night, Bea worried she'd lie awake fretting again, but her exhaustion finally overtook her. After all the confusion and elation and anguish and satisfaction, she found that there was nothing left to do but sleep.

Bea hadn't seen Sam since the ruinous kiss-off ceremony in Amboise, and she hadn't had an actual conversation with him since their date in Champagne, now a full week past—an eternity in *Main Squeeze* time, and seemingly double that in Bea's emotional journey. For their final date, Alison dressed Bea in dove-gray trousers and a black merino sweater, then handed her a silk bag small enough to fit in her palm.

"Eighteen pennies tied with red ribbon—an old superstition of my grandmother's," Alison explained. "She'd give them to us on special days for luck. After she died, my grandfather kept up the tradition, and now all us grandkids do too. They were married sixty years, can you imagine?"

"I honestly can't." Bea turned over the little satchel in her hands.

"Anyway, I just thought—for your last date of the season."

"Thank you." Bea hugged Alison, marveling that this whole experience had lasted only eight weeks, how little that really was compared to a lifetime.

After all the things Bea had seen in the past week—the shock on Luc's face when she caught him with Lauren, the slope in Asher's back as he walked away, the swimming relief in Ray's eyes as she gave in to her desires and kissed him—was there any sight so uncomplicated and welcome as Sam at the base of the Eiffel Tower, beaming as Bea approached him?

"I know it's so touristy, but look how BIG it is!" he exclaimed, his eyes full of wonder.

Bea laughed. "Yeah, that's kind of its thing. You want to ride to the top?"

"No, I absolutely do not!"

He pulled her into a super-tight hug, planting sweet kisses on her forehead and in her hair.

"I missed you so much." She exhaled.

"You've had a big week, huh?"

"Yuh-huh."

"Well, I've got this idea—maybe it's stupid, you tell me— but I've been thinking I might spend the rest of my life making you happy. So maybe today we get a head start?"

"How did you get so good?" Bea looked up at him, her heart swelling with fondness.

"You met my parents—your guess is as good as mine," he joked, and Bea burst out laughing, reveling in how easy it was to be by his side.

After they finished filming at the tower, they loaded into

their vans and went to Bea's all-time favorite department store, the Galeries Lafayette. From the outside, the Galeries looked like any other building, but inside, they were absolutely spectacular: dozens of chambers filled with the most beautiful clothes, all arranged surrounding a soaring atrium topped with a magnificently patterned glass ceiling. From each little *galerie,* you could stand at a railing and look across the atrium to see the whole wonderful place, every room framed in archways of gleaming gold.

"This is not like Macy's," Sam observed, and Bea laughed.

"I'm so glad we got to come here," she told him. "I have a little tradition that every time I'm in Paris, I stop in to buy a tube of Chanel lipstick."

"Wow." Sam grinned. "How'd I land a classy girl like you?"

Bea smiled back. "Just lucky, I guess."

"I know it," Sam murmured, pulling her in for a lingering kiss.

After that, they had to separate for a while: For this portion of the date, they were both given personal shoppers to help them select outfits for their dinner that night, a sunset cruise on the Seine. While Sam was off in menswear with a snooty fellow named Augustin, Bea went up to the specialty department with her shopper, Lorraine—one of those impossibly chic Parisian women in her fifties who looked more fashionable in a black turtleneck than most Americans could in couture.

"Well," she said to Bea in a warm but matter-of-fact tone, "for you I am afraid we do not have many options."

"I know." Bea sighed. "I always try to shop here, but I usually just buy shoes and makeup—I never have much luck with clothes."

"Ah, but this is the fault of backward-thinking designers," Lorraine assured her. "Today, we'll make our own luck."

Lorraine had pulled a few gorgeous dresses for Bea, and while some worked better than others, none were perfect—until Bea stepped into a dress by Tanya Taylor. It was a black silk kimono-style dress embellished with jewel-bright flowers made of rainbow-hued sequins and paillettes that shimmered and caught the light with Bea's every move. Best of all, the dress had pockets, so Bea could keep Alison's satchel of pennies with her for the rest of the date.

"*Parfait,*" Lorraine approved.

An hour later, the sun was beginning to set, and Bea met Sam on a sleek riverboat whose deck was strung with softly glowing lanterns.

"I finally get you on a boat, and *still* no bikini," he teased. "This is just mean, Bea."

"You don't like the dress?"

"No. I love it." He leaned in to kiss her cheek.

"You don't look so bad yourself." She grinned—he was downright dashing in a marine-blue suit worn with a crisp white shirt and open collar. She saw he was holding something—a small black glossy box.

"What's that?" she asked, though she had a feeling she already knew.

"I was done shopping before you were, and I had some time to kill," Sam explained. "Since you couldn't stop by the lipstick counter, I figured . . ."

Bea opened the box and pulled out the tube of Chanel—a rich, vibrant red in shade 104: Passion.

"I hope the name isn't too on the nose," Sam said. "I saw it and I thought, *Yeah. That's the one.*"

"It's perfect." Bea beamed. "You're perfect."

"Well," Sam said, his voice smaller than normal, "maybe you can wear this when you kiss my cheek tomorrow."

As they danced on the deck of the boat to the music of a string quartet playing classic love songs, Bea felt like she was living the epitome of a *Main Squeeze* daydream—the place, the dress, and of course, the man. If she was here to find her happy ending, there wasn't a more perfect one than this. But as she felt the weight of the pennies in her pocket, she thought about Alison's grandmother's sixty years of marriage—the long, extraordinary mundanity of a life like that. Not the performance of a fairy-tale finale, of being seen in a relationship, but the reality of actually being in one: the dumb fights and ER visits and thrilling moments you never forget and all the boring, everyday ones in between. Bea knew she wasn't looking for an ending—not really. She was looking for a beginning.

"Sam," she said softly, "can I ask you something?"

"Of course, anything."

"If it had been some other girl here, instead of me, do you think you would have fallen in love with her?"

Sam looked perplexed. "That's a pretty weird hypothetical."

"I'm sorry, I didn't phrase that well. I guess what I mean is—we met in this specific place, at these specific times in our lives. For me, I was trying to get over someone."

"The guy from the other day?"

Bea nodded. "Did you want to talk about that at all?"

"I don't know," Sam mumbled. "It's not really my business."

"Of course it is." Bea frowned. "If you're considering proposing to me tomorrow, you have a right to know what the hell is going on in my life."

"Are you thinking about a proposal?" Sam's tone was tentative. "Because . . . I definitely have been. And this other guy, obviously, I don't know him, and I don't know what's happened between you. But I trust you, Bea. So if you tell me that you and I are good, that's all I need to hear."

"You always know the perfect thing to say," Bea murmured. "And as for a proposal . . . yeah, I've been thinking about it. A lot, actually. That's kind of what I was trying to ask you about in the first place."

Sam's face turned more serious. "What's on your mind?"

"With everything going on in your life, am I wrong to think that us being together, having a next step, or an anchor point—that that would be a bit of a relief?"

"Are you asking if I would ask you to marry me as an excuse to move out of my parents' house?"

"No! No, I would never say that. You just seem so certain about us, and I guess I'm trying to get to the bottom of why."

"Because there's no way it could be as simple as me being in love with you?"

"I'm not doubting you, Sam," Bea said quietly.

"It feels like you are." He took her by the shoulders. "What are you afraid of?"

Bea met his gaze. "I'm afraid that you're looking for your next chapter, and I'm looking for the whole rest of the book."

"I want to give you that, Bea," Sam assured her. "I promise, I do."

She kissed him gently and told him she believed him.

As day faded into night, their boat docked near the Louvre, and fireworks exploded in showers of sparks and color. Bea thought about the Fourth of July, about the fragile new connection she'd formed with Ray, and about how unknowable life was, how fleeting. In the end, she had only her choices.

As she relaxed into Sam's arms, she felt she was finally ready to make hers.

The next morning, Bea woke up in her beautiful suite for her final day of filming her season of *Main Squeeze*. After she'd been to hair and makeup, she donned a custom silk robe embroidered with her initials and met with celebrity diamond purveyor Nils van der Hoeven, who showed her a vast array of dazzling engagement rings. Per long-standing show tradition, Bea was meant to pick her favorite ring, and somehow, magically, in a highly produced segment, the man she'd chosen to be her husband would pick that very same ring to propose with later that day, proving just how well he understood his beloved's heart's desire.

Bea wasn't even sure she wanted a diamond engagement ring, but Mr. van der Hoeven ("Please, you will call me Nils") had paid good money to advertise his wares on television, so Bea oohed and aahed over his various gaudy confections, all of which were undeniably dazzling, but none of which were remotely her taste.

"I have one more case to show you," he lilted in his accented English. "These are vintage."

He opened a black velvet briefcase filled with twenty rings—mostly large Edwardian cuts, with a few vintage Deco settings thrown in. One caught Bea's eye: The setting was rose gold and considerably less shiny than the rest; upon closer inspection, she saw it had been hammered and carved to resemble a tree branch. The main stone was a round-cut champagne diamond with a couple of obvious flaws, flanked on each side by triangles of three tiny opals that glowed white and blue and green. It was the most beautiful ring Bea had ever seen in her life.

"What's the story with this one?"

"Ah, this is a very interesting choice," Nils said, extracting the ring and holding it up to the light. "It was made for a famed heiress in the 1920s, but she called off the wedding— she never married, and the ring was never sold. I acquired it at auction some time ago, and it's been in my collection ever since. I always wondered why no one snapped it up—but between you and me, I think most brides get skittish when they hear its history. They believe it must be cursed or some such nonsense."

"Cursed," Bea echoed, remembering the times she'd used that word to describe herself. "What happened to the heiress?"

Nils looked confused. "As I said, she never married."

"Sure, but her life—did she do other things? Have a career? Travel the world?"

Nils shrugged. "No one has asked me this before—I would have no way of knowing. Would you like to try it on?"

Bea shook her head and said no, thank you. She told him she preferred a three-carat flawless cushion-cut diamond on a platinum band. He said it was an excellent choice.

After he left, Alison arrived in Bea's suite for their final fitting together.

"I hope you'll forgive me," she said, "but I pulled this for you. We have other options if you don't like it."

She held up a long, flowing dress of soft blush satin with wispy sleeves, a deep neckline, and a dramatic slit, accented with strategic bustles embellished with crystalline camellias. Bea ticked off its flaws on her fingers.

"Unforgiving fabric, light color, no structure, and that slit will *definitely* show my thighs."

"I know, I know, I know, you hate it. Okay, let me show you some others—"

But then she noticed Bea was cracking up.

"It's fabulous." Bea beamed. "Who made it?"

"Actually . . ." Alison said shyly, "I did."

"What?" Bea was overwhelmed. "Alison, this is a gift. *You're* a gift. God, what am I going to do without you?"

"Come on, you're not rid of me yet, I'll see you for the reunion show, all the red carpets in L.A., we're going to be together all the time."

"Promise?" Bea grinned. Alison did, and when she was done tucking and twisting the dress and sweeping one side of Bea's perfectly formed finger waves out of her face with a beaded clip, Bea felt like the most delicate spring flower, ready to burst into bloom.

The proposal was the crown jewel of any season of *Main Squeeze,* and this year, Bea was forced to admit, Lauren had really outdone herself: The proposal was to take place in the middle of the Pont des Arts, the narrow bridge across the Seine where lovers affixed locks emblazoned with their initials to symbolize their eternal love, with a spectacular 360-degree view of Paris all around them. Bea waited at the southern end of the bridge with Lauren and most of the crew; Sam and Ray were stationed at the other end with their respective field producers, both in cars with darkened windows so that neither would know who was visiting Bea first to receive his rejection and who was about to discover he'd won the season—and Bea's heart.

While the lighting and sound crews were getting ready to go (apparently shooting in the center of a bridge, while dramatic, posed a great number of technical challenges), Lauren approached Bea to go over their final shot of the season.

"Are you ready for this?" Lauren asked.

"I am, actually." Bea looked down at her freshly manicured hands, her left ring finger notably bare.

"And you feel sure about your decision? No last-minute changes?"

"Does that happen a lot?" Bea laughed.

"You'd be shocked how often." Lauren rolled her eyes. "But if you're good, I think we're just about ready to film?"

"Do you think I'm making the right choice?" Bea asked.

"Honestly? It's not what I would do," Lauren admitted. "But it's your life, Bea. After everything, you deserve to be happy."

Walking to the center of the bridge, her gown rippling in the breeze, the Île Saint-Louis rising to the east and a pink Paris sunset blazing in the west, Bea took a moment to breathe deeply. She wanted to remember exactly how she felt in this moment: flooded with joy, with warm, rosy sunlight, with the knowledge that, after the most difficult year of her life, everything was finally going to work out exactly as it should.

"Okay, Bea," the field producer called. "We're a go!"

She steadied herself and looked toward the edge of the bridge, where at this very second, in a perfectly fit tuxedo, Sam was emerging from his limo and making his way toward her, a beautiful, brilliant smile on his face.

REUNION SPECIAL

Shot and aired live
at ABS Studios in Los Angeles

@People BREAKING NEWS: @OMBea rejects both suitors in #MainSqueezeFinale! Click through for full story!

@YayStephy WAIT WAIT WAIT SHE SAID NO TO BOTH OF THEM WHAT WAIT WAIT #MainSqueezeFinale #whatishappening

@MichaelLovesSoccer holy fuck I did NOT see that coming #MainSqueezeFinale

@KrisTeeAhNuh AHAHAHAHA she kicked them both to the curb YAAAAAS BEA OH DIP

@TheEllenShow You have so much love in your life, @OMBea, no matter if you're partnered or on your own. Thank you for showing us beauty AND strength!

> **@ChrissyTeigen** also @OMBea thank you for showing us how to have dirty sex with a hot bad French man we'll all be grateful forever

@Data_Emily RIP me I am deceased @OMBea has killed me

@ArianaGrande 👁️👁️ 👁️👁️ 👁️👁️ thank u next @OMBea

@AbyssiniaStapleton Bea Schumacher is a classic example of #SelfSabotage. Rather than marry either of two excellent prospects, she chooses to remain alone. And if she dies that way, she'll have no one to blame but herself—read more in my new book!

@SueSchu614 @AbyssiniaStapleton HOW DARE YOU SPEAK THAT WAY ABOUT MY DAUGHTER SHE MADE A BOLD DECISION TO CHOOSE HER OWN HAPPINESS IN DEFIANCE OF SOCIETAL EXPECTATIONS

@DerringDuncan You tell her, Mom!

@CheshireBob Ms. Stapleton, we're all extremely proud of Bea, and we'll thank *you* not to sabotage *her.*

@TimSchumacher999 Enjoy itsy-bitsy spider, bitch 🕷️ 🕷️ 🕷️

@CoachJonS Tim, that joke is awful. You've got to let it go.

@ChrisEvans81 Wait, does this mean Bea is still single?!? What do I have to do to get her to call me?!?!?! #MainSqueezeFinale #thisisgettingembarassing #seriouslycallme

MAIN SQUEEZE BOMBSHELL: BEA BAILS ON BOTH BEAUX!
by Amy Bello, people.com

BREAKING—*Main Squeeze* star **Bea Schumacher** has turned down not one, but TWO marriage proposals on tonight's bombshell finale! After an emotional reconnection with ex-boyfriend **Ray Moretti** and a fairy-tale day in Paris with fan-favorite **Sam Cox**, Bea was ready to make her final decision—but in a twist no one saw coming, she chose herself!

Sam was the first one out of the limo—and as *Main Squeeze* viewers know, this always spells rejection—but Bea kindly broke the news to Sam before he had a chance to get down on one knee. As soon as he removed a ring box from his jacket pocket, she stopped him from going further, telling him that although she had grown to love him deeply as a person, she truly believed that they were helping each other along their path to find their futures. Sam was clearly devastated, but took the news with characteristic good humor and grace.

Not so Ray, who has proven a shocking and volatile presence from the moment he stepped into the kiss-off ceremony in Amboise. As the second man out of the limo, viewers at home presumed Ray and Bea would be getting engaged—as did Ray himself, when he got down on one knee and proposed using the three-carat cushion-cut diamond Bea had selected from celebrity jeweler Nils van der Hoeven earlier that day. But Bea told Ray that as much as she'd once dreamed of a life together, she now had other, bigger dreams—ones that didn't include a man who'd hurt her so badly for so long. (And instead of calling her parents to announce her engagement, we got to see Bea call her best friend Marin to apologize and tell her she'd been right about Ray all along—a vindicating and relatable moment for best friends the world over.)

The response to the finale on Twitter was fast and furious, with fans and celebs alike weighing in to support Bea as the first *ever* female Main Squeeze to turn down both of her final two suitors. So what's next for Bea? We'll have to wait for next month's live reunion special to get all the details, but *People* will bring you more news as it breaks. For now, we wish *Main Squeeze*'s most controversial leading lady all the happiness in the world.

BLOG POST FROM OMBEA.COM

137,418 Reblogs ↻ · 281,927 Likes ♥

Oh hi there, OMBeauties! I haven't seen you in a hot minute, and I've *missed you!!* So, tell me everything. How's your spring going? You showing off your flirtiest little dresses? As for me, you know, not much is new. Okay, okay, just kidding, my entire life has been turned upside down and shaken miserably, gloriously around again, but after all that, I'm back home and thrilled to be here. It feels like everything is the same and absolutely nothing is, in the best, most exciting way—I can't wait to tell you more about the projects I'm lining up next.

For now, I want to let you know that I'm going to be taking a little break from this blog. So much of what I do here is share the details of my life with you—my plans, my outfits, my hopes, my hottest takes. I have always considered it a privilege that you'd want to hang around with me for all that, and I can never express how grateful I've been for your support. Especially during the insanity of the last two months, knowing you were out there watching me, rooting for me, and sticking by me despite my (many) mistakes made all the difference.

Main Squeeze was an intense experience, and sometime soon, I'll figure out what I want to say about it, and how. For now, I'm excited to take a breath, to NOT have every second of my life available for public consumption for a minute, and to figure out what comes next.

Sending you all the love and sequins in the universe.

xoxo, Bea

Comment from MattyMorgan921: What are the projects????
TELL US THE PROJECTS!!!!! (crosses fingers for remake
of Splash starring Channing Tatum and mermaid Bea????)

Comment from djgy23987359: hi bea youre probably still gonna
die soon bc your so fat but good job on that show, maybe
look into weight watchers???

Reply from DrKamler32998: did you even WATCH
episode 2? Obesity isn't causally associated with most/any
deadly diseases

Comment from Steven929: Bea if you're happy being single,
that's great and everything, but honestly, maybe still call
Chris Evans? The guy seems really upset. Just a thought.
Congrats!

✣

TEXT MESSAGE TRANSCRIPT, MAY 2:
BEA SCHUMACHER & MARIN MENDOZA

Marin [2:28pm]: Hey, have you left yet? I'm running so
behind!!!

Bea [2:30pm]: GET YOUR ASS OVER HERE!!! David just
told us he learned to twerk, and he's going to show us??
Marin he's so drunk it's going to be AWFUL

Marin [2:31pm]: NO! Did Sharon make that sangria again??
That stuff is so dangerous

Bea [2:35pm]: 1) she did 2) I'm wasted 3) would it be a
terrible idea for me to make out with Sneha's hot cousin?

Marin [2:36pm]: Boy cousin or girl cousin

Bea [2:36pm]: Boy cousin I'm still straight Mar

Marin [2:37pm]: Cool then he's all yours!!!! As long as no one's leaking anything to the press, GO FORTH!!!!

Bea [2:37pm]: I'm not really gonna make out with him

Marin [2:38pm]: I know, babe. But you COULD

Bea [2:39pm]: CORRECT, I COULD

Marin [2:42pm]: Ok getting in a car see you soon tell David not to twerk until I get there!!!!!!

Bea [2:47pm]: Too late he just did and it was art

------Forwarded Message------

FROM: Olivia Smythson, The Agency <smythson.olivia@ theagency.com>
TO: Bea Schumacher <bea@ombea.com>
SUBJECT: RE: Projects

Hey, Bea! Just want to do a quick rundown of where we stand on various projects—your call with CondéNast is SET for Thursday, and Jenna Lyons is going to be in town next week, she wants to know if you're avail on Wednesday to talk potential collabs? Katy and Corey will email you to set it up. We're also fielding calls from several publishers about a memoir, but I've told them all you aren't ready for that. Any thoughts on a bone we could throw them in the meantime? A fashion handbook, something like that? Just spitballing here, you're the creative!

And just to double-check, you're sure you don't want to do anything else in television?? I have to tell you, Bea, I'm getting more calls than I know what to do with. Would you remotely consider being a substitute host on The View? Call me when you can!

P.S. I know you're taking a "break" from social media, but can you PLEASE post at least one Insta story a week? We've got to keep your engagement metrics up, or all these new followers will be for NOTHING! Thanks, Bea!

SCRIPT OF *MAIN SQUEEZE* PROMOTIONAL AD RELEASED IN ADVANCE OF SEASON 14 REUNION SPECIAL

OVER FOOTAGE OF THE PARIS SKYLINE AT SUNSET, WE HEAR A VOICE—

VOICEOVER
One month ago in Paris, not one, but *two* men were ready to marry Bea Schumacher.

INSERT FOOTAGE: SAM AND BEA ON THE PONT DES ARTS

SAM
I love you, Bea. I want to spend my life with you.

INSERT FOOTAGE: RAY DOWN ON ONE KNEE

RAY
Bea, will you marry me?

ROMANTIC MUSIC SWELLS AS WE PUSH IN ON BEA'S FACE—BUT THEN WE FREEZE-FRAME AND—

SFX: RECORD SCRATCH

VOICEOVER

But she turned them BOTH down.

SMASH CUT TO A RAPID MONTAGE OF FOOTAGE
FROM THROUGHOUT THE SEASON OVER UPBEAT
MUSIC

VOICEOVER

This Monday, on the LIVE *Main Squeeze* Reunion Special, we'll answer *all* your burning questions. Why did Bea turn down Sam and Ray? Have they forgiven her? Has *she* forgiven Luc? And what will she say when she sees Asher for the first time since he left the show?

INSERT FOOTAGE: BEA, ASHER, GWEN & LINUS
LAUGHING OVER DINNER

VOICEOVER

Don't miss a moment of the dramatic *Main Squeeze* Reunion Special, this Monday night at eight, only on ABS.

Life back in Los Angeles was a little like a parallel universe, one where Bea was mostly the same person, where not many things had changed, but where strangers occasionally gave her odd looks of recognition, and rarely went so far as to offer unsolicited opinions on her romantic choices. Bea didn't frequent the kinds of bars or restaurants where having been on reality television would entitle one to skip the line, much to Marin's chagrin. These days, Bea preferred to lie low; avoiding crowded places and staying as far from social media as her agent would allow, relishing the actual, real-life company of her actual, real-life friends. She hadn't watched any of the episodes of her season yet, even though they were all right there waiting. For now, she was happy to be back in her own house, her own clothes, her own bed.

But as the reunion show neared, one month to the day after the finale, public interest in Bea's life started to perk up again, and Bea felt the familiar nerves return. It was nothing close to the anxiety she'd felt prior to and during her season, but she thought over and over about what it would be like seeing so many of these men for the first time since filming ended—Luc, Sam, Ray, and, if he showed up, Asher.

There wasn't a thing she could do to stop her racing thoughts—but at least she got to bring Marin along for moral support, and the network sent a plush black SUV to chauffeur them to the studio in Burbank.

"Who are you most nervous to see?" Marin asked, helping herself to some M&M's from the car's minibar. "Ray or Asher?"

"Asher's not coming," Bea said quickly.

"You don't know that for sure. TMZ said he might be there."

"Last I heard, he hasn't been responding to any of the producers' emails. They say he's in breach of contract."

"Seriously? Do you think they'll sue him?"

"No, that was just a useful threat to make sure I didn't shut down production. I don't think they'd bother over whether he shows up for one reunion show."

Bea's tone was casual, but the truth was that she thought about Asher more than she liked—when she read something funny, when she wore anything leopard-print, when she stopped into Sephora and found herself browsing for things

Linus might like. As angry as she still felt about the way he'd abandoned her at the first sign of trouble, she found she missed him even more. She'd asked Alison to look into whether he'd be coming to the reunion, which was how she found out he'd cut off contact with the production staff entirely. That was that—he couldn't possibly send a clearer signal that he had absolutely no interest in seeing her again. It stung—and badly—but Bea knew that if she could get over Ray, she could get past Asher too.

"Serious question, though," Marin deadpanned, aiming to lighten the mood, "can I punch Ray when you see him?"

"Marin!" Bea laughed.

"Not like a Krav Maga hit—just a gentle CrossFit hook! Please?"

"He got down on one knee on national television and I said I'd rather be alone than marry him. Isn't it possible he already got his comeuppance?"

Marin scowled. "Not even close."

Once they arrived at the studio, things moved quickly: Bea was back in the hair-and-makeup chair, then off to ward-robe, where Alison dressed her in a custom Jason Wu tuxedo with slim pants, long lapels, and a sheer chiffon camisole that gave the illusion Bea was wearing nothing at all underneath. Her hair was styled in a sleek chignon, her eyes were rimmed with black kohl, and her five-inch black-patent Manolos were completely impossible to walk in. In short, Bea looked like a fierce boss bitch—the total opposite of a typical *Main Squeeze* reunion show look, which was something soft and white and lacy that suggested a glowing bride-to-be.

"Wow," Marin enthused, "if any of these men didn't regret losing you already, they're really going to now."

"Right?" Alison grinned. "My work here is done."

"Ugh," Bea sighed, "your work literally is done."

"Nuh-uh, I'm styling you forever." Alison gave Bea a warm hug, then turned to Marin. "Where are you watching the show? Up in the audience?"

"Oh, I guess." Bea didn't miss Marin's affected nonchalance. "Bea, is that right?"

"You can watch wherever you like," Bea said pointedly. "Do you want to hang with Alison in the green room?"

"I mean, sure, if that'd be cool with you?" Marin turned to Alison, who smiled coyly.

Well, Bea thought, *maybe someone will find love from my time on this show after all.*

But before she could poke any further fun at her two friends, a producer came to grab her—the audience was seated, and it was nearly 5 P.M. Pacific, 8 P.M. Eastern. Time for the show to begin.

@Reali-Tea Okay shippers & sippers, are you ready for the big @MainSqueezeABS reunion show?? Tweet along as we find out the dirty dish on how that finale really went down.

@Reali-Tea Here's Johnny to intro a blooper reel of all the men being idiots in the house, snore. How many times can I watch Trevor get wasted and fall off the diving board?

@Reali-Tea Omfg, they're making all the personal trainers (Kumal, Ben K., and I want to say Ben Q.? maybe?) take a quiz about fatphobia and every time they get one wrong they have to do 10 push-ups hahahahaha I love this show so much

@Reali-Tea OH SHIT they brought Ben G.'s kindergarten class to teach Jefferson why it's bad to be a bully!!!

@Reali-Tea Boss little girl: "Jefferson, do you think it's okay to be mean to people?"

Jefferson: . . .

BLG: "Well, if you don't think it's okay, then why were you mean to Bea?"

Jefferson: . . .

Tiny boy w/glasses: "My mom said that bullies hate themselves. Do you hate yourself?"

@Reali-Tea They're making Jefferson take Michelle Obama's anti-bullying pledge. Y'all, I will go to my grave stanning this show, I swear to god.

@Reali-Tea Awwwww, it's Wyatt!! Hey boo! He's thanking @ombea and all of us for accepting him for who he is, I am cry

@Reali-Tea Johnny's telling Wyatt they have a surprise guest to see him???

@Reali-Tea SHUT UP IT'S WYATT'S MOM HATTIE!!!!! She says she loves him and she's proud he came out, she thinks they should get another set of matching tattoos. Tattoo this family on my face tbqh HATTIE PLS ADOPT ME.

@Reali-Tea Okay, first half of the show is OVER! Queen @ombea herself coming out after the break, so grab your mugs now, because you KNOW she's about to serve some tea.

∝

"Hey, stranger." Lauren grinned at Bea—she was waiting beside the stage door, where Bea would be making her big entrance after the commercial break.

"Hi!" Bea was surprised to see her. "I thought you'd be in the booth with the director?"

"I'm going back in a second," Lauren explained, "but I wanted to see you before you head out there. How've you been? Single life agree with you?"

"Right, something new and different." Bea laughed. "But I have to say, it's exhilarating to wake up every morning and know there's not a single man whose emotional turmoil is my responsibility."

"See?" Lauren grinned. "You're coming around to my way of thinking."

"Really?" Bea was skeptical. "After everything we went through this season, you still have absolutely no interest in finding love?"

"Definitely not," Lauren scoffed. "I mean, you saw the choices I make—Luc, of all people. No one should let me anywhere near a relationship, even if I did want one, you know?"

Bea recalled the first time she'd met Lauren, how envious she'd been of her disaffected attitude toward romance, wishing she could be equally blasé so she wouldn't have to experience the excruciating pain of heartbreak. But now, she found she felt the opposite. Maybe Lauren really didn't want a relationship, or maybe she was putting up a front to protect her own heart (Bea strongly suspected the latter). Either way, Bea had no desire to go backward. She treasured the openness, vulnerability, and wild possibility her life held now, and she wouldn't trade that for anything, no matter how much it had cost to get here.

"Hey," Lauren interrupted her thoughts, "did I do the right thing, asking you to do this? Did you do the right thing, saying yes?"

"Definitely." Bea nodded. "At the very least, you did exactly what I hoped you'd do."

"What's that?"

Lauren looked puzzled, and Bea grinned warmly at her producer. "You changed my life."

"Bea?" the stage manager called. "You're on in thirty!"

He started counting down, and Lauren gave Bea's hand a quick squeeze before she sprinted off toward the booth. As the cameras went live, Bea walked through the stage door and into a blazing spotlight—she waved and smiled, but she couldn't see a damn thing. The audience roar was absolutely deafening; Bea had never experienced anything like it in her life. They were cheering and stomping and screaming her name, and Johnny came to guide her to the stage in the middle of the studio, where the infamous *Main Squeeze* couch awaited her.

"Wow," Johnny said, once the screaming of the crowd had finally abated, "I don't know that any Main Squeeze has ever gotten a reception like that one!"

That started the crowd cheering again.

"Thank you!" Bea exclaimed. "Honestly, it means so much to me that you're here, and to have your support."

"Let's talk about that, Bea." Johnny steered the conversation to the list of topics the producers had prepped for her. "What has all the public controversy around your season been like for you?"

"Obviously, some people didn't think I looked the part of a romantic leading lady"—boos from the crowd—"but I knew that would be the case going into this. It's one of the reasons I said yes to being on this show."

"You said yes *because* you knew some people would object?"

"I wanted to prove that I had every right to be here," Bea answered. "That I could star in a show about love just like any other woman."

"How do you think that worked out, given that you were

the first female Main Squeeze in history to turn down two proposals?"

Bea laughed. "I guess I showed that I deserve love *and* to be picky about it."

The audience laughed, and applauded too.

"You talked about how the audience saw you—but what about how you see yourself? Did the show change that?"

"Yes," Bea said, "definitely. The show took so many unexpected turns for me, right from the moment the first man stepped onstage the very first night. Seeing all these men who *did* conform to conventional ideals of what makes someone attractive—I was humiliated. Obviously, some of those men gave me reason to believe that they found me repulsive. And I'm ashamed to say this, but I think it's important to be honest: There were moments when I believed them. I felt myself being dragged under by every bad thing that's ever been said about me, and worse, every bad thing I've ever thought about myself."

"In a way, you were your own worst enemy."

"I don't know that I was worse than Jefferson, but yeah, it wasn't great."

The audience laughed gently at this.

"And the hardest part was, because I was believing these terrible things about myself, I *wasn't* believing the men who genuinely wanted to get to know me. I wasn't even giving them a chance."

"You were in a pretty bad funk, and you had to pull yourself out of it."

"That's right."

"And how did you do that?"

"How does anyone do anything? With help! My best friend, Marin, came to set pretty early on, that was a real game changer for me. Then we went to Ohio, and I got to be with my family, which was great."

"That was also the week you started getting closer with Wyatt," Johnny pointed out.

"Yes, absolutely," Bea agreed. "Wyatt and Sam in particular were so good to me in helping me believe that I deserved more than to shut myself away from the possibility of finding love."

"And Asher?" Johnny urged.

"Things were more complex with Asher—and with Luc. I had beautiful moments with both of them, and tough ones too."

"Luc has been pegged as the villain of your season—maybe one of the worst villains in the history of *Main Squeeze*. But it sounds like you don't see him that way?"

"I don't," Bea said. "I can't. It's not that simple for me. Luc hurt me badly, but he also made me feel beautiful when none of the other men could. He was the first man in my life to show me how that felt."

"Well, you're about to have a chance to tell him exactly what you think about him—let's welcome Luc to the show!"

A spotlight illuminated Luc as he made his way toward the stage in tight jeans and a strategically undone black button-down, his hair long enough now to be pulled back in a loose little ponytail. The audience reaction was mixed—they cheered for him like they knew they shouldn't, but they just couldn't help themselves. Bea understood exactly how they felt.

"Bea." He kissed her cheek, and he smelled the same—salt and smoke. "It is good to see you."

"You as well," she said politely.

"The last time we saw you two together was at that unforgettable kiss-off ceremony in Amboise. Have you communicated since then?" Johnny asked.

They both shook their heads—they hadn't.

"The public didn't find out until after the episode had aired that Luc was having an affair with a producer of this show. But Bea, did you know? Is that the reason Luc went home that day?"

"I did know," Bea answered.

"Of course she knew," Luc added. "She saw us herself."

This prompted a smattering of gasps from the audience, and Bea shook her head—even now, Luc always had to cause drama.

"Well." Johnny's eyes widened. "That's news! Bea, is this true?"

"Yes," Bea admitted. "That morning, I walked in on them."

"How did you feel when that happened?"

"You know, it was tough, to have that happen within hours of spending the night with Luc, something which was very meaningful to me—and still is."

"Because he was the first person you'd been with since Ray?"

Bea sighed. If America was going to know the truth about her sex life, they might as well know all of it. "He's still the only person I've been with since Ray."

Concerned murmurs from the audience—poor Bea!

"Do you regret your decision to spend the night with him?"

"No, not at all," Bea said forcefully. "Luc and I have incredible chemistry, and we acted on it. I always doubted whether we could make a relationship work outside the confines of the show, and I know now I was right—and in that way, Luc helped me figure out that even though being with him was so exciting, I don't have to settle for a relationship that isn't fully what I want. Do I wish we'd been able to part on better terms? Of course. But I don't hold a grudge. On the whole, Luc was really good to me, really genuine, and a really important part of my journey on this show."

"Luc, are you surprised to hear this?"

"Yes, I am very surprised." He turned to Bea. "I thought you were furious with me."

"I was furious with you, then. I mean, could you not have waited twenty-four hours after sleeping with me to sleep with someone else?"

Luc grinned sheepishly, eliciting an "Oh, you are *bad*!" from a woman in the audience.

"Yes, Luc is very bad," Johnny teased, "and that's why we think he'll be very *good* in the Main Squeeze Mansion. What do you say, Luc? Will you join us for another round this summer?"

"Ah yes, and why not?" Luc grinned, clearly thrilled to be featured on a *Main Squeeze* spin-off. Johnny took them to commercial break, and as Bea rose to give Luc a polite hug goodbye, he murmured in her ear.

"I am leaving my phone number with Alison for you. Call me anytime you like, yes?"

Bea smiled. "Don't hold your breath."

He laughed as he pulled away, his breath tickling her ear.

"We were good together, no? Goodbye, my Bea."

He kissed her cheek and made his way offstage, leaving room for the next guest. As he walked toward her, Bea prepared herself for a far less pleasant interaction.

"Hey," Ray said curtly as he sat down beside Bea. He was stunningly handsome as ever, but he looked a little worn, a little gaunt. He refused to make eye contact, and before they could say anything more to each other, a producer was counting them in, and they were back on live TV.

"Welcome back," Johnny said smoothly. "Our next guest

is a man who Bea knows well, but who the rest of us just met recently. Ray, welcome to the studio."

"Thanks," Ray said flatly. Bea wondered what sort of contract he'd signed—she couldn't imagine why he'd agreed to do this.

"First off, Bea, same question I asked Luc—have you two been in touch since the show finished filming?"

"No," Bea said at the same moment Ray said, "Yes."

"Well, this is interesting. Ray, you've contacted Bea?"

"Yes, I've texted and emailed her."

"Bea, have you seen those messages?"

"No, um. After the show finished filming, I reached out to Sarah, Ray's ex-fiancée, to apologize for my behavior, and for contributing to a situation that must have been really painful for her on a lot of levels. I never heard back from her—not that I expected to, she certainly doesn't owe me anything—but sending her that note really solidified for me that it would be best for everyone if Ray and I sever ties for good. So I blocked his phone number and set up a filter to send any emails from him straight to spam."

"You did?" Ray looked genuinely hurt.

"Ray, I can't keep doing this with you. It's been too many years. I need to move on."

"But *you're* the one who rejected *me*," he said, almost whining. Bea had to remind herself not to feel sorry for him.

"You're not good for me, Ray." She forced the bitter words out of her mouth. "You say you didn't really know how you felt about me when we lived in L.A., but you knew well enough to get drunk and kiss me. And you knew well enough to sleep with me when you were engaged to someone else."

"Then why did you kiss me in Paris? Why did you make me think we could be together?"

"I was reeling. I was so hurt by Luc and Asher, and there

you were, showing up to declare your love for me like I'd always dreamed you would. I wanted to believe that maybe after everything, we could be each other's happy ending. Except you were still the same person who spent all those years hurting me. The same person who wasn't brave enough to date me when you could have, when you wanted to, because you couldn't picture getting serious with someone who looked like me."

"But I got over that!" Ray protested. "I went on television to tell the whole world I love you—doesn't that count for something?"

"My body isn't something you 'get over,'" Bea said coolly. "I have no intention of devoting the rest of my life to a man who's ashamed of me."

"I know I've given you reason not to trust me," Ray pleaded. "But Bea, I promise, I won't hurt you again."

"I know you won't." Bea's tone was sad but resolute. "Because I'm not going to let you. All these years, you put your needs above mine—which is exactly what you did when you showed up in Paris, by the way—and I couldn't see it, because I idealized you as the perfect man. But I see who you are now, Ray. And I know that I deserve better."

The audience applauded heartily, and Johnny took them to commercial. A sound guy came to collect Ray's mic, but Ray told him to hold on just one second before turning back to Bea.

"So that's it?" he demanded. "We're just never going to speak again?"

"Yeah, Ray. I think that's it." Bea fought to maintain composure as Ray's face crinkled and cracked.

"We love each other. I know we do."

"Maybe," she whispered. "But I want more than you can give me."

The sound guy tugged on Ray's arm, and he turned to go—watching him leave was awful. Bea took a deep breath, and Alison swooped in for one last touch-up, giving her hair an unnecessary zhuzh.

"You're doing great," she whispered. "Keep going."

Bea nodded, and when the show started back up and Johnny welcomed Sam to the stage, it all felt so much easier.

"Hey, beautiful." Sam hugged Bea warmly, and seeing him was pure joy, same as always.

"God, I was an idiot to let you go." She smiled, then turned to the audience. "Wasn't I? Wasn't I just the worst to turn him down?"

"YES!" came the resounding cheer from the crowd, and everyone laughed together.

"Why did you, then?" Johnny pressed. "I know for me, and for a lot of the audience, it came as a real shock. You and Sam seemed like a perfect couple."

"I hope it's clear to everyone that I think Sam is an absolutely amazing man, and he was nothing but wonderful to me. And in some ways, that's why I knew we weren't meant to be together."

"That sounds a little twisted." Sam made a face at Bea.

"Ha, I know, my mother would be screaming about my tendency to self-sabotage, but that's not what I mean. It's more that—there was something not quite real about our relationship. We had a great rapport, great chemistry, but we never really argued or had any conflict, and I think that's because we never connected at that serious a level. So for me, at the end of the show, the question was what would happen if we took away the fantasy of *Main Squeeze,* all the travel and limos and hot-air balloons."

"To be real clear, I could have lived without the hot-air balloons."

Bea laughed. "See? Dating Sam, that seemed like a perfect fantasy. But in the end, I finally had to be honest with myself that we weren't right for each other in reality. I couldn't shake the idea that I was helping Sam on his journey to meet his future wife, but that that person wasn't me."

"Sam, do you agree with that assessment?"

"You know, I'm not going to lie, I was hurt when Bea turned me down. She's the first woman I ever really loved, and that's going to stick with me a long time. But ultimately, I do think she made the right decision for both of us, and I know we both care for each other and wish each other the best."

"Do you think you're ready to search for love again?" Johnny raised an eyebrow.

"You know what?" Sam grinned. "I think I just might be."

"On that note, I hear you have some news, is that right, Sam?"

"For the first time in history," he hammed, his voice low and dramatic, "your next Main Squeeze is going to have a mustache."

The crowd cheered, and Bea hugged Sam—she couldn't have imagined a better pick for the next Main Squeeze.

"You know I'm gonna be coming to you for advice," he said to Bea.

"Anytime!" she effused, praying silently that this didn't mean she'd have to be on the show again next season.

"And I want to say one thing publicly, while I have the chance," he went on after the applause had died down. "I think it's great that Bea broke some new ground on this show, and I know I'm doing the same thing by being the first Black man to be the Main Squeeze. But I don't want us to go backward on body diversity—I want the women I meet to represent a range of sizes, and I'm going to be really upset if the producers don't come through for me on that."

Predictably, the audience lost their minds at this, clapping and cheering. It was a great moment, and Bea was happy to end the night on a high note—but Johnny told her they still had one more segment to film after Sam left the stage.

"Bea," he said, "I'm sorry if this is tough, but I have to ask: Are you disappointed you didn't find love on your journey?"

"Definitely." Bea nodded. "It took me a long time to believe—truly believe—that it was even possible for me to find a lasting relationship on a show like this one, so of course I'm disappointed things didn't turn out the way I pictured. But you know, in a way, what happened was even better."

"What do you mean by that?"

"If you had come to me the week before we started filming and told me that Ray was going to leave his fiancée for me, I would have cried for joy. I would have run to him so fast—and it would have been a terrible decision."

"So your happy ending is getting over your feelings for Ray?"

"That's part of it." Bea considered. "But it's more than that. I've told myself for so many years that I'm afraid of men rejecting me for the way I look, of them refusing to look past my size. But I was wrong—I don't need a man to look past my size. I need someone who'll see me and love me exactly as I am. For all its flaws, this show made me believe that that's possible."

"You're not the only one who thinks so," Johnny said. "We talked earlier about the people who weren't so nice about you being on this show. But I hear you also received a lot of support from the plus-size community?"

"Yes!" Bea chirped. "That's been one of the best parts of

this whole experience. So many women and girls have shared their stories with me, have told me about all these acts of bravery they've been inspired to take in their own lives."

"Any favorites?"

"Oh gosh." Bea grinned, thinking back on all the terrific letters. "One girl told me that she was nervous to put her name in to be considered for prom court, but then she saw me on TV."

"And did she become prom queen?"

"No. She decided to run for class president instead."

The audience broke out in a thunderous ovation, and Bea beamed.

"Well," Johnny said, "we have a surprise for you, Bea."

"Uh-oh," Bea's response was involuntary, and the audience laughed good-naturedly.

"As you know, a lot of these letters came to us at *Main Squeeze,* and we passed them on to you. We loved the letters as much as you did, and we wanted to celebrate the women who wrote them. Can we get the lights up on the studio audience?"

On Johnny's cue, the lighting in the studio changed dramatically: The hot lights on the stage dimmed, the house lights came up, and for the first time, Bea was actually able to see the audience.

Every single woman in the crowd was plus-size. And they were rising to their feet to applaud.

"What? What is this?" Bea grabbed Johnny's hand, and to her great surprise, he held it tightly, keeping her steady as the tears streamed down her face.

"Every member of the audience is a woman who wrote to you, Bea," Johnny explained. "We thought you deserved a chance to meet, live and in person, some of the many people who see themselves in you."

"I can't believe I finally liked a twist on *Main Squeeze*," Bea blurted, and everyone laughed and cheered some more.

"I hope you won't mind, but we have just one more." Johnny guided Bea back to the couch as the studio lights returned to normal. "I'm guessing you noticed that one man from your *Main Squeeze* journey hasn't made an appearance tonight?"

Bea's pulse sped up—was he here after all? She looked wildly toward the stage door, thinking of how good it would feel to hold him, to tell him that, after all of this, he was the only one she wanted.

"I'm sorry to tell you that Asher declined our invitation to be here."

"Oh." Bea's voice caught in her throat, and she couldn't say anything more.

"But we do have a surprise guest—a certain celebrity who's made it quite public that he's interested in making your acquaintance. From the new film *Lieutenant Luxembourg: Blast from the Past,* please welcome Chris Evans!"

As a movie star made his way to the stage to give her a friendly hug hello, Bea swallowed her hurt over Asher and tried to stay in the moment, to marvel at the absurdity of her life. To think that less than a year ago, she was lying in bed, counting the days until Ray would be visiting for the Fourth of July, and now here she was, on live television, exchanging niceties with a Hollywood superhero because some publicist or executive had thought it would help sell movie tickets.

Or maybe, Bea stopped to remind herself, he actually was interested in dating her. As she gazed into his dreamy blue eyes, she couldn't rule it out completely.

∽

Three thousand miles away, in a cozy rental house utterly buried in mess and half-packed moving boxes, Gwen and Linus sat rapt in front of the TV.

"Dad!" Linus screamed. "Will you please come in here for one minute?? It's IMPORTANT."

Asher rushed in from the kitchen, packing tape still in hand.

"What is it, buddy? Is everything okay?"

"We need you to see something," Gwen said matter-of-factly, but when Asher saw whose face was on the TV, he turned quickly on his heel.

"Come on, guys, we've been through this. No *Main Squeeze* stuff, okay?"

"But Dad, they ASKED her about you," Linus emphasized. "She was so, so sad you weren't there."

"I'm sure you're exaggerating," Asher clipped. But looking at the screen, he noted that Bea did seem upset, even as she chatted with a handsome man Asher vaguely recognized as a popular film actor.

"Linus isn't exaggerating," Gwen responded. "No one in history has been that disappointed to see Chris Evans."

"I don't know," Asher mumbled, but Linus broke in.

"Dad, it's not even debatable. She *loves* you!" He leapt off the couch, wearing a bright-red T-shirt he'd fastidiously bedazzled with fringe and sparkles.

"Guys, give me a break," Asher pleaded. "It's complicated."

Gwen turned off the television and gave her father a knowing stare. "You're the one who told us to be open-minded about how much Bea could change our lives for the better, even if it felt scary. Did that advice only apply when it felt scary to us? Are you too afraid to take a risk in order to be happy?"

"Why are you so invested in this?" Asher asked, sinking onto the couch. "Aren't we happy already, just the three of us?"

Linus climbed onto the couch and curled up beside his father.

"But Dad, you're not happy. You haven't been happy since you came home."

"That's not true," Asher protested, his voice breaking ever so slightly. "Being with you two makes me happy every day."

Gwen sat down on Asher's other side. "Dad, come on. It's obvious how much you miss her."

Asher appraised his daughter. "You're a little terrifying, you know that?"

"Just promise us you'll think about it, okay?" Gwen pressed.

"I promise," Asher said. "But for now, I'm tired of thinking—and packing. You guys want to watch a movie?"

"It's my turn to pick!" Linus jumped up. "Can we watch *Bringing Up Baby*?"

"Dad said we can't watch that anymore," Gwen chided.

Asher paused for a moment. "I think it might be okay tonight."

Gwen opened her mouth to say more—but then thought better of it and grabbed the remote instead.

"Can we make microwave popcorn?" she asked.

"I'm on it." Asher got up to grab a bag. Once he was out of earshot, Gwen grabbed Linus to whisper in his ear.

"It's gonna happen," she said.

Linus's eyes got wide. "What is?"

Just like her father, Gwen's lips twitched into a barely perceptible grin.

"Everything we wanted."

⌘

Once the reunion show was done, Bea was really and truly finished with her responsibilities for *Main Squeeze*—sure, there were a couple of interviews left to give, and she'd have to appear on a red carpet from time to time, but for all intents and purposes, it was time to go back to her real life, and she was absolutely thrilled. A few days after the reunion show, Bea realized she had an entire day with nothing on her calendar, so she decided to treat herself to an L.A. day of fun. She put on a breezy Mary Katrantzou sundress in a Technicolor mess of floral patterns and drove around aimlessly in Kermit the Car—top down, breeze in her hair, Taylor Swift turned all the way up.

Before she really realized where she was driving, she found herself heading west on Wilshire, and after a few minutes, the rows of LACMA lanterns came into view.

Her membership entitled her to visit the museum anytime she liked, but she hadn't been back since the show finished filming, for obvious reasons. Today, though, it seemed like the right thing to do. She pulled into the parking garage and snapped a selfie among the lanterns on her way in—she figured this was as good an opportunity as any to fulfill Olivia's mandate of one Insta story per week.

Time for a one-on-one—just me and Monet!

She posted the photo and went inside.

The moment she walked through the doors, the memory of him was everywhere. The Rothkos and Picassos, the wide staircase they'd walked down side by side. The exhibit with the car and the music was already gone; if Bea wanted to relive that moment, she'd have to watch it on television. It had been real, hadn't it? He had felt the same things she did, had cared for her as much as she cared for him?

Her memories of him were too vivid, too present here: the feel of his hands at her waist, the way he jerked away rather than kiss her. The release of giving in to her feelings for him in Ohio, his painstaking doubts in Morocco. The highs of visiting his home, meeting his children, sharing each other's jagged secrets—then the devastating nothingness as he pulled back and back and back, leaving her alone with her nightmares in that big, romantic suite in Moustiers, and then, two days later, leaving her for good.

A liar, he called her. A cheat. He didn't even have the courage or the decency to come back and face her, to tell her the truth about why he'd left, how he'd retreated into his own insecurities rather than reach for her hand. He just dumped it all on her shoulders and walked away.

She prowled the museum for hours, sweeping through one room after another, all of it bearing down, all of it too much, until finally her feet steered her of their own volition back to the impressionist gallery—the room where everything had started, where they'd truly seen each other for the very first time.

The gallery was empty as usual; late-afternoon sunlight flowed in, dusty and golden, and the only other person there was a man in navy chinos and a soft gray T-shirt gazing at one of the Monets. His back was facing Bea, but she was immediately drawn to his salt-and-pepper hair—no. Her eyes were playing tricks on her. There was no way . . .

But when her sandals clacked on the hardwood floor, he spun around—and God, he looked the same, his glasses and the crinkles around his eyes, his broad shoulders and sloping frame.

"Bea?" He wasn't asking whether it was her. He was asking something else.

"How did you know where to find me?" she finally choked out.

"I was at the rental counter at LAX when I saw your story,"

he explained. "Gwen put notifications for all of your posts on my phone."

"Really?" Bea was taken aback. "Gwen did?"

Asher smiled. "She's become one of your greatest proponents."

He stepped toward her but she bristled, her whole body suddenly tense.

"I don't understand why you came," she said curtly.

"I—" He stopped short. "Isn't it obvious? I flew across the country to see you."

"And what?" Bea wanted to feel overjoyed, to run to him, but she couldn't—her anger was churning. "That's supposed to make up for what you did?"

"Wow." Asher sniffed. "This is not how I thought you'd react."

"What did you think, Asher? That I've just been mooning over you? Dreaming that you'd show up on my doorstep so I could beg you to take me back, even though you're the one who ran out on me?"

"What are you doing here, then?" he demanded. "If you don't miss me, why are you in this museum?"

"Because I love art!" Bea fumed. "Art isn't about *you,* not everything is about you."

His lips twitched with one of his infuriating smiles, but no—not this time—it wasn't going to work.

"Oh stop it," she spat, "stop smiling like you know everything. This was my place before you ever came along, okay? I'm not some powerless woman, my life didn't begin the night I met you."

"Bea, no." He shook his head and started walking toward her again. "If anyone is powerless, it's me, okay? You think

I don't know how colossally I screwed up in Amboise? You think I haven't gone back to that morning every single day, wondering how I could have ruined something so good? These last six weeks have been a waking nightmare."

"Then why?" Bea's voice broke. "Why did you leave?"

He was close enough now to reach for her, but looking like he didn't know whether he should.

"You know that being on the show was difficult for me," he said, "but the truth is it was even worse than I let on. Imagining you with other men was such torture—my mind couldn't parse the difference between you with Sam or Luc and seeing Vanessa cheat on me in broad daylight. It felt the same to me, like you were waving it in my face and I was just supposed to take it. That morning, knowing you had slept with Luc, yet you were still struggling to trust *me*? I felt insane, like I was reliving my past. Then Ray showed up, and that sealed it. In my mind, it was all the proof I needed that you were just another Vanessa, and that I was supposed to be the same old Asher, still reliable, letting you walk all over me, breaking my heart all over again. I couldn't take it—I just snapped. My only choice was to leave."

"Do you still feel that way?" Bea asked.

Asher sighed. "Bea, I didn't even feel that way the next morning. When I got back to Vermont, I expected this rush of relief—but all I felt was regret. All these years, I've thought of myself as the person who gets left behind. Being the person who ran felt so much worse."

"You could have called me," Bea said softly. "You could have shown up for the reunion."

Asher hung his head. "I was desperate to convince myself I'd done the right thing. If I could just believe I was better off without you, then that would mean I didn't make the worst mistake of my life in France. When I saw your face on TV Monday night after they told you I wasn't coming . . . I've never been so ashamed, Bea. Never."

Bea closed her eyes. She wanted to believe him so badly. So why couldn't she?

"Bea . . ." He took her hand, and he was shaking—they both were. "Do you remember what you told us in Vermont? What your stepdad said, about choosing your family?"

Bea nodded and met his eyes for the first time. Of course she remembered.

"I keep thinking," he went on. "What if it's supposed to be us?"

"All those years," Bea said, her voice quivering, "telling myself I would end up with Ray, when he wouldn't date me, when he didn't live here, even when he proposed to someone else. I was running, Asher, just like you did in Amboise. It felt so much safer to hide from anyone who might actually want to see me."

"And now?" Asher asked, his voice hoarse.

"Now, I think, you and I have seen the worst of each other." Bea's voice cracked, and she felt the first tears start to fall. "But I just want to keep looking at you every single day."

"I should have done this the first time we were here," he said gently, and then he leaned in and kissed her.

It was silent in the gallery—no orchestra, no fireworks, no whir of generators and cameras. The only sounds were her breath and his, just Bea and the man she loved. He wasn't a fantasy, he wasn't a dream, and he wasn't a happy ending. He was warmth and wit and kindness, a certainty and a surprise. He was the person who could hurt her most in the world, and he was worth the risk.

"Hey," Bea said quietly. "I choose you."

EPILOGUE

(One man left)

Cat: Well. Well, well, well, well, well.

Ruby: Wow, this is going to be insufferable, isn't it?

Cat: Why would you say that, Ruby?

Ruby: Because you're the sorest winner in the history of mankind?

Cat: BUT I'M JUST SO HAPPY FOR ASHER AND BEA!

Ruby: And for yourself for having correctly called the winner of yet another season of *Main Squeeze*?

Cat: That too, but like ninety percent happy for Asher and Bea, ten percent proud of my streak remaining unbroken?

Ruby: Seventy-thirty?

Cat: Let's call it eighty-twenty.

Ruby: For those of you who haven't heard, Bea Schumacher and Asher Chang-Reitman from this season of *Main Squeeze* were photographed together watching fireworks with his kids on the Fourth of July, and the whole Internet basically erupted with joy.

Cat: It's so nice to feel proud of this country again!

Ruby: And even nicer to see those two crazy kids found a way to work things out. Do you think we'll be getting a wedding special?

Cat: If only! Sadly, Bea's agent released a statement confirming the two are together, but apparently they're refusing any press requests whatsoever, and have asked that we respect their privacy. Which is pretty understandable, given the run those two had during the show.

Ruby: Definitely, but it doesn't mean I have to be happy about it!

Cat: No, but you know what you can be happy about?

Ruby: What's that, Cat?

Cat: Next week is the premiere of *Main Squeeze Mansion*!

Ruby: Oh my God, I have to watch another one of these things?

Cat: This is your life now, Ruby. You watch one season, you get attached to all the people, and then you can never stop tuning in to see what happens next. Besides, aren't you excited to see which women—and men, frankly—Luc is going to sleep with this time around?

Ruby: Come on, Cat, did you even watch last season? The answer is everyone. Luc is going to sleep with everyone.

Cat: Too right, he is. And if you're going to sleep with everyone, first of all, well done you, but second of all, you might want a monthly shipment of condoms delivered directly to your door. SafetyGirl condoms are made without any harmful chemicals that can be absorbed into your vagina, and you can customize your shipment so you're always prepared to have as much sex as you want, whether that's with a million different partners like Luc or with one person you're going to love forever and ever, just like Bea and Asher because I am always right.

Ruby: Had to get that last one in there, didn't you?

Cat: You know it! We'll be back right after this.

TRANSCRIPT OF CHAT FROM #SQUEEZE-MAINIACS SLACK CHANNEL
Direct Message: Colin7784 and Beth.Malone

Colin7784: Hey, I have a question.

Beth.Malone: What's going on?

Colin7784: Is there going to be a retroactive winner of the league this season now that Asher and Bea are together?

Beth.Malone: OMFG SERIOUSLY COLIN? I HAVE BEEN *VERY CLEAR* ABOUT THE RULES OF THE LEAGUE, WE WENT THROUGH THIS WITH THE WYATT THING, POINTS ARE AWARDED AT THE TIME OF THE BROADCAST

Colin7784: Beth, I'm messing with you

Beth.Malone: What.

Colin7784: So are we going to do another league for Main Squeeze Mansion? Or not until Sam's season?

Beth.Malone: Wow, you really got into it, huh?

Colin7784: Yeah yeah, you were right, it was fun

Colin7784: Do you have plans, by the way? For the Main Squeeze Mansion premiere? Because if you don't, I mean,

I don't know. I thought it would be cool if we could watch together or something. If you want.

Beth.Malone: Oh. Yeah. Yeah, I think that could be cool.

Colin7784: Yeah? Cool.

Beth.Malone: Cool.

LAUREN MATHERS RE-UPPED AS *MAIN SQUEEZE* EP IN 4-YEAR DEAL
by Tia Sussman, deadline.com

Following the highest-rated season in years, controversial *Main Squeeze* showrunner Lauren Mathers has inked a four-year deal with ABS to helm the reality behemoth. Mathers made headlines for her illicit affair with one of the show's contestants, but according to our source at ABS, that wasn't a problem for the brass.

"Numbers don't lie, and this season of *Main Squeeze* was huge," says the source. "Besides, all the men who run these shows have done way worse than Lauren for years, so why would her affair with Luc be a problem? That episode KILLED in the ratings."

Mathers's seven-figure deal encompasses all banners under the *Main Squeeze* umbrella franchise, including this fall's upcoming season starring fan-favorite Sam Cox. We're also told Mathers is developing a new series starring her former paramour, Luc Dupond. More details on that as we receive them.

MAIN SQUEEZE SPECIAL: WHERE ARE THEY NOW?
by Kellie McGinty, usweekly.com

It's hard to believe it's been a whole year since **Bea Schu-macher**'s season of *Main Squeeze* premiered—between the exes, the cheating, and the surprise departures, her season finally lived up to the hype of being the most dramatic one *ever*! But where are the *Main Squeeze* main players now? We caught up with the ones you love—and the ones you love to hate!

- Farm-fresh favorite **Wyatt Ames** isn't just raising barns these days—he's also raising awareness! Wyatt is working to promote outreach and acceptance for the asexual and aromantic communities, and he says he's never been happier. *(CLICK THROUGH to see photos of Wyatt and Bea on the red carpet at the GLAAD Media Awards!)*

- After bad-boy **Luc Dupond** slept his way through popular spin-off series *Main Squeeze Mansion,* he landed the biggest catch of all: his own show! Luc's new series about life in the kitchen, *Can't Stand the Heat?,* will premiere this summer on Bravo. As for his love life, Luc says he is happily single. (Big surprise!)

- Being rejected in the finale turned out to be great news for **Sam Cox**, whose season of *Main Squeeze* finished airing in December—that's where he met his now-fiancée, **Meghan Vazkin**! The couple is getting ready to head off for a year of travel around the world; Sam says he's ready for marriage, but not a 9-to-5.

- As for Bea's ex, **Ray Moretti**, he's still single, and working as an entertainment lawyer in Los Angeles. (We hope he didn't move there to be with Bea, because she doesn't live there anymore!)

So where is the leading lady herself? She tells *Us* she's loving life in Brooklyn, where she lives with former suitor (and current love!) **Asher Chang-Reitman**. He's a history professor at Columbia University (lucky undergrads! sign *Us* up for every class), and Bea is working as a contributing editor for *Teen Vogue,* collaborating on a size-inclusive line with stylist **Alison Sommers**, and writing a fashion guidebook to show how her favorite looks can be worn by women of every size. Phew! We're exhausted just thinking about her busy life—but we couldn't be more thrilled that she's found so much success and so much love.

So what's next for Bea and Asher? With two kids and two booming careers, the private couple says they love their life exactly the way it is. With such a great life to live, who could blame them?

Life with Asher in Brooklyn just fit; it felt right to Bea the way you sometimes pull on a great pair of jeans and intuitively know they're going to button. She loved their ramshackle apartment in a Park Slope brownstone, loved Saturday mornings at street fairs with the kids and Saturday nights cooking at home, loved her wild and motley coworkers at *Teen Vogue,* loved weekly Sunday dim sum with Asher's parents, loved long weekends in L.A. drinking wine with Marin and Alison, loved falling asleep with her head on Asher's chest, loved waking up to his truly horrible morning breath.

She did not love winter. But you couldn't have everything in life—it wouldn't be fair.

This particular day was a perfect New York spring—lovely and cool with a soft breeze that made the whole city smell like fresh-cut flowers. Bea had been running around to meetings all day (the samples had just come in for her collaboration with Alison, and everyone was freaking out about the changes that still needed making). Her feet were killing her and she would have murdered ten men for an iced latte, but she needed to get to the *Vogue* offices at CondéNast, because she had angled for months for this appointment, and she absolutely could not be late.

"Sorry, sorry, I'm so sorry!" She rushed into the lobby, where Asher, Gwen, and Linus were waiting—Linus looked positively smashing in a long, structured kimono, which he'd paired with chunky brogues.

"You look *amazing,*" Bea said, pulling him into a hug. "You're going to be the best-dressed person at *Vogue.*"

"Are you sure? I changed my outfit so many times." He wrung his hands nervously.

Bea could tell from the way Asher tilted his head that the phrase "many times" was not an exaggeration.

"Hi," she said, kissing Asher quickly and leading the group to the elevators. "Your day okay?"

"Better now," he said with a smile.

"Dad, I hate to say it, but you've become a sap," Gwen observed.

"Come on, Gwen," Bea teased. "He's been a secret sap all along."

Once they arrived at *Vogue,* a colleague of Bea's met them at reception for the main event: a tour of the fabled *Vogue* closet. Linus had been begging for a visit ever since Bea started her job, and after many months of finagling, it was finally happening. He was absolutely beside himself as they toured the rooms of slacks and ball gowns, raincoats and rompers. Bea was pretty impressed herself—it wasn't every day you got to share a room with couture from the annals of fashion history.

The tour ended with the fabulous accessories closet, which was filled with scarves, belts, shoes galore, and even a couple of capes. Bea's colleague told Linus it was okay for him to try some things on, and Bea thought he might actually pass out right there.

"I think he's having the best day of his life." Bea linked her arm through Asher's.

"Maybe he's not the only one," Asher said, his lips twitching in a cryptic little smile.

"You're enjoying this that much?" Bea laughed. "Do you have a shoe fetish you haven't told me about?"

"Now that you mention it, I've been thinking you could use a new accessory. I have a pretty specific idea in mind."

"Oh yeah?" Bea stammered. "Are you picturing, like, some sunglasses? Or a hat?"

"No," Asher said as he dropped to one knee. He took a black velvet box from his jacket pocket, and as he opened it, Bea saw a glimmer of rose gold and opals through her tears. "I was thinking more like a ring."

∞

ACKNOWLEDGMENTS

Emma Caruso, thank you for reading a proposal on a train and fighting like hell for three years to make it into a book. Thank you for your sharp instincts and tireless commitment, for pushing me at every turn to make this novel better—and for wrestling my laptop away when I was hell-bent on making it worse. If I aspire to be the literary Ashley I. (after all, this book was my first), then you are the Rhode Island Jared I've dreamed of my whole life. And the single-space editorial letters were our Paradise. And Caitlin McKenna was Chris Harrison. Emma, I'm sorry to say this, but I don't see any way around it: We *did* the damn thing. Thank you forever.

Morgan Matson, thank you for being the first person to tell me I should write a book, for your inexhaustible reservoirs of guidance, and for your miraculous/infuriating ability to solve the toughest story problems in twenty seconds flat. (Seriously, how do you do that?? Whatever, let's go to Vegas and watch a Marvel movie.)

Julia Cox and Ali Schouten, thank you for the hundreds of pages of manuscripts you've read and the thousands of glasses of wine we've shared. Thank you to Jenna Lowenstein, Sharon Greene, Amanda Litman, Sonia Kharkar, and Sneha Koorse for reading various drafts and giving invaluable feedback, to Meg Vázquez for your insight on all things visual (and my fabulous author photo!), and to Megan Lubin and Shareeza Bhola for being my personal PR gurus.

I'm indebted to the many writers who've influenced my thinking on fat acceptance, including Your Fat Friend, Roxane Gay, Michael Hobbes (whose article "Everything You Know About Obesity Is Wrong" should be required reading for every human), Michelle V. Scott, and Lindy West. I'm grateful to Samantha Puc, Tracy Russo, and Sabrina Hersi Issa for helping me think through changes to earlier versions of this novel to make Bea more inclusive and relatable for women of all sizes, and to Jenna Lowenstein, Jess Morales Rocketto, Amanda Litman, and Danielle Kantor for the endlessly wonderful text threads about life in (and fashion for!) plus-size bodies.

If Marin gives Bea any good advice in this book, it's because Sonia Kharkar, Megan Lubin, and Meg Vázquez gave it to me first. I'm sorry for plagiarizing you so rampantly; it's your own fault for being so fucking smart. Thank you. I love you.

Thank you to my family: Dad and Dede, who always believe in me (and who generously put me up in a problematic cabin when I flipped out that I ABSOLUTELY COULD NOT FINISH THIS DRAFT); Rebecca, Rob, Zoe, and Jessica, who drag me into nature against my will and make me happier than any other humans on the planet; Jill (and Liz and Rich), who graciously hosted me for dozens of writing retreats by the lake; my grandmother Bobby Stayman, whose indomitable spirit has inspired me all my life; Florence, who taught me colors, kindness, and French; Liz, Norah, and especially Arlene, who made me a reader, and then a writer.

I've been lucky to have some truly amazing teachers, and I want to mention a few of them here: Thank you to Dolores Antoine, Marcia Greenwald, Gail Ciecierski, Dennis Murray, Tom Manos, Shana Stein, Brad Riddell, Ted Braun, Janet Scott Batchler, Aaron Rahsaan Thomas, Michael Saltzman, Steven Bochco, Trey Callaway, and particularly Connie Congdon, who taught me how to listen, and how not to be afraid.

Thank you to Whitney Frick for steering the ship so peerlessly, to Sarah Horgan for our gorgeous cover, and to everyone at Random House who worked so hard to get us across the finish line: Jess Bonet, Melissa Sanford, Avideh Bashirrad, Cindy Berman, Maria Braeckel, Susan Corcoran, Barbara Fillon, Rachelle Mandik, Jen Valero, Sasha Sadikot, and the incredible RH sales force, whose enthusiasm made my heart grow about fifty sizes. Thanks also to Fiona Davis for helping us launch this book with a bang.

Thank you to Corey Ackerman and Katy McCaffrey for championing me and my writing, and to Helen Land for showing me how much better my life could get (then helping me through the door). Thank you to Trish Welte, Erin Kamler, Rachel LaBruyere, Tia Subramanian, and Taylor Salditch. As some artists thank God at the Grammys, so now would I like to thank Hillary Rodham Clinton. Thank you for inspiring the HFA family every day to do all the good we can.

Okay. Last one.

Thank you, Julia Masnik. Thanks for signing me off a makeup blog. Thank you for Sondra. Thank you for giving me a reason to keep going in 2016 when I couldn't get out of bed, then for gently pointing out that while writing three pages might *feel* like a big accomplishment, it was not enough to sell a book. Thank you for knowing immediately that this idea was the one. Thank you for being my favorite snob, for ebbing my panic one jillion times per annum, for bringing Lisa Van-derpump levels of elegant real talk into my life on the daily. And that one time, when I was in a genuine crisis and you stayed on the phone with me until I was better, and I thanked you for being a really good agent? Thank you for reminding me that you are also, in point of fact, my friend. Champagne wishes and all the rest of it. We're here because of you.

ONE TO WATCH

Kate Stayman-London

Random House
Book Club
Because
Stories Are
Better Shared ™

A BOOK CLUB GUIDE

QUESTIONS AND TOPICS FOR DISCUSSION

1. *One to Watch* examines what it's like to have every move you make documented by cameras and consumed by an audience of millions. Lots of us choose to live some version of this reality by documenting our lives on social media—with both positive and negative impacts! Did you identify with any of Bea's experiences of being on camera in your own life? How do you think the advent of platforms like Instagram has affected your life, if at all?

2. Before Bea ever stars on *Main Squeeze,* she loves it as a viewer, even though she has some serious criticisms of the show. What shows (or movies, or books) do you love, even though you have problems with them? How do those problems affect your experience as an audience member?

3. Would you ever go on a show like *Main Squeeze*? What would the pros and cons be for you? If you were chosen as the star, what types of suitors would you want to date? What would you list as options for your "dream date" locations, both at home and overseas?

4. Bea argues throughout the book that the notion of a plus-size woman starring in a reality dating show is not radical, despite the fact that we've never seen it. What do you think? Would it be radical if a show like *The Bachelorette* cast a plus-size star? How would Americans react? Would you watch?

    a. Follow-up question: What if a plus-size man was cast to star in *The Bachelor* instead? How would that change the dynamic?

5. Bea dates a lot of different types of men in the book—the exuberant younger man, the analytical academic, the sexy European, the alluring ex-boyfriend—and learns something different from each one. Which men did you like best (and least!)? What lessons did they offer you about what you're looking for in your own life?

6. Luc believes it's possible to love someone without being possessive of them. Do you agree, or is this just an excuse to be unfaithful?

7. By the end of the book, Bea realizes that Ray was never the right guy for her (though, of course, her best friend, Marin, knew that all along). Why do you think she fixated on him for so many years, to the exclusion of giving anyone else a real chance? Have you ever struggled to let go of someone in your life?

8. Bea's stepdad, Bob, plays an incredibly important role in her life, and she ultimately chooses to play the same role for Gwen and Linus. This is one way to "choose your family," but there are many others. How has the idea of choosing your family played out in your life?

9. Bea fights against stereotypes of plus-size people (i.e., that it means you're lazy and unhealthy), but it's often an uphill battle. Do you notice stereotypes of plus-size people in your everyday life? Where do you see these stereotypes? What can be done to fight them?

10. Bea argues for the importance of inclusive representation on *Main Squeeze*—not just body diversity but racial and ethnic diversity and LGBTQ inclusion as well. What are other areas of society that could benefit from more inclusion? What are the barriers preventing increased diversity? What effects (if any) do you think increased representation would have?

11. In the beginning of the book, Bea experiences the positive and negative effects of her blog post "going viral": On the one hand, she experiences serious harassment and even death threats, but on the other, all the attention boosts her career and ultimately leads to her being offered a starring role on *Main Squeeze*. Do you dream of winning fifteen minutes of Internet fame? Do you think it would be worth it? Why do you think women, in particular, experience so much harassment when they achieve this kind of fame?

12. Shows like *Main Squeeze* set the expectation that the only way to have a "happy ending" is to fall in love and get engaged, but Bea strives to prove that it's just as valid to live on your own terms as a happy and fulfilled single person. Have you ever experienced a version of this tension? What are some ways our society can be more supportive of single people and reset the expectation that the only way to be happy is if you find a partner?

A Q&A WITH AUTHOR
KATE STAYMAN-LONDON

Q. What have you learned from writing this book? Did the writing process go as you expected?

A. When I started this book, I thought it would be a light-hearted romantic comedy—and it is, but it also explores some really dark and tough emotions, which could be pretty grueling from a writing perspective! Writing this book forced me to get really vulnerable in grappling with my own insecurities with body image, my past self-destructive romantic choices, and, ultimately, my desire to be the arbiter of my own happiness. Bea says in the book that there's a difference between *knowing* something and *feeling* it, and I think writing this book helped me to really feel a lot of things I already knew.

Q. What were some of the decisions your characters made that you might have made differently?

A. The first and biggest one is that I probably wouldn't go on *Main Squeeze*! I think Bea is so brave to make that decision;

it's one of the reasons I really admire her and root for her as a character. I love that she's ambitious and wants a huge career for herself, and she's willing to endure a lot of harassment and criticism in order to get there. But there's a reason I'm a writer and not an actor! I'm much happier typing away in my pajamas than I think I ever could be in front of a camera.

Another really difficult choice is Asher's decision to allow cameras into his home, even as he's worried about how that might affect Linus. I love what Bea says about showing Linus that Asher thinks he's perfect just the way he is. As a member of the LGBTQ community, that's what I would hope for from every parent. I think ultimately Asher made the right choice to celebrate Linus's identity on camera, but for me, that decision is probably the toughest one in the book because of how hard it is to know whether you're doing the right thing for your child, especially given how absolutely brutal commenters can be on social media. (Parenting seems tough! Congrats to all of you who are working hard at it!!)

Q. You say you wouldn't go on a reality show, but you've obviously thought a lot about what it would be like to star in one. Did any experiences in your life inform the way you imagined this?

A. Yes! In 2016, I worked as lead digital writer for Hillary Rodham Clinton's presidential campaign. I'd spent a lot of my career working for various political causes, but nothing prepared me for the intense scrutiny we received on that campaign. I would write a line for Secretary Clinton in a fundraising email and see it quoted the next day in *The Economist*. We posted a picture of me dressed as Hillary for Halloween on our campaign Instagram, and then Stephen Colbert discussed it with her (and showed her the photo) on national television. I was sitting at my desk one day squinting at something on my computer when a photographer snapped a photo that ran the next week in *Time* magazine—it's still on my grandma's fridge. Every time I visit her, I can revisit exactly how tired and haggard I felt that week in September.

It was almost comical, this feeling that everyone was watching everything we did, that we were working eighteen-hour days with no weekends and no end in sight; so tired we could barely see straight, and we couldn't make a single mistake without the entire world knowing about it. There was an element of absurdity about the whole experience—like, how is it possible that this is my life? Do you guys know that I'm just some regular girl who doesn't have time to do laundry and eats cold Pop-Tarts for dinner at least two nights a week? (Oh, tenth-floor vending machine, you really saved me.) But in those circumstances, I wasn't some regular girl; I was a part of a major facet of American culture. So in crafting Bea's story, I really wanted to capture that experience of feeling like you're totally normal, you're just *you*, but suddenly millions of people are interested in every single thing you do. It's the most wild feeling I've ever had.

Q. Why did you decide to write about fashion? Does fashion play a big role in your life?

A. I *love* fashion. In 1997, I bought an issue of *People* magazine that changed my life: It was the Oscars' red carpet round-up, and Nicole Kidman was on the cover wearing a chartreuse Dior dress embroidered with flowers and trimmed with fur. The dress was outrageous and over-the-top but still elegant and refined, totally groundbreaking for its time. After that,

I was hooked. My best friend from college and I still text incessantly during the red carpet of almost every major awards show, and I even had my own short-lived fashion blog in the mid-2000s. But I also have a lot of criticisms of the fashion industry, especially when it comes to body inclusivity. So in writing this book, I wanted to indulge my love of fashion, but I also wanted to call out the industry in a really positive way: by celebrating inclusive designers and creating an explicitly plus-size fashion fantasy. Every single garment Bea wears in this book is made by a designer who makes true plus-size clothes going up to at least a size 20 and often larger. I think fashion can be such a joyous way to express yourself, *for* yourself (and not to make a man think you're beautiful), and there's no reason in the world that every single woman shouldn't have equal access to that joy. (If she wants it!)

Q. In the book, you explored not only reality shows but the cottage industry of gossip and commentary that surround them, from podcasts to Twitter to TMZ. Why was it important to you to include that material?

A. I've spent the past twelve years or so writing for the Internet professionally, and I spend a lot of time thinking about the impacts, both positive and negative, of this huge commentary culture that's exploded online. On the one hand, I obviously wanted to show the darker sides of Internet conversation, and particularly the freedom that men online feel to comment about women's opinions and appearances, often in really nasty, vitriolic ways. That's something I've experienced occasionally, and I knew Bea would experience it on a much more massive scale by agreeing to star on *Main Squeeze*. For me, writing about that was a really important component of criticizing a culture that can be absolutely suffocating in its misogyny and anti-fatness—and for women of color, it's even worse.

However, there are also so many really wonderful things about online culture, and I wanted to illustrate that, too! For example, cultural criticism used to be a really rarefied space where only a few voices (predominantly white, male, rich, cis, straight, etc.) backed by large institutions got to weigh in on what was happening in the world (or on TV!). I think it's amazing that the Internet has really democratized the cultural conversation, and that so many really important voices (particularly from people of color) have so much of a wider reach than they otherwise might have when traditional gatekeepers were the only ones in control.

I also love the way Internet conversations can create community, and I wanted to celebrate that—like when Cat, the cohost of "Boob Tube," is also in a *Main Squeeze* betting league with her friends. Maybe some of the people in that Slack channel were originally Boob Tube listeners who made friends with Cat on Twitter. Maybe they've never even met in real life! But they've bonded over their shared love of this show (and their love of snarking about it), and talking about it really enriches their viewing experience. Maybe they even love that part of it more than they love watching the show itself. (This is certainly true for me with some shows I watch.)

So all of this is a long way of saying that in 2020, I don't think we can talk about fame of any stripe without also talking about the positive and negative ways you can experience that fame online. It was really important to me to capture both sides of that coin in the book.

Q. You're a screenwriter as well as a novelist. What are some of the differences between writing a script and writing a novel?

A. The main difference is that screenwriting is *much* more collaborative. You're working with producers and executives to develop an idea and getting notes from them throughout (or if you're writing for TV, you're generally working with a room full of other writers), and then if you're lucky enough to go into production, you're working with a director and actors and a whole host of other really talented people who are bringing their own ideas to the project.

But with a novel, it's pretty much just me! Of course, I got so much help from my editor and agent and other amazing readers, but ultimately, it's my name on the cover. In some ways, that's so freeing and exciting—I get to do whatever I want now, suckers! But on the other hand, there's nowhere to hide. I can't say, "Oh, that was the director's dumb choice" if someone doesn't like a particular scene. In some ways, writing a novel feels much riskier than writing a screenplay. I'm inviting you into my innermost thoughts and hoping you don't hate what you see.

Q. Say you were the star of *Main Squeeze,* and every character in the book was in the cast. Who would you pick for an overnight date? Who would be the first person you would kick off the show? Who would you choose to win the whole season?

A. Wow, this is a tough one!! Well, let's all be honest here, I'm definitely picking Luc for an overnight date, so we can get that out of the way. (The tattoos? The accent? The outrageous chemistry? The cassoulet?!? Yes, yes, yes, and yes.)

For the first person I'd kick off the show, Nash and Cooper are both strong contenders, but I think I have to go with Jefferson. I'm extremely done with men who project their insecurities onto women's bodies. (Honorable mentions for Marco, Kumal, Abyssinia Stapleton, and that one columnist who writes about "the fatpocalypse.")

Choosing a winner might be the hardest decision of all. I obviously have a soft spot for Asher, but I ultimately think his rigidity and trouble being emotive would be really frustrating for me. And Sam is completely wonderful, but I'd love to have a partner who's as career-driven as I am. I think I'd have to pick Alison so we could spend our whole lives wearing beautiful clothes—and if we got married, we'd both carry eighteen pennies tied with red ribbon down the aisle.

Q. Who are some of your influences as a writer? Did anyone have a particularly big impact on *One to Watch*?

A. Oh man, I have so many influences! I love Maria Semple, and the epistolary style of *Where'd You Go, Bernadette* was definitely a big inspiration for the way I wrote this book—ditto for Rainbow Rowell's *Attachments* and Morgan Matson's *Amy & Roger's Epic Detour*. Stephen Sondheim's books on writing (*Finishing the Hat* and *Look, I Made a Hat*) are basically sacred texts to me, and his ability to view his own work with a critical eye is something I'm forever striving to emulate. But my biggest influence for this book was definitely Nora Ephron. There's a line in *Sleepless in Seattle* that I absolutely love where Becky (Rosie O'Donnell) says to Annie (Meg Ryan), "That's your problem: You don't want to be in love. You want to be in love in a movie." I wrote a whole paper about that line in college (of course I did), and it really gets at the heart of what

I'm exploring in this novel: the fantasy of a picture-perfect love story versus the actual experience of messy, real-life love. I adore how self-aware Nora was in crafting her romantic comedies; even as she told these big, archetypal stories, she always kept them grounded in the emotions of her incredibly charming and relatable characters. Whenever I couldn't crack a scene in this novel, I'd think, *What would Nora do?* Then I'd come back to the truth of the way the characters would feel in a particular moment and let them be my guide. I'm so grateful she gave us so much beautiful work to make us laugh, make us cry, and teach us how to have lives full of love, wit, and truly fabulous dinner parties.

Kate Stayman-London is a novelist, screenwriter, and political strategist. She served as lead digital writer for Hillary Rodham Clinton's 2016 presidential campaign and has written for notable figures ranging from President Obama and Malala Yousafzai to Anna Wintour and Cher. When not writing or traveling, Kate can be found obsessively ranking Taylor Swift songs, laughing loudly with friends over really good bottles of wine, and, of course, watching reality TV. She lives in Los Angeles.

katestaymanlondon.com
Twitter: @_ksl
Instagram: @__ksl